# CARLA NEGGERS
## Finding You

**POCKET BOOKS**
New York   London   Toronto   Sydney   Tokyo   Singapore

This book is a work of fiction. Names, characters, places and
incidents are products of the author's imagination or are used
fictitiously. Any resemblance to actual events or locales or persons,
living or dead, is entirely coincidental.

An *Original* Publication of POCKET BOOKS

POCKET BOOKS, a division of Simon & Schuster Inc.
1230 Avenue of the Americas, New York, NY 10020

Copyright © 1995 by Carla Neggers

All rights reserved, including the right to reproduce
this book or portions thereof in any form whatsoever.
For information address Pocket Books, 1230 Avenue
of the Americas, New York, NY 10020

ISBN: 0-671-88320-8

First Pocket Books printing March 1996

10  9  8  7  6  5  4  3  2  1

POCKET and colophon are registered trademarks of
Simon & Schuster Inc.

Printed in the U.S.A.

For Joe, Kate and Zachary

Special thanks to Bill Deevy of Beaumont, Texas, for answering my questions and thinking up questions I needed answered, and to Deon Youngkin and Al Harmon for their technical expertise. Any mistakes are mine, not theirs. Many thanks also to Brenda Hamilton, Zita Christian, Leslie O'Grady, Linda Harmon, Nancy Martin, and Anna Eberhardt. Finally, I am grateful to my editor, Claire Zion, for her insight and skill and—always—to my agent, Denise Marcil, for everything.

Woodstock, Vermont, is a real—and very pretty—town in central Vermont. The *Vermont Citizen* and its building on Main Street, however, are imaginary, as is Hawthorne Orchard Road, although I did grow up in a house similar to Cozie Hawthorne's, complete with the occasional bat and snake and—of course—bird feeders in the front yard.

# CHAPTER
## 1

Daniel Foxworth ignored the crushing Texas heat and his own blood and pain as he jumped from the Coast Guard rescue helicopter. Reporters, already down from Houston, surged around him. An oil tanker was on fire in the Gulf of Mexico, a major spill imminent. He'd been hired to put it out. Except that the helicopter he and his partner had flown out to survey the fire had crashed into the warm, shallow waters of the gulf. It was a big story, made bigger because the pilot of the downed helicopter was a Foxworth.

The rescue team raced toward the hospital emergency room with the stretcher carrying the huge figure of James Dell Maguire. A mess of blood, oil, saltwater, shredded clothes, and broken bones, J.D. had been Daniel's sole passenger and was still cursing him for damned near getting them both killed.

J.D. wasn't out of the woods yet.

Daniel felt only the searing anger of helplessness and guilt. After they'd hit the water, he'd dragged the

1

semiconscious J.D. from the damaged helicopter before it could sink, drowning them both. Daniel had managed to dial up the emergency frequency in the seconds before they'd plunged into the gulf, but he'd never believed anyone would get there in time. He'd thought J.D. was dead or close to it.

The swarm of reporters and medical staff cut him off from J.D. Daniel fought back waves of nausea and pain. He had a pretty good gash on his right arm, a cut above his left ear, various scrapes and bruises. His clothes, stiff and still damp from saltwater, seemed branded onto his skin. But he couldn't take time to have a doctor look at him.

He turned from the emergency entrance and headed back toward the parking lot. There was nothing more he could do for J.D.

The reporters quickly figured out what he was doing and ran to catch up with him, shouting questions.

"Was this a daredevil stunt that backfired?"

"What caused the crash?"

"The fire on the tanker is still raging out of control —can you handle it without Maguire?"

"Wasn't Julia Vanackern supposed to be on board with you? Aren't you two an item?"

"Any truth to the rumors that your grandfather is coming down from Houston to take over?"

Daniel kept moving in the hot midday sun. An attractive television reporter came up on his elbow and shoved a microphone at him. He looked at her without a word, and she backed off.

Another helicopter was waiting in the parking lot, piloted by another refugee from Fox Oil—one not related to its founder. Daniel could feel the hot wind from the whirling helicopter blades and wished it could just blow him into another time and place. But he climbed aboard. He had no choice. He had a fire to fight. A tanker engine room was on fire. If the fire spread to the cargo area, the tanks would rupture and there would be one hell of an oil spill. He had to stop it.

Only then—when he was finished—could he find out who had blown him and J.D. out of the sky.

Cozie Hawthorne stared into her posh Chicago hotel closet, unable to decide between Bette Davis and Katharine Hepburn. How her life had changed, she thought, to have choosing a dress for a formal dinner party be her most pressing problem.

The Bette Davis dress was from the scene in *Now, Voyager* when Paul Henreid lights a cigarette for Davis, back in the days when lighting cigarettes was sexy. Cozie had taken the video to an old high school classmate who lived in a trailer way up on Hawthorne Orchard Road, back home in Vermont. She had four kids, an alcoholic husband, and an ancient Singer sewing machine. She could stitch together anything, including copies of dresses off videos of old movies.

The Hepburn dress, one of Cozie's favorites, was from the scene in *Adam's Rib* when Katharine Hepburn tells Spencer Tracy she's representing the infamous Doris, the woman who shot her philandering husband. He, of course, is representing the husband. Cozie didn't pull off the low neckline as well as Hepburn did, but it was still a wonderful dress.

She sighed. She was in her stockings and slip and didn't feel much like Katharine Hepburn or Bette Davis. Her hair—ordinarily her best feature, with its unusual mix of blonds and reds—was still a mess from the Chicago wind because she'd insisted on walking across Grant Park to see Lake Michigan. A rough fall wind was blowing in off the water, and the lake really was spectacular.

Tonight's dinner party was her first appearance on her latest—and final—book tour, which would take her from Chicago to Phoenix, San Diego, Seattle, Denver, and then back to New York and, finally, home to Vermont. Her rusted Jeep was waiting for her in long-term parking at the Burlington airport. She'd be back in time for peak foliage week.

By now her publicist would be in the lobby, waiting with her usual impatience. She hadn't caught on to Cozie's source of evening wear, just muttered occasionally about getting her a makeover in New York. Cozie had struggled for money until *Mountain Views,* a collection of her commentaries on everything from international diplomacy to life in Vermont, had unexpectedly hit the best-seller lists—and stuck—six months ago. She had yet to see the point of owning a dress worth more than her Jeep.

The telephone rang. She groaned and padded across the thick carpet to the extension on her bedside table. It was, of course, a king-size bed. As if she needed it.

"Two more minutes. I promise—"

"Hello, Cozie Cornelia. Running late?"

Not again. Her knees wobbling, she sank onto the bed. It was the obviously disguised voice that had followed her for weeks: disembodied, unrecognizable, neither male nor female.

Suddenly she was shaking, goose bumps sprouting on her arms and legs. Her fingers and toes turned cold.

"Chicago's a fun town," the voice went on. "Enjoy your stay. Be good."

*Click.*

Cozie waited for the dial tone, then slammed the phone down.

She had to keep her wits about her. Anger and panic

4

weren't going to help. She knew that from experience. Still trembling, she grabbed her handbag from the bedside table and fumbled for the spiral memo notebook she'd hoped she wouldn't need on this trip. She found a ballpoint pen and carefully wrote down the time, the place, and an exact transcript of the call. Never mind that she was suddenly famous for her wit, humor, and incisiveness, she was a journalist by training and instinct. She had developed a knack for remembering what people said.

Her task completed, she returned the notebook to her handbag and did a series of breathing exercises to calm herself down.

The calls had started two road trips ago, in July. They came at unpredictable times, in unpredictable places—at her hotel, at book signings, dinners, parties. Although not overtly threatening, they were unsettling. Someone was keeping track of her every move when she was on the road. Whoever it was had never bothered her at home in Vermont—a small consolation.

But she hadn't mentioned the calls to anyone. Word would get out, and she was sure that was just what the caller wanted: notoriety. Proof Cozie Hawthorne was rattled. She didn't want to play into the caller's hands. For now she would continue to keep her log and hope he—or she—just gave up. She promised herself that if the calls became more frequent, if they ever held even a hint of a threat, she wouldn't hesitate to go to the police, never mind her publicist.

She went back to the closet and dragged out the Katharine Hepburn dress. It was classy and a little daring, and wearing it always gave her a boost.

A pair of black heels, a fresh coat of mascara and red lipstick, and she was off. She'd enjoy her stay in Chicago all right. She'd be good. Soon she'd be back in the Green Mountains of northern New England, finished with road trips, and finally—finally—able to get her life back to normal.

J. D. Maguire was transferred to a Houston hospital, near where he and Daniel Foxworth had set up shop as petroleum product fire-fighting experts three years ago. Daniel came to visit on a rainy Sunday afternoon six days after the accident. J.D.'s doctors and nurses said he was making a steady recovery, his broken ribs and arm and multiple bruises and lacerations all healing nicely, but he was one ornery patient. Daniel told them J.D.'s orneriness had saved more than one person's life, his own included.

Then they told him J.D.'s shattered left leg still had them worried. It was still possible he could lose it. They were particularly worried about infection setting in.

J.D. was conscious and reasonably coherent when Daniel entered the private room he'd arranged for his partner to have. The medical types had shaved off his big black beard, but even after being hauled from a sinking helicopter, James Dell Maguire looked huge and very competent, his spirit undiminished by his suffering. He was on IVs, his eyes sunken and yellowed, his color lousy. Bruises had blossomed and spread on his arms and face, probably over his entire body.

"Hey, Danny Boy," he said. J.D. didn't believe any self-respecting Texan, even one as rich and educated as his partner, ought to be called Daniel. "We get the fire out?"

"Yeah, J.D., we got the fire out. Took about twice as long as it would have if you'd been there."

J.D. looked satisfied. "It would have been a hell of a mess if the fire had reached that crude. You still beat?"

6

He smiled. "I look better than you do, so I must be doing all right."

"Hell, Danny Boy, you ain't never gonna look better'n me."

In fact, days after he'd got the fire out, exhaustion still clung to Daniel like a stubborn fog. A long, hot shower and George Dickel had helped ease some of his fatigue. A woman would have helped even more. But he needed to keep his edge.

He needed to find out who'd tried to kill him and J.D.

J.D. grew serious. "They find out why our copter went down?"

"Something caused an explosion and busted out a bunch of stuff a copter needs to stay in the air, and into the drink we went. Near as I can figure, the tail rotor drive shaft was damaged and we lost control. Best guess is a couple detonator caps I had stored in back ignited."

"Why?"

Daniel shrugged. "Bad luck."

"Bad luck, hell."

"The easy answer is I was reckless and negligent— in too big a hurry to get to the fire—and screwed up, didn't pre-flight something I was supposed to. But detonator caps don't just up and explode."

"So what the hell happened?"

"That's what I'd like to know. Someone could have snuck aboard and attached a timing device to a couple of the blasting caps we had stored. It wouldn't be much of a bomb, but in a strategic place it could do a lot of damage—like blow a tail rotor drive shaft to hell. I was in the military a long time, J.D., and I know—"

But J.D. had risen up. "You talking sabotage, Danny?"

7

"I'm saying I want to know what caused the explosion that put us in the water. I want answers."

"You're saying someone tried to kill us."

"Maybe not us. Julia Vanackern was supposed to be on board. She could have been the target."

J.D. snorted. "This is nuts. You talk to her?"

Daniel shook his head. "I've never even met her. She and her parents didn't waste any time beating a path out of here after the crash. Julia witnessed it. Guess she was pretty upset."

"Poor thing." J.D. didn't think much of Julia Vanackern. "You never got to meet her?"

"Nope."

"Ain't that a shame. Thought we might see Fox Oil and Vanackern Media in one family. You two'd be so goddamned rich no one could stand you."

Daniel had no interest in pursuing a relationship, romantic or otherwise, with Julia Vanackern, especially since he'd never met the woman. He leaned over J.D.'s hospital bed. "I've done some investigating on my own this week. Remember when you came on board, you mentioned some kid had been bugging Julia before she backed out of going with us. He'd come down from the Vanackern country place in Vermont—he worked for them."

"Yeah, I remember. He and Julia were really going at it. I asked her if she needed me to knock him on his ass, but she said she could handle him." J.D. sank deep into his pillow, his energy waning. He swallowed and slowly licked his chapped, raw lips, the pain showing in his yellowed eyes. "After that she changed her mind about going with us. Must have been upset."

"I checked this guy out," Daniel said. "His name's Seth Hawthorne. He's the younger brother of a Vermont writer named Cozie Hawthorne, who has a best-selling book out; I picked up a copy."

He had it with him, a neatly packaged hardcover collection of commentaries on subjects ranging from the simple pleasures of cidermaking to the problems in the Balkans. Daniel had read it cover to cover on the porch of the dilapidated log cabin on the small ranch he'd bought a couple of months ago outside Houston. Cozie Hawthorne had a wry humor, a straightforward, distinctly Yankee point of view, and an infectious optimism that permeated everything she wrote. He could see why the book had surged onto the best-seller lists.

J.D. squinted at the color photograph on the back cover of *Mountain Views*. She was standing in front of a woodpile, wearing a sand-colored field jacket, dark brown jeans, and half-laced L. L. Bean boots, her reddish blond hair pulled back rather inexpertly. Several wisps had escaped and hung in her angular face. Her eyes, Daniel had noticed, were a dark, vivid green.

"Not bad for a Yankee," J.D. allowed. "She could use some time in the beauty parlor, but they all could up there." He managed a grin as he sank back into his pillow. J.D. didn't go for the outdoor look in women. "Wonder what she'd look like in a leopard-skin swimsuit."

Daniel laughed. "At least your mind wasn't damaged in the crash."

"Damn right. What the hell kind of name's Cozie?"

"Apparently it's short for Cornelia."

J.D. made a face.

"Yeah." Daniel left the book on the bedside table for J.D. to read. "She runs a paper up in Woodstock, Vermont."

"That where they had that damned rock concert?"

J.D. listened exclusively to country-western music, had lost a brother to Vietnam, and had no truck—

9

none—with anything that reminded him of the up-heavals of the sixties.

"No, that Woodstock's in New York," Daniel said. "This one's supposed to be one of the six prettiest villages in America. I picked up a Vermont guidebook. Cozie Hawthorne runs a respected weekly newspaper there. Her family started it back during the American Revolution."

"Bully for them." J.D.'s family had crawled out of East Texas poverty, only to be knocked back down into it by the Foxworths of Fox Oil. It was one wrong Daniel had committed himself to righting.

"Vanackern Media bought the paper two years ago when it was about to go bankrupt. The Vanackerns' country place is in Woodstock, off—get this—Haw-thorne Orchard Road."

J.D. was fully awake again. "So Cozie and Seth Hawthorne both work for the Vanackerns. She's got to be making a fortune on this book." He picked at the adhesive tape around the IV on his wrist, his brow furrowed in concentration. "Meanwhile the brother's a glorified handyman. Can't sit too well."

"You saw him with Julia. Do you think she had herself a little affair with the hired help?"

"And he came down here looking for her, she told him to suck eggs, and he had enough and decided to blow her rich ass out of the sky. It's possible." J.D. heaved a sigh. "If that's the case, we were just a frigging bonus."

Daniel was staring at Cozie Hawthorne's picture on the back of her book. How had she taken to her unexpected success? From her book, he'd guess money impressed her about as much as it did J.D. "I don't like being a bonus."

"Me neither. Hell, you know what they say: I'd rather be shot at and hit than shit at and missed."

"We're way ahead of ourselves, you know." Daniel maintained an outward calm. "Our copter's under water. I can't even prove it was sabotaged."

J.D.'s black eyes narrowed. "Maybe it wasn't."

"I know. Maybe it wasn't. Maybe I'm just poking under other people's rocks to keep from seeing what's under my own." He turned away from J.D.'s probing gaze. They'd been partners and friends a long time, he and James Dell Maguire. "I've been calling realtors in Woodstock. Turns out Cozie Hawthorne herself has a place for rent right on Hawthorne Orchard Road."

"You rented it?"

Daniel smiled. J.D. knew him well. "Under an assumed name. No point in stirring the bottom unless I've got good reason. Right now, I don't. I leave in the morning. I'm driving up, giving myself time to think. I don't want to be hunting a scapegoat when the real culprit's staring at me in the mirror. But I want to know what Seth Hawthorne was doing down here."

"Keep me posted," J.D. said quietly.

"I will." He nodded to *Mountain Views.* "Make sure you read her piece on the moose-sighting craze. It's probably the only one that won't piss you off."

"Can't wait."

"Take care, J.D." His eyes drifted to J.D.'s mangled leg. "I'll be in touch."

He was halfway to the door when J.D. said, "If Seth Hawthorne didn't put me here, Daniel, you did. When I'm on my feet, you'll answer for it."

Daniel looked back at his broken, bruised, and bloodied friend. A full recovery seemed impossible. "You get back on your feet, J.D., and I'll answer for anything."

# CHAPTER
# 2

The smell of apples sweetened the crisp Vermont morning air as Cozie cranked her ancient cider press. Even with getting home from New York after midnight, she'd been up early and out in the field collecting apples. She'd put on baggy jeans and ratty mud shoes and pulled her hair back with a thick rubber band off a bunch of broccoli, then threw on her father's old black-and-red checked wool shirt. Cider-making was a fall Hawthorne family tradition. Nothing could make her feel more at home, more like herself again.

Clear, amber-colored cider dribbled into the spotless bucket she'd set under the spout. Behind her was the white clapboard house Elijah Hawthorne had built in 1790, all around her the land he had settled—the rolling fields, the woods, the old stone walls. This was her childhood home, where generations of Hawthornes had grown up. For the past ten years she'd lived up the road in an early nineteenth-century sawmill she'd renovated.

But in July all that had changed when she'd bought the Hawthorne house and surrounding land from her widowed mother, whose strapped financial condition was about to force her to sell to strangers. Emily Hawthorne had made it clear she wanted to be free—financially, physically, and emotionally—from two centuries of her husband's family traditions. After she and her daughter had closed the deal, she bought a condo in a refurbished building in town, within walking distance of shops, restaurants, and the library, and planned a trip to New Zealand and Australia. Last heard from, she was having a grand time in Perth.

As much as Cozie loved her family's land and the crumbling old house, she had never expected she would end up its sole owner. She'd assumed it would go to her brother or sister, or they'd all share in its ownership.

She paused in her cidermaking, trying to absorb every nuance of the beautiful morning. The sky was a clear, autumnal blue, setting off the dark evergreens and the reds and yellows and oranges of the deciduous trees on the hills around her. Across the unlined road, she could hear Hawthorne Brook rushing over rocks on its mad dash toward the Ottauquechee River. Leaves rustled in the breeze.

*"I know where you are. I can always find you."*

She shuddered. It would take awhile for her to forget her caller's parting words as she'd left her hotel room yesterday afternoon for an early dinner with her agent. She breathed in the smell of the cider, the smell of the clean air. She just needed to be patient. Given time, all would be well.

Her brother's rusting hulk of a truck turned up her loop-shaped dirt driveway, bouncing into the gravel parking area out back where she'd set up the cider press. Seth jumped out. He was twenty-five, six years younger than Cozie, taller and lankier, and darker, but with the same green eyes and sometimes irritatingly practical outlook on life. He lived in a small farmhouse—which Cozie also now owned—on the northern end of the Hawthorne woods.

"Hey, you're back," he said by way of a greeting. "I came by last night but you weren't around."

"Plane was delayed. I didn't get in until after midnight."

"I don't know, Coze." He looked her over, giving her one of his lazy grins. He had on tattered jeans, a cheap, frayed rust-colored flannel shirt, and old work boots. "You don't look any different now that you've been interviewed on the *Today* show."

"Ouch—you saw that?"

"Yep. Rolled out of bed, and here was my sister cackling on TV. How come you didn't call and let us know you were going to be on?"

"It was one of those last-minute things, and I did not cackle." But he'd already started back toward the toolshed, a small outbuilding a long-ago Hawthorne had put up and Grandpa Willard had painted barn red. "What're you up to?"

"I'm bringing a load of wood up to your new tenant. Sal called yesterday and said the guy had just figured out the place was heated with wood and was freezing his ass off. You have an extra splitter he can borrow, right?"

"*Who* can borrow? Seth, I haven't talked to Sal." Sal O'Connor was Cozie's realtor, a transplanted New Yorker who could sell Vermont—at least her vision of

14

it—to anyone. "I don't know anything about a tenant. Who is he?"

She'd followed her brother to the toolshed, where he plucked a heavy, unwieldy splitting maul from a nail just inside the door. "Some flatlander."

"How long has he been here?"

"Two or three days. I haven't met him yet."

"I figured I'd be out of luck finding a renter until ski season, especially the way Sal talked. Maybe I should go up with you, check this guy out."

Seth shrugged. "Climb in back—Zep's got the front."

Zep was the family dog, a half–German shepherd, half–everything else mutt who had certain privileges no one bothered to argue. "Did he behave while I was gone?" Cozie asked.

"He doesn't behave when you're here."

"That's because you spoil him."

Seth tossed her the splitter, which she tucked under one arm as she climbed atop the cordwood. In another minute, they were bouncing down the driveway, Cozie breathing in the smell of bark, sawdust, and wood mold and thinking of herself as a landlady.

At the end of the driveway, while Seth waited for a break in traffic, she looked back at her old white clapboard farmhouse nestled into the rolling hills of south-central Vermont and tried to see not just all the work she had to do, not just her own memories and abandoned dreams, but what the tourists out on Hawthorne Orchard Road saw. The smoke curling from the stone chimney. The wood neatly stacked for winter. The stone walls marking off fields of young Christmas trees and gnarled old apple trees and tall grass glistening in the morning sun. The huge sugar maples with their red-gold leaves, and the fire bushes and yellow mums and gardens of pumpkins and grapes and bushy herbs.

It was all so quintessentially Vermont, so damned beautiful.

The leaf peepers would likely never guess a family of garter snakes had taken up residence in her dirt cellar and a bat was loose upstairs. That a dormer leaked. That there was precious little romance in facing an empty woodbox on a below-zero January night.

Growing up, Cozie would have helped her father dispense with the snakes and told him *she'd* never have snakes in the cellar. But some things were inescapable, and her father had been dead for almost two years.

Seth swooped out onto the road and in less than a mile turned down a steep dirt driveway toward Hawthorne Brook, where her small 1803 sawmill was tucked on a hillside. Constructed of dark, almost black, rough-hewn lumber, it overlooked an old stone dam that formed a tiny pond and ten-foot waterfall on the fast-flowing brook. Cozie loved to lie in her rope hammock out on the porch directly above the pond and listen to the water flow over the dam.

*Used* to love it, she amended. She didn't live here anymore. Some flatlander did. But as she grabbed the splitter and jumped down off the wood, it was as if she'd never left.

Then a dark, long-legged man walked out onto her porch, and she had to admit that here, definitely, was proof that Cozie Hawthorne no longer lived in her little sawmill by the brook.

"Geez, Seth," she muttered as her brother came up beside her, "you could have warned me. This guy looks like he could rope a buffalo."

Seth didn't seem impressed. "I'd have liked to have

seen him crawling out of bed this morning with no heat."

Flatlander though he might be, the man ambling down the porch steps did not look unfamiliar with the basic skills of survival. He was tall—over six feet—and had a thick, muscular build that his black canvas shirt and close-fitting jeans only served to emphasize. His shirtsleeves were rolled to just above his wrist bones. His dark hair was windblown, and his sharp, imperfectly formed features, his alert gray eyes, his tanned skin, suggested a life not spent in an office building of the great megalopolis to the south. He had on scarred black boots distinctly not Vermont in style.

Seth was all business. "Good morning. Sal O'Connor sent me with the wood."

"Great. I could use some."

"Where you want it?"

"Wherever you think best."

His voice was deep and sounded as if it had been rubbed with sandpaper, and his accent was from somewhere decidedly farther south than New Jersey. Cozie glanced at the black truck parked crookedly in her former parking space and noticed its Texas license plate. Well, no wonder he hadn't worried about heat in October. She'd changed planes in Dallas on her latest book tour. It had been stiflingly hot in the jetway.

Seth, who could meditate for hours on where to locate his own woodpile, abruptly started back to his truck. "We'll stack some on the porch where it'll be handy. The rest we'll stack here by the driveway. You'll need to cover it." He cast the Texan a look that, unusual for easygoing Seth Hawthorne, bordered on hostility. "We get snow up here in the winter, you know."

His sarcasm had no apparent effect on its target,

who turned to Cozie after her brother had climbed back into his truck. "Who is he?"

"Oh—I'm sorry, we should have introduced ourselves. My name's Cozie. Cozie Hawthorne. I—um— own the mill. Seth's my brother."

Her tenant gave her a quick but efficient once-over. The gray of his eyes, she saw, was clear and dark, a true slate gray. "So you're my new landlady."

His controlled, laconic manner, coupled with his Texas accent, gave his words an almost possessive quality that Cozie hoped she was just imagining. He seemed to be waiting for her to respond. "Yes, I guess I am."

"I'm Daniel Forrest. Pleased to meet you."

"Likewise." Having never been a landlady, she had no idea what she was supposed to say to a new tenant, especially one for whom she was so totally unprepared. "Everything's okay?"

"Now that I've figured out the place is heated with wood I should be fine." His gaze rested on her. "Rough getting out of the shower on a frosty Vermont morning."

Cozie cleared her throat. She didn't need to be picturing Daniel Forrest running stark naked from the shower into her former loft bedroom.

But she was.

"Did Sal mention that sometimes a bat or flying squirrel might work its way into the loft?"

"No, ma'am," he said, "she didn't."

"Well, it probably won't happen. If there's a problem, just give me a call. I've gotten pretty good at dealing with bats—not that I've had that many. And the flying squirrels aren't bad at all. I've only had four or five in all the time I've been here." *Go ahead, Coze, dig a deeper hole for yourself.*

Daniel Forrest remained quite calm. "I'm sure I'll manage."

Cozie was sure he would, too.

"Anything else?" he asked mildly.

"I'm not sure if Sal . . . there's no garbage disposal, you know, but there is a compost pile on the other side of the house, down this little path." The way he was looking at her, she assumed he had no idea what she was talking about. "You do know what a compost pile is?"

He seemed amused. "Yes, ma'am, I know."

She decided not to mention about not throwing coffee grounds down the drain and using only low-suds detergent in the washing machine. Surely Sal had told him that stuff. She'd warned Cozie that most people wouldn't consider her converted wood-heated sawmill a year-round residence.

Was Daniel Forrest here just temporarily? She'd have to talk to Sal, get the details.

"I live just down the road in the white house with the black shutters, if you need anything."

Before he could respond, Seth honked his horn, and they got out of his way. The truck bed rose up, and logs tumbled out in a huge heap. When Seth got back out, Zep, with no display of grace or manners, jumped out and leaped into the little pond.

"Better show Texas here how to split wood, Coze," Seth said when he rejoined them. "Wouldn't want him lopping off an ankle before he's been here a week."

His words would have set her off, but Daniel Forrest regarded her brother without apparent irritation. "It's all right. I can handle the wood from here on out. Thanks."

Seth was unmoved. "That woodpile's all that stands between you and freezing your butt off on a cold morning."

19

The Texan gave him a tolerant smile. "So I've discovered."

"Show him, Coze."

She had no intention of showing anyone anything, but before she could make up her mind how to handle the situation, Daniel Forrest took a log from the pile and set it upright on her old chopping block on the edge of the driveway. He put a hand out to her. She turned over the splitting maul. She could feel the wind whipping strands of hair from her haphazard ponytail and figured she and Seth weren't coming off too well right now.

"Better stand back," Seth warned her.

She took his advice, just in case.

Using both hands, the Texan raised the heavy splitter above his head with an ease that even Seth, as contemptuous of flatlanders as he was, had to notice. He paused for a beat, then heaved the splitter down onto the log, whacking it neatly in two.

Cozie figured there had to be a column in this somewhere. She picked up the half that landed at her feet. "Well, brother, seems the man's done this before."

But Seth's green eyes remained pinned on the Texan. "You know how to stack wood so it doesn't come down on top of you?"

"I alternate vertical and horizontal rows."

So did Seth. Cozie resisted a laugh, not that her brother deserved her loyalty. In his view, no flatlander —even one from Texas—would survive a week in Vermont without help from the natives. Usually, however, he was more good-natured about his prejudices.

"How much do I owe you?" the Texan asked.

"I'll let you know."

Unchastened, Seth gave Zep a yell. The big mutt

came galloping out of the pond and waited to shake himself off until he was directly behind Cozie's new tenant, who ended up sprayed with cold, muddy water. Daniel Forrest didn't jump in surprise or curse or even wince, but just calmly looked around at the offending beast. "Feel better, fella?"

Cozie observed his reaction with interest. She didn't know what the man did for a living or why he was in Vermont, but he was one controlled individual.

Seth got Zep back in the truck and went around to the driver's side while Cozie climbed in back. She saw the question in the Texan's eyes and grinned. "Zep always gets the front."

He swung the splitter onto one strong shoulder. "I'm sure."

Without warning, the truck lurched up the steep driveway, sending Cozie sprawling. She grabbed the cold tailgate to keep herself from smacking her mouth against it and knocking out a few teeth. She wished she'd worn work gloves. She'd had her nails manicured in San Diego.

Holding on tight as her brother careened up the driveway, she didn't dare duck or even let go long enough to peel back the strands of hair that had blown into her mouth. Her wool shirt, she now noticed, smelled faintly of tractor grease and rotten apples. She probably had a red nose.

Daniel Forrest was standing with the splitter on his shoulder, watching her.

She almost yelled back to him that she was the editor-in-chief of an award-winning newspaper one of her ancestors had founded, that she'd had a book on *The New York Times* best-seller list for weeks and weeks, that she was famous, dammit, and he could quit looking at her as if she were some kind of wild-haired lunatic mountainwoman.

Except, she had to admit, she relished *feeling* like a wild-haired lunatic mountainwoman.

Back out on the main road, she looked down the wooded hill and caught sight of the big Texan setting another log on the chopping block. Without so much as a backward glance, he whacked it in two as easily as he had the first.

Cozie settled back. She wouldn't, she decided, want to get between Daniel Forrest and something he was after.

Daniel swung the heavy splitting maul until his shoulders and arms and even his legs ached, until his lungs burned and he could feel the sweat pouring down his back.

There was no getting around it. Seth Hawthorne didn't look like a man who would sabotage a helicopter and risk killing three people just to get back at a woman who'd spurned him.

Another log split cleanly in two.

But better to sneak off to Vermont looking for a scapegoat than to blame himself, than to be there with J.D. when the doctors came for his leg.

He stopped. He'd stripped off his shirt and was breathing hard. Sweat burned in his eyes—or maybe it was just his own guilt. He set the splitter against an orange-leafed maple and gathered up the scattered chunks of wood. He kept a woodpile at his ranch outside Houston. He should be chopping wood there, in the warm morning sun, not up north in Vermont.

He headed to the edge of the mill pond. In the brook's endless, unthinking rush over the old stone dam, in the quiet stir of leaves in the autumn breeze, he tried to sense a peace he didn't feel.

In his gut he knew Seth Hawthorne had recognized him. Somehow the kid knew his name wasn't Forrest but Foxworth. Daniel Austin Foxworth. Black sheep son of Texas oilmen and generals. Up-and-coming fighter of petroleum product fires anywhere in the world.

At least until his helicopter went down in the Gulf of Mexico. Now no one in the small world of oil fire fighting would dare trust him. He didn't trust himself. And in that world, trust was everything.

He kicked off his boots and stripped off his jeans and plunged into the small pond.

*"Damn!"*

The water was so cold it knocked the breath out of him. But he forced himself to dive once more, and when he came up for air, the water was streaming down his face like the tears of an uncontrolled grief.

"God," he breathed as he swam toward a huge flat rock on the opposite bank, "what am I doing here?"

He was out of his element among the people and hills of northern New England. He didn't know what in hell he expected to accomplish. Heaving himself onto the sun-warmed rock, he saw that after less than ten minutes in the water his skin was splotched with blue and purple from the cold.

Did his landlady ever go skinny-dipping in her icy mill pond?

He pictured her and her rawboned brother as kids, jumping in on a hot summer day. They were a flinty pair of Yankees, Cozie and Seth Hawthorne.

Sliding back into the water, Daniel did a fast breaststroke to the other side, glad for the short distance. He climbed out, grabbed up his jeans and boots, and stole back inside before his landlady came hunting her splitting maul or some tourist up on the road stopped and took his picture.

He dried off and put on fresh clothes, figuring he'd get back to his woodpile, but his eyes drifted to his second copy of *Mountain Views*. J.D. had decided to hang onto the first. Cozie Hawthorne's wry, practical, witty commentaries went with her slouchy clothes, her unlaced mud shoes, her mass of reddish blond curls snarled and beaten down by the stiff Vermont wind.

But her eyes were even more alive, more compelling in person than in her picture. Huge, warm, intelligent, they'd changed from green to blue and back again, it seemed, in the short time she'd helped her brother with the wood. They were eyes that said she was an optimist and a survivor, a woman who wouldn't take to having someone lie to her.

Daniel abruptly returned to his wood. He needed to remember that he hadn't come to Woodstock to contemplate his pretty Yankee landlady's eyes—and he'd already committed himself to his lies.

# CHAPTER
# 3

"The people of Woodstock," the old saying went, "have less of a reason than most to yearn for heaven."

Words, as far as Cozie was concerned, not meant for Friday afternoons during foliage season. Downtown Woodstock was mobbed. Traffic crawled. Parking was, to say the least, a challenge. Yet everyone she saw on the picturesque, tree-lined village streets looked to be having a good time, letting the crowds add to the festive atmosphere rather than detract. All the upscale shops and restaurants and museums were open, the inns full. The Killington ski area, with its hiking trails and autumn gondola rides, was just to the west. The Connecticut River and Dartmouth College were to the east, and the Ottauquechee River flowed right through the middle of town, at one point under a covered bridge. Lots of folks, however, were just strolling about, enjoying Woodstock's famous ellipse-shaped common and its graceful Federal period homes.

The 1832 brick *Vermont Citizen* building—one of Woodstock's most photographed—was located on the common opposite the Woodstock Inn & Resort. Despite its pristine, black-shuttered exterior, it was a creaky old place that barely passed fire inspection. Elijah Hawthorne, whose seditious broadsides in the 1770s had earned him the enmity of King George III, had put up the building the year before he died, back during the one period when the Hawthornes had actually had spare cash. Now it was owned by the Vanackerns. But so was Elijah's paper.

Grateful she had her own space in the *Citizen*'s short driveway, Cozie put on her blinker and started to turn.

She had to slam on her brake to keep from rear-ending a black truck with Texas license plates.

Her new tenant.

Daniel Forrest.

Short of honking her horn and fuming, there was nothing she could do. She backed out into the snaking traffic and had to swing around the common twice before snatching a space just given up by an elderly couple from Rhode Island. She crossed the common in a hurry and gritted her teeth as she headed into the *Citizen*'s center hall entrance.

Nobody messed with her parking space.

Her office was through a six-panel door—presently shut—to her left. The newsroom and production offices, with their Vanackern-purchased state-of-the-art equipment, were upstairs. To her right were advertising, bookkeeping, and her aunt, Ethel Hawthorne, who called her niece into the cluttered but very organized reception area.

Tall, bony, her mostly gray hair in short, loose curls, Ethel Hawthorne was perched behind the long library table she had used as a desk since coming to work for the *Citizen* at age eighteen, close to fifty years ago. She'd never married, and she maintained that she'd never wanted to do anything more at her family's paper than what she was doing, which more often than not was a little of everything. Technically she was supposed to answer the phone, sort the mail, and keep track of people, but every Thursday, when the paper came out, she would critique a copy with a red ballpoint pen and leave it on Cozie's desk. She felt free to make suggestions, solicit advertising, and look over people's shoulders. She had lived in the same ground-floor apartment since moving out of the Hawthorne house—the same one Cozie now owned—at twenty-one, and she walked to work every morning, regardless of the weather. She acknowledged her age to no one not involved with securing her retirement or collecting her taxes. She did not acknowledge the Vanackern ownership of the *Vermont Citizen*.

"There's a man in your office," she told Cozie.

"Tall, dark-haired, Texas accent?"

"That's him."

"And you just let him in." It came out more of an accusation than Cozie had intended.

Aunt Ethel cocked a thick eyebrow at her. "You think I'm going to argue with a man come looking for you?"

"Very funny. He's my new tenant."

"Ah. Well, he's only been here ten minutes. I think he's fiddling around on your computer."

Cozie bristled. "I'd say Daniel Forrest and I need to get a few things straight."

Aunt Ethel, however, was, highly entertained. She liked to think of herself as the Last Spinster of Woodstock and resented any encroachment on her status by her unmarried, over-thirty, lately-of-no-romantic-prospects niece.

27

Leaving her aunt to her chuckling, Cozie went back through the center hall and burst into her office without knocking.

Daniel Forrest was playing solitaire on her computer in front of her window overlooking Woodstock common as if he owned the place. Her computer and computer furniture were the only notably modern pieces in the otherwise nineteenth-century room with its worn Oriental carpets, cherry floors, Vermont marble fireplace, and glass-fronted bookcases.

Cozie flung her oversized leather tote onto the rickety Windsor chair by the door. "Good afternoon," she said coolly. "Is there something wrong with the wood or do you need me to show you how to start a fire in the woodstove?"

He pushed back her ergonomically correct chair and swiveled around, regarding her with a nonchalance that surely would have been beyond anyone else similarly caught. "No, I can manage my own fires." He gave her a long look. "So. This where you think up your smart-aleck columns?"

With some effort, she maintained her deliberately cool demeanor. "It is."

"Quaint. Most of the furniture for show?"

"None of it."

He raised an eyebrow. "Couple of those chairs look pretty old."

"A number of pieces date from the construction of the building in 1832." Her tone was starchy, one way of telling him she didn't plan to humor him for long. "I use them all as needed."

"I'll bet you do." It seemed to her he was deliberately laying on the Texas accent, but maybe not. She hadn't had much to do with Texans. He glanced up at the portrait above the fireplace. "That one of your Yankee kinfolk?"

28

"That's Elijah Hawthorne," she said of her stern-faced, green-eyed ancestor. "He founded the *Citizen* back during the Revolution."

"Which one?"

"The American Revolution." She judiciously kept all sarcasm from her tone. He was just trying to goad her; he knew damned well which revolution. "He settled the land up on Hawthorne Brook and built my family's house, then this building toward the end of his life."

"Kind of dour-looking, isn't he?"

"He was seventy-five when that portrait was painted. That was the style in the early nineteenth century."

"One would hope." He squinted at her, then back up at the portrait. "I think you have his eyes."

Cozie refused to react: she had no idea what this man was up to. "My aunt says you've been here only a few minutes."

"Yep. Three hundred in the hole and I was out of here."

She glanced at her computer screen. "You're close to that now."

"I've never trusted a computer not to cheat."

He leaned back, looking very much at ease and more than a tad full of himself. In the enclosed space of her office, his well-muscled legs seemed even longer than they had outside at her sawmill. He'd changed into a short-sleeved polo shirt, in a cobalt blue that set off the gray of his eyes. Unlike his shirt that morning, it revealed a thick red scar just below his right elbow. Although reasonably healed, the injury appeared recent.

His gray eyes didn't leave her. Since their earlier meeting, Cozie had showered and changed into a squash-colored sweater and black jeans, and she had her hair pulled back neatly with a handmade wooden barrette. Her loafers were a little scuffed and her socks were a print of bright yellow and orange leaves, in honor of the season, but, mercifully, she no longer smelled like rotten apples.

"Well," she said, "what can I do for you?"

"Just figured you could tell me where your brother lives. I ought to pay him for the wood."

"Aunt Ethel could have told you."

"Didn't know she was your aunt."

Cozie warned herself to think before she spoke—not her long suit. She didn't know why she felt so violated. It wasn't as if she'd never had to deal with a surprise visitor. Of course, Daniel Forrest wasn't just a visitor. He was her tenant, and she wasn't sure how she should treat a tenant, especially when questioning his behavior. Should she throw him out and tell him not to bother her at work? Inform him in no uncertain terms that just because he'd rented her sawmill didn't mean he could steal her parking space and barge into her office?

An unnatural caution won out. "Seth has a place on a dirt road up past the sawmill; it's your first left. His house is the red one about a mile up on the right. The only other house on the road is further up. It belongs to the Vanackern family. I don't know how much you've had a chance to look around . . ."

"I know the road."

"I doubt he's there. It's too nice a day. He might be working out at the Vanackern place. You could leave me with the money, but I don't know how much he's charging you."

"It's okay. He's your baby brother?"

"He's a few years younger than I am, yes."

"What's he do for a living?"

"Property management and forestry work, and he serves as a guide for canoeing and hiking trips whenever he gets the chance."

"Doesn't work on the family paper?"

"It's not the family paper anymore. My father sold it to Vanackern Media before his death two years ago. Mr. Forrest, I've been away for a couple of weeks, and I have things I need to do. If I see Seth, I'll tell him you stopped by—but he's not one to forget someone owes him money."

Her lame attempt at humor didn't draw a smile from her tenant. "I'll bet not." As he rose, she noticed the rock-hard muscles in his upper arms and another recent scar above his left ear and wondered, again, what he did for a living. She'd have to give Sal a call. "I'll let you get to work, Ms. Hawthorne. Thanks."

"You can call me Cozie, you know. Everyone around here does."

Still no smile. His slate eyes, however, drifted to hers. "Okay, Cozie. Make it Daniel for me."

A car outside her window drew her eye: a familiar champagne-colored Mercedes with Connecticut license plates. It was double-parked because the driver would be convinced no one would ever dare ticket a Vanackern car. Cozie felt herself tense up.

Tall, leanly built, aristocratic Thaddeus Wythering Vanackern slid from behind the wheel, shut the door, and hesitated a moment before squaring his shoulders and proceeding onto the sidewalk in front of the *Vermont Citizen* building.

"Looks like he's about to confront the Medusa," Daniel commented.

Cozie scowled. "He's here to see me. He's one of your neighbors: Thad Vanackern."

"Your boss?"

"Not to the degree he thinks," she muttered under her breath.

But Daniel heard her and grinned, and the results were so unexpectedly sexy, so earthy and frankly sensual, that Cozie found her throat going tight and dry with an awareness of him that was very physical and very much out of order. She needed to get this man out of her office before she faced Thad Vanackern.

"If you'll excuse me . . ."

But the chairman of Vanackern Media, already in the center hall entrance, strode in without waiting for an invitation or even speaking to Aunt Ethel, which wouldn't sit well with her. "Cozie—so good to see you," he said, taking both her hands into his and kissing her on the cheek.

Daniel Forrest made no move to leave.

"Hello, Thad."

She'd never been good at phony charm. Thad Vanackern hadn't approved of her since the day, at ten years old, she'd wandered onto his property in her fruitless search for a yellow lady's slipper. He'd refused to believe she knew her way back and insisted on calling her father to come fetch her.

Thad was, at sixty-five, a fair, square-jawed, handsome man who looked as rich and educated as he was. He had on his weekend-in-the-country clothes: expensive charcoal wool trousers, a cabled burgundy cotton sweater over a matching turtleneck, light hikers. He lived, he often said, for his favorite pastimes of golf, tennis, running, and fly-fishing. Business had never gripped his soul the way it had those of previous Vanackerns or he never would have urged Vanackern Media to purchase the Hawthornes' little paper, an act, he argued proudly, of historical preservation, not of true capitalism.

"You look wonderful," he said. "I understand you got in late last night?"

She nodded. "It's good to be home. I don't think I'll ever be much on flying. Gives me chapped lips and makes my feet swell—and I inevitably have the ugliest suitcase at baggage claim."

"You're not still using your Grandpa Willard's old suitcase, are you?"

"It's still got a lot of wear left in it."

Thad shook his head as if there were no reforming her. "You sound just like him. You could afford to buy a new one, you know."

She knew. A year ago she'd had to scramble to make ends meet, but the success of *Mountain Views* had changed all that. Still, her old clunker of a suitcase had been a peculiar source of comfort to her on the road. She remembered dragging it out of the back of a closet at eighteen, cleaning it up, packing her things for the university up in Burlington. Her big adventure.

Thad glanced around at Daniel Forrest, who was watching and listening with apparent interest. The man did have his nerve. Why couldn't Sal have found a retired banker to rent the sawmill?

Cozie sighed. In her best diplomatic voice, she said, "Thad, I'd like you to meet Daniel Forrest. He's moved into the sawmill. Daniel, Thad Vanackern."

Thad extended his hand. "Well, then, we're neighbors. Welcome to Woodstock, Mr. Forrest."

"Thank you."

She thought that was plenty enough hint to get moving, but Forrest shook hands with his neighbor and continued to stand there as if he had every right to horn in on his landlady's conversation with her "boss."

Short of being rude, which he would never deliberately be, Thad had little choice but to resume. He

33

turned back to Cozie. "I understand you were in New York yesterday. I wish you had come by."

Vanackern Media had its headquarters in New York City, and she was still one of their employees. Of course they would keep track of her now that she was on the edges of the limelight. But Cozie could feel her stomach flip-flop at the thought of more Vanackern scrutiny, more Vanackern expectations. "It was just overnight. My publisher had lined up a couple of interviews. It was fun; a little nuts, but fun."

Thad smiled indulgently, as if no one knew her better. "The reluctant celebrity."

As if on cue, a few strands of her hair loosened from her barrette and dropped into her face. She tucked them behind her ear, more aware of her tenant's eyes on her than Thad Vanackern's. Did he know about her book? "I wouldn't call myself a celebrity."

"No, I'm sure you wouldn't." An unmistakable tension had crept into his voice. He inhaled deeply through his nose. "I admire what you've managed to accomplish, Cozie. We all do."

She tried to ignore his patronizing tone. "I appreciate that."

"Well. I just stopped by to remind you of our annual fall get-together tomorrow evening at the Woodstock Inn. You will be attending, won't you? Frances said she hadn't heard from you."

Frances was his wife, a Woodstock native who, ages ago, had nearly married a Hawthorne—Cozie's father. Knowing Thad's personal request for her presence was more like an order from on high, Cozie forced a polite smile. She avoided looking at Daniel Forrest. This wasn't the lunatic mountainwoman side of her he was seeing. "Thanks for the reminder. I didn't—"

"You didn't respond to your invitation because you'd hoped we'd just forget about you. No such luck, Cozie. You will come?"

Refusal was impossible, and they both knew it. But she gave him an irreverent grin, if only to relieve her own tension—and maybe to salvage her pride with her new tenant looking on. "What's on the menu?"

"I beg your pardon?"

"I've been on the road on and off for months. I just got back last night from my last trip. About all that appeals to me is canned tomato soup by the wood-stove."

Thad surprised her with a modest laugh; he was never certain how to react to her. "We're not having canned soup, I can tell you that. I believe Frances requested roast native Vermont turkey."

"I guess that beats tomato soup."

"You, Cornelia Hawthorne, are your father's daughter."

"Is that a compliment?"

He sighed. "An observation. Frances will be delighted to know you're coming. So will Julia. She's in town, you know. She's had quite a time the past month or so. I'm sure she'll tell you all about it."

Julia Vanackern was always having "quite a time," usually involving men. "It'll be nice to see her. Thanks for stopping by."

"Always a pleasure. I'll see you tomorrow evening." He acknowledged Daniel with a slight nod, his manners as smooth as ever. "Mr. Forrest, good to meet you."

In ten seconds, he was out the door.

Cozie contained her irritation with her new tenant until she saw Thad back outside on the sidewalk. Then she flung herself around at Daniel Forrest. He had his arms crossed over his chest and was looking totally unembarrassed and unapologetic. "Anything wrong with a Massachusetts turkey?" he asked.

"I'm sure there isn't." She quickly talked herself out of giving him a lecture on manners. There was something about the deliberateness of his stance, about the calculating expression in his gray eyes, that told her this was a man from whom she'd be smart to keep her distance. "Look, I've got work to do. Things have piled up while I was away."

"Okay. Need an escort tomorrow night?"

He said it so casually Cozie almost missed what he was asking. "So swiping my parking space and insinuating yourself into a private conversation haven't exhausted your nerve. No, Mr. Forrest, I do not need an escort tomorrow night."

He grinned. "Now I can see the resemblance between you and your aunt Ethel."

"Mr. Forrest—"

"Daniel. Vanackerns don't mind you gallivanting all over the countryside promoting your book?"

"My hours are flexible. I have a competent staff. I have vacation time. I negotiated for what I needed. Now, is there anything else you want to know?"

"Lots." His cocky grin faded, replaced by a seriousness—a weightiness—that she wouldn't have expected from so relentlessly controlled a man. "But I'd best get back to my wood. Don't forget to tell your brother I was looking for him."

"I won't."

He was into the center hall entry.

Cozie licked her lips, not wanting her relationship with her first-ever tenant to remain on such shaky ground. "I hope . . . well, if you need anything else, just let me know."

He looked around at her. "Oh, I will."

She waited until she saw him back his truck out of her parking space before walking across the hall to see Aunt Ethel. "Did Sal O'Connor leave me any information on my tenant?"

"Folder's on your desk. She said he paid his security deposit and first month's rent in cash, which she deposited in her account; she wrote you a check. I've got it in the safe."

"Cash?"

"That's right," Aunt Ethel said. "Cash."

Cozie shrugged. "Maybe Texans prefer cash."

Daniel figured pissing Cozie Hawthorne off hadn't been one of his smarter moves, but who could resist? She was your basic uptight Yankee. Somebody needed to jerk her chain once in a while. From what he'd seen so far of pretty little Woodstock, there weren't too many candidates for that particular job.

And going to that Vanackern dinner tomorrow night could be useful—unless he had his business in Vermont wrapped up by then. In which case he'd fill up his gas tank and head on home to Texas.

He drove past the sawmill to the narrow, unmarked dirt road on the left. It took him through a stand of birches and slender, young trees whose leaves all seemed to have turned a golden yellow. After a half-mile, the road curved upward and the woods gave way to rolling fields of apple trees, dozens of them, overgrown and unkempt. Even his untrained eye could see the orchard was in rough shape. To restore it, many of the trees would need to be uprooted altogether, new ones planted in their place. He thought of his own long-neglected ranch outside Houston; he hoped to plant fruit trees, he didn't know what kind. J.D. said he was crazy, but the land had become Daniel's refuge—though not *from* anything

37

in particular. Until his helicopter went down, his life was pretty much what he wanted it to be.

The view of the hills of southern Vermont around him was so stunning that he lifted his foot off the gas and rolled down his window. He thought he could smell apples on the breeze even as he imagined his landlady and her brother's ancestors coming to this place more than two hundred years ago, carving out an existence in the thin, rocky soil and sometimes brutal climate. They must have been hardy folks.

He continued around another curve, coming to a small red clapboard farmhouse tucked into the hillside overlooking the far end of the old orchard. Its roof was sagging, it needed paint, its landscaping probably hadn't been updated in a hundred years. A huge butternut tree dripped yellow-tinted leaves in the beaten-down front yard. In a side yard, a vegetable garden was being readied for winter, a pitchfork embedded in a pile of mulch. At the end of the short dirt driveway were the skeletal remains of a rusted Land Rover, its engine hanging from the thick branch of a pine.

Seth Hawthorne's truck was nowhere in sight.

Daniel pulled over to the edge of the dirt road, alongside the front yard, and turned off his engine, debating whether to search the place while he had the chance. Maybe he'd find something that would help explain what his landlady's little brother had been up to in Texas last month.

But as he climbed out, the front door of the farmhouse opened. A woman with a half-bushel basket propped on one shapely hip stepped out onto the cracked slab of concrete and rock that served as a landing. She pulled the door shut with her free hand, turned, spotted Daniel coming around the front of his truck, and gasped. She had straight, silken blond hair that hung to just below her shoulders, and her eyes were huge and blue and staring at him as if she knew for sure he was a mass murderer. She was one very attractive woman.

"Hello," he said. "Didn't mean to startle you. I'm Daniel Forrest. I just moved in down the road. I'm looking for Seth Hawthorne."

"Oh." She looked less scared, brushing back a few strands of hair with her free hand. "You're Cozie's new tenant?"

He acknowledged that he was.

"Well, we're neighbors, I guess. I'm Julia Vanackern. My family has a place up the road."

Daniel manufactured a charming smile. So this was the woman who had changed her mind about going aboard his doomed helicopter—*after* she'd argued with Seth Hawthorne. Yet here she was, coming out of his house. "Nice to meet you, Julia. I just ran into your father in town. I need to pay Seth for some wood . . ."

"He's not here."

As Daniel moved closer, he could see her features were delicate, perfectly proportioned. She wore heavy black stirrups and an oversized white winter sweater that made her look even smaller than she was, made her eyes seem even bluer, a dark sapphire. He'd learned, before he'd headed north, she had no real career. She'd tried various jobs, most abandoned for one grand adventure or another—like checking out a burning oil tanker.

"He's working up at your place?" Daniel asked.

She shook her head. "I don't know what he's up to. I'm just here to pick apples. He said I could anytime. The trees aren't in the best shape, but the fruit's good

39

for pies and sauce." She smiled, self-deprecating in an appealing way, and Daniel could see how Seth Hawthorne could have fallen for her. "I'm thinking about trying apple butter this year."

"Sounds like fun. I won't keep you."

As he started back to his truck, he heard her inhale, and she said, "You're from Texas?"

He turned warily. "That's right."

She licked her lips; he hadn't realized until now she had on no makeup. "I—I was in Texas a few weeks ago. The Houston area."

"That's where I'm from," he said without elaborating.

"My parents and I were there for a broadcasting awards ceremony. I was nearly killed in a helicopter crash."

A hell of an exaggeration so far as Daniel was concerned.

She shot him an embarrassed look, as if guessing what he was thinking. "Actually, I wasn't even on board. Well. I'm sure we'll see each other around."

She left it at that and headed across the dirt road with her basket for apples. Daniel couldn't think of a subtle way to bring up her relationship with Seth Hawthorne. He had time, he reminded himself—but he'd never been a patient man.

"I hope you like Vermont," Julia Vanackern said.

"Thanks. So far Vermont's just fine."

He retreated to his truck, glancing in his rearview mirror as he drove back down toward Hawthorne Orchard Road. Rich, beautiful Julia Vanackern dropped her bushel basket under a gnarled old apple tree where the Tin Man himself might have rusted. In the golden sunlight, she reached up high above her head and plucked an apple.

So why, if he gave her permission to pick apples, had Seth Hawthorne tried to kill her?

"Because he didn't try to kill her, you idiot."

Okay. But he had followed her to Texas. They'd argued. The helicopter on which she was scheduled to ride had gone down, damned near killing the two men aboard. They were facts no one could dispute—unless the man J.D. had seen arguing with Julia Vanackern *wasn't* Seth Hawthorne. Could Daniel be chasing the wrong man?

As he negotiated a downward curve on the narrow dirt road, he decided that Julia Vanackern wasn't in any immediate danger from Seth. He could, theoretically, have sabotaged Daniel's helicopter in a mindless fit of anger and in the meantime pulled himself together and put the incident behind him.

As, perhaps, Daniel should.

But he thought of J.D., his shattered leg and possibly shattered future, of the damaged reputation to their company, and he knew that whatever it cost, he had to know the truth.

Two hours at her desk convinced Cozie the *Citizen* had survived her absence. All was well. She could go home and harvest the pumpkins, mulch the roses, pick apples, make more cider, put up the storm windows, confront the snakes in the cellar. Sneak up on the bat upstairs in the end bedroom. There was plenty to do.

But when she got home and she and Zep started inside together, she felt on edge, unfocused, off her routines. Before leaving her office, her agent had called from New York with another national syndication offer. It was a good one. "Think of it," he'd said, "as writing for dozens of small-town newspapers instead of just one. Come on, Cozie, what do you owe the Vanackerns?"

Saving her family's newspaper, her family's land. Perhaps even saving her family. But more to the point, what did she owe her family history? She and Aunt Ethel were the last Hawthornes at the *Citizen*.

She'd promised to get back to him next week.

Now, on her unheated back porch, she stared at the shelves of empty canning jars, jumper cables, baskets of onions and winter squash, rows of green and half-ripened tomatoes Seth had picked while she was away. Jackets, overshirts, and rain gear hung on a Shaker-type pegboard next to the door, under them a jumble of boots in various sizes and states of disrepair, a kind for every season. One of these days she would have to get in here and clean everything out.

She half expected to find her father in the back room, smoking a pipe and peeling potatoes, keeping a fire going in the old cast-iron cookstove. But the stove was cold, and she was alone in the creaky, narrow, two-hundred-year-old house. She lit a fire and put the copper kettle on for tea.

While the water was coming to a boil on the woodstove, she went down a short hall into the kitchen. Like the rest of the house, it needed work. The wide pineboard floor was bowed, the countertops were scarred, the old-fashioned appliances were charming but inefficient, and the cabinets no longer hung straight—if they ever had. Since the house was so narrow, she could sit at the long pine table and watch the birds at the feeders in the front yard and look out the window above the sink directly across the room and see the fields out back.

She got out a mug and tea bag and returned to the back room. Zep had curled up next to the woodstove, but Cozie couldn't get herself to relax and, finally, abandoned her tea. She had to be outside, unconfined.

Zep stirred, following her, and she headed past the toolshed and a flowering crab, down to the garden. The scents of mint and thyme and lemon balm mingled together, easing some of her franticness. Dry, once-purple oregano blossoms brushed against her legs. Everything looked so wild and overgrown. Even the perennial herbs needed some care. She yanked a giant pigweed from the middle of the chives and threw it over the rail fence.

The few broccoli and tomato plants her mother had planted in the spring, the row of peas, the beans, had all succumbed to weeds, neglect, frost. There was nothing to put away for winter. Her father's reluctant sale of the paper to the Vanackerns before his death had kept her mother going for a while, but finances had continued to tighten. She would have had to sell the house and land within the year. Ever eager to buy the Hawthorne land, the Vanackerns would have stepped in, perhaps permitting Emily Hawthorne to keep her house and a few surrounding acres. But the success of Cozie's book had allowed her to intervene. Now her mother had the money to travel, to live the kind of life she wanted to live, and the Hawthorne place remained in Hawthorne hands.

The wind picked up, penetrating her cotton sweater. She hadn't bothered adding a jacket. Zep thrashed through the maze of herbs, weeds, and wilted vegetable plants. "Hey, boy," Cozie said. "I should throw a rock at you, you know. Pop never allowed dogs in the garden."

But there was little to protect from a dog. Together they walked through the pumpkin patch, where dozens of pumpkins ripened in the autumn sun. Most were on the scrawny side, but a few would make respectable jack-o'-lanterns, and there were sugar pumpkins for soup and pies.

At the far end of the garden, wild grapes tangled on the rail fence and filled the air with their pungent smell. Her mother claimed wild grapes made the best jelly, although she seldom got around to making any before they rotted on the vine. Her father had considered them glorified weeds.

Cozie climbed over the waist-high fence and headed back along the garden, then up a sloping field behind the toolshed, through tall, yellowing grass to a trio of gnarled apple trees Johnny Appleseed himself might have planted. Knobby, misshapen fruit hung from their overladen branches. They needed pruning, spraying, care. The main orchards on the northern end of the property, across from Seth's place, were in similar condition. Her father and brother had started to restore them, but in the two years since Duncan Hawthorne's death, the orchard restoration had gone the way of most of Seth's plans.

Facing the back of the house, down the hill, Cozie could see glimpses of Hawthorne Brook across the road at an angle to her left, through the bright-leafed trees. Behind her to the right were more fields and woods. Seth had planted Christmas trees in one of the fields. So far, he'd managed to keep them trimmed and fertilized.

She plucked an old-fashioned Baldwin and bit into its tart, dry fruit as she swung up onto a low branch of the apple tree and leaned against its rough, old bark. A cardinal swooped among the trees and the crows wheeled overhead, and after a while her thoughts quieted, her muscles relaxed.

She closed her eyes and listened to the wind and smelled the grass and the trees and all the outdoor

smells of a Vermont autumn. She let her mind drift.
Suddenly she could see her father gathering dropped
apples for making sauce and cider. He was wearing his
red-and-black checked wool shirt and had calluses
and tiny cuts on his hands that would heal slowly
because of the blood thinners he was on. She could
smell the applesauce he would make at lunch and
leave on the kitchen table for when she and Meg and
Seth came home from school.

Concentrating on the image, she allowed herself to
hear her father's laugh and see his smile and his eyes,
green like hers, and after a while longer, sitting up in
the apple tree with her eyes shut tight, she could
almost believe that when she opened them, he would
be there. She would talk to him about her uneasiness
about owning the house and land that had been in her
family for generations, about working for the Vanackerns, about pretending the anonymous calls she'd
received on the road had never happened. She would
talk to him about how her career had seemed to take
on a momentum of its own, carrying her along with it,
and she wasn't sure who she was anymore, and they
would pick apples together. He would help her finish
the cider and tell her not to be squeamish about the
few bugs that might get into it.

"Geez, you're lucky the neighbors don't call the
men in white coats."

Her sister Meg's voice came out of nowhere, startling Cozie so that she almost fell out of the tree.

Meg didn't seem to notice. "Aren't you getting a
little long in the tooth for climbing trees?"

Cozie jumped down from the branch and grinned at
her older sister. "Look who's talking."

"You don't see me parked up in a tree. I brought
Matt and Ethan up to go apple picking. Tom's keeping
a lid on things at the farm." Tom Strout was Meg's

laid-back, dairy farmer husband. "The trees are in a sorry state, aren't they?"

"At least they've got apples."

Ducking under a low-hanging branch, Cozie joined her older sister in the sunshine. Her two nephews were walking up from the driveway, each carrying a half-bushel basket. Sara, the littlest, must have stayed with her dad at the farm where Meg ran a popular nursery school/day care center. Unlike Cozie, who was athletic in build, Meg had inherited their mother's pear shape and slightly darker coloring, although she, too, had the Hawthorne green eyes.

"Welcome back," she said.

"Thanks."

"You look a bit done in still. Hey—heard you scrounged up someone to rent the sawmill. Rumor has it he's quite the stud and not likely to complain about not having a dishwasher."

"Have you been talking to Aunt Ethel?"

"And Sal and anyone else who's seen this guy."

"Well, he's a human being, not a prize bull."

But Cozie had to fight off an image that had materialized, unbidden, of her tenant whacking a log in two. She could see the muscles in his forearm tighten. His look of concentration. Jet lag, she told herself. It was only jet lag that had her mind so unruly.

"So you've met him?" her sister asked.

"Seth and I brought him wood this morning."

"And?"

"And what?"

"Are you going to confirm or deny the rumors?"

"How do you hear so much watching little kids all day?"

"They have mommies and daddies happy to indulge the best child care provider in town."

46

Cozie just scowled and walked past her sister.

Meg laughed. "Let the rumors be confirmed. Only a good-looking guy would make Cozie Hawthorne that fidgety. Want to join us apple picking?"

It was just the antidote she needed. Apple picking, warm cider by the woodstove afterward—inculcating a new generation of Hawthornes in family traditions. "Sure."

Meg yelled to her kids, Ethan, age seven, and Matthew, age five, to hustle or they'd be picking apples in the dark. "Ethan! Ethan, you get that basket off your brother's head!"

Then Zep leaped onto all fours and streaked down the hill toward the driveway, barking as if he meant it.

"My, my," Meg said, ignoring her boys for a moment. "Who have we here?"

Cozie squinted at the tall figure walking up her driveway. "My new tenant."

"Oh?"

"Shut up, Meg."

Hoping her sister wouldn't follow, Cozie headed down to the driveway, where Daniel Forrest was standing with her splitting maul slung on his shoulder like a too-light baseball bat. Despite the drop in temperature and the stiffening breeze, he still had on his short-sleeved pullover, no jacket. She couldn't help noticing the close fit of his jeans over his narrow hips and long, long legs. He swung the splitter off his shoulder and stood it next to him. His movements were smooth and confident, unhurried.

He patted Zep on the head. "Figured I'd return your splitter while I was thinking about it. Nice spot you've got up here."

"Thank you. You're finished with the wood?"

"Not yet. I bought my own splitter in town." If he

47

felt any lingering awkwardness from their last encounter, it wasn't in evidence. He grinned. "Reckon I'm on my way to becoming a real Vermonter?"

She smiled. "Would I be a real Texan after just a couple of days in Texas?"

The gray eyes flashed with a mix of amusement and frank sexiness. "Honey, I don't think you'd be a real Texan after forty years in Texas."

No one had ever called her honey. Not ever. Cozie straightened her shoulders, reminding herself she was this man's landlady. She rubbed her wrist where she'd scraped it jumping from the apple tree. "So, what exactly brings you to Vermont?"

"I'm here for some R and R," he said without elaborating. He nodded at her wrist. "You okay?"

She dropped her hand. "Yes, fine."

"That was you up in the tree?"

"I was checking the apples."

He appraised her with a deliberate frankness that reminded her she had no idea who this man was. She saw that he had a small white scar at the corner of his left eye. What did he do to get so many scars?

"You can lean the splitter against the toolshed," she told him. "I'll put it away later."

He did as requested and returned to where she was standing at the edge of the driveway. The hard lines of his face gave away nothing of what he was thinking, feeling. "Thanks for the loan of the splitter."

"Anytime. By the way, did you catch up with my brother?"

Daniel looked around at her as he started down the driveway. "Not yet. There's no hurry. I'm not going anywhere."

"If you want," she said, "there's a path that goes along Hawthorne Brook right up to the sawmill. I used to take it all the time. Beats the road."

"Thanks for the tip."

Refusing to give him a backward glance, Cozie grabbed a ragged bushel basket from the toolshed and charged back up to the apple trees. Physical work, she'd always believed, was an antidote to most anything, even, she hoped, a gray-eyed Texan with an obvious agenda of his own.

# CHAPTER
# 4

———

Cozie let her sister talk her into dinner at the Strout farm. She picked up Aunt Ethel on her way across town, Seth having passed on joining them so he could work in his garden. They caught up with each other over beef stew and dumplings, but Cozie never mentioned the weird phone calls she'd received on the road. She wanted to put them behind her. She presented T-shirts to her nephews and niece and headed back home to her quiet house, still feeling strange there alone.

The smell of warm cinnamon and coffee brought her down to the kitchen the next morning just before eight. She'd pulled on some clothes in case it wasn't her brother, but it could hardly have been anyone else. He was pouring coffee at the counter, making himself at home. "Doughnuts are on the table," he said, his back to her. "They're still warm."

Cozie sighed. "One day you're going to barge in here without knocking and embarrass yourself."

He looked around at her and grinned. "I don't get embarrassed."

No doubt true. Unless she started locking her doors, which would involve buying locks and maybe even new doors, Cozie suspected she would just have to get used to her brother's unannounced entrances. He wasn't about to change his behavior because his older sister owned the house in which they'd both grown up. What would he have done, she wondered, if her mother had had to sell to strangers? If she *hadn't* been in a position to buy the old house and its two hundred acres at fair market value? She didn't care whether he made a lot of money, but his presumptuousness sometimes irritated her.

She helped herself to a cider doughnut. It was soft and sweet, rolled in cinnamon sugar, a family tradition kept alive by her otherwise unambitious brother. Their mother had taught him. Cozie couldn't make doughnuts to save her soul. "Delicious as always, Seth."

He set a mug in front of her on the long pine table before throwing one lean, well-muscled leg over the bench and sitting down himself. Nothing in his expression or demeanor indicated he had anything more pressing on his mind than how many doughnuts he would eat. But that was Seth. He took life as it came.

He made a face when he tried his coffee. "What the hell is this stuff?"

Cozie sipped hers to find out. "Hazelnut."

"Geez, Coze, you turning into a flatlander now that you're loaded? That stuff's awful. I'll bring my Maxwell House next time." He set down his mug. "Mind if I work up in the field? I've got to check the Christmas trees, see if we've got any worth selling this year."

"Of course not. They're your trees."

"Your land."

51

Good of him to notice. Yet it bothered her that he did. "Did Daniel Forrest finally catch up with you? He was looking to pay you for the wood."

"Haven't seen him since yesterday morning. He bugging you?"

"I wouldn't say that." She studied her brother a moment. "You don't like him, do you?"

"Guess he just rubbed me the wrong way. You should watch yourself around him." He swung up off the bench. "See you around."

Calling Zep, he loped down the short hall to the back room and outside to his field of Fraser firs and Scotch pine. Her brother was, Cozie thought, the most infuriating combination of high energy and devil-may-care she had ever encountered.

She took her coffee and a second doughnut outside and walked around the yard. It was a bright, clear, chilly, beautiful morning, the kind that made the long Vermont winter no price to pay. Fully awake now, she headed back inside and spent the morning and part of the afternoon cleaning house, brushing Zep, filling the bird feeders, clearing some of the junk out of the garden, and making another gallon of cider. The work chased away her lingering jet lag and plunged her back into some semblance of her old life, even if she did have a Texan living in her sawmill. She felt more in control of herself than she had in months.

By midafternoon she wound her way into town to spend a couple hours at her computer.

There was no black truck with Texas license plates or champagne-colored Mercedes with Connecticut license plates anywhere in sight. She let herself in through the back. Since it was Saturday, the *Vermont Citizen* building was quiet. Even Aunt Ethel took the day off. Freelancers and staff reporters would still cover their stories, but one of the perks of a weekly newspaper was being able to shut the place down on weekends.

As she entered her office, Cozie had a sudden image of her father and Grandpa Willard poring over the galleys of a Thanksgiving issue of the *Citizen,* back in the days before computers. Had they ever imagined their paper would end up in Vanackern hands?

Tourists had crowded onto the Woodstock common. A walking tour was getting started, a young couple strolled arm in arm, a balding man swung a toddler onto his shoulders. Cozie watched, clearing her mind, as she booted up her computer.

An hour later, she hadn't typed a word worth saving when Aunt Ethel unexpectedly turned up. She peered over her niece's shoulder. "Why don't you take a walk if you're stuck?"

"I'm not stuck. I'm thinking."

She grunted. "I don't know how you can stand having that thing blinking at you for hours on end."

"It's called a cursor."

"How appropriate."

Cozie sighed and backed away from her desk. She hated having people look over her shoulder while she was working, even if there was nothing to see. "What's up?"

"I saw your Jeep parked outside and decided I'd better stop in and tell you what's been going on." She stood back, arms folded under her breasts. She had on an elastic-waist navy twill skirt, a navy turtleneck, and a tweed jacket that had probably seen her through the Eisenhower administration. "Thelma was at the library this morning—they have some new large-print mysteries in. Anyway, she said some fellow came in to research the Hawthorne family."

"Us? What for?"

"Hold the interrogation and let me finish. Thelma described this gentleman as tall, dark, kind of mean-looking; said he wears cowboy boots and has a southern accent." Aunt Ethel let her arms drop to her sides. "Sounds like your Texan to me."

Her Texan. Cozie jumped to her feet. "That man's up to something and I intend to find out what."

"From what Thelma could tell he checked back issues of the paper, a couple of histories of Woodstock. She tried to peek over his shoulder to see if he was after anything particular, but she thinks he must have caught on because he got up and left."

Cozie snatched up her field jacket. With no one at the office, she hadn't changed from the jeans and work shirt she'd put on that morning. What was Daniel Forrest up to? Maybe Seth's instincts were on target and she shouldn't trust him.

"There's more," Aunt Ethel said. "The gossip about you two has already started."

"What two?"

Her elderly aunt pursed her lips. "Don't be disingenuous with me, Cornelia Hawthorne. You had to know the minute you laid eyes on that man that people would talk—which is exactly what they're doing."

"Aunt Ethel," Cozie said. "The details, please."

"All right. You know I'm not one to repeat gossip, but Thelma said she has it on good authority that you and your tenant are going to the Vanackern dinner together tonight."

Cozie groaned, kicked her chair under her desk, and switched off her computer.

"I take it you're not," her aunt said mildly.

"No. We are not. Thanks for the information. I have

a feeling this Forrest character is in town for something besides rest and relaxation. But don't you worry about it, Aunt Ethel. I'll handle him myself."

Daniel had his feet propped up on the sawmill porch rail and his chair tilted back and was reconciling himself to Vermont not being Texas when Cozie Hawthorne marched up the stairs in that hurried Yankee way of hers. She was back to looking like hell again. Blue chambray shirt that needed ironing, baggy pants, hair pulled back with a rolled-up purple bandanna. He didn't know how a woman could be so damned sexy dressed as if she'd just stepped out of the barn. He noticed she had a half-gallon plastic milk jug hooked around one finger. It seemed to be filled with a tea-colored liquid.

Her eyes were huge and damned near spitting fire.

"Afternoon." He deliberately laid on the drawl. "Nice out for Vermont."

"Good afternoon."

Clipped. Uptight Yankee. He crossed his ankles. "No feet on the porch rail?"

"I don't care where you put your feet."

He savored several rejoinders, all designed to make her blush, if she were the blushing type, which he'd already figured she wasn't, but—judicious for a change—he kept them to himself.

She thrust the jug at him. "I brought you some cider. It's homemade. You might watch for the odd spider leg."

"I see. Thanks."

He dropped his feet to the floor and rose, aware of how much taller and bigger he was than Cozie Hawthorne, not that she seemed to notice. Had she found out he'd lied to her? Doubtful. She wouldn't be bringing him cider, with or without spider legs. He set the jug on the rail. She had her eyes narrowed on him as if he slithered instead of walked on two legs, and it occurred to him that probably not too many people gave Miss Cornelia Hawthorne a hard time.

"Why have you been snooping on my family?"

So that was it. "The old lady at the library talked?"

"Her name is Thelma Higgins, and she and my aunt have been friends all their lives."

"So that's why she was so interested in what I was doing. I wouldn't say I was 'snooping' on anyone. I was just doing a little research."

"Why?"

"Curiosity."

"I don't believe you."

He shrugged. "That's your choice."

He could see irritation roll right up her spine. "And I guess it's your choice not to tell the truth. I suggest you don't stir up any unnecessary trouble."

"As you wish, ma'am." He studied her a moment. "You're one straightforward woman, aren't you?"

She stiffened. He was bugging the hell out of her. No question. "I see no point in beating around the bush."

"So I gathered. You want a glass of cider?"

"No."

"You know, maybe I'm not just the nosy bastard you think I am. Your family goes way back in this area. Maybe I'm a historian. Maybe I'm a fellow reporter doing a feature on the newly famous Cozie Hawthorne."

"I thought you were a Texan in Vermont for rest and relaxation."

He was undeterred. "Maybe I'm killing two birds with one stone."

She laughed, rather nastily, he thought. But with her

head thrown back, the sun hit her eyes and made him wonder what she'd be like really happy, really laughing.

A dangerous thing to be wondering when he'd come to Vermont to find out if her brother had tried to kill him and J.D.

"I don't suppose," she said, back to business, "you'd know why people are saying we're going to the Vanackern dinner together."

Daniel didn't have to ponder that one. "Because I told some old geezer at the general store in town we were. Must have been another of your auntie's buddies. He figured out I was your new tenant—God knows how—"

"Your boots. And maybe your accent. Everyone knows I rented to a Texan."

"I'm the only Texan in Woodstock?"

"It's possible."

"That's enough to keep me awake nights."

His landlady scoffed. "I doubt, Mr. Forrest, that much of anything keeps you awake nights."

Oh, Ms. Cozie. He dropped back down to his chair and planted his feet back up on the porch rail. "Well, I don't know about that."

He thought he saw a bit of added color in her cheeks, a surprise. "What about this old guy?" she demanded.

"He warned me about being a gentleman. He doesn't think much of a single woman renting to a single man. I gather people in town are protective of you?"

"Not necessarily. Some just feel they have a right to know about and comment upon my every move. Did you tell him you were going with me tonight?"

Daniel shrugged. "Just figured I'd rattle his chain."

"Who I rent this place to is no one's business but mine, and I'll tell anyone so who asks. *You* quit telling lies and stirring up trouble."

"Like taking the world on by yourself, Ms. Cozie?"

She balled her hands into tight fists at her sides. "If you want to attend the Vanackern dinner this evening, I suggest you speak to the Vanackerns."

"Should you change your mind about needing an escort," he said, "you know where to find me. Thanks for the cider."

She didn't soften and didn't say another word, just marched back down off the porch and onto the path that wound down along Hawthorne Brook, kicking small stones as she went, a lot madder going even than she had been coming. A hardcase Yankee, Cozie Hawthorne. She knew damned well he was up to something in her little hometown.

But he didn't regret his trip to the library. The Hawthornes had been outspoken, up on their moral high horse, and mostly broke since they'd traveled up the Connecticut River and settled in its picturesque upper valley. Their lives, however, hadn't been easy. There had been deprivation, disease, early deaths, tragedy. Yet, right from the beginning, there had also, he found, been a commitment to the highest ideals of American democracy. That commitment could be seen in the long history of the *Vermont Citizen*. Never a big moneymaker, the Hawthornes had managed to keep it going until Duncan Hawthorne had been forced to choose between losing his family home and land or losing his family paper. He'd made his choice.

Daniel wondered how Cozie felt about that choice, how her brother did. From what he could gather, Seth Hawthorne didn't fit in with the rest of his family. He clearly didn't have his sister's drive. In his teens and a bit beyond he'd had his share of scrapes with the law: mostly bar brawls and motor vehicle violations of a nature more serious than the odd parking ticket. If he had gotten mixed up with Julia Vanackern and she'd dumped him while Cozie was riding the best-seller lists—well, who knew?

"I sure as hell don't," Daniel muttered. He put his jug of cider in the refrigerator. Sneaking around the Woodstock town library wasn't going to get him the answers he needed.

Neither, he thought, was thinking about how Cozie Hawthorne's mesmerizing eyes could change from green to blue in the afternoon sun.

The temperature had dropped precipitously by late afternoon, giving Cozie the excuse to curl up under an old quilt on the couch in the back room, with a fire in the cookstove and her notebook computer on her lap. She still wasn't getting much done. She kept thinking about why Daniel Forrest wanted to go to the Vanackern dinner so badly tonight that he'd stirred up rumors about the two of them. Or did he just enjoy stirring up rumors?

She sighed, disgusted with herself. She was supposed to be *writing*. Work was her refuge. She was doing what she liked best: brainstorming ideas, just typing whatever popped into her mind, no matter how unusable.

So far she'd typed "autumn foliage." How original. But she wasn't feeling witty, pithy, or creative, and it wasn't just the town talk about her and her new tenant. It was also her, her surroundings. Sitting near the old cast-iron cookstove, she could smell her mother's baked beans on a cool autumn night, she could hear her father coming in with a load of wood. She could see herself and her brother and sister playing Monopoly, arguing politics, plotting mischief.

She could remember similar chilly autumn nights at her sawmill. Tucked on the hillside above the brook, it had always seemed so snug, enveloping her with a warmth and cheerfulness that must have influenced her work. At home, she was always fighting memories. Maybe it would be different after she'd been here awhile.

Then again, maybe she'd kick Daniel Forrest out of her sawmill, move back, and let Seth have the house.

"I give up."

She cleared her computer screen—nowhere near as satisfying as balling up a sheet of paper and shoving it in the fire.

But it was six o'clock and she had a dinner to attend. At least she knew exactly what she would wear. No doubt in her mind, it was an Ingrid Bergman night.

Seth Hawthorne was working on his Land Rover when Daniel turned down the short driveway beside the sagging red farmhouse. He'd walked up from the sawmill. He'd needed air, exercise. It felt good to be out, even in the chilly early evening air.

"Hello," he said.

Seth looked up. He had a rusted metal toolbox opened at his feet, tools scattered around him. Not an organized worker. His sinewy arms were blackened up to the elbows with grease. "Yeah," he said, "Cozie mentioned you were looking for me."

"Just wanted to pay you for the wood. How much do I owe you?"

"Two hundred should cover it."

Seeing how it was about twice the going rate, Daniel would bet the hell it would. But he fished out his wallet without arguing and handed over two one-hundred-dollar bills.

Seth slid them into his jeans pockets. "Figured you'd pay in cash."

"Still works." Daniel gestured with one hand at the wooded hillside behind the farmhouse, the orchard across the road. "You like living way out here?"

"Yep."

"Ever think of moving?"

"Where to?"

As if there were no other place worth considering besides Vermont. "I don't know, another part of the country, maybe. What about Texas?"

"Texas is probably an okay place for Texans." Seth picked up an old rag and started wiping the grease off his hands, one finger at a time. He seemed basically easygoing, a contrast to his older sister's hard-driving, compulsive nature. "When're you going back?"

"I might not. Maybe I'll become a Vermonter."

For a moment Seth looked as if he might laugh, but he didn't. "You either are a Vermonter or you're not. You don't become one. You know," he went on, attacking a thick coating of grease on his left thumb, "some people might want to take advantage of Cozie now that her book's done so well. I'm not saying you're one of them . . ."

"But you're giving me fair warning in case I am," Daniel said.

"That's right."

"I didn't come here to make trouble for anyone."

Didn't he? Why else was he in Vermont if not for trouble? *You could hire someone if you're looking for answers,* his grandfather had told him. *You don't have to do this yourself.* But he did. He owed J.D., he owed himself.

Seth dropped his rag back on the ground. "Thanks for bringing me my money, but I'd have come and got it. You need a ride back or you going to walk?"

With those green Hawthorne eyes on him, Daniel was convinced Seth knew damned well who he was and why he'd come to Vermont. They were both playing games—and getting nowhere.

"I'll walk," Daniel said.

"See you around, then. Help yourself to some apples anytime."

"Thanks. I might do that."

Daniel took his time making his way back to Hawthorne Orchard Road, enjoying the play of the fading light on the brightly colored leaves. The temperature was dropping. He was glad he'd thrown on his leather jacket before leaving the sawmill.

When he reached the end of the dirt road, a little classic Austin-Healey pulled up, and Julia Vanackern rolled down the window and poked her head out. "Hello, there. Beautiful evening, isn't it?"

It was. Chilly, but pretty.

"I'm heading into town. My parents are putting on their annual fall dinner tonight. Would you like to join us for a drink? We'll be a little early since I've got to play hostess."

"I'm not exactly dressed for a Vanackern dinner."

Her eyes sparkled with her smile. "Oh, who cares? This is Vermont. Come on, jump in."

Despite an initial impulse to turn her down, Daniel walked around the car and climbed into the passenger seat. He had to remember his mission in Vermont. Why had Julia Vanackern really backed out of their helicopter trip? Having a drink with her could prove useful.

She had on a swatch of deep violet that made her look at once sexy and vulnerable, a dangerous combination. Her pale hair glistened, a contrast to her deep rose lips and dramatic charcoal-smudged eyes. She smelled of a light, expensive perfume. Her big adventure in Texas had ended in disaster, but she was in her element now.

Daniel found himself imagining Cozie Hawthorne in her unlaced mud shoes and wondering what she would be wearing tonight among the Vanackerns.

# CHAPTER
# 5

Julia Vanackern found a couple glasses of champagne and a quiet corner in the private dining room of the Woodstock Inn & Resort. According to the many Vermont brochures Daniel had dutifully read, the historic inn that dominated Woodstock common was owned by the Rockefellers. Laurence Rockefeller, grandson of John D., had married the granddaughter of Woodstock native Frederick Billings, the railroad magnate for whom Billings, Montana, was named. The Rockefellers were great benefactors of the town.

Julia had given no indication that she even suspected Daniel was anything but who he said he was. But he suspected Julia Vanackern didn't let on what she was thinking unless it suited her.

"You can stay for dinner if you like," she said.

"Thanks, but I'll just have a drink and be on my way."

Her full lower lip turned down just a little, but she

didn't try to persuade him to stay. "I suppose this is a different sort of crowd from what you're used to."

Not as different as she might want to believe. He smiled. "I'm not used to being around so many Yankees."

She laughed, flashing her sapphire eyes at him. "I've never thought of myself as a Yankee, but some of the folks around here sure are. Of course, I'd never pass for a Texan, either." She waved to someone across the room. "I'm sorry, I've got to run play hostess. Are you sure you won't stay? How will you get back?"

"I'll manage."

"I'm sure you will," she said in a deliberately sultry voice, and glided off among the gathering guests.

Daniel didn't rush through the rest of his champagne. He wasn't much of a champagne drinker. He wondered how many of the guests were locals. Was there any way of differentiating between the part-time residents and the locals?

Then Cozie Hawthorne entered the dining room alone, looking as if she were about to be fed to the lions. Daniel watched her paste on a smile. Her red-gold hair was swept up off her neck, and she had on a cream-colored gown that hugged her slender figure and made her legs seem even longer. In spite of her discomfort, she radiated an ease and elegance that he wouldn't have expected when he saw her yesterday morning atop the cordwood in the back of her brother's truck.

Her green eyes zeroed in on him, and any awkwardness vanished—along with the smile. She marched right over without pausing to greet her host and hostess. "Whose arm did you twist to get in here?"

She was trying to get him ruffled, only Daniel didn't ruffle easily. "Julia Vanackern invited me."

"Just like that."

"You sound dubious, Ms. Cozie." But he motioned to her with his champagne glass. Her cosmetics, he noticed, mostly highlighted her eyes. *"Casablanca?"*

Her eyes widened in surprise. "What?"

"Your dress. Reminds me of Ingrid Bergman in *Casablanca.* The scene where she sees Humphrey Bogart for the first time since Paris and she asks Sam to play 'As Time Goes By.' "

"No one's ever . . ." She stopped, disconcerted; color rose in her cheeks. She bit her lower lip. "It's a copy. Is *Casablanca* one of your favorite movies?"

"I watch a lot of old movies."

Julia Vanackern came up between them, smiling brightly, in her hostess mode. "Cozie Hawthorne— it's been forever. Great to see you."

"You, too, Julia. How have you been?"

"Oh, not bad, all considered." She flipped her silken hair off her shoulder. "I'm coming off a hellish trip to Texas, but I'll tell you about that another time."

Cozie frowned, not one to miss a trick, but if she had any suspicions, she kept them to herself. "Well, you look terrific, as usual," she said diplomatically.

"Thanks. What about you; how have you been? You don't look so bad yourself. Success must agree with you."

"Thanks." She nodded toward Daniel. "I see you two have met."

"Oh, yes. He was up at Seth's yesterday afternoon while I was picking apples. I'm going to take a stab at apple butter this year." Her blue eyes leveled on Daniel, the sultriness back. "Do they make apple butter in Texas?"

"Not my area of expertise," he said.

"Well, I'm still debating whether to do mine on top

of the stove or in the oven. You're the expert, Cozie, what do you do?"

She shrugged. "I'm hardly an expert, but we've always done ours in the woodstove oven. Less stirring."

"We don't have a woodstove. I guess our regular oven will have to do." She touched Cozie's shoulder, smiling graciously. "You two will have to excuse me—I've got gobs of folks I'd better say hello to before I'm cut out of the will."

She winked irreverently and slid off into the crowd, looking totally at ease with herself and her world. But Daniel remembered her reaching for an apple in the Hawthorne orchards, and wondered.

His drink finished, he noticed that the room, with its tasteful early American decor, had filled up with guests. He saw no advantage to sticking around, beyond annoying his landlady. "Enjoy your evening," he told her, resisting temptation.

"I'll try," she said, cool.

He got out of there, fast, before Cozie Hawthorne's green eyes and Ingrid Bergman dress had him doing and saying—even thinking—things he'd regret. No one tried to stop him as he left the private dining room and headed back to the lobby, where guests had gathered on colonial-style chairs and sofas around a fire roaring in the huge stone fireplace. Fighting an urge to linger, he fled outside, across to Woodstock common. He wished he could dive into the tourist fantasy of a picturesque Vermont village, but the wind was brisk and cold, and he needed to think, process, and get on with his business in Vermont.

Cozie swept a glass of champagne from a passing tray and debated how long she had to stay before she could make a polite, unobtrusive exit. Daniel

Forrest's presence had rattled her more than she would ever admit to anyone else. The man was relentless, and she was determined to find out what he was really doing in Vermont.

She spotted Frances Vanackern making her way toward her. Julia's mother was a blue-eyed, fair-haired woman who had started life as the daughter of a quarry worker who'd drunk too much and died too young. But she'd developed a regal bearing in her thirty-five years of marriage to Thad Vanackern.

Ever the warm, natural hostess, Frances greeted Cozie. "It's been a long time; you're looking well. I understand you're just back from another book tour."

Cozie nodded, and they chatted a few minutes, Frances, as always, remembering to ask about the rest of the Hawthorne family. "We invited Ethel, of course, but she couldn't make it. How is she?"

"The same." Aunt Ethel would never attend a Vanackern dinner, and any excuse would do.

"Ethel will never change. My word, I can remember how she and your father and I would warm our bare feet in cow manure together as children." She shuddered, smiling at the same time. "I suppose I can't expect to forget such a thing. How do you like living back home?"

"It was strange at first, but I'm getting used to it."

"But what a wonderful thing for your mother not to have to worry so much anymore. Have you heard from her?"

"I got a postcard today. She says she's having a great time."

"She's earned it. She's had a rough few years."

But Frances Vanackern's warm blue eyes took on an awkwardness unusual for her. "Cozie . . . I wanted to speak to you about our annual autumn hike tomorrow. It's supposed to be beautiful weather. In past years, we've always spilled over onto Hawthorne land. Your parents never minded, but I wouldn't want to impose. . . ."

"It's no imposition," Cozie said, meaning it. "You're welcome to hike on Hawthorne land anytime." She realized she hadn't said "my" land.

"Thank you. Please feel free to join us."

Frances made a point of spotting a familiar face in the crowd, waving and quickly excusing herself. Cozie found herself amidst other guests who asked her about her book, her travels, her various high-profile interviews. Her capacity for small talk, however, had been exhausted by weeks on the road, and her attempts to steer conversation in more substantive directions proved futile. She found herself seizing the first opportunity to duck out early, even before dinner was served. Another week home and she'd be back up to speed, able to deal with the Vanackerns and even a mysterious Texan, on their terms or hers.

It was windy and much colder outside, darker than she'd expected, but she wrapped her mohair shawl tightly around her in a gusting breeze and crossed the street to the common. She wasn't ready to go home to her empty house just yet. The shadows of the leaves danced eerily in the moonlit grass. She pulled pins from her hair. It came down in thick, droopy locks, and she began to feel herself relax.

"Geez," she breathed, "you really are losing it."

More pins came out. She had a handful of them.

"Evening, Ms. Cozie." Daniel Forrest stepped from the shadows of the Civil War statue across from the *Citizen* building. "Party over already?"

She jumped, pins flying everywhere, but she recovered quickly. "No, it's not. I left early. What are you doing out here?"

"Having a chat with old Lieutenant Alonzo here on

the inscrutability of Yankees." He patted the statue's stone boot. "Relative of yours, I take it?"

"And I thought by now you knew everything about me."

His eyes fell on her, and he said in that languid, sandpaper drawl, "Not by half."

An unbidden heat spread through her, making her glad for the darkness. She glanced up at the tall statue of Alonzo Hawthorne in his Union Army lieutenant's uniform, his proud, young face caught in the glare of a streetlight. "He was my great-great-grandfather. He died at Gettysburg."

"It stays with you, losing someone to a war."

"I recited the Gettysburg Address at his feet for a Memorial Day program in high school. I'm not sure I could do it now." She shook off her sudden melancholy. "Did Alonzo give you any insight into Yankees?"

"No, ma'am. He remained inscrutable."

Daniel's eyes were colorless in the darkness, but Cozie felt their relentless intensity, the control of the man behind them. What lengths would he go to to get what he wanted? What *did* he want?

"You're cold," he said.

Her shawl had slipped off her shoulders, but before she could deal with it herself he reached out and gently pulled it up, using both hands. His touch lingered, its intimacy warming her far more than the thin shawl. She wondered if he noticed and decided probably he did. He caught a bobby pin as it fell from her hair and tucked it into her hand with the others. His fingers seemed almost hot compared to hers, never mind that he'd been outside longer.

"I think your lips are purple," he said, and brushed her mouth with one finger.

She swallowed hard. "Actually, the air feels good."

He smiled, dropping his hand from her mouth. "Something only a Yankee would say."

The man knew exactly what he was doing, Cozie thought. Exactly. Daniel Forrest, she was quite sure, did virtually nothing that wasn't calculated and very deliberate, even touch a woman's lips on a chilly Vermont night. What could he possibly hope to gain?

"Did you—did you catch up with my brother?"

His manner changed almost immediately, as if reminded that she was, indeed, his landlady and he ought to mind his manners. "I met him at his place this afternoon and we settled up. So, where're you headed?"

"Nowhere." She tried not to squirm under his probing gaze, tried not to imagine what he thought of her in her Ingrid Bergman dress, so different from the old work clothes he'd seen her in earlier. "I just wanted to walk around, clear my head before I started home. Did you park in my space again?"

"Wouldn't dare. I've learned I was lucky you didn't skin me alive for snatching it. No, Julia Vanackern gave me a ride down. I figured I'd walk home. Exercise'd do me good."

From what Cozie could see, one thing Daniel Forrest didn't lack was enough exercise. "It's a ways. Would you like a ride?"

The offer was out before she could stop herself. The big Texan leaned back on his heels, studying her, and for a moment she thought he'd have the decency to refuse. But he shrugged. "Sure."

There was no graceful way to renege. Cozie glanced up at the Civil War statue, as if her long-dead ancestor could help her out of a mess of her own creation. But she had only herself to rely on, and she walked with Daniel Forrest back across the common, to where she'd parked her Jeep in the inn's front lot.

"I see you didn't buy a new Jeep with your new-found fortune," he said.

"There's nothing wrong with this one. Runs like a top."

"Body's in rough shape."

"Well, nobody would recognize me if I drove a sports car or one of those fancy new Jeeps."

Daniel looked across the rusted roof. "I don't know, I'd bet they would."

But Cozie was distracted by a folded sheet of white paper tucked under her windshield wiper. Assuming it was just an advertisement, she reached over and plucked it free.

"Door's unlocked," she told her passenger as she opened the driver's side door and slid in behind the wheel.

The paper fell open when she flung it between the two front seats.

Her heart stopped, and she cried out in shock.

She stared at the large black letters in the harsh glare of the streetlight.

WELCOME HOME, COZIE CORNELIA.
AREN'T YOU GLAD YOU MADE IT BACK ALIVE?

The message was laser printed in Times Roman bold, probably thirty-two-point type. Being a newspaperwoman, Cozie knew her typefaces.

She was shaking. Her hands felt stiff and cold and too heavy even to hang onto the steering wheel.

"Cozie?"

Her tormentor was in Woodstock . . .

. . . had found her *Jeep*.

"Cozie, are you all right?"

Daniel was in the passenger seat, regarding her with

72

a quiet intensity she found oddly comforting. She had the message in her hand. "I'm fine."

He nodded to the paper. "What's that?"

"It's an ad for a pizza parlor."

"No, it's not."

"It is."

"Then let me have a look."

She shook her head. She couldn't let him see it. But he got to the paper before she could toss it in the back.

He swore softly as he read it.

"I don't want to talk about it," she said.

"This isn't the first one of these, is it?" His voice was quiet, controlled, serious, the sardonic humor of a few moments ago gone.

"My first here. Look, I meant what I said. I don't want to talk about it."

"Do the police know?"

She refused to answer. Of course the police didn't know. What could they do besides tell her what she already knew? Someone was trying to throw her off center, annoy her, even frighten her. But not, they would assure her, trying to hurt her.

"Cozie," Daniel repeated, "do the police know?"

"No."

"Why not?"

"Because I haven't told them," she said, sticking the key in the ignition and starting up the engine.

He settled back into the ragged passenger seat, winced, and reached under him. He pulled out a long, sharp, black needlelike something. "What's this?"

Cozie gave it the barest glance. "Porcupine quill."

"That's what I thought."

"Zep got into a porcupine a few weeks ago. I had to take him to the vet."

"Sounds plausible. You're a prickly lady, Ms. Cozie,

but I don't think you'd booby-trap your passengers."
He cast her a look. Her shawl had slipped off her
shoulders. She was shivering. "If you slide any closer
to that door, you're going to squirt right out onto the
road."

She loosened her tight grip on the wheel by sheer
force of will. "I'm just a little rattled."

"Rightfully so."

She turned onto sparsely populated Hawthorne
Orchard Road. There were no streetlights and few
houses; they met no other cars.

"Do you ever get spooked out here all by yourself?"
Daniel asked.

"Why should I?"

"I didn't say you should, just asked if you did."

"I've lived on this road most of my life. It's what I
know." She licked her lips, dry from the shock she'd
received, and resisted a look at the message she'd
found on her Jeep. "Under ordinary circumstances,
no, I don't get spooked."

She passed the black-shuttered house on the gently
sloping hill, then careened down the steep driveway to
her renovated sawmill, just as she had countless times
in the past ten years.

Except that everything had changed.

She came to a hard stop behind her tenant's black
truck.

"Thanks for the ride," he said, so very close to her.

"You're welcome. Good night."

She sensed his reluctance to leave. He would want
to ask her more about the note on her windshield and
whoever had left it. He wasn't the kind of man to leave
such questions unanswered. But he said, "I'll be
keeping an eye out for you, Cozie Hawthorne."

Her breath caught. "For all I know you could be
responsible."

74

"I'm not."

She gave a small nod. "I have no reason to disbelieve you."

"Cozie . . ." He leaned even closer to her and tucked a finger under her chin, turning her face toward him. "If you believe nothing else about me, believe that. I didn't leave that note on your windshield."

And his mouth grazed hers, and she didn't even consider pushing him away, but the kiss—if that was what it was—didn't last. "If you find you don't want to be alone tonight," he said, still very close to her, "you know where to find me."

He managed to make it sound both like a simple statement of fact and an invitation, a promise.

"Thank you."

But he'd already slid out into the cold, dark night.

Cozie resisted an impulse to leap out after him and instead turned back up the sawmill driveway. The offending message seemed like a live, vicious animal in her Jeep with her, but she couldn't just throw it out onto the road. It was hard evidence that someone, indeed, was harassing her.

But not Daniel Forrest. No, she didn't believe that. Still, he was keeping something from her.

She shook off the thought. She had enough as it was to keep her awake. A nasty note on her windshield, and a brief—too brief—kiss from a sexy, mysterious Texan.

Yes. Definitely enough.

Inside the converted sawmill, Daniel found a few coals still hot in the efficient Vermont-made cast-iron woodstove that dominated the middle of the single downstairs room. He added kindling and in a few minutes had a decent fire going. In the small, simple country kitchen on the far end of the room, he reheated some coffee left over from that afternoon. It was your basic rotgut, but he didn't care. He needed his wits about him. He needed to think.

Or, more specifically, to stop thinking. Whatever had possessed him to kiss Cozie Hawthorne? Hell, to *stop* kissing her?

He stood at the butcher block table, in front of a window looking straight down on the nineteenth-century stone dam and its picturesque ten-foot water-fall. Even with the windows shut, he could hear the rush of water. It was almost soothing. He took his coffee into the living area, which consisted of an old couch and a couple of slip-covered chairs on a hand-hooked rug. A polyurethaned apple crate served as a coffee table. He set his mug on it and sat on one of the chairs and closed his eyes, trying to put it all together, Texas and Julia and Seth and the helicopter crash and the note on his landlady's windshield, because they all fit. Somehow they were connected. He knew it.

But his mind wouldn't cooperate. He kept seeing the fear and worry in Cozie Hawthorne's eyes, a deeper green in the darkness, the bobby pins flying out of her hands when he'd greeted her at the Yankee statue, the tight grip she had on the wheel of her Jeep. Things were going on in the lady's life that she'd never expected, never counted on. She didn't know what to do, how to react—to her sudden success, to someone out to scare her. Maybe to an angry, troubled younger brother.

"Leave it, my man," he said aloud.

He jumped up, putting another log on the fire, then reached for the phone in the kitchen and dialed J.D.'s hospital room. Central Time made it an hour earlier than in Vermont, but it was still late. A nurse an-

76

swered. She reluctantly admitted J.D. was awake and put him on.

Daniel filled him in. "Our smart-mouthed Yankee friend found a nasty little note on her windshield tonight. I'd say someone's been messing with her head for a while, and I'll bet she hasn't told a soul."

"Any threat?"

"Nothing direct. The implication is the son of a bitch is watching her every move."

J.D. was silent a moment. "The brother?"

"I don't know. He knows who I am but won't admit it."

"Think the little creep's trying to spook his own sister?"

Daniel didn't answer at once. He listened to the quiet sounds of the Vermont night and imagined Cozie Hawthorne alone in her rambling old house. Would she get spooked tonight? Finally, he said, "Something's going on. Maybe it has nothing to do with why our helicopter went down—"

"But you've stuck your hand in the fire."

"That's one way of putting it."

"Stay on the case, Danny Boy. Wish I could be there with you."

"I wish you could be, too." His eyes burned; he could feel the tension building inside him, the frustration with his own helplessness. But he could also hear the fog of fatigue and pain in his partner's voice. "How are you doing?"

"Hell, half the time I don't know. I'm either so doped up I don't know what's going on or I'm hurting so fucking bad I don't care what's going on."

"Right now?"

"If I'm talking, pal, I'm hurting. Mostly it's the leg. I still dream some nights it's gone, they've sawed it off and thrown it to the dogs."

"I wish—"

"It's too late for wishes."

He knew. Only too well he knew. "Take care of yourself, J.D."

"Find out who did this to me."

"I will. I promise."

As he hung up, Daniel could see his reflection in the window overlooking the dam. What if he'd already found out? What if everyone was right and he was an arrogant son of a bitch who'd nearly killed himself and his own partner and best friend, all because he'd wanted to be the first, the best, the toughest. Because it had been a hell of a fire burning out there and he'd been willing to risk his partner's life, Julia Vanackern's life, his own life in his determination to put it down.

He pulled on his jacket and headed outside, plunging through the cold darkness to the path along Hawthorne Brook. He would make sure Ms. Cozie hadn't gone home to some nut on her doorstep.

If nothing else, it would keep him from confronting his own demons.

Cozie was staring at the slanted ceiling in her bedroom, her father's old crowbar stretched out at her side. She'd plucked it off a rusty nail down in the cellar and taken it upstairs with her, in case of what she wasn't quite sure. She only knew she hadn't been so spooked, as Daniel Forrest would say, in years.

She decided to blame her sandpaper-voiced tenant rather than whoever had left the unnerving message on her Jeep.

The wallpaper of small roses and forget-me-nots, yellowed and coming down in places, was the same one she and Meg had hung as teenagers. Because Sal had said it'd be easier to rent her sawmill furnished, she'd only brought her flea-market antique chestnut nightstand with her when she moved back in. The twin bed, the marble-topped bureau, the ladder-back chair, the milk-glass lamp—they were all what she'd had growing up. She wanted to put up new curtains, but she had no real urge to decorate.

She swallowed, her throat tight and dry, and jumped at every creak and groan of the old house, every trick of the wind or ordinary sound of the night. She imagined her anonymous tormentor, someone, creeping around downstairs, outside in the shadows. She thought about ghosts and ghouls and how many times she'd awakened as a kid to a bat flying around and had yelled for her father, until finally she was old enough, brave enough, to catch bats on her own.

Before climbing into bed, she'd shut up the end room where she was sure the bat who'd been flirting with her since she'd moved in was still lurking. She didn't want to deal with bats tonight.

She'd also gotten the crowbar and checked every inch of the house and told Zep, as if he could understand, to keep good watch on the place. She'd stuck her anonymous note in the junk drawer next to the refrigerator, in with the old rubber bands and pieces of aluminum foil and odd nail and screw and pair of scissors. It was where she'd put the cheap steno pad in which she had recorded the times, dates, and transcripts of the calls she'd received on the road. She'd hoped it could just sit in there and collect dust. That her calls were an on-the-road thing, a price of sudden fame and fortune.

Now her tormentor had found her in Woodstock. Was *in* Woodstock.

She shuddered, snuggling deep down under her covers.

The ring of the telephone almost killed her. She

leaped out of bed, swearing and stumbling around, heart pounding, and picked up the extension on her marble-topped bureau.

"Hello, Cozie Cornelia. I hope you had fun at the Woodstock Inn tonight."

Her knees went out from under her, forcing her to grab the edge of the bureau to stay on her feet. She gripped the phone. She'd recognized the voice immediately. Disembodied. Neither male nor female. Underlined with hate and rage, it had followed her across the country and now back again.

"Were you there?" she asked in a tight whisper.

"I can be wherever you are."

*Click.*

Cozie slammed down the receiver. She had to tell someone. The police, her publisher, her agent, Meg, Seth. Daniel Forrest. Someone. She knew she needed to before this nut decided having her scared wasn't enough and everyone got to paw through her things while she was on a slab being autopsied.

But surely if she were in any serious danger, her tormentor would have tried something by now. All he—or she—wanted was to see Cozie Hawthorne scared and frustrated.

Which she was.

And even with the note on her Jeep and now the call—with *knowing* this SOB was in Woodstock—she was aware that her tormentor would be difficult to locate. With no demand, no overt threat, no *reason* for the harassment, she expected that the police would feel much as she did: not knowing what to do, how to react, uncertain if she was in real danger. "You killed my dog and I hate you," they all could understand. "You're famous and I'm not." "I want your money." Even, "You're an asshole and I'm going to make your life miserable."

Still, she had to tell someone the whole nasty story. It was time.

And for no good reason, except that he'd already seen the note on her Jeep, she thought of her big, gray-eyed Texan up the road.

"Geez," she muttered, and crawled back into bed, curling her fingers around the cool steel of the crowbar. She felt only marginally better.

Tomorrow, she thought, she'd go to her office and check the references of the man who'd come all the way from Texas, paid in cash to rent her sawmill, wormed his way into a Vanackern dinner, and looked up the Hawthornes in the town library. He might be as innocent as he said he was, but at least she'd be doing something.

# CHAPTER
# 6

It took under two hours with his rental application, the telephone, and a Vanackern computer for Cozie to find out just how big a liar the Texan who'd rented her sawmill was.

She cranked her Jeep up to the speed limit and charged up Hawthorne Orchard Road from her office, past her white clapboard house and down the steep driveway to her sawmill.

Her slate-eyed tenant was at his truck, fiddling under the hood. If she aimed right, she could launch him straight over the dam into Hawthorne Brook. She could claim it was an accident. She was a native Vermonter. People would believe her.

But she forced her foot off the gas, applied the brakes, and came to a hard stop within maybe eighteen inches of him. He looked around at her. Military-style sunglasses hid his eyes, but he did not appear ruffled by how close her Jeep had come to giving him a few more scars.

Cozie leaped out and slammed the door shut. "How appropriate to find a Texas oilman putting oil in his truck."

He still had the oil can in one hand. "Been busy, have you?"

"I know who you are, Mr. Foxworth. Or are you still called Major even after early retirement?"

He set the oil can on the truck's front fender while he replaced the cap. His movements were precise and steady, in contrast to her own barely contained anger. She was mad enough to pick him up and throw him over the dam herself.

"Checked my references?"

"I did. I got a Houston laundry service, a gas station, and two recordings saying the number I'd called was not in service. It's Sunday, but I checked Houston information for the banks you listed. They don't exist. And you paid my realtor in cash."

"No wonder King George wanted to hang your great-great-whatever-granddaddy." He exaggerated his drawl, making himself sound less like the educated, privileged Texan he was. He adjusted his sunglasses, his gaze pinned on her. "Must have been a pain in the ass, ol' Elijah."

Cozie stood her ground. "Sal should have checked your references, *all* of which are phony."

"Don't be too hard on her."

"Your Texas charm might work on her. It won't on me."

He grinned. "Is that a challenge, Ms. Cozie?"

"Of all the arrogant responses—"

She broke off. Unable to see his eyes behind the impenetrable sunglasses, she had only his straight, hard mouth, his erect stance, the length of his pause to judge what he was thinking—all of which told her he wasn't planning to try charming her anytime soon. He shut the truck hood without banging it and turned back to her. "Look, honey, I'd love to listen to you stand here spitting fire all afternoon, but I've got places to go and things to do."

"Well, that's too damned bad!"

He moved in close to her, and it was all she could do not to take a step back, away from his tall, hard body. But that would only tell him he'd gotten to her, and she didn't want him getting the idea he had the upper hand.

"Don't you want to know what else I found out about you?" she asked.

He picked up the empty oil can and walked back toward the sawmill. "Reckon not or I'd have asked."

"Don't you 'reckon' me. You're about as much a bad-boy Texan as I am."

He glanced back at her, his gaze taking her in from head to toe. Amusement tugged at the corners of his mouth. "I wouldn't count on that, Ms. Cozie."

"Your real name is Daniel Austin Foxworth." She marched across the driveway after him, undeterred. "You're an heir to the Fox Oil fortune. You had an ancestor who really did die at the Alamo, another who was a general in the Spanish-American War, another who was a general in World War I. Your great-grandfather founded the family oil fortune. He was an East Texas wildcatter in the days of Dad Joiner and Glen McCarthy, neither of whom I'd heard of until today, but they were big, big oilmen. Your grandfather is Austin Foxworth, Korean War hero and Cold War general. He served at NATO headquarters before retiring to become chairman of Fox Oil. Your father is a graduate of Texas A & M and CEO of Fox Oil. Your sister, likewise a Texas A & M graduate, is a vice president. Your mother is a tireless volunteer for numerous Houston charities."

Cozie waited for him to comment, but he merely set the oil can on the bottom step of the porch and started back toward his truck. Nothing about the way he moved suggested he gave a merry damn what she knew or what she said.

She resumed her litany of facts. "You're thirty-eight years old. You were educated at a private high school in Texas and graduated from the air force academy. You quit the military three years ago at the rank of major, although everyone thought you had a shot at general. You started up a small oil fire-fighting company with a former Fox Oil employee, J.D. Maguire. He was seriously injured in a helicopter crash in the Gulf of Mexico three weeks ago. You were the pilot."

She paused once again. Still no acknowledgment of her words. Daniel Foxworth was opening the door to his truck as if she were relating the latest weather report.

"Julia Vanackern witnessed the accident. She was in Houston with her parents for a broadcasting awards ceremony. They met your grandfather, and he invited them to his ranch, and then the tanker fire started and the Vanackerns wanted to see what you do—"

"Julia did. I'm not sure Thad and Frances cared. But I wouldn't know since I wasn't there." Daniel leaned against his open truck door, his expression calm but unreadable. "Anything else?"

"You don't want to know how I found out all this stuff?"

"No."

She ignored him. "Remember last night when Julia told me she had a bad experience on a trip to Texas? I put two and two together: you're from Texas and you're interested in the Vanackerns. So I did a computer search on Julia and figured you had to be Daniel Foxworth." She squinted at him in the early afternoon sun. His calm only put her more on edge. "So then I did a search on you."

"I'm flattered," he said, without humor.

"Mr. Foxworth, this is a serious matter."

"Ms. Hawthorne, you can quit telling me about myself. I already know who I am."

She gritted her teeth. Finding out there was no Daniel Forrest of Houston, Texas, at least, had pushed her own troubles to the back of her mind. "I hate being lied to."

"Who doesn't?"

He moved away from the door, coming close to her, too close. She could see the old scar above the left corner of his mouth, and an unbidden spark of pure physical desire ignited. He brushed a stray hair off her face. She wondered if he could tell what was going on inside her.

"Why use an assumed name?" she asked. "The Vanackerns know who you are."

Even through his sunglasses, his gray eyes penetrated right to her bones. He let his hand go from her hairline down her temple to her jaw, leaving her skin tingling, hot. "My helicopter crashed before we could meet them while they were down in Texas. I thought using a different name would cause less trouble, which isn't the first dumb decision I've ever made."

"I presume you would prefer I kept your little lies to myself."

"I presume," he said, mimicking her, "that you're going to do what you need to do. Just as I am."

"And what is it you need to do?"

"Oh, Cozie."

Her jaw still cupped in his hand, he bent his head and kissed her, gently at first, as if giving her time to pull away, smack him one, something. But instead she responded. She closed her eyes and gave herself up to the sensations rushing through her. They kissed deeply, hungrily, with an intimacy that left her breathless and half certain she was crazy.

"I can't be feeling this way," she murmured, more to herself than to him. But she hadn't pulled back.

His dark eyes locked with hers. "Why not?"

"I'm usually . . . more sensible. I mean, you and I have nothing in common."

He straightened, still standing close. One eyebrow went up. "I don't know about that, Ms. Cozie."

She shoved her hands into the pockets of her floppy field jacket. She had to readjust her thinking about this man. He was a Texas Foxworth and he'd come to Vermont under an assumed name. She had to remember that, never mind how tempted she was by his dark eyes, the feel of his mouth on hers.

"Just because I kissed you back," she said, "don't get the idea that you can do anything around here you please. I'll be watching you, Ex-Major Foxworth."

"Ma'am," he said, and gave her a mock bow before he climbed into his truck. He eyed her through the open window as he started the engine. "See you around."

"Where are you going?"

But he'd already backed up, turning the truck around before roaring up the steep dirt driveway. Cozie noticed her hands were balled into tight fists. Kissing Daniel Austin Foxworth hadn't relaxed her at all. It hadn't even made her stop wondering what kissing him would be like. *Now* she was wondering what his tongue would feel like against hers, his body . . .

"Nuts," she muttered, disgusted with herself and all Texans, and ducked down the path along the brook, heading home.

\* \* \* \*

Her house was too quiet, too filled with memories that seemed to grab at her ankles everywhere she went, and she was far too restless after her encounter with Daniel Foxworth. She called Zep and they set off into the fields together, picking up one of the century-old farm roads that crisscrossed the woods. It was overgrown with grass and ferns, flanked by old stone walls.

Relieved to be alone, she breathed in the pungent smell of evergreens and freshly fallen leaves, and as she came to a narrow stream, she scooped up a handful of soft red leaves and tossed them into the clear, shallow water. She watched them float downstream until one caught on a rock, where it struggled for a few seconds before being overtaken by the rush of water.

She crossed the stream in a running leap. One foot squished into a muddy spot on the opposite bank, drenching her sock, but she didn't turn back, didn't slow down as she climbed a short, steep hill to an intersection with another old farm road. She veered off to the right, heading north, deeper into the woods. She'd followed this same route countless times as a kid with her brother and sister, but seldom by herself. She rested a moment in the shade of a tall oak and listened to the woodpeckers and blue jays and crows. The cold had gotten most of the mosquitoes that would have tormented her in the summer.

The woods grew thicker, darker, with more evergreens than hardwoods, and the road narrowed to a winding path. There were no stone walls. The path followed along the top of a ravine with birches and pines growing sideways off its steep bank. One slip and she'd roll a good fifty feet, unless she got hung up on a tree or a rock, like her leaf in the stream.

Zep stayed within yelling distance. He would shoot

up ahead of her and wait, then dash off into the woods, and reappear when he felt like it. He was muddy and slobbery and would be full of burrs when they got back.

After another half-mile, the path descended sharply and the woods lightened, with red and orange and yellow leaves adding a glow around her. More ferns and grasses and goldenrod appeared on the path. She pressed ahead. The light forest thinned even more, and she could see the aging orchard across from the red farmhouse where her brother lived.

She heard voices. Laughter. As she came to the edge of the orchard, she spotted a group of about a dozen hikers among the ancient apple trees. The Vanackern hiking party. She'd forgotten. In no mood for company, she considered diving behind the stone wall among the ferns and fallen leaves and waiting until they'd passed.

But Zep tore out into the orchard, barking and carrying on as if he really were a fierce dog. One woman reached for the branch of an apple tree, clearly prepared to make good her escape.

"Zep!" Cozie called.

She chased after him, but he continued to bark. She started to smile at the hikers. Then she spotted Daniel Foxworth among them. So this was where he'd been in such a hurry to go.

Did the Vanackerns know who he was? Were they keeping his identity their little secret? But if Julia had gone aboard his helicopter, she could have been killed.

Zep trotted up to Daniel and let him pat him on the head, and the woman with her hand on the branch looked reassured now that a big, brawny Texan had taken over. Cozie made a point of grabbing Zep by the collar, but he broke free and loped off through the orchard toward Seth's house. Her brother always had treats. The woman looked annoyed with her.

Cozie, however, had her attention focused on Daniel.

"I didn't expect to see you here." It wasn't a question or a demand, just a simple statement of fact. Not that she cared if Daniel Foxworth took offense.

As far as she could tell, he didn't. "Julia called this morning and invited me."

"You could have told me—"

"Ms. Cozie," he said in a low voice, "you were in no mood to let me tell you anything."

She scowled at him. "Does Julia realize you're—"

"No."

Thad Vanackern made his way to the front of the group, his smile strained as he greeted Cozie. "Well, hello. It's turned out to be quite a lovely afternoon. Would you care to join us?"

"I'll tag along for a while," she said, surprising herself.

But Daniel looked around at his host and said, "I need to be going. Hope you enjoy the rest of your hike." His gaze, impenetrable behind the dark sunglasses, rested on Cozie. "I'll see you around."

Nothing about his demeanor suggested he was worried about her keeping his identity to herself, but she found herself saying, if a bit tartly, "Nice to see you, Mr. Forrest."

He followed Zep's trail back up through the orchard. Since she'd already committed herself, she couldn't very well waltz off with him—at least not with any subtlety. The hikers had meandered off to the shade of the trees along the stone wall leading back toward Vanackern property. It was, truly, a stunning fall afternoon.

Thad Vanackern was still at Cozie's side. "Sorry about the interruption," she said.

"Nonsense. We're used to Zep by now."

They rejoined the party, Thad making some half-hearted joke about never knowing what would pop out of the woods. Cozie just smiled and kept quiet, and Julia fell back and walked with her. She had on taupe-colored flats with sleek wool pants and a hip-length lambskin jacket, a woman much more from the Foxworth world than Cozie could ever pretend to be.

Julia kicked up one foot. "Like my shoes? They're suede. Utterly worthless in a bog."

"They don't look too much the worse for wear."

"My passive-aggressive response to being dragged on a hike," she said good-naturedly, "although I do love looking at the autumn leaves outlined against a blue sky—and having Daniel Forrest along was fun while it lasted. He's not bad, even though three weeks ago I never wanted to step foot in Texas or see another Texan."

"Julia . . . I heard about what happened on your trip." Cozie paused a moment, to gauge Julia's reaction. There was none. She simply continued to glide along; she'd always been adept at controlling her emotions, or at least at not revealing them. "It must have been rough, seeing a helicopter crash, not knowing if those on board had been killed."

She smiled thinly. "It was. How did you find out?"

"You know this town. Word travels fast, especially about Vanackerns."

"I was supposed to be on board. Did you hear that?"

Cozie nodded.

"Not one of my finer experiences. One of the men aboard was nearly killed. Apparently the crash was the other guy—the pilot's fault. He got out with hardly a scratch. I thought—well, from the looks of things I was so sure there wouldn't be any survivors." She bit her lower lip, shuddering. "Thank God that's over."

"I didn't mean to remind you—"

"Oh, you didn't remind me. I haven't gone a day without seeing the smoke billowing out of that helicopter, seeing it spin out of control, crash into the water. It was awful."

There was no easy way to bring up the helicopter pilot himself, one Daniel Austin Foxworth, and Cozie had already decided to keep his identity to herself, not that she owed him a damned thing. She just wanted a few more facts before she gave anything away to anyone, even the woman who could have crashed with him in his downed helicopter.

The orchard gave way to a large, rolling field of tall green grass and goldenrod, with spectacular views of the surrounding hills. Up over a rise, across the dead-end dirt road, a beautiful white colonial was tucked behind a stone wall amidst birches and sugar maples. Cozie remembered driving up there with Grandpa Willard and her father and walking around in the then empty field, and hearing them talk about having no choice, doing what they had to do to save the paper and the rest of the land. At least, they said, Thad Vanackern was married to Frannie, and Frannie was one of them. Cozie had been just four. Later, she remembered, she had watched the bulldozers and cement mixers and front-end loaders and carpenter trucks driving past her house to carve up the pretty field up past the orchard.

At first glance, the house with its slate blue shutters and early New England architecture didn't seem less than thirty years old. The Vanackern "estate" itself didn't seem particularly ostentatious. It took a second or third glance to notice the tennis courts, the resort-style pool, the greenhouse, the stone stables, the riding pasture, the guest cottage, the extensive flower gardens. And one could never tell exactly where the Vanackern land ended and the Hawthorne land began.

Thad exchanged places with his daughter. "I was just telling our guests it took three generations of Hawthornes to clear this land, and just one generation for nature to reclaim it."

"Life wasn't easy back then."

"It never is." He sighed, suddenly serious, almost businesslike, and glanced around as if making sure no one was eavesdropping. "Cozie, I need to discuss something with you. It's an . . . awkward situation."

He knew, she thought. He'd found out her tenant was the man who'd crashed the helicopter Julia was to have been aboard, and he wanted Cozie to kick him out.

But Thad Vanackern said, "I'm afraid we've discovered money and a number of valuables missing from our house here in Woodstock." He paused for a minute, then added, "Your brother has been doing some work for us, you know."

Cozie took a sharp breath. She knew exactly what Thad Vanackern, in his oh-so-polished way, was intimating. "How much is missing?"

"I'm not sure how much cash. Several hundred dollars at least. The valuables are mostly small antiques—porcelain, silver, things that could be sold with relative ease."

"And you think Seth stole them," she said, making it an accusation.

Thad looked miserable. "Always so plainspoken, Cozie. That's certainly not what we want to believe, I assure you. Most of his work is outdoors, but he comes in for lunch, a drink every now and then. We don't restrict him in any way. We consider Seth a friend. We're not snobs, you know." He paused, apparently waiting for Cozie to concur.

"You're accusing my brother of being a thief."

"No, I am not accusing him of anything. All I'm asking is that you have a talk with him to see if he knows anything about what happened. The last thing we want is to bring in the police and create publicity that none of us needs right now." His expression hardened. "But we can't let this continue. If we have to go to the police, we will."

Cozie came to a dead stop, her heart pounding. "Seth has had his problems, but he is not a thief."

Thad slowed his pace. The sun glinted on his graying fair hair, and he looked younger than his years, very fit, intelligent. Powerful. If he put his mind to it, he could make her brother's life very difficult. "Cozie," he said, "we care about you and your family. If Seth couldn't resist temptation, if he has a problem for which he needs money, perhaps it's something we could work out among ourselves."

"There: he's been tried, convicted, and hanged. Enjoy the rest of your hike. I'm going home."

But Thad wasn't ready to give up so easily. "You Hawthornes have always stuck together. It's an admirable trait, but it could hurt you—and others—if you allow your loyalty to insulate you from the truth. I suggest you talk to your brother."

"Is that an order from my employer?"

"It is a request," he said tightly, "from a family friend."

She swallowed, wanting to respond, wanting to be reasonable. But every fiber of her being told her that Thad Vanackern was wrong about her brother. He had no sound evidence to support his suspicion and was acting on prejudice. He was wrong, pure and simple. But coming on top of her discovery about her new tenant, her growing awareness of her totally incorrigible physical attraction to him, she wasn't sure she could trust her reaction.

The lead hikers had turned down another farm road that would take them to a waterfall and eventually connect up with the road she had followed out there. Cozie had no intention of continuing on with them. She about-faced and struck off along the edge of the field, then cut up through the middle of the orchard to the dirt road, about twenty yards up from her brother's house. Why had Thad Vanackern stuck her in the middle? Why couldn't he talk to Seth himself?

*Because you're his employee. He expects you to do what he tells you to do.*

Zep loped up to her from Seth's place, and something caught her eye on the slope behind her brother's vegetable garden. She squinted against the bright sun.

Daniel Foxworth was sitting atop a huge boulder. He didn't jump up and try to run away when she started up the hill toward him. He had one knee up and a long blade of yellowed grass tucked between his lips, as if nothing had ever bothered him in his life. He still had on his military sunglasses.

"You know," she said, "if every time people turn around they see me with a lying Texan richer than God. . . ."

"No one's going to see us," he said, "and it was only a white lie."

"You're not going to deny you're richer than God?"

He plucked the blade of grass from his mouth and flung it backward over his shoulder. "Is that how you measure people? By how much money they make or how much they'll inherit?"

"No, of course not."

"Seems to me you like someone a whole lot better if they're broke. Maybe including yourself."

"I'm in no mood to be analyzed." She realized she sounded more exhausted than annoyed. She put one foot up on the base of the boulder, noticing her muddy sock, wondering if he did, too. "What are you doing up here?"

"Just taking in the view."

"Ha."

He stretched out his bent leg. "You don't believe much of anything I say, do you, Ms. Cozie?"

"Not anymore."

His gaze leveled on her. She almost told him to take off his sunglasses so she could see his eyes, at least try to guess what was going on inside his head. "I don't need you to trust me."

Her mouth had suddenly gone dry. "Seth's not around?"

"Not that I can see."

She sighed. She'd talk to her brother later about Thad Vanackern's missing cash and valuables. Daniel climbed down from the boulder and dropped beside her.

"Why did your helicopter crash into the Gulf of Mexico?" she asked suddenly.

"You are a tenacious woman, Ms. Cozie. But I'll indulge you. In layman terms, a small explosion blew out various things I needed to keep it in the air."

"You couldn't land?"

"No, ma'am. There wasn't a whole hell of a lot I could do except try to keep us from coming apart before we hit water."

He started down the slope toward Seth's driveway. Cozie followed, taking extra-long strides to keep up. She refused to back off. "What caused the explosion?"

"I don't know."

"The papers indicated you had explosives on board that were improperly stored. Most likely a detonator cap, or several detonator caps, ignited and caused the damage."

He didn't look around at her. "That's one theory."

"What's your theory?"

He swung around at her, stopping directly in front of her, two inches from her toes. "Leave it, Cozie. It's not your problem."

"I could have you evicted."

"You could."

"You don't think I will, do you?"

"No, I don't."

She pushed her hair back with one hand, sure his eyes never left her. She wondered what he was thinking. Her hair needed a good brushing? He liked her better in her Ingrid Bergman dress? She was way too combative and direct for his tastes? He wanted to kiss her again? She had no idea. She only knew that right now his reasons for being in Vermont, his lies—they didn't matter.

"Cozie."

There was a raggedness to his voice that told her his lies, whatever had brought him to Vermont, didn't matter to him either, not right now.

But if he even touched her, she knew she would run. She would have no choice. She'd already kissed him back once. Who knew what she'd do now? She didn't trust herself.

He didn't make a move to touch her, but his gaze stayed on her. "I'd bet you'd be like a pitbull in a fight, Cozie Hawthorne. You'd hang on for dear life and stop at nothing. But I'm responsible for putting a man in the hospital. I've got a company in a mess because I screwed up. No matter what caused that crash, I was the pilot, and ultimately I was responsible." He lifted a hand, stopped in midair. "I won't be responsible for anything happening to you."

"You think someone sabotaged your helicopter."

"It's my problem. Stay out of it."

That broke the spell. She hated being ordered around, and what Daniel Foxworth was telling her was an order, not a plea. She tossed her head back. "Well, that's just fine with me. I've got enough problems of my own. Good day, Major Foxworth."

When she was halfway down the driveway, Daniel said laconically, "You want a ride?"

"No."

She kept her back to him. "It's going to be dark soon."

"I'm not afraid of the dark."

But he was beside her, his keys already out. "You're a pigheaded, dyed-in-the-wool Yankee, Ms. Cozie."

"I think I'll wait for my brother."

"Cozie, in the truck."

She sighed. "What about Zep?"

Daniel looked around at her big mutt. Zep was wet, muddy, filthy, and panting hard. He had white slobber all over his snout. Daniel shook his head. "No dogs up front. Where I come from, animals know their place."

In the end, however, Zep had his way and rode up front between his master and her new pal from Texas.

# CHAPTER
# 7

———————➤

Fool that he was, Daniel accepted Cozie's halfhearted invitation to come inside for a mug of hot cider. She made the dog stay out. The big cookstove in the back room was still warm. Cozie lifted a cast-iron lid and stirred the coals, then added a couple small chunks of wood from the overflowing woodbox. Daniel stayed out of her way. The house had a homey character, its age apparent in the wide pineboard floor and drafty windows. A long, slipcovered couch occupied most of the wall opposite the cookstove, with two old wooden-armed chairs angled at each end, nothing fancy. He noticed the collection of videos of old movies on a shelf next to the television: they had to be Cozie's contribution. He wondered how many more Ingrid Bergman dresses she had tucked in her closet.

She fetched a half-gallon of cider from the unheated back porch, pulled a pan off a warmer shelf above the stove top, and splashed cider into it.

Daniel stood next to her. "No bug parts?"

"I don't think so."

She was matter of fact. Inspecting cider was, he realized, part of her experience, something she considered perfectly natural.

"You must have had quite a childhood, growing up here."

"It had its moments." The fire crackled as the wood reignited. "I loved being outside. We all did. We'd climb trees, follow streams and stone walls, go sledding in the winter. I guess we never thought much about what went into maintaining this place."

"Kids aren't supposed to worry about those things," Daniel said.

"Well, we sure didn't." She chose a larger log from the woodbox and, opening the stovetop lid, shoved it onto the fire. "It'll take just a minute for the cider to heat up. What was your childhood like?"

"More ordinary than you probably would believe. My grandfather—"

"The general?"

He nodded, refusing to be baited. "He has a ranch southwest of Houston. I practically grew up there."

"With the expectation of your becoming a general or an oilman?"

"I didn't realize it until I was older, but yes, that expectation was there."

"Did you rebel?"

"I just did as I pleased."

"Isn't that a kind of rebellion?"

He smiled. "I didn't think so."

She slid the pan of cider onto the hottest part of the stove, directly over the fire. "My father never pressured any of us to take over the paper. I guess we all assumed he would be around longer than he was.

100

Grandpa Willard lived well into his eighties, and he and my father worked together for years. They always managed to avoid total disaster but never made much money. But when my father got sick and the recession hit, he just had no choice. He had to sell to the Vanackerns."

"Still sticks in your craw, does it?"

"There were no other offers."

"Did you see yourself taking over when your father got sick?"

"I never thought . . ." She tested the cider with her finger, licking it off. Daniel tried not to watch the flick of her tongue. "I thought he'd get well. I never planned for him dying when he did. None of us did." She raised her green eyes to him as if she expected him to contradict her. "But we're managing."

"Hawthornes pride themselves on their ability to endure hardship, don't they?"

"We could pride ourselves on worse."

"So what happens when success comes along?"

She gave him a faint, self-deprecating smile. "We endure."

While the cider heated up, she turned from the cookstove, removing her jacket and tossing it on the back of one of the lumpy, wood-handled chairs. Underneath she had on a ginger-colored turtleneck that outlined the soft curve of her breasts, but she didn't seem to notice him looking. She'd turned her attention to an answering machine on the chest next to the chair. Its red light was blinking, indicating she had received calls while she was out. Leaning over the chair, she pressed the button to play back her messages. With the other hand, she reached back and unobtrusively tucked in the straying hem of her turtleneck. So, Daniel thought, she had noticed his interest.

The first message was from her sister, Meg, who invited her to Sunday dinner, "unless you're still off gallivanting with the Vanackerns or that Texas stud of yours."

Cozie shot him a look. "That's just Meg."

"I didn't say a word."

The next message began. "Hello, Cozie Cornelia."

There was a pause, and she went very still. Daniel moved forward, but her ramrod stiffness warned him not to get too close.

The voice on the tape resumed. "How was your walk this afternoon? I hope you enjoyed yourself."

*Click.*

The momentary hum of a dial tone, the snap of the tape ending, then the familiar whirring as it rewound.

In the ensuing silence, Daniel could hear only the popping and hissing of the fire in the woodstove. Cozie placed a hand on the back of the chair in an obvious attempt to steady herself.

"I thought . . ." She paused, regained her self-control, and began again. "I've been receiving anonymous calls since July—but never here. Always just on the road."

"The voice is always disguised?"

She nodded, still not looking at him. "I can't even tell if it's a man or a woman. Sounds as if he—or she—is talking into a tin can or something."

"You could have an expert listen to this tape."

"I might just do that." With a sudden burst of energy, she popped open the answering machine and fumbled with the tiny cassette, her hands shaking visibly. Daniel resisted the urge to help her. Finally, she had the thing clutched in one fist. "I'll put it with my log."

Her log?

102

Daniel followed her to the kitchen, which ran the width of the narrow house and had a cozy, country feel that, under ordinary circumstances, would be immediately soothing. She tore open a drawer next to the refrigerator, dropped in the cassette, and slammed the drawer shut.

She didn't stop him when he walked over to the counter. She was pressed up against the sink, her color beginning to return. He opened the drawer. Inside, amid the junk and general chaos, were the cassette, the note she'd found last night on her Jeep, and a small spiral notebook. He withdrew the notebook and opened it. Cozie didn't protest.

The time, date, place, and transcript of each call she'd received since July were meticulously recorded on page after page of the notebook. *"Hello, Cozie Cornelia . . ."* They all began the same way.

"You've received dozens of these calls," he said.

She acknowledged his words with a small nod.

He scanned the entries. Without being overtly threatening, the calls were still not what he would describe as the work of a harmless nut.

"Who have you told?" he asked.

She licked her lips, and he saw her hesitation. Understood it.

"Cozie," he said, "I know I lied to you about who I am, but I didn't make these calls. I didn't know anything about them until now. They're not why I'm here." But he was already wondering about that.

She shut her eyes as if she could squeeze back the tension, keep it from overwhelming her. "I don't know what to think anymore."

"You've been under a hell of a strain."

Her eyes opened again, and she tried to smile. "I guess."

Daniel replaced the log in the junk drawer while Cozie took two mugs down from a cupboard, her movements stiff and shaky. "I'm thinking—" She breathed in deeply, obviously not liking what she was thinking. "I'm thinking maybe it's time I reported this to the police. There might be something they can do." Without waiting for him to respond, she took the mugs to the back room and ladled hot cider into them. "It's just plain cider. Sometimes I add spices, but not always." She held a steaming mug out to him. "Enjoy."

"Thank you."

The cider was on the tart side but good. Cozie didn't touch hers. "I shouldn't have lied to you," he said.

"I probably overreacted. As you say, I've been under a hell of a strain. I can see you have your reasons for using an assumed name. They have nothing to do with me."

But Daniel was coming around to believing that in order for him to understand what happened to him and J.D. on the Gulf of Mexico, he needed to understand what had been happening to Cozie Hawthorne and her family since fame and fortune had come her way—and an anonymous caller had invaded her life.

"Nobody likes being on the receiving end of a lie," he said.

"I guess some people are more used to it than I am."

"I thought all journalists were skeptics."

She seemed to surprise herself by smiling. "Maybe that's why most people don't try to lie to me."

Daniel searched her face—her eyes, her mouth, the set of her jaw—for a sign of what Cozie Hawthorne was really feeling. Although direct and outspoken, she was, he decided, adept at suppressing especially powerful emotions like fear, grief, guilt, perhaps even love.

104

The major exception was anger. The woman had no trouble letting folks know when she was ticked off.

She blew lightly on her cider, then took a small sip, remaining by the stove, as if she needed its warmth. "If Julia Vanackern wasn't aboard your helicopter when it crashed—if you didn't even see her and her parents when they were in Texas—why do you think the Vanackerns know anything about what happened?"

Not just the Vanackerns, Daniel thought. Your brother, too. But he said carefully, "I'm not sure that they do."

"You've gone to a lot of trouble to find out."

"I'm going to do what I have to do."

"Suppose," she said, unrelenting, "I decide not to keep what I know about you to myself. I could put one of my reporters on the story. That's what any other editor in my position would do."

"Even if it involves a Vanackern?"

"Why not? I wouldn't stay on at the *Citizen* another minute if the Vanackerns tried to interfere with editorial policy." She drank more of her cider, her natural self-assurance returning. "So what would you do if I had someone investigate what you're really doing in Vermont?"

He shrugged. "Nothing."

"Nothing?" Obviously she didn't believe him.

"That's right. You can make what I have to do here more difficult, Cozie, but you can't stop me."

"I never said I wanted to stop you."

"Then you just want me to satisfy your curiosity."

He set his mug on the wooden arm of a chair and moved to her side at the stove. The fire was going good now, radiating a heat that was a damned good measure of his mounting desire for one green-eyed Yankee with a mop of reddish blond hair and a mess of troubles. Her caller, her brother, her new fame and fortune. Him.

But he wanted her. It wasn't something, he now realized, that wasn't going to decrease the more he was around her. Quite to the contrary.

"I'd better go," he said thickly.

She glanced up, taking him in with eyes suddenly more blue than green, trying to guess what he was thinking, maybe even what he wanted. How fast would she kick him out if she knew?

But her common sense prevailed. "Thanks for the ride home."

He managed a smile. "Anytime, Ms. Cozie. I'm just up the road. Someone comes around pestering you, you just give a holler."

She laughed, and her eyes sparkled, the blue in them receding. He could see her tension ease. "Right, Hoss. Thanks."

Back outside, the sun had dipped below the horizon, leaving behind streaks of orange and red that could almost pass for a Texas sunset. At home, Daniel thought, he'd be on his front porch, thinking about all the work his ranch needed, maybe doing a little dreaming. J.D. just had a place by a muddy creek near what he liked to call "company headquarters." He was always ready for the next call, no matter where it was. Their nomadic life suited him. For the past three years, it had suited Daniel.

When he got back to his house, his phone was ringing. He picked up the extension in the sawmill kitchen, and J. D. Maguire said, "I've been cursing your miserable butt all day."

"You're in good company."

"I hurt, Danny Boy. I really hurt."

Daniel listened intently to his friend's words as he

stared out the window, down at the old stone dam. The golden sunset glinted on the still water of the ice-cold pond. "The nurses and doctors treating you all right?"

J.D. grunted. "They haven't killed me yet. How's Vermont?"

"My landlady figured out who I am. Threatened to toss me out on my ear."

That perked up his partner. "Now that I'd like to see."

"J.D., I can't have her meddling."

"You're a big boy. Tell her to back off, keep her nose where it belongs."

"Cozie Hawthorne isn't one to do anything just because someone tells her to."

"So? Make her."

Daniel had to smile at the thought. "Obviously you haven't met the lady. I found out more about the threats she's been receiving." He told J.D. about the message on Cozie's machine, the log of calls she kept in her kitchen junk drawer. "She says she's going to talk to the police. I don't know. I think this business shakes her image of herself. It's not easy to admit someone hates you enough to leave nasty messages on your answering machine. And I'm betting she's beginning to realize it's probably someone she knows."

There was no response on the Texas end of the line. "J.D.?"

Nothing.

In a moment, a nurse picked up. "I'm sorry, Mr. Maguire has dozed off. Can I leave a message for him?"

"He's okay?"

"He's in a great deal of pain today, but his condition is still stable."

It was something, Daniel thought, then added quietly, "There's no message. Just tell him I'll stay in touch."

"You're . . ."

"Foxworth. Daniel Foxworth."

"Oh," she said sharply, and he knew she'd made the connection: he was the reckless SOB who'd put J.D. Maguire in the hospital—but who'd also saved the Texas and Louisiana coastlines from a major oil spill. "Yes, of course. I'll tell him."

When he hung up, Daniel became aware of the blood pounding behind his eyes. He wondered what all Cozie Hawthorne had found out about him. Had she learned that no one who knew him could figure out why he hadn't managed to kill or maim someone before now? That people believed he was arrogant and single-minded, a man addicted to danger, who would put himself and others at risk to get what he wanted? That it was his fault, and his fault alone, that J.D. was burned and broken and might never fight an oil fire again?

If word got out he was in Vermont, people would say he was there to find a scapegoat for something for which he himself was responsible. Because he was a Foxworth and that was the Foxworth tradition: never admitting to weakness, never admitting to making a mistake.

The early-nineteenth-century New England sawmill along Hawthorne Brook seemed even quieter, almost eerie in the shifting shadows of the waning day. The woodstove popped and hissed with a steady efficiency, giving off a welcome heat. Daniel tugged open the refrigerator, trying to repress images of J.D. twisting and turning in pain in his hospital bed, suffering as he shouldn't have to suffer.

*Could* he have done something wrong—something stupid, negligent, arrogant—and caused the explosion?

Could he have reacted faster, better, gotten the damaged copter safely back to land?

He slammed the refrigerator door, frustrated with his own inaction. In nearly a week in Vermont, he'd accomplished precious little besides allowing himself to be hopelessly smitten by his green-eyed, wild-haired, skeptical, and very much in trouble Vermont landlady.

If J.D. had been there, he'd have told Daniel that Cozie Hawthorne was an uptight, big-mouthed Yankee who needed a few more liars and cheats in her life. He could hear his friend's booming laugh.

What would J.D. have made of the message on her answering machine? *"Hello, Cozie Cornelia . . ."* No matter what he thought of his partner's pretty, suddenly famous landlady, J.D. wouldn't take to having someone trying to scare her. Being a man of action, he would do something.

Daniel swore softly under his breath, but he already had his jacket in his hand, and he headed outside, moving fast, needing to do, to act, before the fear and the grief and the guilt could paralyze him.

The sky was clear and black, a perfect background for the stars and quarter moon as Daniel walked along the isolated dirt road toward Seth Hawthorne's small farmhouse. The cold seemed to seep into his soul. He could hear the crunching of tiny rocks under his feet and the occasional lonely cry of an owl, the rustling of some small animal in the brush.

Once again, Seth's truck wasn't in the driveway, and the house was dark, its windows reflecting the shadows of the swaying branches of the butternut tree. Daniel knocked on the front door, not expecting an answer.

None came.

The doorknob, however, turned in his hand.

*Strike while the iron is hot,* his granny—his mother's mother—had always told him.

He pushed open the door and entered the dark, quiet front hall.

"Anybody home?"

Feeling around in the dark, he found a light switch at the bottom of a steep, narrow, uncarpeted staircase. A dim overhead came on.

He entered a living room to his right. It was simply furnished, with a hardwood floor whose gleam suggested a recent sanding and oiling. Two tall windows, with plain off-white curtains, looked out onto the front yard, two more onto the side yard opposite the driveway. An overstuffed couch that had a grandmother's-attic look about it was pushed up against the wall between two of the windows, directly across from a fairly up-to-date entertainment center. There were also two Craftsman-style rocking chairs and a big, worn, comfortable-looking upholstered chair.

The one print on the wall, Daniel noticed, was of a hawk in flight.

He scanned a stack of periodicals on a rickety side table: *Vermont Life,* gardening catalogs, guides for skiers, hikers, canoeists. No *Texas Highways.*

A double doorway led to a dining room, its floor also hardwood and recently redone. With the light from the front hall insufficient, Daniel flipped on another dim overhead. Seth Hawthorne didn't waste any money on lightbulbs.

An oval oak table occupied what had to be the best

spot in the house: a bay window with views to the southeast, across the rolling apple orchard. Daniel could see rangy Seth Hawthorne drinking his morning coffee and watching the Vermont sunrise. There were worse fates.

He turned his attention to a massive oak rolltop desk that must have come with the place. It was in poor condition, dividers missing, the oak veneer scarred and dirty. The front of one drawer was off, others were misaligned.

Feeling only a twinge of disgust at prying through another man's affairs, Daniel started with the overflowing nooks and crannies. He found old books of matches, rubber bands, paper clips, yellowed index cards, canceled checks, bank statements, receipts for payments received for forestry work, cordwood, guide work, brush clearing, even for building a stone wall. There were cash register receipts for everything from groceries to chainsaw parts.

A family of savers, the Hawthornes.

His latest bank statement revealed a hand-to-mouth existence, not, Daniel thought, atypical for an unattached man in his mid-twenties.

But his eye was drawn to the familiar red lettering of a canceled airline ticket, stuck under a mason jar of pennies. He tugged it free.

In the dim light of the overhead, the destination and departure and return dates were still clearly visible.

Here was irrefutable proof that Seth Hawthorne had flown into Houston the day before the helicopter crash and departed—by design—the day after. He'd paid top dollar for his ticket, an indication it had been a spontaneous trip. Given what Daniel had seen of his neighbor's financial situation, the cost must have cleaned him out.

He set aside the ticket and continued on through the pile under the mason jar, discovering a small white envelope in a heavy, expensive paper, addressed to Seth in a distinctly female hand. Daniel withdrew a simple white notecard. The handwriting was graceful and fluid, in black ink. There was no date, just:

> *Dear Seth,*
>     *I'm sorry for how I treated you in Texas—I was upset. I hope you can forgive me. You don't know how much you mean to me. I only wish things could be different, for both of us.*
>
> *Always,*
> *Julia*

"Well, well." His voice seemed to echo in the isolated, empty house.

Seth Hawthorne, indeed, had a fling going—or gone—with Julia Vanackern, and they'd argued in Texas, just like J.D. had said.

Had Seth, several years younger than Julia, taken their relationship more seriously than she had? Daniel had seen it before. A privileged, beautiful woman looking for fun with a safe, good-looking, regular sort of guy. The guy smitten.

He'd also, he thought, seen the reverse.

But could Seth have been so upset at finding he'd been used he tried to blow Julia Vanackern out of the sky?

He still didn't seem the type. As hard to pin down as the guy was, Daniel couldn't peg him as someone who'd fly into a rage and commit murder.

"And maybe," he muttered, "you're letting your attraction to Ms. Cozie interfere with your judgment."

Tough questions remained to be asked. Why, for

instance, had Seth apparently told no one—including his wild-haired sister—he'd gone to Texas? Why hadn't he told Daniel he recognized him? *How* did he recognize him?

And what about the harassing calls and messages Cozie had been enduring? Were they the work of a secretly jealous and troubled younger brother?

Daniel shoved the note back into the envelope. He had to keep an open mind, and he had to get the answers he needed to be able to go back to Texas and face J.D., face his family, face himself. He returned the ticket and note to their spot under the mason jar and continued into the kitchen.

It was small and badly designed, with the stove, refrigerator, and sink all on different walls and virtually no counter space. He opened up the refrigerator and checked the cupboards, just blindly rooting around. He found a glass quart of whole milk, a half-gallon jug of homemade cider, rapidly browning ground beef, a pint of Ben & Jerry's Vanilla Heath Bar Crunch, a couple of boxes of dry cereal, a few cans of soup, dried beans, two brown-spotted bananas, and about a half-dozen apples.

That told him a hell of a lot.

Tempted to call it quits, he took the steep stairs up to the second floor. Straight ahead on the landing was a tiny bathroom. He skipped it and went into the larger of the two bedrooms. With just a double bed on a simple metal frame and an oak dresser, it, too, had that life-on-a-shoestring look. But the front window would have a view of the orchards and the mountains beyond.

A copy of *Mountain Views* was on the floor by the bed. It wasn't sliced to ribbons or marred in a fit of anger in any way that Daniel could see, but it didn't look dog-eared either. He opened up the front cover.

In a scrawl that only slightly resembled the precise handwriting in the log she'd kept of her harassing calls, Cozie had autographed the book for her brother.

*Take care of yourself, brother. Thanks for always being there. Cheers, Cozie.*

Nice sentiment, no lingering sibling tensions evident between the lines. Daniel shut the book and put it back where he'd found it. He knew he was pushing his luck. Seth could drive up at any moment, and a confrontation on an isolated hilltop in the dead of night wasn't how Daniel wanted to top off his day. He scooted back downstairs, shutting off all the lights behind him, and slipped out the back door through the kitchen.

Standing still a minute or two, he let his eyes adjust to the dark. The cold helped clear his head. He headed along the back of the house, opposite the driveway, the grass soft under his feet. As he was about to cross into the side yard, he heard the putter of an engine. In another few seconds he saw headlights, and Cozie Hawthorne's Jeep pulled alongside her brother's house.

Daniel didn't move in the pitch dark shadows of the old house.

She climbed out, trotted up onto the cracked landing, and knocked on the front door. "Seth? Seth—you home? It's me, Cozie. I need to talk to you."

About who her tenant really was? Did she know about her brother's trip to Texas after all? But obviously Seth wasn't home, and after another couple of knocks Cozie gave up and started back to her Jeep.

It was maybe twenty degrees out, and Daniel hunched his shoulders against the cold, wishing he'd worn a sweater under his jacket. His northerner landlady seemed unaffected by the precipitous drop in temperature.

114

He heard a sound at his feet and looked around. A skunk waddled calmly within a yard of him, its white stripe plainly visible. Daniel swore and automatically stepped out of its path.

He backed right into a wheelbarrow, upending the thing and almost breaking his damned neck. He swore some more, just managing to stay on his feet.

Cozie spun around. "Seth? Is that you?"

Daniel was more interested in the skunk, but the beast apparently had slipped off to quieter haunts. He righted the wheelbarrow, a heavy, old contraption with wooden handles. "No—it's me, Daniel."

*"You!"*

He thought he might rather take his chances with the skunk. Cozie came barreling around to the side of the house, her hands shoved in the pockets of her field jacket. He couldn't make out her features in the darkness, but he would guess she wasn't thrilled to see him. Under the circumstances, he didn't blame her.

He emerged from the shadows. "Evening."

"I don't believe you. What are you doing up here?"

"Looking for your brother."

"He's not here."

"I know." He decided to give it to her straight. "I searched his place. It's not the sort of thing I usually do in my spare time, but I'm not apologizing. He was in Texas when my chopper went down, Cozie. I found his canceled airline ticket if you want proof."

She stared at him. "Seth was in Texas?"

"That's right. J.D. saw him with Julia Vanackern."

"Julia? But he never said—"

"They argued right before our helicopter went up. After he left she changed her mind about going with us."

Cozie had begun to shiver in the cold. Daniel could sense her rising confusion and indignation, wondered how he'd feel if someone showed up out of the blue and made similar insinuations about his sister as he was about Cozie's brother. He'd probably knock the son of a bitch silly.

Give the lady time to sort things out, he thought.

But he couldn't let her stop him.

"So that's why you're in Vermont," she said without drama. She swore out loud, coming to life. "All right. That's it. Either you tell me what in the hell's going on here or I'm calling the police and having you arrested for breaking and entering."

A cold wind was whipping up strange sounds in the orchard, rustles and creaks and the unfamiliar cries of nocturnal animals. Vermont, Daniel thought, could give a man the creeps.

"I'm just here," he said, "to find out if the Vanackerns or your brother know anything about what happened to my helicopter."

"You think—" She had to gulp for air. "You bastard—you think Seth sabotaged your helicopter, don't you?"

"I haven't come to any conclusions."

"But your partner saw Seth with Julia Vanackern, and the two of you figured he must know something or be responsible. Why?"

Daniel hung onto his calm. "Not the two of us. J.D. thinks I'm chasing dust. He thinks I'm responsible."

"Are you?"

He knew what she was asking: did he know, in his gut, that there'd been no sabotage? Was he picking on her brother because he couldn't admit his own guilt? "I was the pilot," he said. "That makes me responsible."

"You don't like to make mistakes," she said.

"Not that kind of mistake."

116

"I know my brother. You don't. He couldn't have sabotaged your helicopter. He wouldn't do something like that."

Daniel sighed. It was so cold his breath formed a cloud in front of his mouth. "Maybe he wouldn't. But I still need to talk to him about what he was doing in Texas."

"Fine. Go ahead." She shoved her hands even deeper into her field coat pockets—probably as much an attempt to control her anger as to stay warm.

"What are you doing up here?" he asked.

"Looking at the stars," she said evasively, turning back.

The stars, Daniel had to admit, were worth looking at against the dark Vermont sky. But the sky was dark down the road, too. He had the feeling Cozie Hawthorne wasn't telling him the truth.

"You walked up?" she asked. "Or do you have your truck hidden in the bushes?"

"I walked."

"Well, I'm not leaving you here to lie in wait for Seth. Get in the Jeep. I'll give you a ride back to the sawmill."

"You'd think you'd busted your head against enough brick walls for one day."

"What's that supposed to mean?"

"It means," he said, following her to her Jeep, "if I don't choose to let you drive me back, there's not a damned thing you can do about it."

She cast him a long, unworried look. "Is that a threat, Major Foxworth?"

"An observation."

"I'd call the police."

If he let her into Seth's house. But she seemed pretty confident she could handle him, and Daniel wasn't going to doubt her. Who knew what else besides skunks and wheelbarrows the Hawthornes had handy. He smiled. "I'd love a ride, Ms. Cozie."

He got into the Jeep beside her. She took the twisting dirt road fast. Daniel reminded himself this was her territory. She would know every curve, every rock in the road. Either that or she was really pissed off and scared and just didn't give a damn if they ended up flipping over a stone wall.

They didn't meet a single car out on Hawthorne Orchard Road. Daniel noticed tangles in her hair, thought of himself easing them out with his fingers, one by one. He noticed the slender shape of her hands as they gripped the battered steering wheel.

As they approached the sawmill, he said, "You can go on to your house and drop me off there. I'll walk on back."

"Why?" She sounded suspicious. "You think Seth's there?"

"Cozie, I was with you last night when you found that note on your windshield. I heard your caller this afternoon, I saw your log—I'd like to make sure you get home all right."

"None of that has *anything* to do with my brother."

"I didn't say it did."

Silence. She stepped hard on the gas, raced past the sawmill, and shot up her driveway. Daniel got out, patting Zep on the head, but Cozie just marched to the back porch without a word.

"You shouldn't stay here alone," he said, following her.

She looked around at him. "I'll be fine. I've lived on this road almost my whole life."

He tried to imagine it. "I guess you're in no mood to listen to me right now. I don't blame you. But if you need me, you know where to find me."

"Thank you." Stiffly polite. As if she couldn't ever fathom needing him.

"And if you do see your brother—"

"I'll tell him everything."

"Go ahead. Then ask him about his trip to Texas."

Daniel could tell it galled her that she hadn't known about it. She straightened. "Good night."

She grabbed Zep's dish off the landing and tore open the back door, and Daniel waited, not moving, as she dug into a monstrous bag of dog food just inside the porch. She came back outside and plopped the dish unceremoniously onto the landing, to Zep's apparent disinterest.

Strands of hair had fallen into her face. She was breathing hard as she squinted at Daniel in the darkness. "You're still here?"

"I'm waiting until you're inside."

"You don't have to."

"I know I don't. Zep staying out here?"

She shook her head. She seemed calmer, or at least not as angry. "I'll bring him in with me."

"Good."

"I—thank you for giving a damn that I'm okay up here."

"I do give a damn. But you might not want to thank me for it."

He climbed onto the landing with her, and he could see her confusion of emotions, felt his own. Stars glittered overhead and nearby trees creaked and groaned in the sharp wind. Cozie could have ducked onto the porch and slammed the door in his face. But she didn't. Nor did she jump back when he touched her mouth, first with two fingers, then with his lips. The taste of her warmed him. He almost didn't feel the wind.

She brushed his cheek with her fingertips.

Her mouth opened into his, and he eased his tongue between her soft lips, tasted even more of her. A thundering ache swept through him. He wanted this woman. Badly. Her quick wit, her unfettered anger, her optimism, her wild hair and the soft swell of her breasts and the changeable eyes—everything about her captivated him, aroused him.

But she didn't trust him.

How the hell could she?

"It would be easy," she whispered as if reading his mind, "so easy just to invite you inside. But I can't. I don't trust myself right now."

He understood. The temptation was to dive into the physical. To let herself be carried away with it. To avoid thinking. But Cozie Hawthorne was a woman who resisted temptation. She would have to think. Before she climbed into bed with him, she would have to know it was right.

And knowing that about her made Daniel want her all the more.

But he said, "Good night, Cozie," and started back down her dark driveway. He heard her soft call for her dog, the creak as she pulled her back door shut, and he wondered what rock he'd turned over in her life by coming to Hawthorne Orchard Road.

# CHAPTER
# 8

A hard, killing frost always came earlier than Cozie expected, and before she could get to work the next morning, she had to dig her scraper out of the toolshed to get the frost off her windshield. Her Hawthorne forebears—even the car owners among them—had never seen fit to build a garage.

Because she refused to wear gloves until November first, she kept switching back and forth between hands as she scraped her windshield. She kept the free hand in the pocket of the teal-colored wool blazer she'd thrown on over a matching silk sweater. She was using her short-handled scraper. The long-handled scraper with the attached brush she didn't break out until the first measurable snow.

She wondered if there was a commentary in these mindless little pre-winter rituals.

"Yes," she said aloud, "the brain is working again."

There had been no anonymous message waiting on her answering machine when she got in last night.

That had helped calm her down. So had drinking a glass of milk and taking an objective look at what she'd had thrown at her on one long, trying day. Her new tenant was a rich Texan out for blood—possibly her brother's blood. Seth had been in Texas when said rich Texan's helicopter went down, nearly killing him and his partner.

Seth and Julia Vanackern had some sort of relationship that had prompted him to go to Texas in the first place.

He hadn't told either of his sisters about his trip.

The Vanackerns thought he might be stealing from them.

On top of which, her tormentor was in Vermont and getting frighteningly bold.

Cozie could admit her brother's behavior did provoke questions, but they were questions, she felt, that he'd be able to answer, given the chance.

Her milk finished, she'd gone up to bed. Imagining Daniel Foxworth under her comforter with her instead of her crowbar had not helped calm her. But she had, eventually, slept.

Now she had her day planned. She would spend the morning in the office and reacquaint herself with her job and her staff and her life as she'd once known it. She would look up Seth and have a serious heart-to-heart with him about the Vanackerns and one rich Texan who was after his hide. What her brother told her would determine whether or not she marched down to her sawmill and packed Daniel Foxworth's things for him. She had no intention of bothering with the finery of an eviction notice.

Leaning over the hood, she attacked the middle of the windshield. Her fingers were red and stiff with the cold. She had refused to drag out her winter coat because it was supposed to get up into the fifties later, even if the thermometer in her kitchen window indicated it was below freezing. She hurried around to the other side of the Jeep, anxious to get the job done.

Something moved inside.

She went still, her fingers tightening around the scraper. Zep was off in the fields. Her crowbar was upstairs in her bed. She stepped back away from the Jeep. She could, she thought, run down the driveway and flag a passing car. If she had to, she could beeline for the toolshed and have her pick of weapons.

But the passenger window creaked down, and Daniel Foxworth said, "You know, Ms. Cozie, there's a nice little Firebird somewhere in your future."

Her relief was immediate and lasted just long enough for him to pry open the door and unfold himself from the confines of her Jeep. She glared at him. "Now what?"

He rubbed the back of his neck, his hair sticking up in odd places, his shirt untucked, his leather jacket open—and the effect unreasonably sexy. "I had it in my mind to protect you from intruders."

"I have a dog for that," she said.

His mouth twisted, she couldn't tell whether in amusement or what. "Zep might alert you to an intruder. I'd *deal* with an intruder."

"How long have you been out here?"

"Just since dawn. Couldn't sleep."

Because he was worried about her—or because he was afraid he'd miss something? "Looks to me as if all your macho inclinations got you was a rough night. Which, I might add, serves you right. Don't think I'm going to thank you—"

"Now why would I think that?" His sarcasm was unmistakable. He picked what appeared to be a Zep hair off his chin. Dark stubble had erupted over his jawline, adding to his overall air of earthy sensuality.

123

"I'll bet you're hell on men, Ms. Cozie. Any anonymous phone calls last night?"

"No. Now move aside and let me finish. I've got to get to work. Some of us still have to work for a living, you know."

Ignoring her halfhearted jibe, he shut the passenger door and leaned against it, one leg bent, arms folded over his chest. "That little ice scraper of yours wouldn't hold me off for long if I had a mind to come at you. You keep a gun in the house?"

"No, I do not."

"You don't have locks for your door. What if someone snuck in during the night?"

"No one ever has," she said.

"No one's ever left nasty notes on your windshield either."

She let him stand there while she leaned over and resumed scraping. Despite the clear, cold morning, clouds were due to roll in later in the day, with a forecast of evening showers.

"Cozie, you're no longer just a small-town journalist. You're a national celebrity. Your life has changed. Someone here in this area—very likely someone you know—is trying to scare you. You can't go on pretending nothing's happened."

"I'm not." She shook the icy frost off her scraper. "I've taken up sleeping with a crowbar."

She knew her mistake at once. She could feel Daniel's presence close behind her. "Well, now," he murmured, "that's something we could work on."

The man was impossible. Lecturing her with all sincerity one minute and melting her bones with his sandpaper drawl the next. She went around to the driver's side of the Jeep and tore open the door, determined to stick to her plan. Office, work, normal

124

life. Those were her priorities for the day. And, of course, finding Seth and talking to him.

"Bugs you, doesn't it?" Daniel addressed her over the rusting, pitted roof of the Jeep. "Bugs you that in spite of my being everything that scares you, you still wish I'd come over there and kiss you."

"Your arrogance astounds me, Major Foxworth." And it did, but it also intrigued her. She'd never met a man quite like him. "You need a shower. And I need to get moving."

But he was already around the Jeep, taking her by the elbow before she could get behind the wheel. She thought, that's it, he's going to kiss me, and when she whipped her head back to glare at him, she couldn't quite pull it off. With the dark circles under his eyes, the stubble of beard, the dog hair clinging to him, he seemed even more real, even more desirable. Had he really endured hours in her Jeep on her behalf? Suddenly she wanted to take a shower with him. She wanted to soap up his hard body and feel his hands on her.

"I've got to go," she said quickly.

"You're afraid to fall for me." His voice was low and intense now, just hinting at the depth of his tenacity. He wasn't a man who gave up easily. Who gave up at all. He moved in even closer to her. "I'm not what you expected. I don't need you to rescue me, I don't give a damn if you try to push me away with your smart mouth or talk of spider legs in the cider. Falling for me, Cozie Hawthorne," he went on, releasing her elbow but not moving away, "means you aren't what you think you are."

"And what's that, pray tell?"

He didn't hesitate. "The self-controlled, self-contained Cozie Hawthorne. Nothing would get this town talking more than the idea of you and me together up here on this hill."

Her throat was so tight she couldn't swallow. Every nerve ending of her body seemed focused on the thought—the feel—of him. His mouth on hers. His palms on her breasts. His tongue on her heated skin. She didn't have to keep standing there. She could just jump into her Jeep and stick the key in the ignition and shove the gearshift into reverse and be off.

But she didn't. "You just want me in your bed because I don't want to be there. I know your kind. Once you had me you'd be off like a shot."

A thick, dark brow went up. He tried to suppress a grin. Then he gave up and threw back his head and laughed.

He laughed hard.

"That does it," Cozie muttered, offended.

She scooped her leather tote from where she'd left it in the driveway while she scraped her windshield, tossed it onto the passenger seat, and climbed in behind the wheel. She fumbled for her key. Her fingers were frozen, and she was shaking all over with indignation. Humiliation. The bastard was laughing at her!

"Darlin'," he said, leaning in through the open door, unrepentant, "you've got me all wrong. You know what I'm afraid of?"

"Nothing you'd admit to."

But his expression was suddenly serious. He reached inside and touched her chin with one finger in a caress so gentle, so erotic, she almost melted to the floor. There'd be nothing left of her. Like the Wicked Witch of the West.

"I'm afraid once I had you I'd never want to leave," he said. "And I'm not sure I belong in your world, Cozie Hawthorne. I'm not sure that the answers I'm looking for up here would ever let me stay." He straightened, leaving her unable to speak. "Have a good day at work. I'll be seeing you."

She pulled the door shut and backed out onto the driveway, and it wasn't until she was in her parking space at the *Vermont Citizen* that she finally had her breathing back under control. Even so, when Meg, camped out on the stone terrace at the back entrance, spotted her, she said, "What happened to you? Your face is all red."

"I'm cold. I couldn't get the heat to come on in my Jeep. What's up?"

Her sister shrugged. "I've still got an hour before the onslaught of little ones. I rode my bike into town." She unzipped her anorak, a bright turquoise and orange that a passing car would have no excuse for not seeing. "Seth tell you he's got a guide job? Some hikers wanted to go up in the mountains."

"No, he didn't mention it. When did he leave?"

"Yesterday, I guess. He told Tom—I wasn't around. Cozie, is there something going on with him?"

"I don't know. I hope not. Why?"

"He's just been hard to connect with the last few days. He seems to have something on his mind that he doesn't want to explain."

Cozie sighed, then told her sister about Thad Vanackern's suspicion that Seth could be stealing. She didn't mention the helicopter crash and Daniel Foxworth. It was just too complicated, too damned ridiculous.

Meg groaned, kicking a loose pebble. "I was afraid of something like this. Seth's working for the Vanackerns has just been a disaster waiting to happen."

"You don't think he'd steal from them, do you?"

"No, of course not. Seth's no thief. I think he's got a thing for Julia and Daddy Vanackern doesn't approve

—Mommy, either—and would love to nail him for something. Not enough to put him in jail but enough to keep him from sniffing around."

"Then why did they hire him?"

"Maybe he fell for Julia after he started working up there. Anyway, I'm not saying the Vanackerns are setting him up; I'm sure this money and stuff's legitimately missing. I'm just saying I think they've got their own reasons for not minding if Seth turned out to be the culprit."

"You've never liked them," Cozie said.

"Nope. I never have."

"They say they only want to help. That's why they haven't been to the police."

"Bully for them," Meg scoffed. "They've already decided he's guilty. That's the point, Cozie. And basically there's not much either of us can do. Seth keeps pretending our lives haven't changed since we were kids. They have. I've got kids of my own. You've got all this fame and fortune. Pop's dead. Mother's off in Australia." Another pebble went skipping off into the parking area off the end of her shoe. "Things change. We all have to move on."

"I need to talk to him," Cozie said.

"Yeah. He's always listened to you more than me. I'll ask Tom if he knows where he went." Meg peered at her younger sister. "What about you, Coze? You okay?"

"Yeah, basically. Meg—look, there's stuff you don't know . . . that I haven't . . ." Cozie ran a hand through her hair. "I know you've got to get back up the hill before your staff panics. But there's more I need to tell you."

Her older sister regarded her with a mix of consternation and morbid satisfaction. "I kind of figured there was. I'll come up to the house as soon as I can after work."

Meg walked her bicycle out to the road, and Cozie headed in through the back, down the narrow hall to the main office where Aunt Ethel was already on the telephone. She hung up when she saw Cozie. Her expression was grave. "You'd best take a look at your front door."

"What's wrong?"

But Cozie was in the front hall before Aunt Ethel had a chance to answer.

The door was swinging loose on its hinges, its simple brass lock still attached to the molding. It looked as if it had been neatly and effectively smashed in with a crowbar or something.

Behind her, Aunt Ethel said, "Someone must have broken in during the night or early this morning. I came in through the back myself and only just noticed it. I was just trying to phone you."

Cozie nodded without comment, staring at the splinters where the lock had been. Was this a new way for her caller to unnerve her? Or had Daniel Foxworth just moseyed on down after he'd searched Seth's place and searched her office as well? If Seth's door had had locks, Daniel might have resorted to smashing it in, too. And thinking him responsible seemed preferable to some unknown figure who'd been harassing her for weeks and just might be getting dangerous now.

"Shall I call the police?" Aunt Ethel asked.

"I think that would be a good idea. I'll check my office for anything missing."

"Mine hasn't been touched that I can see. I'll check upstairs after I notify the police."

"Thanks, Aunt Ethel."

"Could be kids. I remember back in 1957 we caught

a couple of rascals going through the place for money." She cackled. "Fat lot of good it did them."

Taking deep breaths to calm herself, Cozie saw that her office door was shut, just as she'd left it, no sign of forced entry—not a surprise since it didn't have a lock. She turned the knob. Her head was spinning, her heart pounding uncomfortably. Classic response to unpleasant stimuli. *Anything* could be in there. Maybe she should wait for the police.

But, holding her breath, she pushed open the door.

No body on the floor. Nothing scattered, trashed, or even, that she could see, taken. Her computer was on her desk. Her glass-fronted shelf of first-edition books was intact. Elijah Hawthorne still stared down from above the mantel, his slightly disapproving, puritanical expression unchanged.

She looked around for a laser-printed note like the one she'd found on her windshield Saturday night. There was nothing. She turned on her computer, just in case her tormentor had left a message there. But, again, nothing.

It wasn't like him—or her—not to leave some kind of calling card. To make sure Cozie knew her every move was being kept track of, that someone was out there, watching.

Aunt Ethel appeared in the doorway. "I can't find anything missing or damaged upstairs."

"Nothing in here, either." Her voice shook.

"It's possible the miscreants didn't get past the front door. Someone or something could have interrupted their festivities for the night. Cornelia, are you all right? It's just a little break-in. No one was harmed."

Cozie nodded, distracted. "I know. I'm just a little jumpy, I guess. Will you deal with the police? I want to run up to the house for a minute. I need to check something and . . ." She looked at her elderly aunt, not wanting to explain further. "Would you mind?"

Aunt Ethel pursed her lips. She knew dissembling when she heard it. "I won't lie for you."

"Of course not. Just tell the police I'll be back in a few minutes."

Cozie could tell she still didn't like it. "Do you want me to call the Vanackerns?" her aunt asked. It was a rare acknowledgment that the *Citizen* was no longer in Hawthorne hands.

"The Vanackerns? Good God, no."

Aunt Ethel grinned. On that subject, she and her niece were in total agreement. "Go. Hurry up. Do whatever skulking about you have to do and then get back here and talk to the police."

"You're okay?"

She simply scowled, and Cozie dashed through the back, hoping she was being overly dramatic and that the break-in was an isolated event in her already hectic return home. Yeah, her life could return to normal after her last road trip. Right. Maybe *this* was normal.

*Why* did Seth have to take off for the mountains now?

Because it was the easy way out or because he had something to hide?

A hot shower in the sawmill's loft bathroom loosened the muscles that had cramped up during his insane night in Cozie Hawthorne's Jeep but did nothing to ease Daniel's frustrations. With her, with her brother, with the Vanackerns. With himself and his mission in Vermont. He pulled on a pair of jeans and headed down to the kitchen, where he had a pot of coffee brewing. With the fire in the woodstove going strong, he was, for the first time in hours, finally

131

warm. He could dare to walk around bare-chested without risking freezing to death. It was, he noted, all of eight-fifteen. Any sane man would be in bed making love—

No. He had to stop that line of thinking.

Then his front door banged open, and Cozie Hawthorne breezed in like an apparition, red-gold hair flying, eyes wide, face pale with a near-palpable mix of anger and fear that she was desperately trying to control. "I should have called the police last night when I had the chance," she said.

Daniel took a mug from an open shelf and set it on the almond-tiled counter. "Cozie, what happened?"

She seemed not to hear him. "I don't care if you're a former air force major, I don't care if Foxworths single-handedly defeated the Mexicans, the Communists, *and* the Nazis—I don't care how rich you are or how many damned oil fires you've put out. I will *not*"—she had to stop to breathe—"allow you to invade my privacy just so you can prove you aren't the reckless son of a bitch everyone thinks you are."

Removing the pot from the warming pad, Daniel filled his mug. The smell of fresh-brewed coffee seemed to have no calming effect on Cozie—nor, any longer, on him. Tension gripped him. He could feel it but refused to let it control him. He chose his words carefully before he spoke. "Cozie, if you think I searched your house last night while you were asleep—"

"My office," she said. "I'm talking about my office."

He tried his coffee, but it turned to acid even before it hit his stomach. "I haven't been to your office since I saw you there on Friday."

She shut her eyes. He watched her silken throat as she swallowed. She was rigid and trying not to shake, and every part of him—and not just the nice parts—

wanted to go over to her and take her into his arms. But a cold, hard voice kept telling him that his presence had indeed turned over a rock in Cozie Hawthorne's life, and ugly things were squirming out into the sunlight. He needed to look at them. Maybe she did, too.

"Tell me what happened," he said.

Her eyes opened. They were clear and alert, their anger and fear abating if not gone. "It wasn't you?"

"No."

"I wish it had been," she said without embarrassment.

"Should I say thank you?"

She almost smiled. "Probably not. Maybe I'm jumping to conclusions and it was just rascals like Aunt Ethel said—"

"Cozie. Tell me what happened."

She sighed, her shoulders sagging. The teal of her jacket and sweater brought out both the blue and the green in her eyes; she looked competent and polished, a woman to reckon with. Using both hands, she pushed her hair back behind her ears and seemed, just for a passing moment, ready to rip it out by the roots. But she dropped her hands to her sides, and said, the reporter in her taking over, "The *Citizen* was broken into last night. The front door was jimmied open, but nothing was taken."

"You're sure?"

"As sure as I can be from a brief look around the place."

"Anything damaged?"

"No."

"Do you keep cash around—would it be missing?"

"Believe me, nobody would break into the *Citizen* building looking for cash. The Vanackerns may own the paper, but a Hawthorne runs it."

133

"A Hawthorne," Daniel pointed out, "with a book on the best-seller lists."

She grimaced. "I know who I am. There was no cash for anyone to take, all right?"

Daniel took another sip of the hot coffee, his eyes never leaving Cozie Hawthorne. He kept his manner steady, but nothing about him was calm. A tight coil of anger was burning its way straight into his gut. She was suffering; someone was doing his or her level best to get under her skin, scare her, make her less the optimistic, confident survivor she was. Maybe it had nothing to do with his helicopter going down. Maybe it did.

"What about information?" he asked. "Could whoever broke in have been after something in your files or on your computer?"

"It's possible, but I can't imagine what."

He set his mug on the counter. "What about your caller?"

Her mouth snapped shut, a fresh wave of color draining from her face. He hated to see her fear, but he didn't withdraw his question. She said tightly, "That was my first thought, but . . . I don't know. Look, I've got to go. I left Aunt Ethel alone to deal with the police. Enjoy your coffee. Sorry I disturbed you."

She was halfway to the door. "Cozie," Daniel said, knowing he had to, "where's your brother?"

His question had the effect he'd anticipated. She whipped around at him, her jaw set hard and color rising in her pale cheeks. But she didn't say a word.

"Does he have a key to the *Citizen* building?" Daniel asked.

"I know what you're getting at, and you're wrong."

The woman definitely had no problem standing up

to him. "I could be. I hope I am. But right now all I'm doing is asking questions you refuse to ask."

She took a step toward him, her gaze as icy as the morning wind. "If you're suggesting I refuse to consider my brother a would-be murderer, a man capable of harassing his own sister—then you're right. I refuse to consider it."

"Cozie . . ."

"I'm not so cynical I distrust everything and everyone around me."

The implication being, Daniel realized, that he was. He leaned back against the counter and quietly warned himself to gather up the last shreds of his objectivity and back off. Her red-blond hair was hanging in her face, making her look more vulnerable and out of control than he suspected she was. Underestimating Cozie Hawthorne could get a man in deep, dark trouble.

"You're right," he said. "You'd better go."

She was already on her way. She tore open the door, slammed it shut, and was gone.

Daniel finished his coffee and made a couple of pieces of toast from Baba-Louis anadama bread he'd picked up in town. After that he went up to the loft and pulled on a clean shirt, socks, and his boots, and grabbed his jacket and keys. Stick to your mission, he told himself. And his mission didn't include falling for a green-eyed Yankee.

Once again, Seth Hawthorne's truck was not in his driveway. Daniel did a quick run through the house: nothing had changed since last night. He figured the kid had cleared out. Did Cozie know where he was? Would she tell him?

"Like hell she would," he muttered to himself as he climbed back into his truck.

Two minutes later he pulled into a cobblestone driveway at the Vanackern country estate. He had no idea what they'd be up to on a brisk Monday morning —or even if they'd be up. But seeing how nothing else seemed to be working, he figured he might as well confront them with who he was and what he was doing in Vermont and see what happened. Maybe their reaction would tell him something.

A stone walk took him through a large landscaped area of rhododendrons, boxwood, quince, ferns, all on a blanket of thick, waxy-leafed myrtle. He mounted perfectly laid stone steps to a black-painted door with a grapevine wreath decorated with dried yarrow and autumn-colored straw flowers and sprigs of bitter-sweet—vegetation he could identify thanks to his mother.

He rang the doorbell. He had no real plan. He'd just tell the Vanackerns the truth. Stir the pot a little.

Julia Vanackern herself answered the door. She had on a cut-off sweatshirt over a black exercise unitard that outlined every curve of her slender body; her pale hair was pulled back in a neat French braid. Daniel saw no evidence of perspiration or strain and assumed he'd caught her before she'd started whatever routine she did.

"Oh, hello," she said, smiling broadly. "You're out and about bright and early."

"I hope I'm not disturbing you. I was wondering if we could talk a minute."

"Of course. I was about to go for a run, but that can always wait. What happened to you yesterday? I hope our little hike didn't bore you to death."

"Not at all." He didn't explain further. "Are your parents around?"

"They just got in. We're all up early in the country. Mum was off bird-watching, Dad fishing. They're in the sunroom having coffee right now." She moved back from the door. "Come in. I hope nothing's wrong?"

Daniel didn't answer as he shut the door behind him and followed Julia into an elegant living room of antique furnishings and a Wyeth print over a massive brown marble fireplace. The house was relatively new but constructed and decorated to look old. It had none of the Hawthorne house's worn homeyness, nor, undoubtedly, its problems.

Julia perched on the arm of a slate-blue wingback chair. Daniel noticed she was wearing brand-new cross-trainers and thick exercise socks. He wondered what she did for a run. A couple miles? Whatever she felt like? Self-discipline, he would guess, was not one of Julia Vanackern's character traits.

He remained on his feet. "I'd like to ask you about what happened to you when you were in Texas last month."

She frowned. "In Texas? You know—"

"I was there."

She twisted her small hands together in her lap, her frown deepening as her sapphire eyes narrowed on him. Daniel couldn't tell if her confusion was an act or not. He would hate to have to put money on an accurate read of what Julia Vanackern was thinking or what she'd do next. "But we didn't meet you there."

"My name is Daniel Foxworth."

Her eyes widened, and she covered her mouth with one hand as she made the connection. "Oh, my God—you're not Daniel Forrest. . . . You're the one . . . you were the pilot. . . ."

"That's right."

"But what are you doing in Vermont? What do you want with me?"

Daniel didn't blame her for being upset, but she

wasn't the one who'd ended up in the hospital with multiple injuries and the possibility of losing a leg. She'd *watched* his copter go down. She hadn't been on board.

"Julia, I'm not here just to remind you of something you want to forget. I only—"

"Does Cozie know who you are? Did you lie to her as well?"

Why wouldn't he? He decided to keep his answer simple, not to give Julia anything to work with. "Yes, I lied to her as well."

She tugged on the end of her braid, fidgeting. "I'm sorry." She faked a laugh. "Here I am getting all hysterical and you were the one who crashed. Actually, I wondered when you said you were from Texas if you might be here because of what happened to me."

To her?

She caught herself. "I didn't mean it that way."

Daniel took her off the hook. "It's okay."

"I just never expected that Daniel Foxworth—that you would be—I mean—" She stopped herself, flushing. She looked much younger than she was. Then she smiled, and the flustered girlishness disappeared. A practiced sultriness came into her eyes. "Well, you don't look anything like your grandfather."

Daniel smiled. "One would hope."

But Thad and Frances Vanackern came into the room, dressed in casual country clothes that made them look surprisingly alike. Julia thrust an accusing hand in Daniel's direction. "Mum, Dad, this is Austin Foxworth's grandson."

"We heard," Thad Vanackern said coldly. He fastened his gaze on Daniel as if Daniel had just been caught stealing the china. "By God, you've got gall."

It was about the reaction Daniel expected, given

Julia's attitude toward her near-miss in Texas. "I didn't come here to argue."

"I don't care why you came. Just get out."

"Thad," Frances Vanackern said in a soft, pleading voice, "at least let's hear what he has to say."

Her husband sucked in a sharp breath, his gaze still locked on Daniel. "I'm quite certain your father and grandfather haven't sanctioned this fishing expedition of yours. You're here to stir up trouble, that's all. You could have killed my daughter with your recklessness, your lack of consideration for her safety or anyone else's—"

"Father," Julia interjected, embarrassment—or something—clouding her sapphire eyes.

Frances was visibly taken aback by her husband's vehemence. "Thad, isn't that a little extreme?"

He shook his head. "No, it's not." He sounded very sure of himself. "I know his reputation. He's always been a seat-of-the-pants player. It's why he stalled in the air force at major, and it's why he'll never run Fox Oil. Don't look so surprised, young man. Your grandfather and I had quite a conversation about you when we were in Houston. He was smart to let you go off to fight oil fires."

Daniel refused to rise to the bait. "You're entitled to your opinion."

But Thad wasn't finished with him. "Your helicopter crashed and you and your partner were nearly killed for one reason and one reason alone: you were negligent in your responsibilities as pilot. Thank God Julia wasn't on board with you."

"That's one of the questions I have: why did she change her mind?"

"She—"

"I can answer for myself, Dad," Julia said quietly,

without any hint of irritation. She turned to Daniel. "There was really no reason. I just decided at the last minute I didn't want to go. I'm afraid as intrigued as I was about what you do, I don't like helicopters all that much."

No mention of Seth Hawthorne and their argument. Was she protecting him or protecting herself? Had he warned her not to mention his visit to Texas? What Julia left out of her story, Daniel thought, could be as informative as what she included.

"She was still forced to witness the crash," her father said.

That one got to Daniel. "Who forced her?"

"Oh, yes," Thad sneered. "I suppose you think she could have just looked away from a helicopter going down. I suppose, in her place, you would have turned your head."

"I wasn't in her place," Daniel said. "I was flying the damned thing."

"That's right: *you* were flying it. And now my daughter can't stop thinking about how close she came to death—to witnessing the death of others. It was a shattering experience for her. I don't care to have you here, *reminding* her of what she saw, dredging up what we would all prefer to forget."

Daniel considered throttling Thaddeus Vanackern. Maybe just shoving his snotty ass up against the wall and giving him a damned good scare. It would serve the bastard right.

It would also accomplish nothing.

"My apologies for disturbing your morning." Daniel didn't know how sincere he sounded and didn't care. He nodded to the two women. He'd been taught manners. "Have a good day."

Without waiting for a response, he walked back

through to the foyer and pulled open the front door, but he couldn't resist turning back to the Vanackerns. "You all wanted to see what an oil fire was like. You wanted a taste of adventure. Don't complain to me because you got more than you bargained for."

He was outside on the brick walk, breathing the cool Vermont air, even as the memory of J.D.'s screams and the stifling heat of that hot Texas morning swarmed over him. *Daniel—what the fuck did you do? Jesus! What did you do?*

A small explosion had taken out their tail rotor driveshaft, and they'd autorotated into the gulf. It was, at the root of it, as simple as that. Vermont, Seth Hawthorne, Julia Vanackern—maybe they didn't matter. Maybe Cozie Hawthorne and her threats didn't matter. Maybe all that mattered was that Daniel had taken up a helicopter and it had crashed. Period. End of story.

"Daniel—Daniel, please wait."

Frances Vanackern caught up with him at his truck. He had the door open. He could see a little of Julia in her mother's eyes, the delicacy of her nose and mouth.

"I hope you'll forgive Thad." She smiled weakly at him. "He's very protective of Julia, and she's only just begun to get over what happened in Texas. I know it's nothing compared to what you and your partner have had to endure, but it's been difficult for her. How is Mr. Maguire?"

"Holding his own."

"He'll make a full recovery?"

"He'll live," Daniel said.

"I'm sure this has all been a tremendous ordeal for you and your family. If I thought . . ." She hesitated, ill at ease; hers wasn't a world of sabotaged helicopters. "If I thought we were responsible in any way for what happened . . . if our being there distracted you from your job, made mistakes more likely—"

"I wasn't distracted, Mrs. Vanackern. I never saw you or your husband, or even your daughter." But that didn't mean he couldn't have made a mistake.

"But then I don't understand. . . ." She trailed off, looking to Daniel. She was used to having other people do her confronting for her. "Then I don't understand why you're here."

"I'm just looking for answers that for all I know you can't provide. Maybe no one can. Good day, Mrs. Vanackern." Without further explanation, he climbed into his truck.

But before he could shut the door, Frances Vanackern shot forward. "You saw Seth Hawthorne with Julia, didn't you?"

She seemed to know the answer already. "My partner did," Daniel said.

She twisted her fingers together, clearly unaccustomed to the role she was playing. "He—Seth does outdoor work for us on occasion. He's had a difficult time, and his father's death hit him very hard. They'd been restoring the orchards together. Seth seemed to be getting himself straightened out." She sighed, pained. "We've tried to help, but he became infatuated with Julia this summer. When she realized it, she tried to stay away from him, hoping he would understand she didn't return his feelings and just give up. But when she came here for Labor Day weekend, he pressed his case, and she had to tell him in no uncertain terms there could be nothing between them. Then he followed her to Texas. Julia had to be very frank with him, Mr. Foxworth. I can't imagine it was easy for either of them."

"Probably not."

"Julia never reciprocated Seth's feelings for her or encouraged him in any way."

Daniel remained noncommittal. "I see. Does he still work for you?"

She pursed her lips. "We have nothing for him right now."

A diplomatic, if transparent, answer. "I was just over at his place. Any idea where he is?"

"No. None." She looked away a moment, hesitating, then turned back to Daniel. "Mr. Foxworth, I'm afraid there's something else you should perhaps know. We've discovered money and valuables missing from our place here."

"A lot?"

"Several thousand dollars' worth, yes. The cash is insignificant—a few hundred at most."

From what Daniel had seen of Seth Hawthorne's finances, a few hundred wouldn't be insignificant to him.

"Frankly, we suspect Seth," Frances Vanackern went on. "His trip to Texas must have been very expensive, impulsive as it was, and he could very easily have decided we 'owed' him a kind of reimbursal, because of Julia. He's had difficulties with the law in the past."

"Have you gone to the police?"

She shook her head, continuing to wring her hands together as if that would somehow change the nature of her words. "We would like him to come to us. We've always had a soft spot for the Hawthornes. But they're self-reliant people; they don't like asking for help. It hasn't been easy for them since Duncan died. He tried to ease their burden by selling the paper—but there were so many debts. For a while we thought they would lose the land, too. Fortunately, the success

143

Cozie's had with her writing saved it." Frances backed away from the truck. "I'm sure at times Seth must feel left behind."

Daniel pulled his door shut. "Thanks for the information."

"I hope we can count on your discretion, Mr. Foxworth. Julia—well, she wouldn't want to see Seth hurt. None of us would."

"Mrs. Vanackern, you can count on me keeping an open mind until I get the answers I came for. After that, I make no promises."

She gave a curt nod, somewhat offended, and moved back onto the plush green lawn. Some of Seth Hawthorne's work? Daniel headed off down the dirt road, seeing no sign of life at the sagging red farmhouse. He figured he might as well scoot on down Hawthorne Orchard Road and make sure Cozie didn't have her little brother tucked up a tree or stuck in a closet.

# CHAPTER
# 9

Will Rubeno, the Woodstock cop dispatched in response to Aunt Ethel's call, shook his head as he inspected the *Citizen*'s splintered door. "I've been telling you Hawthornes for years to get better locks."

He and Cozie had graduated from high school together, and she trusted him, even if he considered all Hawthornes—particularly her—too opinionated. He was a big man, although not tall, and his hair had started to gray; he had a schoolteacher wife and two kids in elementary school.

Aunt Ethel snorted in disgust. "Maybe if we had better police protection we wouldn't need better locks."

Will opened his mouth to argue—he and Aunt Ethel had been arguing for years—but Cozie intervened. "Vanackern Media has been bugging us to put in a security system since they bought us all that new equipment. Now I'm sure they'll insist, so no need to worry about the future. Look, Will, let's not waste your time or mine. You're not going to find anything that will lead us to whoever's responsible for this, and I'm supposed to be at a staff meeting. . . ."

"Gee," Will said sarcastically, "I wouldn't want to interfere with your schedule."

Cozie sighed. She was, she thought, surprisingly calm after her encounter with a bare-chested Daniel Foxworth, a sight not easily put out of her mind. "That wasn't my point. Aunt Ethel told you nothing was stolen, didn't she?"

He nodded, tight-lipped. "You want to do my job for me?"

"Don't be so defensive."

"Has it occurred to you, Cozie, that someone could think you have a lot of money now that you're famous?"

"I don't keep cash around, and I'm not that famous. I don't have all *that* much money, not compared even to a lot of folks around Woodstock. Most of what I do have is tied up in property or in the hands of the IRS. Next year I should see more—"

Will held up a hand. "Who's going to know all that? Consider yourself lucky this time. When you order a new door, order one that's not so easy to kick in."

"Sure," Aunt Ethel piped in. "Next time they can just come through the window."

Will ignored her, far more annoying to her than flat-out arguing—and he knew it. "I agree with Vanackern Media. Your security's too light here. It has been for years. You want some advice, I'll be glad to come by on my off hours."

Cozie nodded. "Thanks."

"Right now, though, there's not much I can do. If someone saw anything it might help. But I doubt anyone did. Anything else?"

Her head ached. She couldn't seem to think straight. She needed to pull herself together before she tried to explain. "No," she told him, "there's nothing else I can think of right now."

"Better work on your security up at your house, too. No point inviting trouble. Vermont may be one of the safest states in the country, but I manage to stay busy."

He started out on the short brick walk to his cruiser. Cozie's hands were clammy. Her heart was thumping so hard her chest hurt. Before she consciously decided what she was going to do, she burst down the steps after him, grabbing his arm. "Will, I need to talk to you. Not about the break-in. About something else. It might— I don't know if it's related."

His eyes narrowed on her, all cop. He nodded thoughtfully. "All right."

"Not here. Up at the house. Can you meet me there?"

He sighed. "Okay."

"Give me an hour."

He made no sarcastic comment about her rescheduling her staff meeting.

Back inside, Aunt Ethel hadn't budged from the front hall. "So, Cornelia, when are you going to tell me what's really going on?"

"I will—"

"When you get around to it. Your Texan," she said. "Does he know anything about the helicopter crash Julia Vanackern witnessed while she was down there?"

"You know about that?"

"I keep track."

Although she claimed never to repeat gossip, Aunt Ethel did listen to it, something she was ever reluctant to admit. "I'll explain everything as soon as I can.

147

Right now, I need everyone who's here in my office in ten minutes. You'll see about a new door?"

"You're the boss."

No, she wasn't. Vanackern Media was the boss. But Aunt Ethel was already miffed enough without Cozie reminding her that Hawthornes no longer owned the *Vermont Citizen*.

The moment Daniel entered Cozie's back room, he knew whoever had been to her office had been to her house, probably after he'd gone back to the sawmill to shower.

Whoever it was could be there now.

And he thought he knew what the sneaky bastard had been after.

A familiar tension gripped him. He'd faced difficult and dangerous situations before and understood his reactions, had learned to use them to his advantage.

Alert to any sound, any movement, he walked past the cold cast-iron cookstove and turned down the narrow hall to the kitchen. Birds fluttered at the feeders outside the front window. Mourning doves and chickadees and a pair of cardinals, robins ready to bolt south for the winter. Way at the back of his mind, unrelated to the part that remained vigilant, he could see Cozie coming down on a cool autumn morning, alone in a kitchen, a house, meant for a family. There was a sense of permanence to the place—of continuity between the generations—that was nearly palpable. He wondered if he could feel it because of the lack of continuity and permanence in his own life.

But his attention was directed at the open cupboards and drawers, their contents spilled out as if a mad cook had been through, hunting a missing ingredient needed quickly before the soup was ruined.

Daniel knew better.

He focused on the drawer next to the refrigerator. It was neatly shut. Still alert to an intruder's presence, he walked across the scarred pine floor and opened the drawer.

The spiral notebook "log" containing the time, place, and transcript of each call Cozie had received was gone. So was the message she'd found on her windshield. So was the cassette from her answering machine. They provided the hard evidence that she was being harassed—evidence that could possibly lead to the caller's identity.

He shut the drawer.

Careful not to let his thoughts get away from him, he returned to the back room and took the cast-iron poker from beside the cookstove. Methodically, concentrating on the task at hand, he checked the cellar, then came back upstairs and checked the kitchen, the adjoining dining room, the living room at the far end of the house, and then headed up the steep stairs between the living and dining rooms. There was another set of stairs, he'd noticed, in the back room.

He started with the bedroom to the right of the landing. Its furnishings were solid and old: a brass double bed covered in a bright quilt; two maple dressers; a small rocking chair; an unwieldy blanket chest. There were framed photographs everywhere of what he took to be a wide assortment of Hawthornes. With no intruder in evidence, he didn't allow himself to linger.

Across the landing were three more bedrooms in a row, barracks-style under the slanting roof of the narrow house, separated by white-painted doors with black wrought-iron hardware. The first was obviously Cozie's, sun streaming in through a dormer window. The bed was unmade, a nightgown heaped on the floor, a cluttered marble-topped dresser not dusted in days. Even with her untidy habits, Daniel could see the intruder had been thorough: her mattress was askew, too many drawers half shut, too many dresses off their hangers on the closet floor, jewelry boxes dumped out on her nightstand.

"Hope the bastard got everything," he muttered sarcastically.

He moved on through the two end rooms. Again, the furnishings had a sturdy charm suggesting they'd serviced more than one generation of Hawthornes. There were more photographs. But he kept moving, down the stairs into the back room. He went back out through the porch, taking the poker with him. The air was noticeably warmer, but clouds had begun to roll in from the west—not that a man could see the weather coming with all the damned Vermont hills in the way. He walked around the house, alert to footprints or someone hiding in the bushes. With the weekend over, there were fewer tourists out "leaf peeping." He heard crows up in the field, the rush of the brook over rocks.

Life, he thought, could get pretty damned stark out on Hawthorne Orchard Road.

When he returned to the back room, satisfied the intruder must have made good his—or her—retreat, the phone was ringing. He picked up the receiver, but he didn't get a chance to say anything.

"Hello, Cozie Cornelia."

Well, well.

"I'm glad you didn't let your answering machine take the call," the disembodied voice went on. "I would have hung up."

"Coward that you are," Daniel said.

There was a small gasp, then a *click,* and, finally a dial tone. Daniel hung up only marginally satisfied. He should have continued to listen, found out what the caller wanted this time. To crow about stealing Cozie's evidence?

Not two minutes later, she came through the back porch looking none too pleased to find him there. He didn't wait for her to start griping. "You've had company," he said.

He got halfway into explaining what he'd found before she had to go into the kitchen and check her junk drawer for herself. She banged it shut, flying around at him. "It wasn't you?"

"No, Cozie, it wasn't me."

He told her about his search of the premises, and then about the call. She listened without interruption. When he finished, she shook her head, still taking it all in. "I should have told someone about the calls weeks ago. I thought ignoring them made the most sense."

"At the time maybe it did."

"They seemed so innocuous at first—annoying, of course, but not as unnerving as you might think. But now . . ." She pushed both hands through her hair, tearing at small tangles. "I could scream."

"Go ahead. Might make you feel better."

She eyed him. "How about you? Would it make you feel better if I screamed?"

"Sure. I dream about screaming women every night." He gave her a sardonic look. "Ms. Cozie, you are the damnedest woman I've ever met. Where do you get these ideas? Must be the mountain air. Scream if you need to. But don't think it's going to make *me* feel better."

She didn't back off. Not Cozie Hawthorne. No way. "You know what I mean. You've got a macho streak about as wide as the Rio Grande."

He wondered if she had any idea how wide the Rio Grande was. "So?"

"Don't go thick-headed Texan on me."

"Okay. You stay away from uppity Yankee and we'll do just fine." He moved closer to her, close enough to make her really think about just how wide his macho streak was. "If you're suggesting screaming might make me think you're vulnerable and I'd want you more—hell, sweetheart, I can't imagine wanting you more than I already do."

A small breath escaped her tightly compressed lips. She wasn't looking at her junk drawer, her trashed kitchen. She was, he knew, trying not to think about who had invaded her house—her life—and why. Her eyes reached his, and he saw the pain, the confusion, the anger—and the desire. He felt a small stab of guilt.

"Cozie, I shouldn't have said that."

"Are you going to take it back?"

He didn't answer at once. Then, slowly, he shook his head. "I'd be lying if I did, and I don't want any more lying between us."

"Neither do I."

Standing so close, the smell of her, the possibility of her, assaulted his senses. He ran one finger along the angular line of her jaw. "I never thought I'd want to kiss a smart-mouthed Yankee."

She almost smiled. "Believe me, rich, macho Texans haven't been high on my list."

She could have drawn away. He wasn't even holding her. But she didn't move, and he touched the corner of her mouth, dragged his finger across her lower lip. He saw her swallow.

"Cozie," he said, "stop me."

"I don't think I want to." Her voice wasn't even a whisper.

He cupped her chin and tilted her head toward him, and if she looked away he'd have gotten the hell out of there. But she met his gaze dead-on. A different kind of tension gripped him, one he wasn't nearly as comfortable with as when he faced down unwelcome intruders.

Lightly, gently, he touched her mouth with his, but she seized his upper arm and held on, and he opened his mouth, opened himself to her urgency—to his own. Her lips parted. He drew his arms around her, pulled her against him as he explored her mouth with his tongue, tasting her, wanting her as he'd never wanted a woman before. The ache spread all through him, taking his breath away.

Moaning softly, she clasped her hands at the back of his neck and tilted back her head so that he could kiss her throat. He obliged. Her skin was soft and smooth and tasted of a fragrant, feminine soap. She pressed herself against his throbbing maleness, and shut her eyes, and Daniel found her mouth again, probing harder, deeper, in a rhythm that told her in no uncertain terms what he wanted.

Then his eye caught the shut junk drawer, the swinging cupboard above it, and he remembered the voice on the phone. *Hello, Cozie Cornelia . . .*

He knew what she was doing. What he was doing.

And he pulled away. Forced himself to do it.

Her mouth was swollen with the same heady desire that shuddered through him, but she looked neither embarrassed nor angry—at him or herself. "Why did you stop?"

Because he was crazy. But he said, "Because we have a few things we need to deal with before I haul you upstairs and make love to you until we loosen the rafters—"

"We weren't to that stage yet," she said primly.

"Oh, yes, we were."

She licked her lips, uncertainty creeping into her eyes. "I don't even know you. You used to fly fast, expensive airplanes, and now you fight out-of-control oil fires—and something about me . . ." She struggled for the right words. "Seems to appeal to you. Or maybe it's just because I'm here and available. Lord. I don't know what's happening to me."

"Well, then, honey, you'd best thank me for stopping when I did. Because when we do make love," he said, "I want you to know exactly what's happening."

She turned to the sink, pouring herself a tall glass of water and drinking it down. "Guess it's just as well," she said when she came up for air. "I've got a cop friend coming. Will Rubeno. We went to school together."

"You're going to tell him about the calls?"

"I was planning to, but without proof, I'm not sure he can do anything." She set her empty glass on the counter. "Well, I'm glad you stopped kissing me because I've got to think."

Daniel chose not to remind her that she'd done some kissing of her own. As she'd said, she needed to think.

She leaned against the counter. "I told Meg—my sister—about the calls. She was going to come out here after work but I couldn't wait, not after the break-in. She wasn't too happy, and she'll skin me alive if I don't tell Will everything. I was going to tell Seth as well, but . . ."

"But he's taken off."

"What do you mean, 'taken off'? He's taken a job as a hiking guide up in the mountains. He'll be back in a few days."

"When did this job come up?" he asked as neutrally as he could manage.

He must not have sounded particularly neutral. She shot him a nasty look. "What is this, guilty until proven innocent?"

"It's just a question."

She sprang away from the counter. "That's all that matters to you: getting your damned answers."

"I owe J.D. that much," Daniel said quietly.

"Well, give me some credit for knowing my own brother."

"He didn't tell you about his relationship with Julia Vanackern or his trip to see her in Texas."

"I haven't been around."

"He didn't tell Meg either, did he?"

"That's not so unusual. She doesn't like the Vanackerns."

Daniel hesitated but figured he might as well press on. "What about his previous troubles with the law?"

Cozie stiffened. "That's in the past—and most of his problems were because he was too quick to jump to the aid of a friend in trouble. He has a tendency to act first and think later. But he hasn't been in trouble in years."

"Your father's death hasn't been easy on him."

"It hasn't been easy on any of us."

"Then your success—he ever feel inadequate?"

"Why should he?"

Through the window above the sink, Daniel saw a police car pull in behind Cozie's Jeep. "Tell your cop friend everything, Cozie." His gaze fell on her, and even as mad as she was at him, as suspicious as he was of her brother, he wanted to kiss her again. "Everything—including the Vanackerns' concern that your brother's been stealing from them."

Anger and no small measure of surprise flashed in her green eyes. "They told you?"

He sighed. "I figured you knew. Thought you weren't going to lie to me either."

"I didn't lie. I just didn't tell you."

"Hair-splitting."

There was a knock out on the back porch. Cozie gritted her teeth. "You're going to hunt down my brother, aren't you?"

"Your brother's a big boy. He can take care of himself."

Daniel met the cop, a beefy guy older looking than he'd expected, coming through the back porch. "Who're you?" the cop asked.

"Ms. Hawthorne's new tenant." It was a pretty decent fudge. "Excuse me."

He headed out, resisting telling the cop that Cozie Hawthorne was the stubbornest woman he'd ever encountered. If Will Rubeno had spent any time in Woodstock, if he'd grown up with her, he had to know already.

Cozie changed her mind about telling Will anything. What could he do with no proof? Nothing to take back to the lab and analyze? He would only tell her—she knew Will—to lock her doors, start a new log, and let him know if her caller actually threatened her. Right now the calls were just a nuisance. If by some miracle he did start nosing around, talking to Daniel Foxworth and the Vanackerns, learning about Texas and the thefts, he could jump to the erroneous, off-base, outrageous conclusion that her brother had it in for her. First she wanted to talk to Seth herself. Then, maybe, she'd reconsider telling Will everything.

He didn't take her change of heart well. He knew she was holding back on him. "You decide you want to cooperate," he said on his way out, "give me a call. You've got my number."

"I'm just jumpy after this morning."

"Yeah. Making money hand over fist would make any Hawthorne jumpy. Tough to feel sorry for you."

"I'm not asking you or anyone to feel sorry for me."

"No, you're just wasting my time."

She couldn't argue with that. "I'm sorry."

"Yeah, right. Call me at home if you need to." He regarded her with one of his grave cop expressions. "Go easy on yourself, Cozie, before you crash and burn."

"That's not going to happen, Will."

He shook his head and laughed. "I should have known better. God forbid Cozie Hawthorne should ever bite off more than she can chew. I'm out of here. I'll go help people who want my help."

"Thanks for stopping by."

He waved a dismissive hand as he went through the back porch, at least as disgusted with her as she was with herself.

By the time Cozie had stuffed things back in the cabinets and drawers and returned to the *Citizen*, Aunt Ethel was impatient for a full accounting from her niece. "Saved my lunch," she said, following Cozie into her office with a crumpled brown paper bag. Every night she washed out her plastic sandwich bags and hung them to dry. Planting herself on a rickety Windsor chair, she unwrapped a ham salad sandwich smothered in her own butter pickles.

Cozie, however, could only bring herself to tell her aunt about the Vanackerns' suspicions of her brother.

When she finished, Aunt Ethel gave her a look of painful dissatisfaction. "Meg warned me you'd lie."

"I didn't lie!"

"You didn't tell me about those anonymous calls you've been getting."

"Meg told you?"

"Of course she did. She knows I'm not some crazy old bat who can't be trusted with the naked truth."

"Aunt Ethel . . ."

"Don't think I'm feeling sorry for myself."

"*You?*"

She pursed her lips. "Now back up and add what's been going on with those calls."

"It's all so complicated."

Aunt Ethel glared at her.

"Not for you to understand. For me to explain. I've got a column to write, and I need to call my agent and—"

"Okay." Her aunt picked up an untouched half of sandwich and climbed to her feet. "I'll come by the house this afternoon and you can fill me in. Have the kettle on for tea. Shall I bring my shotgun?"

"No," Cozie said, taking the offer seriously, "I've been sleeping with a crowbar."

"Well, I suppose it's better than sleeping with that Texan. I'll want to know his role in this sordid affair as well. Messages are on your desk. I'm across the hall if you need me."

After Aunt Ethel had marched out, Cozie went through the scraps of paper—no "While You Were Out" forms for the *Citizen*'s receptionist—and marveled at Mondays. She had umpteen calls to return, complaints to answer, and tasks to delegate. There was even a call from Julia Vanackern. But there was nothing that couldn't wait. She could always go home and carve jack-o'-lanterns and pretend her house and office hadn't been broken into and searched. That her life hadn't been turned upside down by a relentless Texan who was far from "hers" or anybody else's. Daniel Foxworth was very much his own man.

She snatched her Rolodex and got the number of an inn that often hired Seth to serve as a hiking or canoeing guide for their guests. She didn't care if he was on some mountaintop somewhere. She needed to track him down and get some straight answers from him.

But the inn hadn't hired him.

She swore. Who else? There were other inns. Outdoor sporting goods stores. Hiking clubs. Friends.

An hour later, she gave up. No luck. Daniel Foxworth, it seemed, had the same idea: several of the places she called had just heard from him.

She switched on her computer and stared at the blank screen, determined to forget the whole damned mess for a while and do her work. But her muse had departed. She had long vowed that when she had nothing to say, she wouldn't say anything. She'd rather run fillers in her space than have her name on something inane.

But she'd been thinking about pumpkins, and pumpkins were what she *wanted* to think about, and maybe they were what other people wanted to think about, too, and she could get that across somehow. Pumpkins as diversion. As savers of sanity.

The words came, the calls went unreturned, the complaints went unanswered, her brother and Daniel Foxworth and Julia Vanackern went right out of her mind. Her staff, no idiots, were left to their own devices. Assignments were generally routine: state and local governments, education, arts and entertainment, business, police. That she herself was at the center of a brewing story was, at the very least, a good reminder that the press didn't always know as much as it thought it did.

Without reading them back—she was too close to be a good judge yet—Cozie saved her jumble of words and switched off her computer. She decided she should at least return Julia Vanackern's call before she headed out.

Frances answered. "I'm returning Julia's call,"

Cozie said as casually as she could manage—never mind that the Vanackerns thought her brother was a crook.

"Oh, I know what that's about," Frances said cheerfully. "We want to invite you to dinner this evening up here at the house. Several people from Vanackern Media headquarters are going to be here, and I know they would love to see you."

Under the circumstances, it wasn't the kind of evening entertainment Cozie would have chosen for herself. "Frances, given your suspicions about my brother, I wouldn't think—"

"I wouldn't classify our concern as suspicion. Our primary concern is his welfare. More than anything we want to make sure he's all right. We're not out to punish him. If he has problems that compelled him to resort to—well, to stealing, then we would like to help."

"Seth would never resort to stealing," Cozie said stiffly.

Frances, who had always hated confrontation, didn't argue. "The Hawthornes have always been a close family. I admire that. At any rate, tonight has nothing to do with Seth. Please consider joining us."

Cozie knew she was caught. Without Thad's direct intervention with Vanackern Media, the *Vermont Citizen* would have been relegated to a shelf in a Woodstock Historical Society display. She would likely have had to leave Woodstock, even Vermont, to find similar work. Her family would certainly have lost their land. And that meant if the Vanackerns wanted her to come to dinner now that she was a national "celebrity," she needed a damned good excuse to turn them down.

But perhaps, while she was there, she could get Julia into a quiet corner and grill her about her relationship with Seth.

160

"We're serving cocktails at six-thirty," Frances said.

"I'll be there. Thanks for the invitation."

Slipping her blazer back on, Cozie headed upstairs, where the nineteenth-century surroundings were overwhelmed by Vanackern Media computers. Tapped into the media conglomerate's computer network, the little Vermont weekly had access to more news than it needed or could ever print—including information on Daniel Austin Foxworth of Houston, Texas.

The half-dozen staffers up there all wanted to know if she had anything more on the break-in that morning.

"Do any of you need my guidance pertaining to your *jobs?*" Cozie asked.

No one did.

Downstairs, Aunt Ethel was waiting. Tea and the gory details. She wasn't one to forget.

"Can you drive me or shall I go 'round for my car?"

Her car, a 1972 Dodge Dart, was like new, largely because Aunt Ethel was very good at getting other people to drive her around. Cozie, of course, offered to drive.

Daniel's truck was still parked in her driveway. She hoped nothing in her demeanor suggested she and her tenant had kissed and then some in the kitchen. Zep trotted out to greet her, but he'd learned the hard way not to come within a yard of Aunt Ethel.

Daniel had a fire going in the woodstove and was sitting on the couch with a detailed road atlas of Vermont opened on his lap. Cozie hoped her aunt didn't notice her sudden shortness of breath, but the man was, she now accepted, going to have that effect on her.

"Made yourself right at home, I see," Aunt Ethel said.

He shut the atlas and rose, giving her a gentlemanly nod. "Afternoon, Miss Hawthorne."

"We're having tea," Cozie said, hoping he would take the hint.

Aunt Ethel checked the fire in the woodstove, a fixture in the back room even since her own childhood. "Aren't you even going to ask what he's doing here?" she asked Cozie.

"He's been out looking for Seth. He doesn't believe he's on any hiking trip. Look, I'll get the teapot. You two decide what you want to say to each other."

But as Cozie headed for the kitchen, she heard her aunt say, "I don't believe you're any Daniel *Forrest*— you're that Foxworth fellow whose helicopter crashed down in Texas. I knew something wasn't right about you the minute I laid eyes on you. Just took a while for me to come to what it was."

Leave it to Aunt Ethel.

"Did you check my references?" Daniel asked mildly.

"I didn't have access to your references." Her tone suggested that if Cozie were any kind of niece she would have provided such access. "I just used common sense, which most folks around here are bound to do sooner or later. Everyone but Cornelia keeps up on Vanackern goings-on. Well. You *are* Daniel Foxworth, aren't you?"

"I am."

"Your family as rich as the Vanackerns—or richer?"

Cozie shot in from the hall. "Aunt Ethel."

She scoffed. "I don't know how you can call yourself a newspaperwoman and squirm at an honest question."

Daniel, however, was looking amused. "I'm afraid I

162

have no idea how much the Vanackerns are worth. I'm not even sure about my own family."

Aunt Ethel slid the copper kettle onto the hot end of the stove, directly over the fire. "I've yet to meet a rich person who doesn't know how much he's worth down to the last dime. Cornelia? Just regular orange pekoe tea for me, none of that purple stuff you tried serving me last time." She turned her attention back to Daniel. "What about you? I daresay you don't look much like a tea drinker."

"Just iced tea," he said.

"You're out of luck there. We stop icing the tea up here after Labor Day."

Marveling at her aunt's nerve, Cozie retreated to the kitchen for the stoneware teapot, a couple of orange pekoe teabags, and two mugs. Daniel was on his feet when she returned, his atlas tucked under one arm. "If you'll excuse me, I have somewhere else I need to be."

"Where?" Cozie asked.

He ignored her. "A pleasure to see you again, ma'am," he said to Aunt Ethel, who plainly wasn't charmed; then, to Cozie, "I'll be seeing you."

His words held a double meaning that in no way was lost on her. He went through the back porch and out, and she breathed again.

"Don't let me keep you from following him," her aunt said.

"It wouldn't do any good." She set the tea paraphernalia on the chest between her father's chair and the couch. "He thinks Seth tried to blow up his helicopter."

"Well. My goodness. Do begin at the beginning."

# CHAPTER

# 10

Cozie had always loved the expression "fair play's turnabout" because it usually helped her justify things her other favorite expression, "two wrongs don't make a right," told her she shouldn't be doing.

Like breaking into the renovated sawmill she'd rented to Daniel Foxworth.

"Breaking into," she reminded herself, was an exaggeration. It wasn't as if she had to smash a window or kick in a door. She was, after all, a landlady with a key.

Shortly after returning an unusually pensive Aunt Ethel to town, Cozie had taken the path along Hawthorne Orchard Brook, trotted up the front porch, stuck her key in the lock, turned it, and pushed open the front door as she had countless times in the past.

She wasn't entirely sure what she thought she'd find. Something incriminating against her brother—or at least something *Daniel* would consider incriminating? Maybe she was just looking for proof he really was on the level and her attraction to him wasn't completely insane.

Just inside the door, she found a black leather jacket hanging on the pegboard instead of her barn jacket or one of her sweatshirts. In the kitchen, the coffeepot and a mug were rinsed and turned over to dry on a towel on the counter. A stick of butter, unmarred by crumbs or gobs of jam, was in a glass butter dish she'd forgotten she owned. A partial loaf of homemade bread was neatly encased in plastic wrap. The compost bucket under the sink was empty. The living area was equally tidy, a copy of her book and last week's *Citizen* the only indications Daniel had even moved in. She had no interest in his belongings beyond anything that would help her make sure he'd told her absolutely everything about why he'd come to Vermont. Forget her instincts. If he needed facts, she needed facts.

Peeling off her field jacket, she ventured up the uncarpeted stairs to the loft, where she'd built a small bathroom and bedroom, both with skylights in the slanted roof. The double bed was made up with her hunter green flannel sheets. Towels in the bathroom were hung. Clothes were put away.

"My, my, Major Foxworth," she said, just to relieve some of her own tension, "aren't we the neatnick."

Maybe it was his military training.

She peeked out the loft window overlooking the driveway. No sign of him. Probably he was out combing the countryside for her brother. She wouldn't blame Seth if he'd ducked out expressly to avoid Daniel Foxworth. She wouldn't put it past her brother to give Daniel room to figure out he'd had nothing to do with the downing of his helicopter. Once he was back in Texas, Seth would turn up.

Cozie exhaled, suddenly sensing the silence of the

sawmill, its uniqueness. Daniel Foxworth, she thought, did not belong in Vermont. He *would* leave.

She pulled herself away from the window and started with the maple chest of drawers she'd found at an auction, her first real piece of furniture. On top, she picked through loose change, a stack of Vermont brochures and maps, and a small leather address book she'd check later if she had time. The top drawer contained items decidedly male in origin and she skipped right past it. The second drawer was equally, if less interestingly, personal, containing a couple of stacks of shirts and sweaters. Next, logically, was a drawer of jeans and sweats.

What a great criminal she'd make, she thought sarcastically.

The telephone rang, sending her sprawling back on her behind and damned near giving her a heart attack. She immediately decided to ignore it.

Then she wondered: who would be calling Daniel Foxworth?

The bill was still in her name. Heck, she had rights. She jumped up and flopped across the bed to pick up the extension on the night table. "Good afternoon, Cozie Hawthorne speaking." What else was she supposed to say?

Silence on the other end. She tensed, anticipating her caller's disembodied voice. But a decidedly male voice with a strong Texas accent said, "You cough up your little brother yet?"

She sat up slowly. "Who are you?"

"The bad-ass Texan he put in the hospital."

"J. D. Maguire."

"Danny said you were a smart lady."

Danny?

There was a brief, suspicious pause before Maguire went on. "You addling his brain?"

"Am I what?" Then she got it. "No, I most certainly am not."

"Ha."

But she remembered their lingering kiss in her kitchen: *her* brain certainly had been addled. It wasn't, however, something she had any intention of sharing with the man on the other end of the line. "Mr. Maguire, I suggest instead of plotting against my brother, you and your partner start considering who *else* could have sabotaged your helicopter. From what I can gather, you two have quite a list of enemies yourselves."

The Texan grunted. "You talk to Danny like that?"

"Why shouldn't I?"

"Because one of these days he's going to turn you over his knee and give your behind a good swat, that's why."

Cozie was incensed. "Excuse me? How dare you—"

"Hey, this is on my nickel. I'll dare what I damned well please. Put him on."

*Right. Now you're caught, you idiot.* She had to remind herself that J. D. Maguire was thousands of miles from Woodstock, Vermont, and in no position to be intimidating anyone. "I'm afraid Daniel isn't here."

"Ah-huh. And you wouldn't be cooking dinner for him, would you?"

"I would not."

He coughed, a racking, pain-filled cough he finished with a string of curses that sounded well-practiced. "I'd love to be there," he went on hoarsely, "when Danny catches you. He hates sneaks."

She couldn't let that one slide. "That's a street that runs two ways, Mr. Maguire. Did you want to leave him a message?"

"You'd give it to him?"

"Sure. I have nothing to hide."

Maguire chuckled. "If I were you, sweet cheeks, I'd get my fanny out of there before he comes home and finds you. I'll probably go back to sleep and forget we even talked."

"Don't do me any favors, Mr. Maguire."

"I don't do anybody any favors. You tell Danny Boy," he said, "that this time he's bit off more than he can chew, and I'm not talking about who tried to kill us. Afternoon, Ms. Hawthorne. You thank your lucky stars I'm hooked up to tubes and shit and can't take the next plane north."

He hung up.

Cozie replaced the receiver, her face hot. J. D. Maguire had sounded lucid and every bit as difficult and relentless as his partner, if, indeed, more offensive. She pictured the two of them cruising the world for oil fires. A couple of macho, nomadic Texans, one of them also rich. How different their lives were from her own, she thought, sliding off the bed.

An engine sounded in the driveway. It was too much to believe it would be someone other than one Daniel Austin Foxworth. She peeked out the window and through the gathering gloom saw the black truck and its Texas license plate.

She could hide under the bed. No: with no dust ruffle he would see her the moment he came up the stairs.

She could stand there and face him. She hadn't, after all, found a damned thing of interest.

But J. D. Maguire's assessment of his partner—whom he knew better than she did—echoed in her head and she thought maybe that wasn't a good idea. Not that she was a coward, of course. She just preferred to choose her own battles.

She ducked into the loft closet, pushing past a battered soft-leather duffel and an oilcloth coat right out of *Bonanza*. It would be just her luck if Daniel were in for the night.

The porch door opened and shut, and he headed straight for the loft, his footsteps heavy on the stairs, then on the six-inch pine floorboards she and her father had laid one blustery spring weekend.

Two seconds later he tore open the closet door. "Out."

"I can explain—"

"Out," he repeated.

She examined her options, not a time-consuming task since she had few. "Move aside first."

"You're in no position to be making demands."

"I can stay in here and rot. Once I had a field mouse die in between the walls and the smell—"

"Cozie."

"Well, I can't go through you, you know."

He opened the door wider and stepped back, giving her a partial escape route. His idea of moving aside and hers, however, were clearly two different things. "Okay. Out."

Noting that she was feeling less mortified than she would have expected, Cozie pushed her way out of the closet without tripping over his damned duffel. "I suppose," she said, adjusting her shirt, "just because you've had POW training and have put out zillions of big fires you think you're tough enough to intimidate an innocent woman."

"You're not intimidated, Cozie Hawthorne, and you're damned sure not innocent." He shut the closet door. He was, she observed, in a rather uncompromising mood. His eyes could shred steel. "Tell me what you're doing here."

She refused to turn away from his hard gaze. "Well. I see you can dish it out but you can't take it."

"Meaning?"

"Meaning you've searched my brother's place, you've searched my place—"

"I was looking for an intruder."

She made a dismissive sound. "The break-in just gave you an excuse."

"How did you get in?"

"I used my key."

He put out his palm. "Give it to me."

"I most certainly will not. This is my property."

His eyes darkened, capable of melting steel now instead of merely shredding it. "Then I'll get it from you myself."

"The hell you will," Cozie said, and bolted.

She got approximately half a step before an iron arm clamped around her middle and she was swung up off her feet and tossed onto the bed like a sack of laundry.

The moment he released her she shot upright. "You bastard!"

He smirked. "Tell me you wouldn't have taken a poker to me if you'd had the chance when you caught me at your brother's place last night."

"If it'd been a hot poker."

He started muttering things under his breath that she had a fair idea were uncomplimentary to her. His hair was damp from the misting rain, and he had a masculine scent about him that reminded her of his mouth on hers, his hardness pressed up against her.

She cleared her throat, and he smiled nastily, as if reading her mind. He pointed a finger at her. *"Don't* move."

"Or you'll what?"

Right away she knew it was a dumb question.

170

Dumb, dumb, dumb. He leaned over and caught up a length of her hair in his hand and tilted her head back, not ungently, so that they were eye to eye. "You're a complication I don't need, Cozie Hawthorne." His sandpaper voice was low and hoarse with an intensity she could see in his eyes, in his stiffened muscles. "Did you find anything of interest?"

"No, but J.D. called."

Daniel pulled back, once more the remote, controlled professional. "We talked earlier. He's having a good day—he hates it that he's not here."

"I got that impression."

He gave her a mild look, the passion he'd displayed only a moment before no longer in evidence, buried somewhere deep inside him. "He thinks you're a bad influence on me."

"If that's because I'm insisting you think twice before damning my brother, then I hope I am."

"That wasn't it," Daniel said, an unexpected, sardonic smile twitching at the corners of his mouth. "J.D. operates on a more elemental level than that."

She swallowed. "Oh."

"I'd better call him before he runs out of energy. You," he said, "stay put."

He went around the bed and picked up the extension, dialing J.D.'s hospital number from memory.

But Cozie quickly decided there was no advantage in sticking around for their conversation. Daniel would have to crawl over the bed to get to her. Even he wasn't that good.

Seizing the moment, she lunged for the stairs, bounded down them in two well-practiced leaps, and was out the door, onto the porch, and up and over the rail, scurrying down the path toward the brook like a panicked squirrel.

But why? She hadn't really done anything wrong.

Besides which, if Daniel were going to throttle her, he would have done so by now. She groaned, stopping. Running would accomplish nothing—a point she'd make to her brother when she found him.

She walked back up the path. There was a cold, steady drizzle now, the kind that penetrated to the bone. In her haste, she'd left her field jacket on the stair rail, which, she belatedly realized, must have given her away. Being an ex-military type, Daniel was more than up to the challenge of figuring out she was hiding in the closet.

He was standing in the doorway when she climbed back onto the porch. "J.D. gave me permission to go after you."

"I'll bet he did."

"Change your mind about running?"

"I decided running would only make you think you had the upper hand. And you don't." She paused, giving him a chance to respond. But he didn't. He merely leaned against the doorjamb and waited for her to go on. "Did J.D. tell you what he wanted?"

"He started to. He's getting a team together to salvage our helicopter."

"From his hospital bed?"

"It gives him something to do," Daniel said neutrally.

Cozie acknowledged his words with a small nod. "You feel responsible for him, don't you? I don't mean just for his injuries."

"I know what you mean. J.D. and I go way back." His tone shut off further questions. "I'll get your coat."

She debated following him inside but decided she'd pushed her luck enough for one day. When he returned, he held the jacket for her to slip into, and she did, feeling his solid presence so close to her, a part of her wanting just to fall back against his chest and let his strong arms envelop her. But she quickly drew away from him and said, "If your salvage crew can bring up your helicopter, do you think they'll find evidence of what caused the explosion?"

"I don't know."

"But you're hoping."

"I'm not hoping anything. I haven't closed off any options. Believe it or not, I am trying to keep an open mind."

She registered her doubt with deliberately raised eyebrows. "My brother is your chief suspect, though, isn't he?"

"I'd like to talk to him about his trip to Texas. I'm not saying what he's done or what he hasn't done. I haven't got a shred of evidence against him." His tone was all business, with no hint he was in any danger of letting her—or anyone else—provoke him into doing something not directly related to getting what he wanted. "I suggest if you know where he is, you at least tell him he's got some explaining to do."

Cozie buttoned her jacket, just to have an excuse to avoid Daniel's probing gaze. "I don't know where he is."

"I'll bet if you thought real hard you could come up with some ideas."

She ignored him. "I'll see you around, Major Foxworth."

"You use your key again," he said as she started down the porch steps, "it had best be for reasons you and I both can understand. No more sneaking around."

"That goes for you, too, bub."

"Darlin', if you catch me in your bedroom, there won't be any question of why I'm there."

She slid down the path, welcoming the cold drizzle

173

and the smells of the wet woods, reminders of who she was and where she came from. But, in the swirling fog above her, she could hear Daniel's low laugh, arousing her, challenging her, and she pushed through dripping, wilted ferns, getting as far away from him as quickly as she could—not, she thought, that it would do any good.

"How bad are you hit?" J.D. asked when, a few minutes after Cozie departed into the fog, Daniel called him back.

He knew what his friend meant. He thought about Cozie's luminous eyes and how much he wanted to see them radiating the warmth and passion she was trying so hard to keep at bay. Grabbing hold of her in the snug, intimate loft, he had known he was damned close to sacrificing anything, even the answers to what had happened to him and J.D. over the Gulf of Mexico, just to make love to Cozie Hawthorne. But he couldn't be that irresponsible. Not to J.D., not to himself. Not to her.

"It's just a flesh wound," he lied. "Nothing I can't handle."

"Yeah, right." J.D. was dubious. "Well, fill me in before I konk out. I've felt almost human again instead of like some steer being hung from a meat hook and gutted alive."

Daniel inhaled. "J.D.—"

"Skip it, Danny Boy. I know you'd be in my place if you could." He chuckled. "Though maybe I wouldn't trade with you with that Yankee spitfire on your case."

"She's protective of her brother."

"Right."

Time for a change of subject. "I haven't had any luck locating him. I checked inns and outdoor-gear stores around town. Nothing. Nobody has hired him.

Nobody knows who hired him. Trying to find a Hawthorne in Hawthorne country . . ." He sighed. "I'll keep looking."

"Hell, if that little weasel's guilty and we were just a goddamned bonus—"

"I know, J.D."

"Rubs me the wrong way."

"In the course of the afternoon," Daniel went on, "I ran into Julia Vanackern. She asked me to meet her for a drink about thirty minutes from now."

"You didn't turn her down, did you?" J.D.'s voice, even his intermittent cough, was weakening.

"Nope. I'd best make myself decent. Tell the salvage boys to do what they have to do. Spare no expense."

"When you're footing the bill, Danny Boy, I never do. My advice? Cut the bullet out and disinfect the wound with alcohol. Then stay the hell away from Cozie Hawthorne."

It was good advice. "She can lead me to her brother."

"Just don't let her lead you to anything you'll regret. Keep your head and other vital body parts screwed on straight. I know it's tough without me there to do it for you."

Daniel laughed. "Yeah, J.D., it's real tough. I'd pay money to see you and our Ms. Cozie go toe-to-toe. Look, take care of yourself, and trust me: I'm not going to forget why I'm here."

Fifteen minutes later, he was in his truck cruising down Hawthorne Orchard Road, and as he passed the white clapboard farmhouse with the black shutters and orange-leafed maple trees, with the pumpkin patch and the bird feeders all barely visible in the fog and the rain, he felt Cozie's loneliness tugging at him. She wasn't a kid anymore, growing up on her pretty Vermont road with her brother and sister and parents, with her hard-bitten old aunt and a grandfather who'd lived into his eighties, and God only knew who else. She couldn't be what she had been. Her life had changed.

The parking crunch in downtown Woodstock had eased with the rain and the passing of the weekend. He found a space across from the *Vermont Citizen* and walked through the common, giving Alonzo Hawthorne a nod. He wondered what the old Civil War hero would think of a Texan falling for his great-great-whatever-granddaughter.

J.D. was right. Daniel was hit bad. Dig out the bullet and pour on the alcohol and forge ahead.

Julia Vanackern was at the bar of a dark, crowded restaurant with an eclectic Victorian decor. Daniel slid onto the stool next to her and ordered George Dickel, over ice. When he got that straightened out, he turned to Julia. Her hair shimmered in the dim light. She had on a black jumpsuit and long silver earrings and a dark red lipstick, and her eyes seemed an even deeper sapphire. She twirled a turquoise ring with the thumb of the same hand as she nursed a nearly full glass of champagne. Daniel had the feeling it wasn't her first.

"Hello, Major Foxworth."

"Just Daniel will be fine."

She smiled, flirtatious. "I like Major better. It's sexier."

"Ms. Vanackern—"

"Oh, don't be so serious. And it's Julia. Elegant name, isn't it? *Julia.*" She curled it on her tongue. "To think, if dear Mummy had married Duncan Hawthorne after all I could have been a Cornelia. What would we be, rolled up into one? Julia and Cornelia. Juzie?"

Daniel's bourbon arrived. He paid the bartender

and took a sip, and Julia swallowed more of her champagne. Her hand was trembling. Her eyes shone with tears. "Julia," he said gently, "I can see you another time. . . ."

She seized his arm. "No. Don't go. Please. This is fine."

Her grip eased, and Daniel extricated himself. If he'd met Julia Vanackern in Houston as planned, before the crash, before Cozie, would he have fallen for her—at least for a while?

"I'm sorry." She took a couple of deep breaths, calming herself. "It's just that seeing you this morning, realizing who you were—it's reminded me of so much I'm trying to forget. I had only met your partner for a short time. I never did get to meet you. It made witnessing your helicopter go down . . ." She fumbled for words. "Not easier. That's not right: less personal. I could almost talk myself into believing I was watching it all on television."

"I can understand that."

"Can you? Then can you understand that seeing you now, meeting you, dredges it all up, makes it all very real?"

He looked at her. "It is real."

Her lower lip trembled with her feeble smile. "Yes."

Daniel drank more of his bourbon, waiting for Julia to go on. This was her show. The bar was uncrowded, the clientele young, out for a good time. Did Cozie ever come here? Or did she stay up on Hawthorne Orchard Road, her nose to the grindstone?

Julia snatched up her glass and took a huge gulp of her champagne, her eyes focused straight ahead, at nothing. "You already know why I changed my mind about going up with you at the last minute." It came out as an accusation, and she motioned for another champagne, still not looking at him. "Your partner saw me with Seth Hawthorne while you were racing around getting things ready to tackle your oil fire. He must have told you."

The bartender returned with a fresh glass of champagne. Daniel paid without a murmur of protest from Julia Vanackern. Cozie, he felt sure, would have been all over him for being presumptuous, a macho Texan, Lord only knew what.

Julia held her glass by the stem and swirled the contents, studying the reaction. "J. D. Maguire . . . your partner . . ." She tipped her glass, taking another big swallow. "He nearly died, didn't he?"

"Yes. It was pure luck we both weren't killed."

She gave him a sideways glance, her gleaming hair hiding one eye. "Your considerable skill as a pilot certainly helped," she said with a sultry smile.

Flattery had never worked on him; it didn't now. "J.D. might not make a full recovery. If that's the case, he won't fight another oil fire. It'd be a hell of a loss. He's damned good at it."

"What about you? Will you go back?"

He shrugged.

She gave her head a little shake, and her hair tumbled straight down her back, catching, it seemed, every bit of available light. "You have options J.D. doesn't have."

It was obvious enough, so Daniel refrained from comment. He was going slow on his bourbon. A woman like Julia Vanackern required a man to keep his wits about him.

"Seth and I . . ." She breathed out, as if releasing the part of her that had to posture and pretend. "We had a brief fling this summer. At least I looked upon it as a fling. I know my mother told you he's infatuated with me and I never returned his feelings, but she doesn't know the whole story. I did. For a while I

178

really did. Oh, I thought we had an understanding—a little fun, sex, a few laughs, friendship. But nothing more than that."

"Why not?"

Bitterness swept across her pretty, delicate features. "A thousand reasons, and don't pretend you don't understand them all, Daniel Austin Foxworth."

He took another sip of bourbon, asking himself if he did understand; if he'd ever treated a woman the way Julia Vanackern said she'd treated Seth Hawthorne.

"But it's different for a man," she went on, lightly sarcastic. "You can even marry 'beneath' you and get away with it. My father did. Frannie Tucker was just a pretty local girl when Dad met her. About all she knew how to do was milk cows and boil down sap into maple syrup. She considers herself lucky for having escaped that life."

"Did she object to your relationship with Seth?"

"I told you: she didn't even know about it."

"Because you knew she'd object."

"Because I knew it would never last and I might as well spare her the worry."

"What about your father?"

She gave a short, bitter laugh. "I could have made love to Seth on the front lawn and Dad wouldn't have noticed."

Daniel didn't touch that one. Around them, the bar began to fill up with tourists and locals, laughing, talking among themselves. Julia seemed to draw even more into herself.

"Seth Hawthorne works for my parents on occasion, as you well know. We built our house on his family's land, bought his family's paper. They've been struggling and scraping for two hundred years."

"But they've hung on."

"Thanks to us." She drank more champagne, not as

fast. "There was no other buyer for the *Citizen,* at least none that would have paid what we did. Maybe we should have just let it go bankrupt. I don't know. I certainly don't feel sorry for them. Their land is tremendously valuable. Three hundred acres in Woodstock? Give me a break. They could have sold it for a fortune when land values were so high in the eighties."

"Maybe making a fortune isn't what they're about."

"Being mule-headed is what they're about. Do you think Seth needs to clear brush for a living? He could have been so much more if his father hadn't been so stubborn—"

"Whoa," Daniel said, holding up a hand. "I thought he's the one who sold the paper."

"He is. But he could have sold us everything—the land and the paper—and Seth wouldn't have had to suffer. He could have gone back to school, he could have gotten out of Vermont if he'd wanted to, instead of being so tied to the land, that damned apple orchard. And his mother . . . You haven't met Emily, but she's an absolute joy. She's suffered, too."

Julia seemed to sense her rising intensity and took a moment to calm herself. Daniel didn't interrupt, just kept close watch on her reactions, the rise and fall of tears in her sapphire eyes. What was real, he wondered? What was just a show? She seemed to relish a certain level of drama in her life.

"Seth's a lot like his mother," she went on quietly. "Laid-back, easy to talk to. Cozie's more like her father: your basic rock-headed Vermonter. Meg—I don't know her very well, but she seems to have carved out a place for herself in all that Hawthorne family history. Seth hasn't. But they all, every one of them, suffered because Duncan Hawthorne refused to face reality: his paper was bankrupt and he couldn't afford to sit on three hundred acres of prime Vermont land."

"Cozie's success with her book must help take the edge off," Daniel said.

"For her. It doesn't do a damned thing for Seth except remind him that he couldn't save his family's land himself."

"Is that so important?"

"He cuts down trees and shows hikers around the woods, does a little of what he calls 'property management.' Don't get me wrong: I'm not putting that down. But he has no future—and don't think he doesn't know it."

But was that his sister's fault? Daniel skipped the last of his bourbon. He'd had enough. "Do you think he resents Cozie for her success?"

She lifted her shoulders and let them fall, aware, Daniel thought, of how dramatic she was being. "I don't know. I only know that when I realized he wanted more from me than I was willing to give—than I *could* give—I broke off our relationship."

"How did he take it?"

"All right, I thought. Half the reason I went to Houston was to put some distance between us, psychic as well as physical distance. But I couldn't not see him when he showed up. He just wanted to talk. I tried to be kind."

They were not, Daniel thought, discussing a rabid dog that had to be put down. Bottom line, Julia Vanackern shot the guy out of the saddle. She was conscious of who and what she was, and she wasn't a woman who would have more than a "fling" with a Seth Hawthorne.

She leaned toward him, brushing her soft shoulder against his upper arm as if by accident. "I don't blame you for wanting to know for sure what happened to your helicopter," she said in a half-whisper. "I saw it go down. I can understand your need to know."

"Julia—"

She placed a hand on his thigh, as if supporting herself to keep from falling off the stool. She looked vulnerable and, Daniel had to admit, very beautiful. "But don't get the idea I would share my private life with just anyone, for any reason. It cost Seth a good deal of time and money to fly down to Texas. Summer and fall are his biggest moneymaking seasons. And there was no point: he saw that right away. What we had was over. Is over. He agreed, finally, and went home."

Daniel, however, was nothing if not persistent. "I thought you two argued."

"It wasn't an easy conversation. We both lost our tempers."

"Did you tell him you'd changed your mind about going up with J.D. and me?"

"No. He'd already left when I changed my mind. My parents had caught up with me, and I decided to bag flying over an oil fire with a couple of Texans. If I'd met you first . . ." She managed a coy smile. "I don't know, I might have gone up anyway."

"Be glad you didn't."

She shrugged. "I suppose so."

"Your parents didn't stick around?"

"No. They were worried about getting in the way; your people were really hustling to get equipment together. I decided to stay awhile and watch from a safe distance. I saw your helicopter go up, and I saw it spin out of control and crash into the water. I didn't know what to do. I started screaming. I couldn't actually see your chopper in the water—it was too far out—and I'm not sure people believed me when I said it had gone down. Here I was, some hysterical rich girl from New York, and you were Daniel Foxworth—but you'd already radioed you were in trouble?"

Daniel nodded, remembering.

*Hell, Danny Boy. We're goners this time. Your granddaddy's going to be pissed. He made me promise I'd keep you alive.*

Julia slid off the tall bar stool. "I'm glad you weren't killed. I don't know if I'd ever have recovered. I like to think if I'd have been on board I would have come out all right, but I'll never know." She lifted her eyes to his. "I wish we could have met under different circumstances, Daniel Austin Foxworth."

He nodded, leaving it at that. "Just one more question. Did you ever feel in any danger from Seth Hawthorne?"

"No. Never." The tears were back, shining, damned close, this time, to spilling down her pale cheeks. "I never could. If you'll excuse me, I have to get back for a dinner my parents are having. I'd love to invite you, but Dad . . ."

"It's okay. Another time."

She smiled, her eyes sparkling. "Yes. Another time."

When she'd gone, Daniel asked for a menu. Dinner out, alone, sounded good to him.

# CHAPTER
## 11

Cozie stopped at her brother's place on her way to the Vanackern dinner. With the rain and fog, she'd opted for plain black wool pants and an evergreen silk charmeuse blouse, but she wished she'd tossed her mud shoes into her Jeep when she had to tramp across Seth's sodden yard. She'd decided Daniel was right about one thing: her brother had cleared out. His story about taking hikers into the mountains was bogus. She'd checked everywhere and no one had hired him as a guide. He was in trouble. And running only made him look guilty.

She was one of the last to arrive at the small dinner party. The rain had done a job on her hair, which she'd fortuitously pulled back with a handmade barrette. Julia greeted her at the door. "I just had a drink in town with your new tenant," she said, leading Cozie into the living room. "You've heard he misled us about his identity?"

"I'd say he more than 'misled' us; he outright lied."

Julia looked amused. "Well, let's have him drawn and quartered. Come on in."

"Wait a second. Julia, I know Seth went to Texas to see you." Cozie hesitated as laughter drifted from the next room; this was hardly the time or the place for grilling Julia Vanackern. But she plunged ahead. "You two argued before you were to go aboard the helicopter with Daniel Foxworth. . . ."

"Seth and I saw each other just before I was due to board the helicopter," Julia said coolly. "It was pure coincidence. If Daniel thinks Seth had anything to do with the crash, he's dead wrong."

Cozie straightened. "I agree."

"It was just an unfortunate accident. Seth—well, you'll have to ask him about our relationship." Something, her tone communicated quite clearly, she considered none of Cozie's business. "I understand he's on a hiking job?"

"As far as I know. Julia, about the thefts—"

"I don't know anything about them. Now, do come in. Mum's delighted you decided to join us tonight. I think she wants to show you off."

As if Cozie were a project—a quilt or a pottery vase—that had come out unexpectedly well. But when she entered the living room, Frances Vanackern immediately took her by the arm and introduced her to the other guests as if nothing else was going on. Cozie tried to relax and enjoy herself.

Halfway through a simple "country" dinner of New England chicken pot pie, Thad Vanackern brought up the break-in at the *Citizen* building. "I spoke to the police late this afternoon. They suspect kids."

"That's what Aunt Ethel thinks," Cozie said diplomatically, suspecting that her aunt, now that she'd been filled in on the various goings-on in the lives of her late brother's children, thought no such thing.

Julia, who'd been unusually quiet, said, "No one's immune to crime," and the conversation moved on to a general discussion of crime and violence in America.

When Cozie left, Thad insisted on accompanying her to her Jeep despite a steady, soft rain. "We'll know you've finally accepted your new life when you trade this dinosaur in," he said good-naturedly. "Thank you for coming tonight, Cozie. Those who hadn't met you wanted to, and those who had wanted to see you again."

"That's kind of you to say."

"It happens to be true." He gave her an indulgent, paternal smile. "Your small talk is improving. You managed not to throw a single stick of dynamite into the conversation the entire evening."

She laughed. "What's the point? You well-bred types always put out the fuse before it can go off."

He opened her Jeep door for her and held it while she climbed in. "Good night, Cozie. I'm sure we'll see you again before we leave."

"When will that be?"

"Don't sound so eager."

"I wasn't—"

"It's all right. We plan to stay through next weekend, at least Frances and I do. I'm not sure how long Julia will be staying. She's got a half dozen irons in the fire, as usual." He inhaled, suddenly awkward. "Have you had a chance to talk to your brother?"

"Not yet. He's gone hiking."

Thad frowned, but his skepticism was plain.

"I suggest," Cozie said, unable to keep the sharpness out of her voice, "you notify the police about your missing things."

"Perhaps we will," he said without emotion, and shut the door firmly as she started the engine.

She gripped the wheel in frustration and set off too fast down the dark, foggy dirt road. She careened around a bend, nearly taking out part of a stone wall, and slowed down. The fog was mercurial, impenetrable on one curve, gone on another, the bright autumn leaves adding an eerie glow to the night. She didn't look forward to walking into her empty house.

But Daniel's truck was parked out back as if it belonged there. Cozie was surprised at her relief—and distressed. She had no business, none, getting mixed up with a rich Texan after her brother's hide. She was exhibiting about as much common sense as Seth had when he'd gotten involved with Julia Vanackern.

She found Daniel stretched out on the couch under a tattered quilt with a fire in the stove and Bullwinkle on television. "Don't you people believe in remote control?"

"The day I can't get up to turn off the television or switch the channel—"

"Don't get started." He swung off the couch and turned off the television. He'd pulled off his boots, sexy even in his ragg wool socks. He didn't, however, stray from his stated mission. "Any word from your brother?"

"My brother," she said, "is guiding tourists through the wilds of Vermont."

The slate eyes darkened. "That's a bullshit story and you know it."

"I'm going to bed. Good night. Thank you for keeping the fire going." She paused in the doorway. "You can go home now."

She breezed on into the kitchen. Her stomach was churning. She opened the front door and yelled for Zep, and stood there in the cold, damp draft until he finally came running. He was confused. He never got to use the front door. He tucked his tail between his legs and beelined for the back room as if he'd done something wrong.

"Hello, fella," Daniel greeted him.

Cozie flounced back down the short hall to the back room. Daniel was patting the big mutt on the head. "You have to leave," she told him.

Zep darted for the stove. The place was already smelling like wet dog. Daniel dominated the room with its low ceilings and barnboard walls. He looked very tall, very much a man accustomed to doing as he pleased. "I'll leave only if you come with me."

"Not a chance."

"There are no locks on your doors, Cozie. Your dog and your crowbar aren't enough protection against the caller I heard on your phone today."

"And you are?"

He didn't even hesitate. "Yep."

"Damned arrogant of you, isn't it?"

"Let's just say I'd hope just having my truck here would keep whoever slipped in this morning from coming back."

"Okay. Leave your truck and walk back."

She might as well have saved her breath. "If it didn't, I reckon you, me, Zep, and your crowbar could handle the situation." The man wasn't willing to yield even an inch. He moved toward her. "I've put my things in the end room. There'll be one whole room between us, if that's what you're afraid of."

"It isn't."

A smile tugged at the corners of his mouth. "You said that awful quick, Ms. Cozie."

She had indeed, but she didn't care. The prospect of spending an entire night with Daniel Foxworth within yards of her wasn't something she needed to dwell on. "You just want to stay in case Seth shows up."

Daniel shrugged, impassive. "Think whatever you want to think. I'm not spending another night in your Jeep."

"Who asked you—"

"Ms. Cozie, I've only known you a short time, but I've already figured out you don't like asking anybody for anything. So I'm not waiting to be asked."

She threw up her hands and headed for the bathroom. "Fine, do what you want. I suppose I'd rather know where you are than not. Now if you'll excuse me, I'm going to wash up and go to bed. If you need anything, I'm sure you know where to find it."

"If I don't," he said from the back room in his deep, sandpaper drawl, "I know where to find you."

Right then and there she decided not to tell him that the room he'd picked was where Horace, the bat who'd been eluding her for weeks, liked to hang out. Literally. Let the major find out for himself.

Around midnight Daniel figured he had a goddamned bat in his room. Probably the biggest one he'd ever encountered. Had the wingspan of a damned eagle. It darted around under the low, slanted ceilings, its wings and erratic movements creating shadows right out of *Dracula*.

He assumed it was looking for a way out—or maybe a juicy neck. Hell, what did he know about Vermont bats?

His landlady, he suspected, knew a lot.

Keeping his head low, he rolled out of bed and made for the door, which he'd been reasonable enough to shut, given Cozie's reluctance to have him there. As he pushed it open, the bat dove, just missing Daniel's head. He heard—felt—the flutter of wings at his scalp.

He swore.

The bat streaked into the adjoining bedroom. Daniel could easily have shut his door and gone back to bed and left his housemate to her fate. But he could see that the door into her room was open. The bat, no doubt, was already in there.

Walking away from a fight just wasn't in him.

He fumbled around in the dark and found the lamp on his bedside table. It gave off only a faint glow, not enough, he presumed, to deter a bat. He pulled on his jeans, his eyes adjusting to the light. No point having Cozie wake up to a bat and a naked man. She'd probably have at them both with her trusty crowbar.

Venturing into the next room, he remained alert to any movement, any fluttering sound, any sharp teeth. He paused in Cozie's doorway. He couldn't hear the bat, couldn't see it. Most likely it had lit somewhere.

He glanced over at the bed, prepared to explain his presence.

But Cozie wasn't in it.

Her voice came from the darkness. "I see you've met Horace."

She was pressed up against the wall to the left of the door, holding a blanket under her chin in the moonlight. Daniel could have smothered her with it. "Horace?"

"The bat." As if he should have known. "He's gone into the end room. I think he's the same one who's been haunting me all summer. I never can catch him."

Catch him? Daniel stepped over the threshold. "You could have warned me."

"That's an interesting point of etiquette, isn't it? Should one warn one's guests a bat might show up or let them sleep, with the hope one doesn't?" The woman was enjoying herself. "You don't like bats, Major?"

"Not in my bedroom. Where's your crowbar?"

"What are you going to do, beat the poor thing to a pulp?"

"That's the general idea, yes."

"You don't need to kill him. Just go on into the next room and flush him out. I'll take care of him."

Just go flush him out. Right. "Are you testing my courage?"

"I hope not. I shouldn't think a big macho Texan like you would be afraid of a little old bat."

If she'd seen Horace, she knew he was no little old bat.

"You can turn on a light," she said. "That should do the trick. Bats get disoriented in the light. There's a switch by the stairs."

First he'd deal with the bat, he thought, then the woman.

He started onto the landing to the end room. There was a fluttering sound to his right, a movement, and the bat suddenly swooped up the stairs. For a split second they were eyeball to eyeball. Daniel swore and ducked. If he'd had Cozie's crowbar, that would have been the end of one bat.

The creature darted into the end room.

Cozie charged out of her bedroom with her blanket. Feeling along the wall, Daniel found the switch, and when the light came on, it caught her stalking the flying bat with her blanket at the ready, exactly for what he could only guess.

"Well," she said, "he certainly is a big one."

Good of her to notice. "What are you doing?"

"I'm going to capture him and throw him out the window."

"Be easier to knock him on the head."

The bat lit on the curtain, not a smart move. Cozie eased toward him. Daniel leaned against the wall. He wasn't going to interfere. Cozie and Horace, so far as he could see, had been through this little routine before.

"Some people," she said, never taking her eye off the bat, "just use their hands and pluck them out of the air."

Daniel refrained from comment.

She gave the curtain a good shake. The bat dropped off, spread its wings, and prepared to get the hell out of there. But she tossed her blanket and had him. She let go, and the blanket and the trapped bat dropped to the floor.

"Bravo," Daniel said.

She cast him a look. "At least he has a chance."

She was breathing hard, her cheeks were flushed, and her hair was sticking up, a stark reminder that she'd just crawled out of bed. She had on a blue plaid nightshirt that covered her from chin to toe and managed to fire his imagination as to what she looked like—felt like—underneath all that flannel. Probably not the effect she'd intended.

The bat twitched and squeaked under the blanket.

"Now what?" Daniel asked.

"Open the window."

He obliged, stepping over the blanket and its prey. The old window took some work to open. There was no screen. Behind him, Cozie scooped up blanket and bat and hurried to the window and shook the bat loose.

"Hasn't one ever flown back into your face?"

"Yep." She pulled in the blanket and shut the window. "I'm more careful now."

"I suppose this is what passes for excitement up here in the woods?"

"Are you demeaning my lifestyle?"

"Just asking a question."

"I'll take a bat loose in the house for excitement

anytime over what I've been putting up with the past few weeks." She started past him, tucking stray hairs back off her face, aware, he suspected, of the wild figure she cut. "I'm going back to bed."

"Do you have any idea how damned sexy you look?" he asked as he followed her back into her room. At the very least he owed her a tweak after leaving him to Horace.

"What? Aunt Ethel gave me this nightgown. It can't be . . ." She wouldn't say it.

"Well, it is. Sexy as hell, Ms. Cozie."

In the dark he couldn't see if she blushed. He doubted it. She crawled under her comforter and drew it up to her neck like the proverbial reluctant virgin.

Daniel looked out her dormer window at the sparkling night sky. "Do you always name your bats?"

She shook her head. "No; seldom, in fact. This one's just been around so long I figured I might as well name him."

Her eyes, he noticed, were carefully avoiding lingering on his bare chest. She switched on her bedside lamp. "I'll probably read for a few minutes. I'm always a little wired after dispensing with a bat."

"Wired, hell. You're distracted, same as I am."

"By a bat?"

He grinned. "By the possibilities of us both being wide awake at midnight with the adrenaline running high and hard."

Her knuckles were white where she was holding on tight to the comforter. "We could take a walk," she said.

"Is that what you want?"

She settled back against her pillow. "I don't know what I want. That's not like me, you know. Not knowing what I want."

He sat beside her, feeling the chill of the night air,

knowing she was talking about more than whether or not she wanted to make love to him. The life of Cozie Hawthorne of Woodstock, Vermont, was changing so fast she couldn't keep up.

"That's one thing we have in common," he said. "When I went into the air force academy, I *knew* I wanted to become a fighter pilot. No question. Then that certainty just wasn't there anymore. It was sort of like making a sand castle, and everything's perfect, and then the waves come and it slowly washes away, but it's not any one wave that does it in."

"Why did you go into fighting oil fires?"

"It was something I got into even when I was in the military. J.D. and I have been friends for a long time—I knew it was his dream to have his own outfit. He couldn't get the money together."

"But that's one thing that's not a problem for you," Cozie said.

"I owe J.D." He sighed heavily, not wanting to imagine his partner and friend suffering in his hospital bed. "All J.D.'s ever wanted was a chance. When that copter dropped out of the sky—hell, his chance could have gone down with it. The business we're in is unforgiving. It has to be. The stakes are too high: people's lives, property, millions of barrels of oil, the environment. You can't risk that on someone who'd let his own helicopter blow out from under him."

Cozie leaned forward, touching his arm, igniting something within him he'd thought he'd given up on, desires that went beyond a need for mere physical satisfaction. "I'm sorry for J.D.'s loss. For yours. But you can't blame the wrong person."

He looked at her. "I won't."

She nodded. "I believe you."

"Cozie . . ."

His mouth found hers in the shadows. A cool hand

brushed his cheek, trailed down his arm. His entire body tensed with the need to hold her, to touch that slim body beneath all that flannel and down. Her hand, warmer now, came around his back, and she sank against her pillows, bringing him with her.

Their kiss deepened. He felt an urgency mounting inside him, threatening to overwhelm him, as her mouth opened into his and her fingers tangled in his hair. A small voice warned him to be careful, go easy. More than anything, he didn't want to hurt her.

The comforter had slid down to her waist, allowing him to slip his arms around her, feel the heat of her skin through the flannel, the warmth of her bed.

She ran her palm down his back, and he thought he would die right there. He tugged on her nightgown until he could feel the soft, warm skin of her hip under him. His mouth never left hers. He tasted her, made it crystal clear what he wanted, what he was offering, with the primitive rhythm of his tongue. She moaned beneath him.

"Daniel, I've never . . . this isn't something I do—"

"I know, honey." He raised up slightly, locking his eyes with hers. "Are you okay?"

She didn't hesitate. "Yes."

He drew the nightgown up higher, gazing at the milky length of her legs in the starlight, the dark patch between her legs, the firm abdomen. Breathing in at the sight of her, he slid his palms up the warm, smooth skin, raising the nightgown above her breasts. The nipples were dark and hard in the cool night air. He took one in his mouth, tasting it, licking it.

"Don't stop," she whispered, passion straining her voice.

"I can't imagine ever wanting to."

She moved beneath him, her hand skimming the

front of his jeans where his own state of arousal was obvious. There was no hesitation, no embarrassment in her caress. In his mad dash for the bat he'd never snapped his jeans. She caught the zipper, started to slide it down. He imagined his shaft in her cool fingers.

And bolted straight up and out of her bed, nearly banging his damned fool head on the slanted ceiling.

She didn't pull her nightgown down. She lay before him in the starlight, a temptation like no other he'd known. A beautiful, green-eyed, bat-chasing Yankee.

"I must be crazy," he muttered darkly.

But she smiled, knowing that what he'd done had nothing to do with rejecting her. "I know. Me, too."

"We can't—"

"We *can*. That's plainly obvious to us both, I think. But we shouldn't. We—" She swallowed. "We just shouldn't."

She wiggled into a sitting position, a maneuver that almost had him back in bed with her, never mind that he'd come to Vermont to find out if her brother had blown him and J.D. out of the sky.

Mercifully her nightgown fell over her breasts, and she pulled the comforter onto her lap.

"If you want to do something useful with my crowbar," she said, only her hoarseness giving away her own continued state of arousal, "there's a family of garter snakes down in the cellar." She slid down under the comforter. "I don't mind bats, but I really do hate snakes."

"Cozie . . ." He sighed, raking one hand through his hair. He wasn't accustomed to suppressing his desire for a woman, especially one he desired as much as Cozie Hawthorne. "Good night."

"Pleasant dreams," she murmured.

He headed back through the adjoining room. He

couldn't remember ever leaving a woman alone in bed when it was damned obvious she wanted him to stay. But this time he did. They needed to find Seth. Talk to him. Hear his side of the story. Daniel didn't want to push things too far with Cozie until he was sure her brother hadn't tried to kill him. *Then* they could tackle the issues between them, because no matter what Seth had been doing in Texas, his big sister was still a woman with roots, with family. A woman of wit and charm and an insight Daniel found both compelling and mystifying. And he was a nomadic firefighter. The black-sheep heir to a Texas oil fortune. He didn't fit in her world. She didn't fit in his.

Back in his bedroom, he switched off his light and climbed under several layers of quilts and blankets. He watched the shadows on the slanted ceiling and listened to the quiet sounds of the night, hoping they would work their soothing wonders not just on his mind but his entire body.

He'd be willing to bet Cozie Hawthorne was making similar efforts.

It was craziness. He should be in there having good, heated, rousing sex with her. She should be in here with him.

A solitary car whooshed by out on Hawthorne Orchard Road. He pretended he heard Cozie's footsteps in the next room, coming to him.

"Hell," he muttered, and rolled over onto his side.

When Cozie slipped down to the kitchen at six the next morning, nuthatches and finches and a slew of chickadees, undeterred by the milky fog, were at the feeders out front. She opted not to light the woodstove. Rattling around directly beneath her slumbering guest would be rude—and she needed time to pull herself together. She made coffee and drank a glass of orange juice at the table just as if it were an ordinary fall morning.

But just as she started her second cup of coffee, the telephone rang, and she stiffened as she never would have if her life were back to normal. She didn't answer it. She went into the back room to listen while her answering machine took the call. If it was Seth or Meg or someone from the paper, she'd pick up. But whoever it was heard her taped message kick in and hung up.

She shut her eyes and tried to keep calm. Her caller. It had to be. He or she had gone to the trouble of stealing the evidence Cozie had collected and didn't plan to provide her with any more.

She heard the creak of bedsprings and Daniel's feet landing on the floor above her.

The phone rang again. It was a challenge, a dare.

"Let it ring," Daniel called down from upstairs.

Cozie picked up. "Hi, I'm just getting up. Did you call a minute ago?"

"Hello, Cozie Cornelia."

Her caller's routine wasn't going to change no matter what Cozie did. She gripped the phone but kept her fear and anger out of her voice as she tried a new tactic. "Good morning. Fog's going to burn off, don't you think?"

"You want to know who I am, don't you, Cozie Cornelia?"

"I don't care who you are. I just want you to stop."

"You *know* who I am. Think about it. You really do know."

*Click.*

Daniel came down the back room stairs, in close-fitting jeans and an unbuttoned flannel shirt. Cozie turned away from him. It was as if he'd just walked into a private, nasty part of her life, one she didn't like and couldn't control. She felt vulnerable, victimized.

"You okay?" he asked.

"Yes." It was an obvious lie, but she didn't care.

She went past him, through the door and out onto the back porch, grabbing her sand-colored field jacket.

"Where are you going?"

His tone was undemanding, as if it didn't matter to him whether or not she answered. But she knew it did, and not just so she wouldn't sneak off behind his back to find her brother. He really was concerned about her. It was a complication probably neither of them needed.

"I'm going for a walk," she said. "I need some air."

"You want any company?"

She turned around, and he was there, within arm's length. She absorbed the sight of him, the dark slate of his eyes, the odd scar here and there, the muscles of his chest, the way his jeans hung low on his hips.

She had to get out of there.

"I'll take Zep with me," she said, slipping her stockinged feet into her mud shoes.

Daniel leaned against the doorjamb. "I'll start a fire while you're out, take the chill out of the air."

"It's not that cold, but you do what you want." She left her shoes unlaced and was out the door, into the damp chill of the fog. "If you do start a fire, you could fill up the woodbox while you're at it."

"Be glad to." He followed her out the back door and stood on the landing, his arms crossed on his chest, a man absolutely unlike any other in her life. "If you find your brother, tell him he's going to have to talk to me sooner or later."

His words went right up her spine and stopped her dead in her tracks. "Forget the fire. Pack up your toothbrush and be gone by the time I get back."

"Why?"

"You know damned well why. You'll do anything—

*anything*—to get what you want. You're not hanging around just to make sure my caller doesn't come after me. You're hoping I'll lead you to my brother. The other stuff—what almost happened last night—that's just because I was . . . convenient."

A laconic smile tugged at the corners of his mouth. "Honey, you're anything but convenient."

"You know what I mean. You're going to get your precious answers and beat a path out of Vermont as fast as you can."

Bare feet and unbuttoned shirt and all, he walked out into the cold, damp grass, right up to her. His toe touched her mud shoe; he was boldly—consciously—invading her space, forcing her to step back or endure his closeness. He brushed her chin with the tip of one finger. "I hope you find Seth."

Before she could respond, he about-faced and headed back toward the porch, giving no indication that the cold bothered him. "You know," she yelled to his back, "not every woman in the world wants to go to bed with you."

"Nope." He glanced around at her. "Not every woman."

He was determined to have the last word no matter what she said or did. So she let him. Calling Zep, she plunged through the fog up into the field above the toolshed, trying to adjust her own frantic state to the quiet and stillness of the autumn morning.

# CHAPTER
# 12

⟶

The tall grass, still wet from yesterday's rain, soaked the legs of Cozie's jeans, and the fog seemed to hold the damp, earthy smells of the field and woods. Some of the brightest, reddest leaves had fallen with the rain. Autumn was flying by. She thought of all the work she'd planned to do: till and mulch the garden, plant bulbs, put up applesauce and apple butter, maybe some pear butter, rake leaves, trim the deadwood in the trees around the house. Wash the windows. Put up the storms. But even as she listed it all—the simple, mundane tasks of the life she led, wanted to lead—the disembodied voice of her anonymous caller came to her.

*You know who I am. Think about it. You really do know.*

Did she? Was she just too afraid to admit it?

"Seth," she said aloud, "where the devil are you?"

She pressed on into the woods, taking the familiar

farm road over the rocky stream. Pockets of fog made everything damp and cold. Zep had charged ahead, chasing a rabbit in the brush. If she were Seth, where would she go? He was an experienced hiker and camper. He could get along easily in the woods; it was where he was most comfortable.

The monk hut.

She would take shelter in what they called the monk hut, a cavelike structure located on a steep hillside en route to the orchard.

She picked up her pace, hoping Daniel Foxworth wasn't following her. But here she had the advantage: she knew the woods, knew their sounds and their paths and old farm roads and stone walls. He didn't.

Refusing to take a break, she kept moving until the road narrowed as it cut through the woods at the top of a ravine. She was above the fog. A light breeze stirred in the pine and hemlock overhead. Birds and squirrels and chipmunks went about their morning routines, oblivious to her tension. Leaving the path, she ducked through a stand of gray birches. Fog shifted and swirled at the bottom of the ravine. The steep grade of the hill forced her to crabwalk, to keep from sliding uncontrollably to the bottom. Sodden pine needles and brown, crumbling leaves from autumns past clung to her wet pants and socks and oozed between her fingers. About a third of the way down the hill, she started moving horizontally, over the trunk of one of several fallen pines. Thick, smelly pitch stuck to her hands, and she scraped her forearm on a broken branch.

But up ahead she could see the cluster of boulders that marked the spot where, just beyond them, it was said ancient Celtic pagan priests—Druids—had built a small, stone-lined chamber into the hillside, hundreds of years before Columbus. The monk hut, she and her brother and sister called it. Scholars disagreed as to the authenticity of the claim that Bronze Age Europeans had traveled across the Atlantic and constructed their megaliths throughout central and northern New England. Grandpa Willard had insisted the hut was more likely something the Abenaki Indians built, or was just an old root cellar.

Cozie made her way to the opening, under a large, flat slab that served as roofing. The drystone construction kept the chamber at a relatively even temperature and protected anyone inside from the elements—and gave Cozie the creeps because the "anyone" could have been a dead body. Many scholars thought the megaliths were burial chambers. As she peered inside, Cozie preferred to think about stored potatoes.

"Bingo," she said softly, seeing her brother's sleeping bag and camping paraphernalia.

He, however, was not in sight.

Twigs crunched behind her. She flew around, and Seth dropped down from a huge boulder. "I should have figured you'd find me."

Unshaven and in need of a hot shower, he looked fit enough. He was accustomed to long spells in the woods. But Cozie noticed his jeans were worn at the knees, patched and frayed, and one of the lesser brands. His chamois shirt had a button missing, a facing ripped half off. His hiking shoes needed replacing. Because he'd never indicated he gave a damn about whether or not he had money, she'd never considered he might be struggling financially—enough, she wondered, to steal from the Vanackerns?

"Seth," she said, "we need to talk."

He shook his head, not countering her so much as willing her away. "You don't have to worry about me, Coze. I don't *want* you worrying about me. I'm doing just fine."

"Then why did you come out here?"

He didn't answer, just sat on one of the smaller boulders, adopting an expression she knew only too well. It said he'd just sit there and wait her out. So she plunged right in. "Seth, the Vanackerns think you've been stealing from them. Thad spoke to me about it on Sunday. He wants me to talk to you."

"Why doesn't the chickenshit talk to me himself?"

"Because he can order me to, I suppose. He found some cash and valuables missing—"

"And figured I'd stolen them. I work my stinking butt off for that bastard and he accuses me of stealing. Real nice. But he shouldn't be sticking you in the middle."

Cozie picked pine needles off her wet pants legs. "That's the least of my worries."

"He going to the police?"

"He said he doesn't want to."

"What, I can hand over the missing stuff and all will be forgiven? He thinks I'm stealing, fine: let him prove it."

"Do you have any idea who it could be?"

"No. I just know it's not me." He looked at her, the question in his eyes plain. "What about you?"

"*I* know you're not a thief! Geez, Seth, how could you even ask?"

"A lot's been going on the past few months." He gave her a wan smile. "All that hobnobbing with the rich and famous you've been doing could've loosened a screw or two."

"Could have," she allowed. "But it hasn't. Seth, there's more."

He breathed out. "Daniel Foxworth."

"He knows you were in Texas."

Seth shut his eyes, looking pained and—rare for him—embarrassed.

"His partner saw you and Julia arguing before their helicopter went up. He came up here looking for an explanation. Then he finds out you didn't tell anyone about your trip to Texas or your relationship with Julia, and the Vanackerns think you've been stealing from them—and you take off."

"Yeah." He launched himself to his feet. "I didn't know what else to do. Coze, you don't have to bail me out. It's not your problem."

She thought of the harassing calls and knew, in her gut, he was wrong: whatever was going on, it was her problem, too. But she said, "I'm not trying to bail you out."

He said nothing, just stared up at the sky.

"What about you and Julia?" she asked quietly.

"There is no me and Julia, not anymore." He squinted at her. "I didn't sabotage Foxworth's helicopter. If that's what he wants to believe, that's his business."

"Did you recognize him when you brought him the wood on Friday?"

He nodded. "We never met face to face, but somebody pointed him out when I was looking for Julia at the base camp his outfit had set up for fighting the tanker fire. I figured he'd come here looking for a scapegoat."

"You."

"He could have wondered if I'd sabotaged his helicopter in a fit of—I don't know what, anger, I guess. Julia had really given me the heave-ho. I left thinking she was going on board with him."

"You went to Texas specifically to see her?"

"Sounds pretty stupid now, but, yeah, I did. Guess I was too dumb to take a hint. I thought we had something going. Then next thing I know, she won't talk to me, won't even come to Vermont; I couldn't

205

figure out what went wrong. So when I found out she was in Houston, I hopped a plane and went down to see her. Sounds like a lovesick, dumb-ass thing to do, doesn't it?"

"You're hardly the first," Cozie said, remembering herself last night with Daniel Foxworth.

Seth shook his head. "I guess I was supposed to divine it somehow. She wasn't too happy to see me, I'll say that. She basically told me to get lost, and so I did. Packed up and headed on home."

"Seth . . ." She hesitated. "You don't need money, do you? There's no way anyone can demonstrate you'd steal from the Vanackerns because you're in debt up to your eyeballs or something?"

He shrugged. "I'd like a new engine for my Rover."

"Your trip to Texas didn't put you back too much?"

"It cleaned me out, but I had the money."

There wasn't a hint of defensiveness in his tone: to her knowledge, money had never been her brother's measure of himself—or anyone else. "What about the helicopter crash?" she asked. "When did you hear about it?"

"Not until I got back home. I figured Julia was lucky not to have been on board, but I never thought—it never occurred to me Foxworth would think I might have sabotaged it."

"Okay," Cozie said, her wet pants legs ice cold in the chilly morning air. "But cutting out like this could make you look guilty."

"I just needed some space to get my head together. I'll be okay." He balled his hands into fists, as if to contain his frustration. "I can keep an eye on the sawmill and the Vanackern place from here, maybe figure out what's really going on—if anything."

An uneasy silence fell between them, interrupted only by the sounds of the woods. Crows called to each other overhead, and the sun made a stab at penetrating the fog.

"Coze?"

She had no choice. She had to tell him about the calls.

When she did, Seth looked at her, serious. "Nobody can lay that one on my doorstep. I got a problem with you, Coze, you'd be the first to know."

"I realize that, but—"

"But it doesn't mean anyone else will," he finished for her.

"What would you like me to do?" she asked softly.

"Be careful." His eyes reached hers, and she realized, as perhaps she never had before, that he wasn't a kid whom trouble always seemed to find, not anymore. "Lay low. Hell, get out of town or go stay with Meg or Aunt Ethel for a while." Suddenly, out of nowhere, came one of his trademark lazy grins. "Geez, I'm starting to sound like you."

She tried to smile. "And count on me paying about as much attention to you as you do to me." But her breath caught, her smile faltered. "This is going to work out, Seth. It will."

"Yeah." But his grin, too, had already faded.

"Do you need anything?"

"No, I'm doing okay. I've been sticking to uncooked food, so a pot roast'll sound good after this mess gets straightened out. But I've survived lots worse conditions. The monk hut's better than a lot of tents I've been in." An awkwardness came over him. "I'll be fine."

"Maybe this will turn out to be a tempest in a teapot."

"Yeah. Watch yourself around Foxworth, okay? From what I heard while I was down in Texas, he's your basic black-sheep rich guy, women falling over him all the time, arrogant—most likely he took that helicopter up without taking proper safety precautions."

Cozie decided not to tell him where Ex-Major Daniel Foxworth had spent the night. "I'll keep that in mind." A gust of wind made her shiver. "Good luck, okay?"

"Yeah," he said, and disappeared through the narrow opening into the drystone monk hut, root cellar, or whatever it was.

The fog had already started to burn off, and Cozie crept back up the hill to the farm road, soaked and cold and not eager to face Daniel Foxworth. Would he be able to guess she'd found her brother? It'd be tough to explain why she looked as if she'd been rolling around in pine pitch and dead leaves.

But when she came down the sloping yard toward her barn-red toolshed, she saw he'd taken her advice and cleared out. His truck was gone. She found a note in the back room: *Be careful what you wish for. DF.*

"Heard your Texan spent the night up at the house," Aunt Ethel announced when Cozie arrived at her office less than two hours after leaving her brother.

She groaned. "What, can't I do anything without half the town knowing by noon the next day?"

"I'd say the whole town was in on this one by eight this morning."

"Should I run an extra edition of the *Citizen*? *NOTHING HAPPENED! TEXAN SLEPT IN DIFFERENT ROOM!*"

"No need. Thelma said she thought someone saw a light on in Seth's old room about midnight."

"We had a bat." Cozie didn't explain further. She'd already decided, on her way into town, not to mention Seth's whereabouts to her aunt, or even, right now,

Meg. She owed her brother a little discretion, and Meg and Aunt Ethel were just the type to grab him by the ear and march in down to Will Rubeno. "And what was one of Thelma's pals doing out at midnight?"

"I didn't say it was one of her friends."

"Who else would know which one was Seth's room?"

"She had them draw her a diagram of the house and point out which room had its light on," Aunt Ethel said matter-of-factly. She eyed the warm cinnamon bagel slathered with maple-walnut-raisin cream cheese Cozie had taken from a paper bag. "You got another of those?"

"You don't deserve it, listening to such gossip."

"Nonsense. You should thank me for keeping you informed of the current talk about you and your affairs. Myself, I prefer to keep abreast of what people are saying behind my back."

Of course, Cozie had seldom had opportunity to generate one of the juicier stories circulating in town. If the "talk" had been about a newcomer to town or one of the transplanted New Yorkers or a part-timer like the Vanackerns, that would be different. But Cozie was a Hawthorne. Her family had been in Vermont's upper valley for generations, and the locals had ideas about who she was, how she ought to behave, indeed how she *would* behave in any given situation. Having a mysterious Texan—with *scars,* for heaven's sake—camp out at her house turned their neat little idea of her right on its head.

Her neat idea of herself, too.

Before she headed into her own office, she relented and handed her aunt the bag with the extra bagel. Aunt Ethel thanked her by informing her the coffee in the pot was fresh, which, in the frugal halls of the *Vermont Citizen,* was by no means always the case.

Work proved a welcome, if fleeting, distraction. There was copy to check, layouts and headlines to approve, photographs to choose among, assignments to make, advertisers to reassure. She rewrote her column and sent it upstairs. After lunch her agent called.

"You've got to make a decision, Cozie."

She knew. Oh, she knew.

"Syndication can give you a national audience on a regular basis. We can try to work something out so your columns originate in the *Citizen,* but it's a Vanackern paper . . ."

"I'll keep thinking. It's nice to have options."

"Cozie, you wowed folks on your television appearances this last trip. The invitations to have you on as a commentator are starting to come in. You need to think about that, too."

She thought of Daniel's note to her. Indeed, indeed: Be careful what you wish for. But she was proud and pleased, even grateful, if also somewhat unnerved. She thought of her anonymous caller's voice, of her brother hiding in the monk hut. "I've got a few fires to put out. I'll call you as soon as I can."

A restored Austin Healey that just about everyone in Woodstock recognized as Julia Vanackern's pulled into a vacant space in front of the *Citizen.* Julia slid out, dressed for town. A two-piece sweater-knit skirt and top in ice blue, hair pulled back, face perfectly made up with subtle, natural-looking cosmetics. Cozie watched her glide up the sidewalk. After her harrowing night in the company of Daniel Foxworth and her jaunt in the woods to find her brother, she herself had bypassed her country-newspaper-editor wardrobe in favor of chocolate-brown jeans and a curry-colored cotton turtleneck sweater.

"Good morning," Julia said from the doorway, "may I come in?"

Cozie pushed her chair back from her computer. "Sure."

"I'm not here on business; Father would never let me near one of his papers on business, even the *Citizen.*" She flushed. "I'm sorry. I didn't mean that the way it sounded."

"It's okay. *The New York Times* we're not. Would you care to sit down?"

"Thank you, but I'll only be a minute." She paused, a cautiousness coming over her that had to be an unfamiliar feeling for someone as freewheeling and self-confident as Julia Vanackern. "I'll just get right to it: Dad's discovered more things missing at the house. Jewelry this time."

"Jewelry? Seth wouldn't—"

Julia pretended not to hear her. "A diamond necklace, a couple of rings. We don't keep much of that sort of thing here in Vermont, just a few favorite pieces. My parents—" She broke off, sighing. "Understandably they're frustrated and upset."

Cozie remained outwardly calm. Inwardly, her stomach was churning. "Seth swipe rings and necklaces? Come on, Julia, that just doesn't wash. A couple of black walnut seedlings, maybe. But not diamonds and rubies. He's just not the type."

"They're quite valuable. He could get a fair amount of cash for them."

"Well, he's not your culprit. He's not even in the area." She lied—as she almost never could manage—with a straight face.

Julia averted her eyes. "That's just it. Dad says he saw Seth skulking about last evening in back of the house, after you left."

"Skulking about? What's that supposed to mean?" Cozie was ready to jump out of her chair and toss Julia Vanackern out, never mind who owned the building and who just worked there.

But Julia showed no sign of taking offense at Cozie's tone. "His choice of words, not mine. He says he called out, but Seth just ran off—and with guests around, and the rain, Dad couldn't very well chase after him. So I don't think . . ." She cleared her throat, and her blue eyes fell on Cozie. "It doesn't seem he's on a hike."

Her words didn't have the impact she was looking for because Cozie already knew that much, if by different means. She kept her mouth shut. As Seth himself had said, hiding in the monk hut allowed him easy access to the Vanackerns—something they would pounce on if she told them. She bit her lower lip, despising herself for the twinge of doubt she felt. Whatever his faults, her brother wasn't a thief.

"Julia, do *you* think Seth is stealing from your family?"

"I don't know!" Julia placed one hand on her temple, her self-control evaporating. "I only know that if he is, I'm partially responsible. I should never . . . our relationship . . ." She dropped her hand from her temple and said boldly, as if she were uttering her first swear words, "I should never have slept with him."

Cozie refrained from comment.

"Seth took what we had together more seriously than I did," Julia went on in a clear, even voice. "I should have known he would. He's a Hawthorne. Everyone knows Hawthornes are all relentless, monogamous—hard on people they feel betray them, never mind the circumstances."

Cozie was mystified. Monogamous? How would

Julia Vanackern know if all Hawthornes were monogamous? And hard on people—where'd she get that idea?

Julia smiled, amused. "Is this news to you, Cozie? I don't believe that. You Hawthornes are all so goddamned honorable it's enough to make us lesser mortals feel inadequate. You've made a virtue of your financial troubles. It's going to be different now, of course, with your success."

"You think we're a bunch of prigs?"

"That's a pejorative term." She was oddly pensive as she paced back and forth on the worn Oriental carpet; Julia Vanackern had never been known as a deep, analytical thinker. "I would say you're idealists. Look at Elijah Hawthorne, taking on the king of England, and then later pressuring George Washington for a bill of rights. Alonzo Hawthorne volunteered for the Union Army and died in the Civil War to defend an ideal. Your grandfather Willard Hawthorne was a model of civic virtue."

A strand of hair fell across Cozie's face as she got to her feet; she wasn't feeling a model of anything. "Grandpa Willard was pretty much an old grump."

Julia turned to her. "And you, Cozie. Your observations and commentaries are in the same tradition of optimism and idealism that have seen your ancestors through the past two centuries. You're down-to-earth, honest, frank, and witty—but you're never cynical. That's why you're so popular. People are tired of cynicism. They read your columns and come away feeling your hope and energy for the future."

"I just write what I think," Cozie said.

"But like all Hawthornes," Julia pressed on, as if Cozie hadn't even spoken, "you're hard on those who are weaker than you are. The selfish, the petty"—she gave a small, self-deprecating laugh—"the rich girl who'd come to town and sleep with a local just for fun."

"So we're a bunch of self-righteous prigs?" Cozie was more nonplussed by Julia's view of her and her family than insulted.

"Let's just say Hawthornes set a high standard for themselves and everyone around them." Julia's smile, the gleam in her deep blue eyes, took some of the edge off her words. "The rest of us aren't all so honorable as you are. Ask your aunt how your father felt when my mother broke their engagement because she had fallen for another man. He never forgave her, Cozie. Never."

Cozie blinked, surprised. "You don't think so?"

"I know so."

How could she know? Neither of them had even been born when Frances Tucker broke her engagement with Duncan Hawthorne. "Pop always maintained that your mother giving him the boot was just one of those things meant to be. If she hadn't, he'd never have met my mother and had us and the life we had together. Of course, he knew Mother already. They just hadn't got around to noticing each other."

"That's not the point," Julia said impatiently.

"Then I don't get the point."

"Duncan Hawthorne went on with his life, but he never again trusted my mother—never allowed her to be a friend."

Cozie thought that one over a moment, then shook her head. "I honestly believe you're projecting an attitude onto my father that he simply didn't have. But look, if it makes you feel any better about what's going on or what's gone on between you and Seth, go ahead and analyze us Hawthornes however it suits you. Just don't expect me to agree. And you can regard my father and brother and me and all

Hawthornes back to the beginning of time as a bunch of holier-than-thou sourpusses if you want, but it doesn't make Seth a thief."

Julia's look was cool, even supercilious. "I never said he was. Neither have my parents. We just want to help."

Didn't they always. But Cozie wasn't about to turn the table and start analyzing the Vanackerns. "I've got some calls to make. Anything else?"

Two bright spots of color rose in Julia's pale, polished cheeks. She swallowed visibly. "I hope you're not angry with me. I—I never said you were a sourpuss. You're too witty, Cozie, to be a sourpuss."

"Okay, scratch sourpuss. Are your folks going to report the thefts to the police?"

"I don't know," Julia said softly.

"Tell them that as far as I'm concerned, they're not doing us any favors by holding off. If they don't want the publicity, that's one thing. But I'm not afraid of what the police will find. Seth isn't your culprit."

"Perhaps you could find him," Julia said, the color receding from her cheeks, "and we could all sit down and discuss this problem together, as friends." She tried to smile. "And that's not an order, Cozie. It's a hope. Everyone in Vermont knows one never orders a Hawthorne to do anything."

She started toward the door but turned back once more. "By the way, I understand Daniel Foxworth spent the night at your house."

"Julia, don't think—"

She held up a hand. "I know it's none of my business. I just wanted to warn you, as a friend, to be careful. I met his family while I was in Texas. He's not—the Foxworths just aren't what you're used to."

"Tell you what, Julia, if you've been listening to

gossip around here, you know I'm not used to much of anything in the romance department." She kept her tone light, ignoring her own general uneasiness.

Julia just smiled knowingly and departed, leaving the light scent of her perfume behind. Cozie went across the hall to her aunt. "Is Julia Vanackern in therapy?" she asked.

"Not that I know of. I heard she'd been seeing one of those psychics who reads Tarot cards, though. Why?"

"She just analyzed the entire Hawthorne family from Elijah on down. I wonder if there's a Tarot card for prigs. Maybe she drew it when she was thinking about us." She shrugged. "How do you think Pop regarded Frances Vanackern after she broke their engagement?"

"I believe," Aunt Ethel said as she flipped through her Rolodex, "that he regarded the entire incident as a bullet dodged."

"Did he trust her?"

"To do what?"

"Just as a human being."

Aunt Ethel looked up from her Rolodex. "What kind of drivel is that?"

Yeah, right: all Hawthornes were idealists. Julia should spend a day with Ethel Hawthorne. "You know what I mean."

"Frannie Tucker became Frances Vanackern when she married. She and your father and I had known each other all our lives. We'd all grown up together. But after she married—well, she used to invite me to Vanackern goings-on in the beginning, but after a while she gave up."

"You couldn't maintain your friendship because she married a Vanackern?"

"That was her way of looking at things, not mine."

"I see." Cozie started back to her office, not sure she did see. She stopped in the doorway. "One more thing. Does everyone in Vermont know not to give a Hawthorne an order?"

"I would hope so," her aunt said tartly.

# CHAPTER
# 13

━━➤

Daniel watched three fiery orange leaves drop onto
the clear, still water of the sawmill's tiny pond, the
slow current drawing them inexorably toward the
stone dam. Around him the trees glowed orange and
red and yellow in the early afternoon sunlight, as if the
woods were on fire.

Closer to the dam, the current picked up, sucking
the leaves over its edge into the fast-flowing, rocky
brook. He could almost smell the water's coldness.

A car sounded in his driveway, and he turned as
Julia Vanackern's Austin Healey slid in behind his
truck. She climbed out, the sunlight catching her hair,
making it sparkle. "Hi," she called. "Hope I'm not
catching you in the middle of something."

"Nothing important."

She came toward him. "I was just wondering—you
haven't seen Seth Hawthorne, have you?"

"No, I haven't. I've checked places that might have
hired him to serve as a hiking guide, but no luck so

far." What he should have done, he thought, was followed Cozie into the woods that morning.

Julia scowled. "He's not on any hike. I don't know what he thinks he's doing, but—" She broke off, inhaling sharply. Some of the edge came off her voice. "I'm sorry. I'm trying to keep an open mind. Dad found more stuff missing, and he's fairly sure he saw Seth up at the house last night, and now he's insisting on going to the police in the morning if Seth doesn't come forward."

Daniel, judicious for a change, said nothing.

Sudden tears shone in Julia's eyes, and she looked up at the sky as if to keep them from spilling. "I don't know what's going on with him."

"He could just be scared," Daniel said. "Me sniffing around, your family asking questions—he doesn't have to be guilty to feel a little intimidated."

She looked at him, and the tears trailed down her cheeks. She didn't brush them away. Julia Vanackern wasn't, Daniel observed, a woman who got uglier when she cried. "Is that what you think?"

"I'm trying to withhold judgment. Would you like to come inside?"

She nodded, and Daniel lead the way up onto the porch, then into the sawmill kitchen. She perked up. "This is such a neat place, isn't it? I've only been in here a couple of times. Cozie did a wonderful job renovating. It was an absolute wreck when she got hold of it but still structurally sound. There was no interior to speak of—she and her father and Seth did all this." She folded her arms on her breasts and gazed out the kitchen window. "The setting's so beautiful."

"Would you like some iced tea?" Daniel asked. "I made up a pitcher, seeing how it's not the easiest thing to find up here this time of year."

She smiled. "I'd love some."

He got two tall glasses down from an open shelf and added ice, then got the pitcher from the refrigerator and filled them with tea. It was from a mix. He didn't mention that as he set the glasses on the table.

"It really is a shame," she said, sitting down, "that we couldn't have met under different circumstances. Does your family know you're here?"

He leaned against the sink. "Yes, they do."

"I'll bet your grandfather doesn't approve."

"I can't say any of them approve, but that's never worried me before."

She tried her tea, made no comment. "You just do as you please, don't you? I wish I could—but I always have to try to please everyone. Most of the time I end up pleasing no one, least of all myself."

Her "fling" with Seth Hawthorne hadn't pleased her family. But, then again, she'd kept the full extent of it from them.

"I don't think I met your sister—Susanna, isn't it?" she asked.

"That's right. She's a few years younger than I am. Once my grandfather accepts I'm not ever going to run Fox Oil, he'll realize what a gold mine the company has in Susanna. Our father already knows."

"Your mother?"

"She's terrific—just wants us all to be happy, so long as it's not doing something that'll get us thrown into jail."

Julia looked right at him. "What about killed?"

Daniel shrugged. "That, too."

"Fighting oil fires is dangerous work."

"Doesn't help matters when someone tries to blow your helicopter out from under you."

"You still think that's what happened?"

"I don't know what happened."

"I can't imagine . . ." She stared at her tea, a

tortured look coming over her. "I can't imagine Seth would try to kill me—or anyone. You don't know him. He's just not the type."

Daniel swallowed some tea. "I'm not accusing anyone of anything."

"It doesn't look good, his taking off—my father spotting him last night."

"He didn't go after him?"

She shook her head. "It was raining, and we had company."

"Wish I'd been there," Daniel said.

Julia was on her feet, moving across the small kitchen toward him, a sudden intensity coming over her. "In your heart of hearts, Daniel, do you think Seth's guilty of sabotaging your helicopter to get at me?" She searched him with her sapphire eyes. "Do you think I could drive a man to do such a thing?"

Daniel was not unmoved. Even J.D., who distrusted inherited wealth, wouldn't have been immune to Julia Vanackern's mix of vulnerability, beauty, and instinctive sexiness. There were layers and layers of mystery to peel away—or maybe that was just what she wanted men to believe. Would a man ever know what he was getting was the real Julia Vanackern or just some manifestation of what she thought he wanted her to be?

Not so, he thought, with Cozie Hawthorne. Come hell or high water, she was what she was.

Julia was so close he could smell her light perfume, see the pale highlights in her hair. "You're not going to give me an answer," she said softly.

"I don't have an answer, except that whatever he did or didn't do, Seth Hawthorne's responsible for his own actions. Not you."

"I can see why your grandfather said you would have made general if you'd stayed in the military.

221

You're an impossible man to read." She spun out away from him, the ends of her hair just missing his chin. "Thanks for the tea."

"Where are you headed?"

"Mum and I have a tennis game scheduled. She's a *brutal* competitor." She gave him a strained smile. "She just wants me to be happy, too—so long as it's doing something she thinks a Vanackern ought to do. Sometimes I think she's more of a Vanackern than Dad is. Well, I'm off. Will you let me know if you run into Seth?"

Daniel pulled himself away from the counter. "I don't see why not."

"And if you see Cozie, tell her my father *will* go to the police. If she knows where Seth is, she'd be doing him a favor by getting him to come forward. She's always had more influence over him than anyone else has."

"I'll tell her, if I see her."

"Oh," Julia said, "I think you'll see her."

After she left, Daniel called J.D. from the extension in the kitchen. He was alert and ornery, more the old J.D. The salvage crew had found the helicopter and thought they could pull it out of the shallow gulf waters in one piece. Then they'd bring in the experts to go over it.

"Oh, and your granddaddy came by this morning," J.D. said. "Told me I looked like death warmed over, which was better than being dead but not much. I think mostly he was checking up on you. I didn't tell him you were falling for some loud-mouthed Yankee. He might have sent in the troops."

Daniel chose not to tell J.D. about last night with Cozie and the bat. "He's not planning on interfering, is he?"

"You don't think he'd tell me?"

"No, I guess I don't."

Then, almost as an aside, J.D. added, "Doctors say I've got an infection in my leg. They've got me on extra doses of antibiotics, but they might have to go in and clean things up."

A cold chill went through Daniel. "J.D.—"

"Yeah, yeah, if it's a choice between saving me and saving my leg, they can have the damned leg. Look, if I have to go under, I won't be able to keep up with the salvage crew until I get coherent again."

"Don't worry about it. You've done plenty."

"It's given me something to do besides watching the talk shows and soaps—and I got myself hooked on C-SPAN. Love those one-minute congressional speeches. Nurse is coming. Gotta go."

"You take care of yourself, J.D."

Daniel hung up and got on his leather jacket, heading out to his truck. He drove into town, getting used to the twisting, hilly, narrow Vermont roads. Cozie's Jeep was in her parking space outside the *Vermont Citizen.* He could see her through her office window and made a point of going slow past it, so she would know he was keeping an eye on her.

Back up Hawthorne Orchard Road, he tried Seth's again, but the sagging red farmhouse was still quiet, no sign he'd been around. Daniel left his truck in the driveway and walked out into the light woods behind the house, not knowing what he was looking for, what he'd find. How far had Cozie gone this morning? Had she found her brother?

About all Daniel accomplished was getting himself thoroughly lost. He managed to thrash his way back to his truck, cursing Cozie Hawthorne most of the way. But, hell, he thought, in her position he wouldn't trust him either. And it wasn't as if he trusted *her.*

He went back to the sawmill, back to the little mill

pond and the falling bright orange leaves. The temperature was tumbling fast. Tucked on the hillside, he couldn't see the night coming, not like he could from the front porch of his dilapidated ranch down home. But he knew it was closing in on dusk. He could tell by the change in the light, the feel of the air.

He wondered how Cozie would respond to a Texas sunset spread out on the horizon.

Without thinking, he launched himself down the narrow path along the edge of Hawthorne Brook. The air was filled with the earthy smells of damp pine needles and rotting ferns, of hemlocks that grew close to the brook. He kept moving, not pausing to reflect, to think about the fear—unarticulated and probably unacknowledged—he had heard in J.D.'s voice. J.D. would bluster his way through even the loss of a limb.

As the brook wound closer to Hawthorne Orchard Road, Daniel took the narrow, well-used path that led up a short, steep hill directly across from the black-shuttered white clapboard house. Smoke was curling out of the stone chimney. He could smell it as he walked up the loop-shaped dirt driveway.

A maroon minivan was parked alongside Cozie's battered Jeep. He spotted kids hauling pumpkins up from the garden, one little towheaded girl of maybe three struggling with a misshapen pumpkin about as big as she was. She wasn't about to abandon it or permit the two older boys, presumably her brothers, to help her.

Had to be a Hawthorne, Daniel thought.

Cozie was standing near the back steps with another woman, shorter, darker, a little heavier. The sister, Meg. They had their backs to him, unaware of his presence until Zep bounded up from the pumpkin patch to greet him.

"Well," the darker woman said, turning around,

"you must be Cozie's infamous new tenant. I'm Meg, her not-so-infamous sister. I saw you from a distance the other day."

She gave him a frank once-over, measuring him, Daniel guessed, against the gossip-generated image she had. Then he noticed the old aunt, Ethel, walking up from the garden with two small pumpkins. Sugar pumpkins, she called them. "I'm making soup," she told him, eyeing him warily. "I'll bet you've never had pumpkin soup."

"No, ma'am, I can honestly say I haven't."

"Thelma puts curry in hers. I just like a touch of cinnamon and nutmeg in mine—tastes like a pumpkin pie without all the sugar."

Sounded lovely.

"Daniel," Cozie intervened, "I'd like you to meet my nephews and niece. Ethan, Matthew, and Sarah, this is my new neighbor, Daniel—" She faltered. The aunt smirked, waiting.

"Hi, guys," Daniel said. What did a last name matter to kids? "Nice pumpkins. Going to make soup out of them?"

No way, they said, theirs were for jack-o'-lanterns, they hated pumpkin soup. "And we're not going to let anybody steal them and roll them down the hill," Ethan, the older boy, said.

Daniel looked to Cozie for translation.

She smiled. "Kids like to swipe pumpkins and roll them down some of the steeper hills, see how far they go before they get smashed. It's a sort of Halloween tradition."

"Charming custom."

Ethel sniffed. "I don't mind so much if they use their own pumpkins, but they ought not to steal somebody else's."

Daniel guessed he'd rather roll a pumpkin down a

225

hill than make soup out of it, but he didn't tell Ethel Hawthorne.

A rangy, fair-haired man around his own age came out the back door. The kids swarmed. At least one pumpkin landed on his toe. He introduced himself as Meg's husband, Tom Strout, and, generally unfazed by the bedlam, proceeded to pile kids and pumpkins into the minivan.

"Nice meeting you, Daniel," Meg said on her way to join her family. "Cozie's keeping me posted. I'm in her corner, you know. And my brother's."

"Message received," he said.

The old aunt, he noted, had no visible means of transportation unless by broomstick. She continued to keep a close eye on him while Cozie saw her sister off. "Meg and Tom are going off shopping over the river in New Hampshire. Cozie's giving me a ride home. I guess it won't matter if she leaves you here alone a few minutes. From what I hear, you'll do as you please regardless."

Under the circumstances, especially with these people, it wasn't a bad reputation to have. "Your nephew hasn't turned up yet, has he?"

"You know, I've gone more than two days without seeing Seth and not worried one bit." She tucked her pumpkins up on one bony arm like she would a fat baby. "Those calls my niece has been getting worry me more than the idea Seth might have swiped a few things from the Vanackerns."

"I can understand that."

"My nephew's not behind them, if that's what you're thinking."

Daniel wondered how many had made the mistake of underestimating Ethel Hawthorne. A breeze stirred, and he could feel the cold right through his leather jacket. He zipped it up. "If he's innocent, all the more reason he should come out of hiding."

The old woman snorted in disbelief. "If you'll excuse my saying so, I wouldn't want to face an interrogation by the likes of you either. So. You *are* watching out for Cozie, aren't you?"

Daniel stared at her but realized she wasn't being inconsistent. As much as she didn't trust him on other accounts, Ethel Hawthorne trusted him to look after her hotheaded niece. He smiled, and laid on the Texas twang. "I am sticking to her like a burr to a dog's hind leg."

"If he is," Cozie snapped behind him, "it's only because he thinks I can lead him to Seth. Come on, Aunt Ethel, I'll run you home. Are you sure you don't want any more pumpkins? I've got plenty. I'm just going to compost them if you don't use them. Tell Thelma she can have as many as she wants."

They headed for the Jeep without any further acknowledgment of Daniel's presence. The aunt climbed into the passenger seat as casually and comfortably as if it had been a Cadillac. She probably could split wood and throw a blanket over a bat, too, and Daniel would bet that a few garter snakes in the cellar didn't give her pause. He patted Zep on the head as he watched the two Hawthorne women depart. He considered heading down to the garden and picking out a couple of pumpkins for the sawmill porch. Just let some bored Vermont kid try to steal them to roll down some damned hill.

Crows wheeled and cawed overhead in the waning sunshine, drawing him out to the side of the house, past a crabapple. He could smell the sweet-sour odor of the rotting fruit, clinging to branches and scattered on the ground.

And he asked himself: why the Hawthorne pow-wow?

He plucked a sorry-looking crabapple. It was soft and wormy, with spreading brown spots. He pitched it up and over the toolshed. Zep, the dope, chased it. Daniel grabbed another.

Meg, Ethel, and Cozie Hawthorne had joined forces to discuss Seth's predicament. If Cozie had found him that morning, she'd told them where he was. If she hadn't, they'd put their heads together and figured it out. He was one of their own. They knew his habits; they knew the territory. They'd figured it out. For all Daniel knew, they could already have fetched him. Cozie could have had him tucked in her Jeep, Meg in her minivan. Aunt Ethel could be making pumpkin soup for him.

The next crabapple splattered on the toolshed roof.

Daniel thought of J.D., of his own family in Texas, imagined what they were doing—would they have a powwow to discuss his trip north? He imagined the heat, the shade of live oak, the cries of migrating birds on their way south to warmer climates.

His next crabapple cleared the toolshed roof. He had a few minutes until Cozie got back—enough time, surely, to take a look around the place and see if Seth Hawthorne was stuck in with the bats and snakes.

Cozie stood at the top of the stairs in the corner by the woodstove, not all that surprised to find Daniel coming up from the cellar. "Hunting snakes, I suppose?"

He grinned at her, totally unembarrassed. "Garter snakes aren't worth hunting. I save my energy for rattlers."

"You're being sarcastic," she said.

He came up beside her. "Smart lady."

She went back around the woodstove and dropped into her father's chair, having promised Aunt Ethel to be circumspect around "her Texan," whom she apparently trusted to keep her niece from bodily harm and not to miss a trick. But everything about him—his untucked shirttail, his western boots—struck Cozie as casual, rugged, sexy. It wasn't going to be easy to keep her focus.

"You didn't find Seth," she said, "because he's not here."

"But you know where he is."

"You know, I can see how people think you're arrogant. You always sound so damned sure of yourself."

"In this case, I am."

She did, of course, know where her brother was. She wanted to sneak out to the monk hut to ask him about the Vanackerns' missing jewelry and what he'd been doing out at their place last night, but now she had Daniel to contend with.

He shoved a log on the woodstove fire. "How long have you had snakes?"

So he wasn't going to badger her about Seth's whereabouts—or he was just buying time, plotting his next move. "I noticed them when I moved in this summer. Who knows how long they've been here. Mother always had a live-and-let-live attitude toward them. Figured they kept the mouse population under control. Not me. I hate snakes."

"Your parents must have been quite a pair," Daniel said, turning to her.

"They were. My mother was devastated by Pop's death, but she gave herself time to recover; she didn't push it. She seems comfortable with her decision to move out. She loves having the freedom to travel."

"And the money, I would think."

229

Cozie shrugged. "It helps."

He came and sat on the couch, near her. "Did you buy this place because of her, or yourself?"

"Both."

"But did you want it?"

"I can't imagine being without it. If Mother had had to sell to strangers . . ." She sighed. "It would have been really hard. But it would be better than seeing her suffer, pass up all the things she's wanted to do. It was her choice."

"What about you? What are you passing up by sinking so much time and money into this place?"

She didn't answer at once. She listened to the crackle of the fire in the woodstove and leaned back against the lumpy cushion of the old chair. "I don't think it's a question of what I've passed up but what I've taken on," she said at length. "Sometimes I miss my sawmill—I rattle around in here like a pea at the bottom of a barrel. And the house needs work. That's obvious. I don't mind that. But the land . . . it's a part of who I am. I don't mind taking that on."

"What about your brother?"

She gave him a sharp look; she'd fallen into the bastard's trap. "What do you mean?"

"It's different, mooching off your mother and mooching off your sister."

"He's not mooching."

Daniel didn't back off. "Your success has changed his life as well as yours and your mother's. When you bought this place, he couldn't pretend anymore that he'd get his act together in time to buy it himself or that your mother might will it to him. You took that option—that fantasy—away."

"I don't know that he ever had that fantasy. You don't either." She tightened her hands into fists on her lap, trying to keep her tension under control. "And even if he did, it doesn't mean he sabotaged your helicopter."

"No," Daniel allowed, "it doesn't."

"Things happen in life that we don't necessarily want to happen—that we don't expect. You didn't want or expect your helicopter to crash. I wanted my book to do well, but I never expected it would do as well as it did. It's how we respond to the unexpected that counts."

"And how have you responded to your unexpected success? By doing everything you can to pretend that nothing's changed when everyone around you knows it has." He leaned forward, not touching her. "You're afraid your success—the fame, the money, the travel —has changed you."

"Afraid it *will* change me, maybe. So far it hasn't."

His eyes held hers. "Hasn't it?"

She scowled. "No."

"I don't believe you."

"You didn't know me before. And you're not one to talk: I could say you're up here because you're afraid to face the results of your helicopter going down in the Gulf of Mexico. Your friend was seriously injured, your reputation tarnished. Better to blame someone else for what happened even when you know you've no one to blame but yourself."

Daniel simply said, "I'm not here to assign blame, I'm here to get answers. If I am responsible, so be it."

His response surprised her, mainly because he hadn't told her to go to hell and gotten up and walked out. "You're not afraid of facing that fact?" she asked.

"Oh, I'm afraid. But I'll do it."

She nodded, believing him. "I admire your courage."

His slate eyes darkened. "It's not courage: J.D.'ll hold my feet to the fire until I admit I screwed up." He got to his feet, his mood lightening as if by sheer will. "I'm up for a little dinner. I suggest we go out and really get the gossip mill churning. And don't say we can eat here. I've checked your refrigerator: slim pickings, Ms. Cozie. Course, I could go down to the cellar and catch us a snake for supper."

"We'll go out," Cozie said.

They ate at a popular Mexican restaurant over in Quechee. Daniel muttered about cultural encroachment, but he finally admitted the food was pretty good. They talked Mexican food and all its regional incarnations and worked their way into politics and farming and airline food, skirting the issues that had brought them together on a chilly October night. Although casual and uninhibited in his remarks, Daniel, Cozie felt, remained on edge, alert, wary, as if he expected her to jump up and pluck a bat out of the air at any moment. Or something.

The wind had picked up by the time they left, and Cozie buttoned up her field jacket as they headed to his truck. Being a man who believed in locks, he had to unlock the passenger door for her. "I can feel winter in the air," she said.

"It's only October."

"Exactly."

Next to her in the truck, she was more aware than ever of his size and strength. He slid his arm across the top of the seat as he looked over his shoulder to back out of their parking space. She watched the muscles in his forearms work as he drove.

When they reached Hawthorne Orchard Road, the wind was howling. "Hope your brother's holed up in a sheltered spot," Daniel said. "Should be a rough night."

"Seth's used to much worse conditions." And she

added stubbornly, "Besides, he never takes a group out that's not properly equipped."

Daniel cast her a look. "I thought we weren't going to lie to each other."

"I'm not lying: he never takes a group out—"

"I heard you." He made a sound of pure disgust. "Has a Hawthorne ever lost an argument?"

She smiled. "Not when we're right."

"What are you going to do when Thad Vanackern goes to the police in the morning?"

Cozie felt herself pale, her smile disappear.

"You didn't know," Daniel said.

She shook her head.

"Julia stopped by the sawmill this afternoon and said if Seth didn't come forward by morning, her father would go to the police. I assumed you knew."

They'd come to her driveway. "You can just drop me off," Cozie said, abruptly. She *had* to get out to see Seth, talk sense into him. "I'll be fine."

Daniel glanced at her, but she couldn't gauge his expression in the darkness. But she could feel his intensity. It virtually crackled in the air between them. "I promised Aunt Ethel I wouldn't let you out of my sight."

She inhaled. "I don't need your protection."

"I know: you, Zep, and your crowbar can ward off any manner of desperado." He turned up her driveway and parked next to her Jeep. "You're still not getting rid of me."

When he climbed out, Cozie didn't even argue. She had no idea why she was cooperating beyond a growing awareness that arguing with Daniel Foxworth was exhausting and futile when he thought someone's safety and his precious answers were at stake.

And, she admitted as she followed him into the house, she really didn't want to be alone. As much as she wanted to see Seth, the wind was howling, the night was dark, and probably no matter what her brother did, the Vanackerns were going to the police in the morning. They had their excuse. They were just waiting so they looked noble, not ones to rush to judgment.

"Heck," she muttered under her breath, "that's enough for me."

But it wasn't all. She knew it wasn't. She'd been dealing with howling winds, dark nights, and Van-ackerns her whole life—but not a slate-eyed Texan who intrigued her in a thousand different ways.

He set about rekindling the fire in her woodstove, making himself right at home. "Temperature drops fast after dark in this part of the country, doesn't it?"

She nodded, returning to the back porch to feed Zep. She could hear the wind pushing against the windows, and Daniel at the stove, moving with a steadiness and purpose she'd come to expect of him. When she returned to the back room, the stove was giving off a welcome heat. She thought of Seth alone in the monk hut. Would the police issue a warrant for his arrest? Should she give Daniel the slip and go warn him?

Had anyone ever succeeded in sneaking out on Daniel Foxworth?

There were no messages on her answering machine. She hadn't heard anything from her caller since morning.

If it was Seth and he hadn't been able to get to a phone . . .

She shut her eyes, refusing to finish the thought. How could she even speculate about such a thing? It was disloyal. Crazy.

"I'll make tea," she said abruptly.

She went to the kitchen for a teapot and a couple of herbal teabags, not wanting to add any caffeine to her system. She brought them and two mugs to the back room. Daniel could join her or not. He was sitting on the couch, watching her.

"Do you have any other theories about what could have happened to your helicopter? Seth couldn't have sabotaged it," she said, "and I have to admit that I can't imagine you just leaving explosives around to blow up by accident. That kind of recklessness doesn't seem within your character. Why were people down in Texas so willing to assume you were arrogant and reckless?"

"Because I'm a Foxworth," he said without bitterness. "We're known for getting what we want, regardless of the cost. I wanted to get to that fire. Why take the time to check the explosives I had tied down in back, make sure nobody had tampered with them?"

"Could the explosion have been a simple accident —spontaneous combustion or something where no one would be to blame?"

"No. Either I screwed up or someone planted a small explosive device on board."

"Seth wouldn't know—"

"He would, Cozie. He's done a lot of forestry work. He'd know how to attach a timing device to a couple of detonator caps. He might not know the explosion wouldn't be enough to blow a helicopter to smithereens, but he'd know it'd cause some serious damage in the right place."

The water in the copper kettle was hot. She poured it over the teabags in the pot, welcoming the warmth of the steam, the spicy scent of the tea. "Couldn't it have been someone else?"

Daniel was on his feet. "I hope it was," he said.

He abruptly started up the back stairs. Cozie gestured to him with an empty mug. "Don't you want any tea?"

"No, thanks. Don't think I could take herbs after Mexican food. Think I'll head on up to a warm bed and a decent book, put this mess out of my mind for a while." And he added in that voice that curled up her spine, "Good night."

That was that. No fireworks, no nothing. Cozie poured herself a mug of tea and sat on the couch, groaning inwardly. She could hear him moving around above her. Her awareness of him, the wave after wave of sensual heat inundating her—none of it was going away. Even the sounds of the floorboards creaking seemed sexy to her, overpowering in their intimacy.

What would he do if she turned up the television real loud?

She sighed and called upstairs, "You have everything you need up there?"

"Not quite," he said.

He didn't need to elaborate. She knew damned well what he meant. She abandoned her tea and headed for the bathroom and a hot shower. But as she peeled off her clothes and climbed under the hot water, sponged her body with an almond soap, it struck her. She jumped from the shower, pulled on the terry-cloth robe she kept on a hook on the bathroom door, and yelled up at the back room ceiling.

"You sneaky bastard, you're hoping I'll take advantage of your being upstairs and go after Seth, so you can follow. You think I know where he is."

Daniel, naturally, hadn't gone to sleep. She could easily hear his voice from upstairs. "I *know* you know where he is."

She flew up the back stairs, well ahead of her

common sense, but it wasn't until she was standing in front of Daniel's bed that she consciously realized she'd made a mistake. He had his bedside light on, a book opened on his lap. But his eyes were on her. Her skin was still warm and damp. Her robe had fallen open in her mad dash upstairs.

He started to say something, but she shook her head. "No, don't. Don't say a word."

And she knew what she wanted; it was all suddenly so very clear in her own mind. She slid her robe off her shoulders, let it drop to the floor. Her eyes stayed on his. He remained very still. He was sitting up in bed, a thriller open on his lap. She took it from him and laid it on the bedside table.

"Cozie . . ."

"It's okay." She drew back the covers, climbing in beside him, feeling his skin warm and hard. "Unless you—"

But he'd already turned to her, his mouth seizing hers, and there was no question in her mind, none, that she wasn't exactly where she wanted to be. A rush of heat inundated her, right to the very center of her.

He pulled her onto him, her hair hanging down her front as she took in the sight of him, felt his masculine body beneath her. She was only marginally surprised by how comfortable she felt, how right. Her body melded with his in all the right spots as she straddled his hips, her wet heat already pressed against him. His hands skimmed slowly up her sides and curved over her breasts, lingering there. She shuddered with a warm, liquid desire.

"I've been imagining you here with me," he murmured.

She ran her fingers through the dark, curling hair on his chest, up along the steely muscles of his shoulders, down his arms. He was tanned and hard everywhere she touched. She noted the scars, big and little, fresh and well healed.

"It's grueling work, isn't it," she said, "doing what you do?"

"Sometimes."

Her fingers were splayed on his chest as if absorbing through the skin everything about him she desired, as if memorizing the feel of him. Tonight was special. She would remember it.

He slid his palms back down her sides, cupping her bottom, lifting her, moving her against him so erotically, so boldly, she gasped and lowered her mouth to his. But before their tongues joined, he whispered, "I can't imagine ever not wanting you," and his words sent a heat pouring through her.

And he tasted her, gently at first, but whatever hunger he had for her, whatever need, rose up from the depths of him, and his tongue explored her mouth with a probing heat matched only by his heavy, swollen, thrusting maleness. Things were going to happen fast between them, she knew. Explosively. Just as she'd imagined.

"I want you, honey." His breath was coming in ragged gasps. "I want you now."

She thought she would explode just with the power of his bridled passion. He clutched her bottom, his fingers digging into her buttocks. He lifted her. She felt the tip of his erection in the hot, wet part of her that was pulsing with a longing wilder, more insatiable, than she'd ever known.

He stroked her, slowly, holding back his own need.

A fierce tremble rocked her to her toes even as an erotic tension seized her and refused to let go, moaning as she turned back her climax. He kept stroking, pushing her throbbing heat up and down the hard length of him. Her world was focused there, on her raw, aching desire. Nothing could penetrate it.

He raised her higher, and when he pulled her down again, he was inside her. For a long moment neither moved. Then they couldn't stop.

"Oh, honey."

His sandpaper drawl only excited her more. He responded, no longer holding back.

When the shattering spasms came, Cozie felt an overwhelming joy, a whirlwind of emotions that compelled her to look at the man beneath her, to see beyond the physical pleasure he was giving her to the human being he was.

She wanted him a part of her life forever. But it didn't seem possible. The odds were so stacked against them. She snuggled against his warm shoulder, her tangled hair spilling over his chest.

"Stop thinking, Cozie," he whispered. "It doesn't do either of us any good."

Trust in others, Daniel decided as he pulled on his boots, was not a Hawthorne long suit.

The sky was brightening with the approach of dawn. Cozie had slipped out of bed and tiptoed down to her room, obviously thinking he was still asleep. He'd groggily thought she just wanted to wake up in her own bed. She had things to figure out. So did he.

But he'd been wrong.

Fully awake now, he snatched up a shirt and stepped over her discarded bathrobe, then took the steep back stairs as fast as he dared. She had a good head start on him. Even when he'd heard her slipping downstairs, he'd figured she couldn't get back to sleep and was just going to put on a pot of coffee and watch the birds.

"Right, bubba," he muttered, bursting onto the cold back porch. He pulled on his shirt.

She hadn't made coffee or lit the woodstove or watched the birds. She'd snuck her little butt out the front door. If Zep hadn't tried to follow her, Daniel would still be oblivious. But she'd had to get her dog back inside, and that was when he'd realized his green-eyed Yankee was up to something. He should have been expecting it.

He stood out on the stone landing and scanned the fields and hills. Dawn was breaking out across the horizon in streaks of lavender and rose and orange, and the air was cold, a heavy frost shrouding the landscape. His breath formed clouds in front of his mouth.

Not a sign of her.

He walked up the slope to the trio of apple trees and stood very still, squinting in the distance, listening. This was her turf. He didn't even know what direction she'd gone. She was on foot: he knew that much because her Jeep was still parked outside beside his truck.

Definitely he should have clamped an arm over her when she'd sneaked out of bed. She wouldn't have gone far after that.

He returned to the chilly, empty house and put on a pot of coffee and started the woodstove. He sat near the fire with a mug of coffee and the atlas he'd had out yesterday, hoping something might pop out that hadn't so far. Wherever Seth Hawthorne was hiding, it was close and Cozie was on her way there. But though she might have gotten the better of him this time, Daniel wasn't concerned. He was in the house where Hawthornes had been living for two centuries. She'd be back.

# CHAPTER
# 14

Cozie slowed as she approached the cluster of boulders that marked the entrance to the monk hut. The woods seemed curiously silent. She could hear only her breathing and the cry of a few birds.

"Seth? It's me, Cozie."

No answer.

She wondered if he was asleep and crept horizontally across the steep hill, closer to the opening. Twigs crunched behind her and there was a rustling of the dried leaves underfoot. She immediately assumed Zep had snuck out of the house and started to turn to call him.

But something hard struck her in the middle of her back, pitching her forward, up off her feet over the steep grade of the hill. She came down on her side, jamming her shoulder into the fallen pine needles and leaves, but her momentum kept her going even as she yelled out in pain, shock, and fear. She tumbled and rolled through the undergrowth of ferns, princess pine, oak and evergreen seedlings. She couldn't grab hold of anything strong enough to stop her. She couldn't breathe. Sticks and rocks and pine cones bit into her hands and arms even as she tried to protect her face.

An image flashed of her and Meg and Seth rolling down hills in blankets as kids. She'd always gotten dizzy, sick to her stomach.

She plunged sideways into a tree that had fallen vertically up the hill. A half-rotted pine. She could smell it.

It was shifting, rolling back toward her. She couldn't scoot out of its path fast enough as it lost whatever precarious balance that had been keeping it from crashing to the bottom of the ravine.

*"No!"*

The thick, rotting trunk slid onto her legs and stopped, having found something else to impede its progress down the hill. Her.

The soft ground and the sharp angle of the hill held some of its weight off her legs. But she couldn't pull them free. By now her head was pointed downhill. Even if she could manage to budge the tree, it could end up rolling over her chest and face, doing worse damage. She lay still. She needed to catch her breath, *think* before she acted.

Was whoever had pushed her coming after her?

She heard only her own labored breathing. Her lungs ached. Her head was spinning. Her stomach had turned. She spit dirt and bits of pine needles and leaves from her mouth. Scratches on her arms and hands and one on her face stung.

She shut her eyes, concentrated on her breathing, on not throwing up. Best, she thought, to feign unconsciousness and let the SOB make good his or her escape.

*Seth.*

Was her brother all right?

She couldn't get ahead of herself. She had to believe Seth was fine unless she had proof otherwise.

*Could he have pushed you?*

No. No, no, no. Whoever had pushed her hadn't given a damn if she'd cracked her head open on a rock and died on the spot. Seth did give a damn. He was her brother.

All this time she'd refused to believe that anyone, least of all herself, was in any real danger. Daniel's near-fatal helicopter crash aside, a few creepy phone calls, thefts, and break-ins hadn't seemed life-threatening. Unnerving, frustrating, annoying, the work of someone who plainly had it in for her—but not someone really, seriously dangerous. What if she were dealing with a killer?

Of course, if the bastard who'd pushed her scooted down the hill and finished the job, she'd know for sure, wouldn't she?

Her gallows humor didn't make her feel any better. She was still trapped under a tree in the middle of the woods, and if she did try to extricate herself, and the tree twisted and fell on her chest or neck, she could end up in a worse mess.

She racked her brain. If not Seth, who could have pushed her? Who'd want to?

"Who wouldn't," she muttered under her breath, opening her eyes and staring up at the clear blue sky above the canopy of pine and oak and yellow-leafed maples and poplars. It was going to be a gorgeous day. Surely she was being overly dramatic. *Surely* she could wriggle out from under the tree without seriously injuring herself.

But when she moved her trapped legs, the tree shifted and creaked ominously, one thick branch, she now noticed, maybe a foot above the back of her head. If it came down on top of her, she'd have a face full of tree. She stopped moving her leg.

She tried to distract herself from her immediate situation. Suppose one person were responsible for all the mayhem—the calls, the helicopter crash, the thefts, the break-ins. That person would have to be someone who had been in Texas when the Maguire-Foxworth helicopter went down and someone who was here now.

Seth, the Vanackerns, Daniel Foxworth.

Or it could be some unknown individual who'd thus far remained out of sight, off everyone's list of suspects.

Cozie sighed. Nothing made any sense. Her leg hurt, and she was going to end up with a caffeine-withdrawal headache to go with everything else.

Why would a Vanackern sabotage a helicopter that Julia was supposed to be aboard?

Of course, she had changed her mind at the last minute and hadn't been on board. So why sabotage a helicopter in which two men the Vanackerns didn't know, one of whom they'd never even met, were flying?

Seth's guilt, Cozie had to admit, sounded more plausible, if only marginally so.

"So forget the chopper." Her voice was hoarse; she sounded rattled—scared—even to herself. "Life is full of bizarre coincidences and the chopper crashing into the Gulf of Mexico could be one of them."

Her head was throbbing now. Her left foot itched where she couldn't reach. What if her assailant had gotten to her brother? What if—

"Don't get ahead of yourself. *Don't.*"

She was thirsty. What she wouldn't give for a glass of cold apple cider.

A rustling sound up on the hill startled her, and even with her pounding heart she shut her eyes and prepared to feign unconsciousness.

But she heard a dog's pant, and then Zep catapulted toward her, saliva flying, tongue wagging. He licked her face.

"What are you doing out? Don't touch the tree, Zep," she warned. "All I need is to be killed or paralyzed by my own damned dog. Where were you twenty minutes ago?"

Something caught his attention, his ears going up. He started barking and streaked back up the hill, out of sight.

"Useless mutt."

Still, she could feel the panic well up inside her. She hated not being able to move, being trapped, a sitting duck. The tree probably had ants. Termites. It'd just be a matter of time before they were crawling over her.

She shuddered. Meg and Aunt Ethel knew Seth was hiding in the monk hut, but it'd be several hours before they figured out she was missing and thought to look there.

"You're going to have to take your chances with the tree, kiddo," she told herself.

Probably she was exaggerating the potential for real damage. If she was quick, prepared, she could get out of its way or flip over onto her stomach and let her back take the blow. The steep incline of the hill could work to her advantage. With its greater weight, the tree would want to keep on rolling, hopefully without her.

Zep's barking died down, and she heard a male voice say, "Hey, Zep, old fellah, where's your sneaky master?"

Hell's bells. Daniel. Cozie didn't know whether to be mortified or relieved. She'd damned near rather take her chances with the tree or wait until Meg and Aunt Ethel found her.

"Cozie? You here?"

Then again, he was your basic military type. He was looking for her and he wouldn't stop until he found her.

"I'm down here," she yelled, trying to sound more in control of her own fate than, from all appearances, she was.

"Where?"

Was that a note of concern in his voice? She called, "Under the damned pine tree."

"Are you all right?"

She could hear him making his way toward her, wasting no time. Give the man a mission. "I'm stuck. I—" She hated this. "I could use a hand."

He was there. He circled around the fallen tree to her prone, trapped body. "You want to repeat that?"

"You heard me."

As he squatted down beside her, Cozie had to acknowledge a relief so powerful and immediate it brought tears to her eyes. Daniel was there. She was going to be all right.

"No broken bones?" he asked.

She shook her head.

His expression was grim, his gray eyes two pits of cold, hard steel. "A pity."

"I can see I don't have to worry about being coddled."

"Not when you insist on putting your head in the lion's mouth. It's a case of getting what you ask for." But he gently pulled a twig from her hair. "I take it you didn't fall."

"I most certainly did not. I know every inch of these woods. I was pushed."

He rose and walked around the tree, surveying the situation. "By whom?"

"I didn't see who—whoever it was hit me from behind. You didn't see anyone?"

"No."

"Seth . . . "

She sighed, warning herself not to jump to conclusions. "Are you going to get me out of here?"

"Would you like me to rush the job and break your leg? On the other hand," he said, walking back toward her, "that might not be a bad idea. It'd slow you down."

"How'd you figure out where I was?"

"Deductive reasoning. With you sneaking around out here yesterday and then again this morning, it made sense Seth would be hiding out nearby. So I took a look at my map of Woodstock and, lo and behold, there was a note of this old Druid's cave. Sounded like a good possibility to me."

"Very clever," she said.

He stood above her, looking very tall in his Texas boots, which were close enough to her head she could smell their leather. "Well, Ms. Cozie, you're in a fix."

She tried to rise up on her elbows, but the movement caused the tree to press painfully into her left leg. "How do I know it wasn't you who attacked me?"

"Honey," he drawled, "after last night I'd think you'd allow that when I attack you, you'll know it."

"Get this tree off me."

"As you wish, ma'am."

Moving to the middle of the tree, he bent at the knees and seized the trunk and raised it up off her. She scrambled free. Then he pretty much tossed the whole damned tree to one side. He wasn't even red in the face.

"Maybe it wasn't as heavy as I thought," she said.

Daniel brushed his hands off on his pants. "Maybe you're not as strong as I am."

She sat up, slowly. Her shin ached. She fought an unreasoning wave of panic now that she was free. "I didn't have good leverage."

He laughed and held out a hand to her. "All right, I suppose if I'd been in your position I'd have needed someone to peel that tree off me, too." His tone, however, was not serious.

"Don't patronize me. You'd have plucked that thing off you like a matchstick."

"Hell of a matchstick." She took his hand, and he pulled her to her feet. "You all in one piece?"

He hadn't released her. Standing close, she could hear his breathing. His hand was warm and steady on hers. "More or less. I just need to get my circulation back in my legs."

"Nice scratch," he said, and gently touched her forehead.

She swallowed. "I'm okay now."

"You sure? You want me to carry you up the hill?"

Her mouth went even drier. "I'm heavier than I look."

His grin was slow and sexy, utterly confident. "Honey, you don't look very heavy at all."

This just wasn't going to do. She backed away, but pain shot up from her left leg and it went out from under her. To her further humiliation, Daniel had to catch her by the elbow to keep her from falling flat on her face. "I'll be fine in a minute," she said, but she could hear her own uncertainty.

"Want me to take a look?"

"Daniel—"

"It's okay," he said softly. "Whoever pushed you is gone."

He seemed to sense that she'd used up all her reserves, her humor, her bravado, the parts of her she could steel to anything, and that what shreds of strength she had left needed a break. She needed just a few minutes to tremble and fight tears and acknowledge she'd been pushed down a hill and damned near killed. She let herself sink against the warmth of his chest, let him take her weight. Circulation returned to her lower legs. She felt the pain of every scratch and scrape. But a little of Aunt Ethel's special antibacterial ointment and all would be well.

She drew away from him and pulled twigs and leaves and pine needles from her hair. "Let's get this over with," she said, and started back up the hill.

She was too sore and shaky to move very fast, but determination and the thought of Daniel right behind her, ready to catch her if she stumbled, kept her going at a steady pace. When she came to the stone-lined chamber in the hillside, she was breathing hard, her badly scraped shin aching. But she didn't hesitate.

"Seth?"

She peered inside. His camping gear was packed, his sleeping bag rolled up. "Maybe he decided to come forward and got his stuff ready," she said as Daniel came up beside her.

"He could also have figured the wind was changing and decided to clear out, but you interrupted him making his exit."

Cozie just scowled and sank onto a small boulder while Daniel disappeared inside the monk hut and Zep wandered about uselessly. If Seth were nearby, Zep would find him.

Daniel emerged a few minutes later, his expression immediately telling her something was seriously wrong. She got stiffly to her feet. Adrenaline still had her heart pumping at a rapid rate.

In one hand he had a small mechanical device with little wires sticking out of it. She had no idea what it was.

But she could guess. "A detonator cap?"

He gave a curt, grim nod. "There are about a half-dozen of them in there. Whoever sabotaged my helicopter could have grabbed more than they could use from the case the caps were stored in. Maybe there was no time to put the extras back—or maybe the timing device was attached to blasting caps *inside* the case and the saboteur needed to make room."

"How convenient," Cozie said, "that they should show up now."

His eyes narrowed on her. "You think someone planted them here?"

"Of course!"

His expression remained intense, uncompromising. She wouldn't, she thought, want to get on the wrong side of Daniel Foxworth. He said, "If they're mine, I'll know it. We keep detailed records."

"Are you going to the police?" Her throat was tight and dry, her body rigid with rising tension.

"I don't take any pleasure in this, Cozie, and I'm still not ready to jump to any conclusions. The police can come out here and search the area, take fingerprints, do whatever it is they do. I'll wait and see what they find out."

"Good of you."

"In the meantime," he said patiently, "we need to get you back to the house and doctored up."

She brushed back strands of tangled hair with a shaking hand. Her fingers were cold and stiff. "I'd like to wait for Seth."

"Cozie, he's not coming back. If he pushed you, he won't risk it. If he didn't, he's probably not too far off and realizes I'm here."

"He didn't push me," she said stubbornly.

He didn't bother arguing it. "Let's go."

But she didn't move.

He sighed. "All right, what's on your mind?"

"You didn't plant those detonator caps yourself, did you? You didn't have them on you already when—"

"No," he said without expression, without hesitation. "No, I didn't."

She nodded, accepting his denial. If he could ask tough questions, so could she. "Then whoever pushed me planted them."

"Cozie—"

"I know it could have been Seth," she said. "Technically."

And she got to her feet unassisted, wincing at the pain shooting up from her left leg. The tree had done a damned good job on it.

Daniel shook his head. "J.D.'s going to have to meet you."

"He'd go ahead and carry me, wouldn't he?"

"Damned straight."

"You're thinking about it?"

He almost managed a smile. "I'll leave that for you to wonder."

As he walked behind Cozie, Daniel didn't want to admit how badly she'd scared him any more than she wanted to admit how much she hurt. She was limping and dazed, but too damned proud even to lean on him.

"You're worse than J.D.," he muttered, staying close to her. "When we were in Scotland putting out an oil fire, he practically blew himself to bits—but damned if he'd let anyone give him a hand. He had so much blood in his eyes he couldn't even see."

"What a charming story," Cozie said as she struggled along.

"I walked behind him and caught him when he passed out. You haven't seen J.D. He's got fifty pounds on me."

She gave him a cool look over her shoulder. He would lay odds she had no idea how pale she was. "I have no intention of passing out."

"Neither did he."

"Well," she said, resuming her limp along the old farm road, "I'm not J.D."

"Thank the good Lord for that. I've never wanted to kiss J.D."

He thought he saw a different kind of hesitation in her gait, one not brought on by pain and exhaustion. "That's not what I meant. You feel responsible for J.D. He's your partner and your friend; you two go back a long ways. You don't need to feel responsible for me."

"Did I say I feel responsible for you? I'm just tired of crawling along behind you waiting for you to collapse when I could be carrying you and moving a whole lot faster."

She dropped to the side of the road. "You can go ahead of me."

He stopped. "Not a chance, sweetheart. I'm not letting you out of my sight."

She frowned. He suspected she had a tough time knowing when he was deliberately trying to get under her skin and when he was doing it by accident.

"How bad's the left leg?" he asked.

"It's just the shin. I must have scraped it worse than I thought."

252

"Let's have a look."

She licked her lips. "It can wait."

"You know," he said, dropping to one knee in front of her, "you'd last about ten seconds in the military before someone beat you senseless. Maybe not even that long." He carefully raised her pant leg, exposing a well-shaped calf and a shinbone that was nastily bruised and scraped. "Looks like a tree fell on it."

"I didn't notice it much before. Adrenaline, I guess."

"Well, it doesn't need stitches—it's hardly bled. But walking on it can't be any fun. We don't have much further to go. You can make it?"

"Of course."

The woods lightened as they crossed the stream, with more birches and poplars and fewer pines and hemlocks. It was a perfect autumn morning by weather and scenery standards. Cozie didn't seem to notice. The scratch on her forehead stood out against her pale skin, and Daniel knew if he'd caught whoever pushed her, he'd probably still be beating the daylights out of the bastard.

But he also knew he was right to have come to Vermont. The answers to what had happened to him and J.D. over the Gulf of Mexico were here.

Cozie seemed to be in more pain than she wanted to admit. He sighed. "I'll bet you don't weigh more than the nozzle of one of my hoses."

His comment gave her a good excuse to stop. "There's enough gossip circulating about me without having my first-ever tenant dropping dead of a heart attack carrying me through a field."

With that, she resumed walking, her limp less pronounced if only through sheer willpower. Daniel followed along in the rear. "According to the old man in the country store, I'm more than your 'first-ever tenant.' I gather there's been a fair amount of speculation about your love life over the years."

Cozie cocked her head around at him. "Who is this old guy?"

"He said he's some friend of Ethel and Thelma."

"Royal. Royal Thornton. It has to be. Kind of on the short side, wears a Red Sox cap? He's been after Aunt Ethel for years. He thinks I'm just like her." She made a face and turned her attention back to the road. "Well, it's none of his business what I do up here or with whom." Another quick look back. "Or are you just making this up?"

"Nope, I'm not making it up. You can ask Royal if you want."

"Oh, sure, count on it."

Daniel noticed Cozie's pace slowing as her house came into view, as if she knew she was about to leave some fantasy world and re-enter reality.

"Are you going to call the police yourself?" he asked.

She pushed back her hair with both hands. "Let me get cleaned up first. Then I'll decide."

Nothing in her tone or expression suggested she believed for one second her brother could have pushed her down that hill. Daniel kept silent as they walked down the field to the house, side by side now. Cozie grimaced with every step. He wondered if she'd been doing that the entire way. But he thought he understood: she was a woman accustomed to carrying on without self-pity, counting on herself and her family. He thought about the work and determination her ancestors had required to clear and cultivate these fields with their thin, rocky soil, to endure the harsh, mercurial Vermont climate. Cozie Hawthorne needed, right now, to know she was a part of that gritty tradition—that she could walk through a field no matter her bruises, her fatigue, her mounting fears for her brother, even for herself.

He saw her stiffen and followed her gaze down to the toolshed, where Thad Vanackern waved to them. Cozie didn't wave back. Julia and Frances were behind him, their Mercedes parked in the loop of the driveway.

"Good morning," Thad called.

Cozie gave him a polite nod as she and Daniel came around the shed. "Good morning."

Thad got right to the point. "Cozie, Frances and I have decided to go to the police about the thefts. We wanted you to know."

She had no obvious reaction. "I see. Thank you for telling me. I'm sure it's best for all concerned."

"Have you seen Seth?" Julia asked, coming up beside her father. She had on slim tan jeans and an oversized Vermont sweatshirt, her hair gleaming in the morning sun.

Cozie picked bits of dead leaves from her tangled hair. "I think I'll save my comments for the police, should they decide to question me or my brother."

Thad gave a low hiss of exasperation. "Cozie, there's no need to be so stubborn. You can't possibly think our loyalty to you and your family would extend to covering up criminal acts."

She balled up her hands into tight fists, and Daniel figured she was just in the mood to take a swing at the snotty bastard. But she held her fire. "I'm quite sure I've never asked you to do anything for me or my family—for any reason."

Frances Vanackern touched her husband's arm. She was dressed in charcoal gray wool pants and a white cashmere turtleneck, a simple, elegant outfit that contributed to her regal bearing. She had an immediate calming effect on Thad. "Cozie, you know how sorry we are about what's been happening. We're all trying to keep an open mind."

"I hope so," Cozie said.

"I want you to know that I understand how difficult this must be for all of you. When I married Thad, my family and many of my friends had a hard time. They projected all their feelings of envy, all their inadequacies, onto me. Seth—"

Cozie's eyes flashed with anger as Frances's words sank in. "No, you don't understand. Seth doesn't care if I sell ten books or ten million books. It's just not an issue for him."

Thad looked as if he wished he could beam himself to a quiet golf course somewhere. "If it's any consolation, Cozie, I believe Seth wants to be caught. Why else would he be so obvious?"

"Obvious! Yeah, you're keeping an open mind all right."

"Your brother is a troubled young man." Thad's tone had hardened. "It's time you saw that."

Cozie swallowed, trembling, holding on to what remained of her self-control. Daniel longed to touch her, to hold her. But this, he knew, was her show. She said through clenched teeth, "My resignation will be faxed to Vanackern Media headquarters in the morning."

Frances gasped, but Thad made a face, impatient. "Don't cut off your nose to spite your face." But he frowned suddenly, searching her face as if seeing her for the first time. "What in God's name happened to you?"

"I fell."

She brushed past him to the back porch, tore open the door, and went inside.

Thad sighed and turned to Daniel. "She doesn't

make life easy on anybody who cares about her. She knows where Seth is, doesn't she?"

"Not anymore."

"You mean he—"

"He wasn't in the woods." Daniel saw no need to be more specific. "I didn't see him."

"What a terrible dilemma we're facing," Thad said. "If only we knew for certain what the right course of action is. Seth clearly has his troubles. He's had them for years. His family's just never wanted to see it."

Frances nodded in pained agreement. "He was never interested in the paper, and yet he never carried through with any of his plans for the land or anything else. He had those scrapes with the law a few years back. I'm afraid Duncan—his father—saw him as aimless and unambitious and was trying to force him into taking some responsibility for his life when he died."

"His death was a tremendous blow to everyone," Thad said, softening, and Daniel sensed a genuine affection for the departed Duncan Hawthorne. "If you look around this place, you can see the entire family struggled with finances for years. It was a terrible strain. I tend to believe Seth just became over-whelmed. His father's death, his sister's success, his failed romance with Julia—they were all too much for him. I think he just cracked."

"Cozie's going to need proof before she believes that," Daniel said, keeping his tone neutral.

"I know. And I believe I owe you an apology, Daniel. You came here thinking Seth might have sabotaged your helicopter, didn't you?"

"I just wanted to know why my partner and I ended up in the Gulf of Mexico. It had to make sense to me before I could move on."

"I hope you find out," Frances cut in softly. "Come, Thad, we should be going."

Thad, in a formal gesture, inclined his head slightly toward Daniel. "Please let us know if we can be of assistance. Say good-bye to Cozie for us."

Daniel nodded. "I will."

As they left, his eyes met Julia's, and she hung back as her parents climbed into their car. "Is Seth all right?" she asked softly.

"I don't know. I really haven't seen him."

"But Cozie did."

"I'm not speaking for her."

Julia compressed her lips in a knowing expression, and inhaled through her nostrils. "Well, I can see there's definitely something going on between you two. God, who'd have ever thought. But it's none of my business. If you do see Seth, I hope . . ." She faltered, her eyes shining. "Just tell him I care about what happens to him."

"When are you going to tell your parents the whole story about your relationship with him?"

She smiled coolly. "You mean that I slept with him?"

"It could come out in the police investigation."

"That," she said, waltzing off to the car, "is my worry."

She tossed him a half-sultry, half-defiant look. "I can handle the police—and my parents." *And,* her eyes, the set of her mouth, said, *I can handle you, too. Just try me.*

Daniel didn't rise to her challenge, and she sauntered off to her parents' car.

# CHAPTER

# 15

Stripped to her underwear, Cozie sat on the edge of the bathtub, prepared to disinfect and, if necessary, bandage her various scratches and scrapes. She had the first-aid kit opened up on the floor. It was in a black metal case about dictionary size, a haphazard collection of Band-Aids, adhesive tape, gauze, sterile cotton, hydrogen peroxide, and Aunt Ethel's miracle ointment, a thick goo that looked like motor oil and smelled a lot worse. Cozie hadn't touched the kit since she'd sliced open a knuckle planting tulips with her father the autumn before his death.

Everything in the old house, she thought, was a reminder of the past—and of how much her life had changed.

She turned on the hot water and let the tub fill. She would just soak her wounds clean. If she did a hurry-up job, as she'd intended, she would have to face Daniel and decide whether to go to the police

about what had happened—and what they'd found—
at the monk hut.

She peeled off her underwear and eased into the hot,
unscented water, biting back a yell when it hit her
various scrapes. But the stinging abated, and the heat
seeped into her, relaxing her tensed muscles.

After a while, a soft knock sounded on the door.
"You okay in there?" Daniel asked.

"Fine."

But the sound of his voice broke the spell, and she
groaned, prying herself from the tub. There was no
point putting off the inevitable any longer. She slathered on some of Aunt Ethel's goo and put her clothes
back on. She combed out her hair, leaving it hanging.
Her body ached right up to her eyelids. Daniel would
only say it served her right.

She returned to the back room, where he was
drinking a cup of coffee on the couch. He watched as
she held her hands over the woodstove, as if to warm
them. In reality, she just wasn't sure what else to do
with herself.

"You were awake the whole time I was sneaking out
this morning, weren't you?"

"Yep," he said, coming beside her.

"Why didn't you stop me?"

"Because I didn't think you'd get yourself up to
anything devious after what we did last night. I
thought you'd trust me more."

"I wasn't being devious."

"Just didn't want to wake me, huh?"

"Sure. Why not?"

"Because that's not how you think, and because it's
a flat-out lie." He stood very still beside her. "Don't
tell me anything if you feel you can't, but don't lie to
me."

His words stung. "I hate lying."

"I know. Cozie . . ."

She knew she was lost. There was a tenderness, a need, in the way he said her name. Cold and damp, suddenly sleepy from her bath and the heat of the woodstove, yet instantly aroused, she was a mass of contradictory sensations. Thad Vanackern was probably at the police station. She should find Seth. She needed to drink her coffee, find something to eat.

But she was sinking against Daniel's hard, warm chest, welcoming the feel of his arms around her, the strength of his body. If he let go, she would drop to the floor.

She made herself look up at him, into those steely eyes, but his mouth covered hers, seized hers with a hunger, a fierceness she'd already discovered lay within him. He immediately lifted her up and pulled her against him, leaving her with nowhere to put her legs except around his hips. His hardness thrust against her, boldly, as if he needed her to know just how much he wanted her.

His tongue plunged into her mouth, taking away her breath. She gasped for air, but he didn't let up, just pressed her more firmly against him, probed more deeply with his tongue. Desire surged through her like a wild fire. They might as well have been naked, making love.

"Sweet Cozie," he murmured, "if only you knew what you do to me."

"I've a fair idea."

"No, you don't. You don't have any idea."

His hands slid under her sweater, and she moaned at the feel of his fingers on her skin. They moved up her back and slipped beneath the damp, filmy fabric of her bra, deftly unclasping it. Then he found the naked flesh of one breast. His tongue thrust into her mouth again and again, in an erotic rhythm, and he lifted her shirt higher, kissing her throat, taking her nipple between his fingers. The sensations were blending—tongue, hands, throat, breast—until his mouth was on her breast and he was licking, tasting, and she cried out.

She thought she heard him moan.

"Take me upstairs," she whispered. "Carry me because I don't think I can walk."

But he pulled her sweater down. She could feel the shudder go through him as he lowered her to the floor, steadying her before he released her. His eyes were dark, hot coals, and the swelling in his jeans betrayed every millimeter of his own arousal. "I guess there won't be any pretending between us from here on out. You know what I want."

"I want the same thing."

"Do you?"

He walked out through the back porch, and she jumped when the door shut behind him. She didn't move until she heard his truck start. Maybe he'd decided to throw in his nickel's worth with the police. *It's possible Seth Hawthorne tried to kill me and my partner in Texas.*

"The hell with him," she said, ignoring the tears burning her eyes as she shoved another log on the fire. What *did* he want from her if not sex? She grabbed her coffee and headed upstairs for fresh clothes. Aunt Ethel and Meg would want their updates, and she had work to do. Let Daniel Foxworth do whatever he needed to do.

Daniel got cleaned up and changed at the sawmill and put Cozie Hawthorne if not out of his mind at least under a trap door somewhere at the back of it. But as he dialed the phone in the kitchen, he could still taste her. Could still feel her skin under his hands.

Not a good sign. He needed to keep his wits about him. He—and Cozie—needed to find her brother and get some straight answers from him.

He contacted the salvage crew directly, and the head of it told him they expected to bring up the helicopter today. Then the experts would have a look at it. He added, "Your grandfather was down last night asking."

That didn't sit well with Daniel. He hung up and called Austin Foxworth on his private line at Fox Oil headquarters. "Thanks," Daniel said, "but I don't need your help."

His grandfather didn't agree. "What the hell do you think you're going to accomplish bringing up that helicopter?"

"I have to know."

"What for? Since when do you care what people think?"

"It's not what people think. It's what I think." He didn't bother telling his grandfather about the detonator caps in Seth's hiding place. It was too complicated, too circumstantial, and it wouldn't change the old man's mind. He wanted Daniel back in Texas and the incident forgotten—or used to get him out of fire fighting and aboard at Fox Oil.

"The press is sniffing around," his grandfather said brusquely. "They get wind of what you're up to, it'll be all over the local papers. You want to take that risk?"

"I already have," Daniel said, starting to hang up.

"You haven't talked to the hospital yet, have you?" Austin Foxworth said. "Maguire's in surgery. They're after the infection. They'll keep the leg if they can. You hop a plane now, you might could see him when he comes to."

A trio of grackles landed on the sawmill's front

porch as Daniel dully thanked his grandfather for the information and hung up. He tried calling the hospital but they only told him what he already knew: J.D. was in surgery and they would know more in a few hours.

The grackles departed. Apparently there was nothing to keep them. Daniel wondered if he should follow their lead. But he filled the woodbox, stoked up the fire, and finally headed out, knowing he couldn't stay there watching the leaves fall and the birds fly.

Aunt Ethel was at her desk when Cozie arrived. In all her time at the paper, she'd never beaten her aunt to the office and doubted her father and grandfather had before her either.

"What in blue blazes happened to you?" her aunt demanded. "You been climbing trees again?"

"No, I went out to the monk hut—"

But Aunt Ethel pressed a finger to her lips, silencing her. "It'll have to wait. Will Rubeno's in your office. He wants to talk to you."

Cozie had no stomach for lying to the police. "I'll sneak out the back."

"No, you won't," Will said behind her.

She whirled around, feigning surprise. "Will, I didn't realize you were here." Technically it wasn't a lie: she could claim by "here" she meant right behind her, not in the building. "What's up? Do you have a suspect for the break-in?"

"You know why I'm here, Cozie. Thad Vanackern said he told you he was reporting the thefts. He should never have waited, but that's water over the dam." Will gave her one of his grim cop looks. "I've got to question Seth."

So Thad hadn't simply reported the money and valuables missing: he'd fingered her brother as a suspect. Sure, they were just trying to help. Then why not let the police investigate with an open mind? "Where's your probable cause?" she demanded.

Will made a sound of disgust mixed with disbelief, one he'd perfected since they were in the eighth grade together. "Probable cause? What the hell are you talking about? I just want to talk to him."

"Dammit, Will, you know Seth's not a thief!"

"We're not talking about what I know and don't know," he said sternly. "Where is he?"

It was a direct question from an officer of the law. "What makes you think I'd know?"

"Because you wouldn't rest until you did. Never mind. I won't tempt you to lie. I already know about the monk hut."

"How—"

Then she saw Daniel coming in from the center hall, behind Will. So that was how. His gray eyes met hers without any hint of his guilt or innocence. Had he told Will about the detonator caps, his belief his helicopter had been sabotaged?

"Tell me about these calls you've been receiving," Will said, but he didn't wait for her to make a denial. He held up a hand, silencing her. "Now don't get your back up: Meg told me that one. Said you'd have gotten around to it yourself if you didn't have so much else on your mind." He sounded highly dubious. "You have any evidence of these calls?"

"I did, but it disappeared."

"Disappeared?"

"That's right." She glanced at Aunt Ethel, who was busying herself at her desk but clearly listening to every word—and not about to rise to her niece's defense against an officer of the law, even Will Rubeno. "That was what the break-in here was about. Someone—presumably the caller or someone he or she hired—wanted to find any evidence I'd collected, didn't find anything here, then went up to the house and tried there."

Will's eyes narrowed on her. "You should have told me. What exactly did they get?"

"A log I'd kept of the calls."

"All of them?"

She nodded.

"They started this summer?"

"In July. I'm not sure of the exact date. I know I was in New York. I can check."

"Do that. Anything else?"

"A cassette from my answering machine recording one of the calls and a note I found on my Jeep Saturday night after the Vanackern dinner."

"You got anyone to corroborate any of this?"

"I saw the note on her Jeep," Daniel said quietly, "and I picked up one of the calls. They're for real."

Cozie was incensed. "Of course they're for real! Do you think I'd make up something like that?"

Will held up a silencing hand. "My point is, were you ever threatened, was there any attempt at blackmail, anything like that?"

She shook her head. "What could you do if there were?"

"We have a few options. You should sit down and tell us everything, let us decide if they might be more than nuisance calls."

"I'll consider it," she said, feeling more and more out of control of what was going on around her.

Will glared at her. "I'm reminding Meg what a pain in the butt you are so she won't chew me out for not doing my job. You don't know where Seth is?"

"No, truthfully, I do not. Are you calling out the dogs and the men with guns and going after him?"

"For God's sake, Cozie, we just want to talk to him. We don't even have a warrant for his arrest."

"Gee, what a relief."

Will spent five seconds staring at her in spitting fury, turning redder and redder. Then he exhaled, bit off a swear, and looked to Aunt Ethel. "I suppose you don't know anything?"

"Young man," she said haughtily, "I know a great deal, but I'm afraid I can't help you so far as my nephew is concerned. I haven't seen him since Sunday morning when he brought me cider doughnuts."

"You Hawthornes," Will muttered, as if that alone summed up his disgust. He scowled at her and turned back to Cozie. "If you hear from your brother, you know where to find me."

He headed out through the front hall.

"Good luck finding the Vanackerns' thief," she called to his retreating back. "It's not Seth."

When she was sure Will was gone, she ignored both Aunt Ethel and Daniel and marched through the back out to her Jeep. She was throwing it into reverse when Daniel pulled open the passenger door and climbed in. "Always count on a Hawthorne not to lock a door," he said mildly and glanced over at her. "You look mighty pissed off, Ms. Cozie. Guess I'd better put on my seat belt."

"Guess you'd better."

"Taking a ride up to see the Vanackerns?"

"You don't have to come. I didn't invite you."

"You'll notice," he said, locking his seat belt, "I didn't wait for an invitation."

With one foot lightly on the brake, the other on the clutch, she regarded him with a steadiness she didn't feel. "Did you tell Will you found detonator caps in the monk hut?"

"I decided to wait." Any amusement left his eyes. "I'm still gathering facts. When I've come to a definite conclusion, I'll let you know."

"Good of you," she said, and roared out of the driveway, around Woodstock common, onto the covered bridge over the Ottauquechee, and finally up onto Hawthorne Orchard Road.

She picked up speed as she passed her house and the sawmill and veered sharply onto the dirt road that led to Seth's and the Vanackern place. Daniel didn't ask her to slow down. He seemed, in fact, perfectly calm. She wondered what scared him. The prospect of his partner losing a leg? Of facing a shattered reputation?

When she rocketed past her brother's house, Will Rubeno's cruiser was already there. Her jaw clamped down tight. Was Seth behind a tree somewhere, watching?

Two minutes later, she pulled the Jeep to a hard stop in front of the Vanackerns' attractive colonial house. She had to pry her fingers loose from the steering wheel. She squinted over at Daniel. "You're not going to try and stop me?"

"Nope. I never get between a ticked-off woman and whatever she's shooting at."

"That's sexist."

"Same philosophy applies to a man. You going to sit here and gripe at me or get on with skewering the Vanackerns?"

"Thad didn't have to implicate Seth."

She climbed out of the Jeep, and Daniel said as she closed the door, "I'll be here whenever you run out of steam."

Thad Vanackern was waiting on the front steps when she got there. He had on tennis clothes that revealed how fit he was for a man in his late sixties. He regarded her for just a moment before saying, "Cozie, I know you're angry, but don't make this any uglier than it already is."

"What are you going to do, fire me? Go ahead. I

don't need your money, and it'd save me from having to resign—"

"It's not *my* money, it's corporation money, and it does no good for you or your brother for you to be so reactive. Think about what you're saying. If Seth would come forward, perhaps we could work something out—perhaps he could convince us of his innocence."

"Guilty until proven innocent, huh?"

He sighed, not a man comfortable with displays of any strong emotion, but especially anger. "Taking off this way leaves an impression of guilt, however unintended or wrong."

Cozie was not mollified just because she'd had the same thought. "Seth *always* takes off, he has since he was a little kid. It means he's upset if it means anything at all."

"Cozie," Thad said through his teeth, "I'm not required to explain my decisions to you. If you're too stubborn to see that we care deeply about you and your family, that, I'm afraid, is your problem. We understand the pressures on your family the past few years. We know it wasn't easy for you to sell the *Citizen* to us—that it was the lesser of two evils so far as you were concerned."

She didn't back down. "This isn't about the *Citizen*. You told the police you think Seth is guilty when you could have just let them investigate with an open mind."

"Don't be disingenuous." Thad seemed pained, anguished by what was going on. "You know this is about the *Citizen;* it's about your father's death, your success, your brother's lack of direction. You're making a great deal of money, Cozie. You're well positioned to make considerably more. You were able to save your family's property, allow your mother to fulfill her dreams. What could Seth do? Nothing. God only knows what effect all this has had on him. He hasn't done a thing with his life. . . ."

Cozie bristled. "That shows how little you understand of him and my entire family. Having money or not having money doesn't determine what we mean to each other or to ourselves. It's not a measure of anything except our bank accounts. I knew that when I couldn't scrape four quarters together for a milk shake and I know it now."

Frances Vanackern had come around the house, and before Thad could fire Cozie on the spot, his wife took her by the hand as if she were a four-year-old throwing a tantrum, so out of control she wasn't really responsible for what she was saying. Frances wouldn't understand that Cozie was simply *furious*. "I know this is a difficult day for you, Cozie," she said soothingly, "but we just want to help. If Seth is innocent, no one will be happier than we are. We would like nothing better than to put this all behind us. But if he's not innocent, all the more reason we needed to bring in the authorities now, before anything worse happens. You do understand?"

"Yeah, I get it. I may be stubborn, but I'm not stupid." She launched herself down the walk, wondering why in blazes she was already feeling guilty for not behaving herself. For not keeping the old stiff upper lip.

When she got to her Jeep, Julia had the door open on the driver's side and was talking to Daniel, about what, Cozie could only imagine. Did Seth have enough time to sneak detonator caps off Daniel's helicopter when they were down in Texas? Little things like that.

Julia, dressed in tennis whites, moved out of Cozie's way. She was visibly upset. "This all makes me ill, Cozie. I want you to know that. And I don't believe Seth is guilty of anything more than falling for the wrong woman. I wish there was something I could do."

Cozie softened. "Thanks. I wish there were, too."

"Father would never fire you," she said quickly. "Having a Hawthorne at the *Citizen* gives it a continuity and a legitimacy it wouldn't have if it were just another Vanackern property. He knows we don't have your reputation for integrity."

"Fat lot of good it's done us. Seth hasn't been in touch with you?"

Julia shook her head, her straight, silky hair pulled back with a sweatband. "I'm sorry."

"It's okay. I know things will work out somehow or another."

"I wish I shared your optimism," Julia said weakly, and slipped off down the path toward the tennis court.

Her anger deflated, Cozie climbed in behind the wheel and sighed heavily, refusing to look at Daniel.

"Lonely lady," he said.

"Julia? That's just what she wants you to believe." A thought struck her. "When you two were in Texas together, did you get the idea that she—I don't know exactly how to put this—that she was attracted to you?"

"I told you: I never even saw her."

"But she could have seen you, heard about you, seen a picture, known you're rich, macho, unmarried."

Daniel's mouth twitched. "Macho?"

"Well, yeah. Geez, you fight oil fires and fly jets, you wear boots. . . ."

"Boots are macho?"

"Yours are."

He laughed. "This from a woman who used to live in a sawmill with no heat."

"You know what I mean." She stuck the key in the ignition and turned it, coaxing her Jeep to a start. "Anyway, my point is, a Foxworth would be a better catch for a Vanackern than a Hawthorne." She glared at him as he sputtered into laughter. "What?"

He continued to laugh. It was a deep, rich sound that vibrated in all her vitals, reminding her of how easily, willingly, she had responded to him just a short time ago.

"Are you trying to embarrass me?" she asked, pulling a U-turn on the dead-end dirt road and heading back out toward Hawthorne Orchard Road.

"You should be embarrassed," he said. "Your reasoning is highly flawed, Ms. Cozie, if you think Julia and I would think ourselves a good 'match' because she's a Vanackern and I'm a Foxworth. I don't think that way. Never have."

"She might."

"Takes two," he pointed out, very sure of himself.

She kept her eyes on the road. "I'm not saying it's just your name that could have attracted her."

"I'm also macho and unmarried."

"Okay, never mind. You're being deliberately obtuse and sarcastic and I'm not going to explain it. Just answer this question: do you or do you not, for whatever reason, think Julia could have dumped Seth to go after you?"

He frowned, considering it. "So Seth sabotaged my helicopter to get rid of me, not to get back at Julia?"

"No!"

"Then what difference does it make if Julia is or was attracted to me?"

She sighed. "I don't know. I'm just trying to make

sense of this whole mess. Maybe your helicopter wasn't sabotaged. Maybe that's just a coincidence."

"The calls, the thefts, the break-ins, Seth's taking off—they're all unrelated coincidences?"

Cozie ignored his sarcasm. "Maybe."

"You don't believe that any more than I do." He leaned back in his seat, one knee up, his seat belt off. Apparently her driving had passed muster. "If Seth did sabotage my helicopter, it's possible he wasn't trying to kill Julia but wanted her to witness the crash, to know she should have been aboard. He wanted to rattle her, let her know the kind of power he has over her."

"That's ridiculous."

But she could feel his eyes on her. Her throat was tight, her fingers once again white as she gripped the wheel. They came to the end of the dirt road, and Cozie continued on into town, dropping Daniel off at his truck, parked, she now saw, up on the west end of the common.

"Will you be spying on me all day?" she asked.

He gave her a frank, sexy, utterly masculine grin. "And all night."

# CHAPTER
# 16

---

**"All right,"** Meg said when Daniel and Cozie arrived in Aunt Ethel's office, "what's going on? The little ones are having a snack. I've got a permissive staff. If I'm not back soon, all the little boys will be playing firefighter on the bathroom wall." She eyed Daniel. "You do that when you were a kid?"

Aunt Ethel gave her older niece a stern look. "Are you going to tell them what you told me?"

"In a minute." Meg's mood had suddenly darkened as she studied her younger sister. "First I want to know what bobcat Cozie had hold of this morning. You look like hell. What happened?"

Cozie grimaced. "I snuck out to see Seth at the monk hut, but he wasn't there and someone shoved me down the hill. I got stuck under a tree."

"I had to rescue her," Daniel put in.

"How mortifying," Meg said. "So. Seth's flown the coop?"

"So it would seem," Cozie acknowledged.

Her sister exhaled. "I figured as much. Hell. His truck's on the farm. Tom found it about twenty minutes ago. I don't know how long it's been there." She let loose with a string of curses not many would expect from so revered a child-care provider. Then she grinned sheepishly. "Excuse my English and don't tell my little kiddies, far too many of whom know the meaning of every word I just said."

"It's okay."

"I know it's okay." She turned to Daniel once more. "Bet you were tempted to drown her in the bathtub when you realized she'd snuck out on you, huh? She never has been clear-eyed where men are concerned. Cozie," she went on, back to her preschool teacher persona, "the man is not putting you in a position of dependency. You need help. So. Call me with any developments. We'll comb the woods for that fool brother of ours, but I wouldn't be surprised if he's just trying to throw us off the scent—or if his stupid truck's been there all along. If this is his idea of heroics . . ." She made a face. "Shit."

Aunt Ethel was stone-faced behind her library-table desk. "Think I'll go home and oil my shotgun on my lunch break. If you ask me, someone's trying to pin a whole lot of things on Seth that he'd never do."

Cozie nodded. "I quite agree."

Daniel, she noticed, was silent.

"You think Seth's being framed?" Meg had paled slightly, clearly not liking even the idea of her younger brother as the target of a nasty setup, rather than just an innocent—and coincidental—suspect. "But who would do such a thing? Why?"

"I haven't figured out that part yet," Cozie said. "But I will."

"Well, when you do, let me know, because I sure can't imagine . . ." She breathed out, leaving it at that. "I've got to get back. Daniel, are you making sure my sister doesn't get into trouble or do I need to cart her back to the farm with me?"

"Meg!"

He smiled. "I see you do know your sister. I'd be happy not to let her out of my sight. But if she'll promise to stay put and get her paper out, I'd like to go back to your farm with you and see if I can help find your brother."

Cozie folded her arms over her chest. "Why don't I go, too?"

But Aunt Ethel provided the answer. "Because you have a staff that awaits your direction and several dozen calls to return. I'm afraid word's getting out fast that Seth's on the run and you've been receiving anonymous threats. This is what happens," she added pointedly, "when you become the subject of headlines instead of the writer of them."

"All right, fine," Cozie said, not pleased. "I can see I'm outnumbered." She turned to Daniel and her sister. "Go ahead, you two. But if you find him—"

"I'll call you here at the paper," Meg promised.

Daniel was less forthcoming. "Do not," he told Cozie, "leave the building until I get back."

The lecture on not ordering her around, she decided, would have to wait. "Just get back soon."

When they'd gone, Cozie warned Aunt Ethel not to say a word and went across the hall to her own office. She suddenly felt every one of her scrapes and bruises. Her head pounded. She took a couple of aspirin and ventured upstairs, where she got updates, checked assignments, discussed articles, decided between several photographs. Routine stuff. Work helped her feel more normal, but she was beginning to wonder if her life ever would return to something familiar, something she recognized as hers.

Back down in her office, her private line was ringing. She pounced on it, hoping Meg or Daniel had news of her brother.

"Hello, Cozie Cornelia . . ."

Every muscle in her body went rigid. She stared out her tall window at Woodstock common. It was a beautiful autumn morning in Vermont. "I'd hoped you'd given up."

"Never. Everything's going my way. I wouldn't give up now. You're scared, aren't you?"

Cozie heard the note of relish in the caller's disembodied voice. She hesitated, but the person on the other end was obviously waiting for an answer. "I'm afraid for you. I think you must be a very sad, desperate person." She bit down on her lower lip, her gaze focused on the statue of her ancestor, Alonzo Hawthorne. He'd faced cannons and bayonets. "I'd like to help you."

It was the wrong answer.

The caller inhaled sharply—pained, taken aback, angry, Cozie couldn't tell what—and slammed down the phone.

Cozie cradled the receiver and flopped back in her chair, annoyed and frustrated and just so damned tired. Her windows, she observed, needed washing before winter. With the clear weather and the approaching weekend, leaf-peeper traffic had again picked up. She watched a toddler kick through freshly fallen leaves on the common, a senior citizen van unload its smiling, eager passengers.

She jumped to her feet and grabbed her field coat, ignoring the pain in her left shin and the residual stiffness of being pushed down a steep hill. She stopped in the front hall and poked her head into her aunt's domain. "I'm going home."

Her thick brows arched. "Cornelia. You promised Daniel you wouldn't leave the building."

"I did not 'promise.' I just didn't argue with him when he gave the order. Aunt Ethel, if whoever's behind all this mess wanted to hurt me, they'd have done it this morning at the monk hut."

Her aunt scowled. "Seems to me they did."

"A rock to the side of the head would have been a lot surer way to be rid of me than pushing me down a hill. I'll be fine up at the house."

"You got another call, didn't you?"

Cozie sighed and, reluctantly, nodded.

"Shall I notify Will Rubeno?" her aunt asked.

"No, I'll call him myself."

"It wasn't . . ." But Ethel Hawthorne was at a rare loss for words. "Seth couldn't have—"

"I hope not. I need to find him, Aunt Ethel. I can't stand sitting around here. I thought I'd go up and have a look around his place. The police have been up there, but they don't know their way around as well as I do; I might see things they've missed. Look, I'll be fine. If you don't hear from me in an hour or so you can call in the cavalry."

"You're going to leave me to explain to your Texan?"

"You can handle him."

"Oh, I know that," she said without doubt.

Cozie joined the leaf-peeper traffic snaking up Hawthorne Orchard Road. She tried to be patient. She forced herself to absorb the nuances of color—the dozen shades of red—around her. It was warm enough that she could roll down the window and suck in deep lungfuls of the crisp air. Seth would do all right out in the countryside today.

A car with Georgia license plates was pulled to the side of the road above her sawmill, a middle-aged couple taking pictures. Cozie felt a surge of pride that her place, which she'd worked on for so long, could bring such pleasure to strangers. Her father had never quite understood tourists, at least ones who crawled up his road during foliage season.

She thought she did. The appeal wasn't just the beautiful scenery, it was also the link they felt with the past, even a nonexistent, romanticized past—something that reminded them of hope and possibility, transported them from the complexities of their own lives. When he drove up Hawthorne Orchard Road, Duncan Hawthorne had seldom seen beyond the complexities of his own life. He would think about the taxes required to keep up the road, he would see the effects of disease and pollution in the trees, he would understand the work and grief and abandoned dreams that the places along the road had experienced. It was all so very real for him. He loved the land not because of any nostalgia—he knew what it was to do without water when a dead chipmunk had contaminated the well—but because it was a part of him, not just something his family had owned for generations, not just an investment.

By buying the land, Cozie wondered, had she been trying, in her own way, to keep her father alive?

She sighed, turning onto the unmarked dirt road up past the sawmill. When she parked in front of her brother's house, Julia Vanackern surprised her, waving from the side yard.

"I was just out for a walk," Julia said when Cozie joined her, "and ended up here. I guess I was hoping against hope Seth would be back."

"No sign of him?"

She shook her head.

"Cozie, I can't tell you how sorry I am." Julia looked away, across the apple orchard, so picturesque in the autumn sun. "Mother and Dad really don't care about the stuff that's missing. They think by reporting the thefts to the police they're ultimately helping Seth."

"That's a hell of a stretch."

Julia's mouth was a grim line. "I never should have let him believe there could have been anything serious between us. The timing was all wrong; I didn't see what kind of stresses he was under."

Cozie glanced at the garden. There were brussels sprouts that needed picking. They were always sweeter after a frost. She and Seth were the brussels sprout eaters of the family. "Did he ever give you any indication that he resented my success, resented my buying our place?"

"Cozie—"

"Did he, Julia?"

"No. Not explicitly. But this hasn't been an easy year for him. I know you and Meg think he just doesn't care about money and success and all that, but he does. His self-esteem is very low right now. I think he believes he failed you and Meg, your mother. . . ." She paused, facing Cozie. "Your father. His memory. But I don't know if that would translate into resentment."

Cozie tried to listen to Julia's assessment without arguing or getting defensive, to look at her brother through another person's eyes.

Julia sighed. "This all must be especially painful for you. Everyone can see what's happening between you and Daniel Foxworth."

There was a sharpness to her voice that drew Cozie's attention. "What do you mean?"

"Oh, please. Don't pretend nothing's going on."

Cozie swallowed, remembering last night, feeling

Daniel's hands on her. "Julia, it's not easy for me to talk about that sort of thing."

"I know. Here you have a real romance going and your family could ruin it for you. If Seth did take down Daniel's helicopter, the two of you—well, it would be impossible."

"You were in Texas. Do you think it's possible? Could Seth have sabotaged Daniel's helicopter?"

"You mean did he have 'motive and opportunity'?" Julia pondered the question a moment. "He definitely had opportunity: Daniel Foxworth wouldn't be here if he didn't. As for motive . . ." She shrugged, the sunlight glistening on the palest highlights of her hair. "He was terribly upset when I broke off our relationship. I told you that. It was a clean, irrevocable break; I don't believe in stringing people along. Then no sooner did we arrive in Houston and meet Austin Foxworth, Daniel's grandfather, than the rumors start about Daniel and me."

Cozie couldn't keep the surprise from her face.

"Oh, I see Daniel hasn't mentioned that little tidbit to you," Julia said coolly. "Well, I'm just giving you the facts. Believe me, all they were were rumors. There's never been a *thing* between us."

Possibly, Cozie thought. But was that what Julia wanted?

"Daniel and I had never even met," she went on. "I suppose it's possible Seth heard the talk and lashed out at Daniel on impulse."

"How would he have heard Texas rumors in Vermont?"

Julia's smile was close to condescending. "Some people here do keep track of me and my family. Seth works for us, so he would be tapped into that network."

"He said he went to Houston because you wouldn't come to Vermont and he wanted to know where he stood with you. I understand you think you'd been clear with him about your relationship, but apparently he didn't get it."

Julia made a face. "He was just being thickheaded. I couldn't have been more plain."

Cozie didn't argue with her.

"Well, it's all so silly. I'm inclined to believe the helicopter crash was just an unfortunate accident that has nothing to do with the rest of what's been going on. Look, I should be going. If there's anything you need—"

"There isn't right now, but thanks for the offer."

Julia started back up the dirt road, and Cozie went into Seth's garden, no longer sure of her purpose in coming here. She broke off a few small brussels sprouts, but they were stubborn little things and she'd need a knife to get a meal's worth.

Where could Seth have gone?

Halfway back to her Jeep, she noticed the passenger door on Seth's skeletal Land Rover was ajar. It hadn't been that way yesterday. She was sure of it. She rushed up to the Rover, a project her brother had been working on for over a year, and peered into the passenger window.

A moth-eaten wool army blanket was pulled over what appeared to be two wooden apple crates, one on the battered backseat, one on the floor. With a shaking hand, Cozie pulled open the stiff door and drew back the blanket.

*"No."*

The crates were filled with jewelry, sterling silver flatware and serving pieces, antique Delft, an antique clock, a few odds and ends in gold. There were a couple of wads of cash.

Cozie's head pounded. She tried to stiffen her muscles to help stop her shaking. Her throat was so tight with tension she could barely swallow. *He wouldn't be this stupid.*

Daniel's truck pulled in behind her Jeep, and he walked up the short dirt driveway, grim-faced in his military-style sunglasses. She fought an urge to slam the door and pretend she hadn't seen a thing.

"Find anything?" she asked with false brightness.

"No. Thad Vanackern called. He talked to your aunt, said he'd just called the police. He saw Seth up here within the past hour."

"But Julia was just here."

"It must have been before she got here. Thad said she was out walking and he was worried about her should she run into Seth."

"Well, he doesn't have to worry," Cozie snapped. "She's on her way back now. She didn't see him."

Daniel had a bad angle on the apple crates. "What are you trying to hide?"

"I'm not—"

"There's something disarming," he said without humor, "about a woman who's as lousy at lying as you are."

She knew she had no choice. He touched her shoulder, forcing her to move aside, but his expression didn't change when he saw the apple crates.

"This stuff could have been planted here to make Seth look guilty," she said.

"By whom? When? Do you have any witnesses?"

Cozie's jaw clenched. "That's for the police to figure out."

His gaze, impenetrable behind the dark glasses, turned on her. "That's right: it's for the police. Your cop friend's on his way. He's going to get the Vanackerns to identify these things. When they do, he'll have no choice except to get a warrant for Seth's arrest."

She didn't back down. "When you start looking at this thing more objectively and rationally and less as your opportunity to nail your saboteur, you'll see that someone is trying to hand my brother to the police on a silver platter for crimes he has not committed. He's being framed, Daniel."

But Will Rubeno had already pulled up in his cruiser, and he joined them at the Land Rover. "Well, well," he said, seeing the apple crates.

"Before you jump to any conclusions," Cozie said, "I suggest you have a thorough conversation with Thad Vanackern."

Will stared at her. "You accusing *him?*"

"I'm not accusing anyone."

"Makes a hell of a lot of sense. You tell me why Thad Vanackern would make those calls to you. Hell, Cozie, you tell me why he'd sabotage the helicopter his own daughter was supposed to have been riding on."

"I never said I had all the answers."

He scoffed. "Wish I had my tape recorder: a Hawthorne admitting to not having all the answers. Come on, Coze. Tell me why Thad Vanackern would steal his own stuff, why he'd risk breaking into your house and office. The guy's known all over town. He'd be recognized."

She gritted her teeth. "So would Seth."

"He doesn't stand out like Thad Vanackern would. He could do stuff and no one would necessarily pay any attention. Thad Vanackern's got no motive; Seth does. If I were you, I'd find your brother before he does something he really regrets. Now go on. Get out of here and let me do my job."

Cozie opened her mouth to protest but shut it again

when she realized Will Rubeno was in just the mood to arrest her. He'd been looking for an excuse since the eighth grade. She headed back to her Jeep, ignoring both men.

But Daniel fell in behind her. "I'll follow you."

"Maybe I'm not going where you're going."

"Honey," he said, "wherever you're going, I'm going."

Daniel was true to his word. Cozie felt only a minor twinge of guilt that she hadn't been true to hers: it wasn't *his* brother on the run. After letting Aunt Ethel know she was alive and well, she took a discreet look around the house in case Seth was there. She began with the toolshed and worked her way inside, not giving a damn if Daniel could guess what she was up to. For all she knew, her brother was hiding in the dirt cellar with the garter snakes.

She straightened. It was a thought. He knew she hated venturing down cellar. He could tuck himself down there in relative safety and comfort.

Daniel was putting together sandwiches in the kitchen.

She slipped into the back room and down the cellar stairs. Half the cellar had been modernized, with concrete floors and finished walls, while the other half had the original dirt floor. She ducked under a low beam and felt through the cobwebs for the overhead light, just a bulb in a socket. She found the string and pulled, and the sixty-watt bulb illuminated the immediate area. The corners behind the furnace and pump, toward the stone walls, remained dark. Her parents had been great do-it-yourselfers, but she planned to hire plumbers and electricians to deal with anything that went wrong down here. It wasn't so much the work, it was the atmosphere.

She could smell dust and mildew, feel them in her nostrils.

A splotch of dark red in the dirt caught her eye. She dropped to one knee, blood pounding in her ears. With one finger, she touched the splotch.

Blood. It was still tacky.

"Seth."

Squinting, her eyes adjusting to the dim light, she could see more splatters of blood. Her brother had been here. He was hurt.

Was he close by now? Had he snuck in here *after* Thad Vanackern spotted him up at the farmhouse?

A snake slithered about six inches in front of her bare foot, and she leaped up, yelling.

The snake disappeared, but the damage was already done. She could hear Daniel upstairs as he bounded into the back room, presumably to her rescue. Cozie groaned.

"Seth," she whispered, "I hope you're not in here."

Because if he were, she was leaving him to the snakes. She pulled the string to the light and backed out, keeping her eyes open for any other slithering intruders.

She was back in the finished part of the cellar when Daniel hit the last stair.

It was speckled with blood. Cozie could feel her knees sinking under her. But she said, "I was startled by a snake. I'm going down to the hardware store in the morning and get some poison. I know they eat mice and bugs and all that, but I really can't have snakes in the cellar."

"Cozie—"

"I suppose you want to know why I'm down here?"

"I don't ask questions when I already know the answer, unless I want to know if the person I'm asking would lie to me." He casually dropped from the

286

bottom step to the floor, standing very close to her, so she could see the little scar at the corner of his eye. "You wouldn't lie to me, would you, Cozie?"

She licked her lips, and he watched. "I wouldn't want to."

"You were looking for your brother," he said.

"He's not down here."

Daniel moved a step closer, seeming even bigger, more muscular, under the low ceiling. "What would you have done if you'd found him?"

"Made sure he was all right."

"I like to think," he said, "that in similar circumstances I would be as loyal to my family as you are to yours. But I can't say that I would be. I've been bred and trained all my life to consider the facts and make judgments accordingly."

"I am considering the facts," she said calmly.

He didn't argue with her. He touched the scrape on her forehead. The warm brush of his fingertips on her skin brought an unwanted, unwelcome surge of physical awareness. "Are you all right?"

She nodded.

But she could see he didn't believe her. "You're hiding something," he said.

"Daniel—"

He dropped down from the bottom step and pushed past her into the old part of the cellar. She didn't stick around. She headed back upstairs to look for any spots of blood she might have missed, any clues as to where Seth might have gone.

Zep was curled up by the woodstove. "If only you could talk," she said.

When Daniel came back upstairs, she could tell at once that he, too, had seen the blood. He said, "We're going down to the police station. You're telling Will Rubeno everything."

But this time she didn't argue. She'd already come to that same conclusion. "I think for once we're on the same wavelength."

He moved close to her, and she could tell from the smoky steel of his eyes that he wasn't thinking about her brother. "What about last night? Were we on the same wavelength then, Cozie, or was that just a fluke?"

"I don't know," she said, and darted past him out the back porch before she could say something she would regret, like how much she hoped, in spite of everything, last night had been anything but a fluke.

# CHAPTER
# 17

It was a long time at the police station. Daniel was impressed at how Cozie, once she'd made up her mind, gave it to Will Rubeno straight. Sneaking out to the monk hut, being pushed from behind and landing under a tree, getting the anonymous call at her office, finding the missing goods in her brother's Land Rover. She even told him about the blood in the cellar.

Daniel was likewise forthcoming. He produced one of the detonator caps he'd found among Seth Hawthorne's things in the monk hut. Rubeno regarded it with interest. "Think it's yours?" he asked.

"I don't know," Daniel said.

The cop got his jacket. "Come on, you two can take me out to this monk hut. Maybe there'll be something you missed."

Under the circumstances, Daniel thought Rubeno was being remarkably restrained. Then again, he lived in Woodstock. He'd known the Hawthornes all his life. As much as they might annoy him, he couldn't

289

take any pleasure in seeing them under this kind of strain.

Not that Cozie was letting it show. The optimism and energy that had put her on the best-seller lists was standing her in good stead. She refused—at least on the surface—to believe that her brother could have committed any of the crimes for which he was under suspicion. He was being framed. Period.

But Daniel wondered if she had her doubts.

Ethel Hawthorne and Meg Hawthorne Strout were up at the house when he and Cozie returned from the monk hut, where nothing had changed since that morning. The police were combing through Seth's abandoned camping gear.

"We haven't turned up any new leads," Meg said as the three Hawthorne women gathered at the kitchen table. "We've looked everywhere we can think of. Tom's checking with Seth's friends." She hesitated, her own worry plain. "Cozie, maybe you should sit tight for a while. You're involved in this thing in a different way from the rest of us. No need to make yourself a tempting target."

Cozie's tension was evident in her pale skin, tight expression, even the super-concentrated way she was staring out at the birds. "I'm doing the best I can, Meg."

"I know. That stuff you found in Seth's Land Rover—"

"It's a set-up. He wouldn't be so stupid as to hide stolen goods in his own Rover—especially when he knew we'd be looking all over the place for him."

"What if he had no choice? He could have stuck the stuff in there in a hurry, figuring it'd only be temporary." Meg threw up her hands, snorting in disgust. "Listen to me!"

"I know, you feel so disloyal when——"

"No point in borrowing trouble," their aunt cut in, climbing to her feet. "We'll know soon enough what Seth's done and hasn't done, and why. If I know Seth Hawthorne, the 'why' will involve putting his neck on the block in place of somebody else's. Most of the trouble he's been in was for that very reason—always had to jump in and protect somebody he felt was out-numbered."

It was a point Daniel had only vaguely considered, being a newcomer among Hawthornes. But was it possible Seth was trying to protect someone?

"High time the stupid bastard looked after himself," Meg muttered. "I've got to get back home. You all keep me posted."

"You do the same," Cozie said.

Ethel Hawthorne reluctantly left with the older of her two nieces, who'd driven her up from town. Cozie walked out to the porch with them. When she returned to the back room, she flopped down on the couch and shut her eyes, more to combat tension, Daniel guessed, than in any serious attempt to sleep. But her fatigue was obvious.

"Can I get you anything?" he asked.

She shook her head, not opening her eyes. "No. Thanks."

He left her alone and used the phone in the living room to call Houston for an update on J.D. He was in stable condition. He still had his leg. There was nothing more anyone could tell him.

But a heaviness settled over Daniel as he rejoined Cozie in the back room. She hadn't moved, but she hadn't fallen asleep, either. The scratch on her forehead was outlined in harsh detail in the fading sunlight. J.D. Maguire, Daniel reminded himself, was his reason for coming to Vermont. His only reason. If Seth Hawthorne had brought down their helicopter in an impulsive act born of jealousy or desperation, he would be held to accounts. Daniel would see to it, no matter how hard and deep Cozie had bored into his soul.

"What are you doing?" Cozie asked, her eyes still closed.

"Just sitting here. You?"

She didn't answer right away. "Mostly I'm trying to talk myself out of worrying about what comes next."

"If I weren't here, you'd be with your sister or your aunt. The three of you could take some of the edge off your worries."

But she opened one eye and looked around at him. "That's not what I meant."

He knew it wasn't. What she'd meant, he could tell from her hesitant tone, was what came next between them. Cozie Hawthorne wasn't the sort for a no-strings-attached toss in the hay. He'd known that last night when she'd climbed into his bed.

"I never in my wildest dreams," she said, sliding off the couch, obviously stiff and sore, "imagined I'd fall for a Texas oil firefighter. I never even imagined meeting one."

"Life sometimes brings the unexpected."

She kept her back to him as she rooted around in her collection of old movies, as if searching for one in particular. But she gave up and turned around, empty-handed. Her eyes were as vivid a green as he'd ever seen. "Tell me something, Daniel. Do you already know you're going to go back to Texas and pick up where you left off?"

He watched her standing in the middle of the bowed pineboard floor, her arms hanging at her sides, her hair as red-gold in the fading afternoon light, it seemed to him, as the autumn leaves. She seemed ready to take whatever he threw at her. But he said, truthfully, "I'm beginning to realize I can't go back to Texas and pick up where I left off. That's just not a possibility."

"Because of J.D.?"

"Because of a lot of things. Being up here, regardless of what happens or why I came, has made me realize I need to make some changes in my life. J.D. could probably go on until he's eighty the way he has been—if his body holds up. I'm not so sure I can. I don't think I was sure even before our copter went down. I just wasn't ready to admit it. I'd bought a ranch. It's not much of a place—it needs work. But in the spring there's a field of bluebonnets. . . ." He smiled, not wanting to burden her with his own demons. "Well, you'll have to come to Texas some spring. There's nothing like a field of bluebonnets in full bloom."

She sat on the edge of the couch, dark circles, he noticed, under her eyes. "Your family has a daunting history. Oil, the military, Texas. Has it been tough finding a place for yourself within the Foxworth traditions?"

He didn't turn away from the question, as he had so often in the past. And he could see that she needed for them to talk about him, about his world. "I guess I've tried to make a place for myself rather than find a place. I want to honor the good those who've come before me have done without being trapped by it— without letting it determine my life for me. It hasn't always been easy. My idea of being responsible to Foxworth traditions isn't necessarily the same as my father's or grandfather's idea."

"You didn't join Fox Oil, and you didn't become a general—at least yet."

He laughed. "Honey, I'll never become a general."

"What about Fox Oil?"

"I don't know. It's a more diversified company these days—it has to be. And I'm not your basic suit-and-tie business type. I'm not sure what good I'd do there. I do know I've felt more of a need than my grandfather or my father to right the wrongs my great-grandfather committed."

"The one who founded Fox Oil."

Daniel nodded. "Stephen Foxworth. He was a hard-driving, competitive man. He swindled J.D.'s grandfather, James Maguire. It's a commonly known fact in my part of the country. James Maguire was a lot younger, and naive, and he trusted my great-grandfather to look after his interests. Instead he got James to surrender the oil rights to his land for next to nothing. Eventually the Maguires lost everything, even their land. James died at forty of tuberculosis. His son—J.D.'s father—went to work as a roustabout for Fox Oil, and J.D. followed in his footsteps. The Maguires have always had a hard life."

"And so you feel responsible for J.D.," Cozie said.

"I felt I owed him a chance, that's all. I don't believe in sons paying for the sins of their fathers, never mind their great-grandfathers. But when I decided to get into fire fighting, I needed his expertise, and I knew he wanted his own company—he'd been working fires for years. I offered him a partnership. He knew what I was doing. He was tempted to say no."

"But he didn't."

"No, he didn't. Now maybe he wishes he had. He's done more for me than I ever have for him."

"I think I understand," she said quietly, coming to

him, "why you have to know what happened that day over the gulf."

His clothes were scattered with hers on the hand-hooked rug under her dormer as they explored each other in the darkness. Coming upstairs together had been totally natural. Maybe, Daniel thought, too natural.

But there was nowhere else he wanted to be, needed to be.

"I don't want to hurt you," he whispered.

She let a palm skim up his arm, across one of his own more recent wounds. "You won't."

But he was careful of her scrapes and bruises even as she shuddered with sensual desire under his touch. Feeling the soft, smooth skin of her body, feeling his own rising desire, Daniel throbbed with a need he'd never known. It wasn't just physical. It went beyond that. Way beyond. As he tasted her mouth, her throat, her breasts, he tried to imagine leaving Vermont without her. He tried to imagine life without her smart mouth and changeable green eyes, without that blend of toughness and vulnerability that made her so intriguing, so maddening and fun and endlessly interesting to be around.

She gave a small cry, and he thought he'd hurt her although he wasn't anywhere near a bruise. Then he realized he hadn't. Her smile came to him even in the darkness. "We'd better get on with it, Major Foxworth. I don't think I'm going to last."

He smiled back, not stopping his stroking of her wet heat. "Going to fall asleep, are you?"

"Uh-uh."

"Cozie . . ."

"I'm so glad we have tonight, Daniel."

And she moved his hand away and guided him into her, and everything they were together became as sparklingly clear to him as the Vermont night sky above him. His eyes focused momentarily on a single, bright star, then shut as he let himself be absorbed by the smell and feel and taste of her, by his own hot, hard need for her . . . for no one, he thought, but her. Not ever again.

Afterward she fell asleep in his arms, and he watched her in the moonlight and tried so very hard not to think.

The call came just before dawn.

Cozie bolted upright, almost dumping Daniel onto the floor. "Oh," she said, feeling his hard, naked body next to hers, "I forgot you were here."

But he was instantly awake. "Don't answer it."

"I have to." She was already reaching across him to the extension. "It could be Meg or Aunt Ethel about Seth."

"Then let me—"

She looked at him, his face silhouetted in the muted predawn light. The phone was on its third ring, but she gazed long enough for him to know that she had no regrets about their lovemaking. To the contrary. But that didn't mean she was going to let him do all the hard things for her, not, she thought, if she expected to retain not only her own self-respect but his respect as well. He was a man with an identity strong enough not to demand that people around him seek his approval, re-cast themselves to his desires.

"No," she said. "I need to make my own decisions, do my own dirty work. I think we're alike in that regard."

He grimaced, then gave a reluctant nod. "We are."

She picked up the receiver.

"Hello, Cozie Cornelia . . ."

And even as she shut her eyes, even as the fear and the disgust rolled through her, she realized it wasn't as bad getting an anonymous call in the middle of the night with Daniel right beside her.

"Are you having fun with Daniel Foxworth tonight?"

"What? Wait a minute—"

*Click.*

She slammed down the receiver. "Bastard. Bitch. Whatever you are, whoever you are . . ." But the tears were already hot on her cheeks, and Daniel pulled the comforter up over her. "Hold me, Daniel. Don't say anything. Just hold me."

Cozie was out refilling the birdfeeders when Julia Vanackern's Austin Healey sped up her driveway, parking in the loop toward the front of the house. She jumped out, leaving her door open, and ran across the lawn. Cozie dumped a handful of thistle into a feeder. Daniel was inside taking a shower. They'd agreed to spend the morning looking for Seth together.

But she tensed when she saw Julia's expression. "Cozie—I'm glad I caught you," Julia said, her voice hoarse as she blinked back tears. "I wanted you to hear this from me."

Fear surged through Cozie as she clenched her hands. "Seth . . . he hasn't . . . he's not . . ."

Julia guessed what she was thinking and quickly reassured her. "No—no, he hasn't been found that I know of. It's nothing like that. Cozie, the police went through Seth's phone records. They didn't find anything on his summer bills, but on his most recent bill there were calls to cities you stayed in while on this last road trip."

Cozie stared at Julia, mute, numb. There was a soft

breeze out of the south, surprisingly warm for October. *Not Seth. It can't be Seth . . .*

"I'm sorry," Julia said weakly. "I know how hard this is for you."

"Thank you for the information." Cozie made herself focus on Julia Vanackern, see her pale hair and face, without makeup, shaken as well by what was happening. "But it still doesn't have to be Seth. He doesn't keep his doors locked. Anyone could have gone in and used his phone when he wasn't around."

"Cozie . . ."

"Please don't argue with me, Julia."

Julia took her hand, squeezed it gently. "I won't. I hope you're right. I know—somehow this will all work out."

"Daniel's inside." Someone else seemed to be speaking; she dipped one hand into the bag of thistle. "Could you go in and tell him? He's in the shower, but you can just give him a yell, tell him you've got news. I want to finish feeding the birds."

"Sure," Julia said, and took the front door into the dining room.

Cozie threw down the bag of thistle.

Her brother as her anonymous caller . . . as the disembodied voice of last night, of so many nights.

She wouldn't believe it.

She found herself running. Her legs were moving as if by some outside force. She could feel the wind in her face and smell the clean autumn air, see the golden leaves all around her, and somewhere deep within her came a calm, centered voice telling her Seth was innocent, he was being set up. Framed. Used.

*By whom?*

She was in her Jeep, digging her spare key from inside the driver's door. In another minute she was swooping out onto Hawthorne Orchard Road. She turned up the dirt road, swallowing hard as she passed the red farmhouse, her eyes pinned straight ahead. It was warm enough to open a window. The feel of the air, its fresh smell, helped calm her.

About a half-mile past Seth's place, she pulled to the side of the road and climbed out, taking a path down a gentle, grassy slope to a small graveyard enclosed in a dilapidated wrought-iron fence. She went through an opening, among the rows of flat, rectangular headstones from the last three centuries, most inscribed with the name Hawthorne. Several graves were marked with black cast-iron stars honoring service in the Revolutionary War, the War of 1812, the War Between the States, the Great War.

Cozie paused in front of a dark granite stone, its lettering worn by time and weather: ELIJAH HAWTHORNE, 1752–1833. There were a few lines from the Bible, and one of the Revolutionary War stars.

The wind gusted, warm, out of the south.

But she heard an engine up on the road, squinted in the sun, and saw Daniel making his way toward her. She turned back to her ancestor's grave.

Daniel came beside her, but he said nothing.

"I wonder what Elijah would think if he could see his descendants now," Cozie said without looking up. "Seth wanted by the police for stealing, maybe even attempted murder. Me driven to suspecting my own brother of resenting me enough to terrorize me. The *Citizen* in Vanackern hands."

"Coming out here must make you feel the weight of your family history."

"Not just coming out here. Being in Vermont. People outside the state—no one's ever heard of Elijah Hawthorne." Her eyes reached his, and she realized she was in no danger of crying. Not now. It was time to face reality, the changes that had occurred in her life. "I noticed that when I was on the road. It was sort of liberating."

He nodded. "I can understand that."

She thought he could. "It was interesting those few days being Daniel Forrest, wasn't it?"

"It was."

A silence fell between them. There was something about the quiet graveyard, the autumn wind, the bright-leafed trees around them that she found reassuring. "I used to come out here often when I was a kid, especially as a teenager. I did charcoal rubbings of each of the stones. Seems kind of morbid, but I was in my American history phase at the time."

"What did you do with them?"

"Hung them on my wall, then stored them somewhere. Rubbings wear out the stones faster, so we don't do them any longer." She touched Elijah's name, not looking at Daniel. "Julia told you about the phone records?"

"Yes."

"I'm trying to reserve judgment." She breathed out. "I've got to find him. If he's hurt—"

She stopped herself, abruptly threading her way back through the gravestones. Daniel followed, not too close. She opened the door to her Jeep and looked around at him. "Back to the world of the living. I guess you're going to follow me?"

He managed a tight smile. "Good guessing."

Cozie had her hand on the phone in the sawmill kitchen, where she'd led Daniel if only because it was closer, when it rang. She automatically picked it up. "Cozie Hawthorne speaking."

"You again." J. D. Maguire didn't sound too happy. "Danny Boy's not letting you out of his sight, I hope."

"That's his intention, yes."

"Good, because if your baby brother tried to kill us—"

"You have proof?"

He growled, and she got the impression not many people interrupted J. D. Maguire. "Close enough."

Cozie swallowed. The receiver slipped in her hand. "You're serious, aren't you?"

"Put the major on."

She handed over the phone and drew away to the woodstove, and Daniel said, "Hey, J.D., how's the leg?" His tone was cheerful, but his gray eyes, his stance, betrayed the tension he was feeling. Cozie mouthed that she was going out for wood.

Halfway to the woodpile, she stopped hard.

No one had checked the sawmill for her brother. Not the police, not Meg or Aunt Ethel, not even Daniel since he'd been so busy keeping an eye on her. But Seth knew the sawmill about as well as anyone— almost as well as she did—and he probably knew, too, that Daniel had been staying at the house.

If he were hiding there, where could he be?

"The root cellar," she whispered.

It was worth a look.

Keeping an eye on the porch door, she hurried along the narrow path just above the stone dam to the opposite side of the sawmill, past the side door off the kitchen, up along where the rock foundation angled into the hillside. She tried to make as little sound as possible, in case Daniel decided to peek out the window.

She came to the five-foot wooden door to a small cellar room under the sawmill's main floor. Originally it must have been some kind of storage room. She called it her root cellar, but she'd never gotten around to putting any roots in it.

The door was cracked open. That didn't necessarily mean anything since it was warped. She yanked on it, and it creaked and groaned, finally sticking about eight inches out.

"Seth?" she called in a whisper.

She gave another hard tug, and there was enough space for her to slip into the damp, gloomy room. The ceiling was just over five feet, and she had to duck to keep from bumping her head. The open door provided very little light.

But she could see her brother slumped up against the drystone wall. "Hey, Coze," he managed to say. "Heard you upstairs. I was just about to call it quits and come on up."

"Good thinking." As her eyes adjusted to the darkness, she could see that he was very pale, looking at once scared and relieved to see her. She crept over to him. "Seth, what happened?"

She saw the dark splotch on his left shoulder.

"I got shot," he said simply.

*"Seth!"*

"It was my own fault; I got too close to the Vanackerns' shooting range. Think I got grazed by a stray bullet when Thad or somebody was out target practicing."

She knelt beside him. "Then the bullet didn't go in?"

"I don't think so. The bleeding's stopped. It was just a stupid accident."

"Are you sure?"

He sighed. "I'm not sure about anything right now."

"I assume you didn't tell Thad he'd shot you."

302

"The way things are going, he'd find a way to blame me—and I don't know that it was him. Julia and her mother like to shoot, and they've always got guests up. Could have been anyone. I should have been more careful."

She quickly peeled back the place where the bullet had torn through his shirt. Blood had soaked through the gauze patches he'd taken from the first-aid kit at the house, but there didn't appear to be any fresh blood. "This could get infected. You need a doctor, Seth."

He grimaced. "I need to find out who the fuck's setting me up. I've been thinking, a dead man's easier to set up than one who can argue for himself."

"Seth, Will Rubeno's got a warrant for your arrest. We've found the Vanackerns' stolen goods in your Land Rover. The police—Seth, there are calls on your bill to me from this last road trip."

"What?"

"You don't know anything about them?"

"Hell, no."

"But your phone bill—"

"Cozie, I haven't gotten my phone bill this month. The police must've checked with the phone company." He bit off a curse. "It's part of the set-up. Somebody waltzed in and used my phone."

They were silent a moment. Cozie could smell her brother's stale sweat, mingling with the dirt and mold and dampness of the small underground room.

Finally he said, "You don't believe I'd make creepy calls to you, do you, Coze?"

"No. None of it." She made sure she didn't hesitate.

"Good."

"About the Vanackerns' missing cash and valuables . . . Thad said he saw you at your house right before I found them in your Rover."

303

"Yeah, I was there," he said wearily. "I was trying to figure out what to do. I saw Julia coming and cleared out, headed back down here."

"You spent the night here?"

"Yeah. It was pretty comfortable." Only her brother would think so. He leaned his head back against the rock wall and managed a feeble grin. "You and Daniel Foxworth, huh, Coze? Geez."

"He's upstairs," she said briskly. "I told him I was getting wood. Seth, I think he can be convinced of your innocence. He says he's keeping an open mind until he collects all the facts. . . ."

"What if all the facts point to me?"

She thought of J.D.'s call. "I don't know."

"What about you, Coze? You still believe me?"

She heard his doubt. Felt it. "Yes." She made herself smile. "You'd do a better job of covering your tracks if you were guilty."

"I don't know, I think I've made plenty of mistakes as it is. Cutting out—it was supposed to make things easier on you, not harder." He drew a deep breath. She had never seen her brother so low. If he hated her, resented her success, he was doing a good job of not showing it. "And I was worried—I don't know, Coze, but I think Julia . . . I think she's pretty messed up. I thought maybe she was involved somehow in what's going on and if I lay low for a while, maybe I could find out what was going on, figure something out. But things have gotten out of hand."

Cozie nodded slowly, studying him in the dim light. "Yes, they have. When were you shot?"

"Just before Thad saw me at my place. I was going to get cleaned up, think about coming forward—then I saw Julia and I just couldn't face her. So I came on down to the house. I cleared out just as you and

Foxworth were coming up the driveway. A wonder you didn't catch me."

"Catch you? Seth . . ."

He gave her a wan smile. "I know. It sounds crazy. But I was scared, not thinking straight."

"What about your truck at Meg's?"

"I left it there the first day. I figured it'd throw you off my scent if you found it. I hiked from the farm out to the monk hut—it wasn't bad."

"Look," Cozie said, rising as much as she dared before she'd hit her head, "I've got to get out of here before Daniel gets suspicious. He's on the phone now with his partner in Texas."

"I didn't sabotage—"

"I know you didn't. I'll be back, Seth. We'll work this thing out."

"Yeah." He sounded dejected and hopeless, not like himself at all. "Thanks, Coze."

She gave him a quick, encouraging smile. "You'd do the same for me."

"I would, you know," he said.

She left him and snuck back to the wood pile, grabbing an armload of logs.

Daniel was sitting on the porch rail when she came up the steps. "Nice try, Cozie."

"What, I can't carry as many logs as you can?"

He was unamused. "How's your brother?"

Refusing to answer, she opened the screen door with her toe and caught it with her elbow, then pushed open the oak door with her shoulder. She dumped the logs in the wood box she and her father had made. Sawdust and tiny wood chips clung to her front. Daniel, she knew even without looking around at him, had followed her inside.

She shoved a log on the fire and whipped around at

him. He was leaning against the door frame, arms crossed, utterly calm. And why shouldn't he be? Seth was trapped under the sawmill with a bullet wound, and she wasn't about to go anywhere with Daniel blocking the doorway. He had both her and her brother right where he wanted them: under his control.

She did not mean more to him than his answers. She did not mean more to him than his sense of responsibility to J. D. Maguire. Than restoring the Foxworth honor and his own shattered reputation.

That much, she thought, was very clear to her.

But was the reverse also true? Did proving her brother innocent mean more to her than her complicated, overpowering feelings for Daniel Foxworth? Would she rather shove him out of her life than admit Seth's guilt?

"The doctors got all the infection in J.D.'s leg," Daniel said.

"That's a relief, I'm sure."

"He's about ready to break out of the hospital and come up here, rattle a few chains."

"Help you find my brother, you mean."

Daniel didn't move. "The experts have gone over our helicopter. They say they've found evidence of sabotage: part of a timing device."

Cozie brushed the sawdust and wood chips off her front. She had nothing to say.

"J.D. and I have been around aircraft and explosives a long time. It wouldn't take someone who knew what they were doing five minutes to slip a timer onto a detonator cap before we took off."

"And that someone had to be Seth?"

"It could have been," Daniel said calmly. "He's in forestry. He knows how to handle explosives."

"That's not proof! That's just speculation."

She shut her mouth. Her pulse was racing. She almost fell back against the stove. She thought she saw Daniel take a step toward her, but he remained in the doorway.

"I'm going to talk to your brother, Cozie, and see what he has to say."

He started back out to the porch. Short of knocking him on the head with a chunk of wood, there was little she could do to stop him.

But her brother was already staggering up the steps, looking even more haggard in the sunlight, as he clung to the railing. Cozie could see Daniel stiffen. "You need a doctor," he said. "I'm calling an ambulance."

"No," Seth said. "It looks worse than it is. And if I don't have any color, it's because I'm waiting for a little vigilante justice to come down on my head."

"That would be premature."

"No kidding," Cozie put in.

Seth paused on the top step, puffing, out of breath— or just scared. "I didn't sabotage your helicopter, and there's no way I'd . . ." His eyes met Cozie's; he was at a loss for words. "She's my sister. I might short-sheet her bed once in a while, but I'd never make those calls."

Daniel sighed. "I think it's high time we brought in the police and let them start sorting things out. It's not easy for me to trust someone else's instincts, but your sister here has been vouching for you since day one, even against increasingly damning evidence. That level of conviction . . ." He paused, not looking at Cozie, the hard lines of his face uncompromising despite his words. "I can't ignore it."

"I shouldn't have ducked out," Seth admitted. He was shaky, and Cozie wondered if he were being too sanguine about how fine his bullet wound was doing.

"It's done now." Daniel's tone was neither condemning nor sympathetic, just that studied neutral Cozie had come to learn was a cover for his deeper, more powerful emotions. "I keep thinking it's interesting that of all that has conveniently turned up to incriminate you, the stuff stolen from Cozie's kitchen hasn't. The log she kept of the calls, the recording, the message she found on her windshield—nobody's seen any of it."

"Because it could clear Seth!" Cozie blurted.

Daniel, however, wasn't ready to go that far. "It's possible."

"I hadn't thought of it," she continued, "but maybe an expert listening to the cassette could eliminate Seth as a suspect; and he might have a foolproof alibi for some of the calls. To complete a successful frame, that evidence would have to be destroyed."

Seth didn't look as hopeful. His bony shoulders sagged. "Either that or the police could say they just haven't found it, or I was better at getting rid of it than the other stuff."

"Does one of you want to call the police," Daniel said quietly, "or shall I?"

"I will," Seth said, taking the final step onto the porch.

A sparkling 1972 Dodge Dart barreled down the steep driveway and careened to a crooked stop. Cozie ran down to it. Her aunt had the door open, but she hadn't moved. "Aunt Ethel, what's wrong?"

She was as pale as Cozie had ever seen her. "Get in the car, Cozie. The house is on fire."

# CHAPTER
## 18

Even before Aunt Ethel turned up the driveway Cozie could smell smoke. Acrid and black, it billowed up from the far end of the house. The porch and back room were engulfed in flames. She was too stricken to cry out. Her aunt braked hard and swerved onto the island created by the loop shape of the dirt driveway. Daniel and Seth barreled in beside them in Daniel's truck.

Cozie staggered out onto the grass. She could feel the heat of the fire. She imagined things burning that shouldn't be burning. The old cookstove. Her father's chair. The television, the canning jars, the old boots and shoes. All her green tomatoes.

The volunteer fire department was out in full force. They'd had to bring a water tanker. One of the fire fighters was dragging a hose down to the brook. There were no fire hydrants on Hawthorne Orchard Road.

Seth yelled, swearing, re-energized, and shot past

Cozie and Aunt Ethel, running and stumbling toward his childhood home. He was a volunteer firefighter himself. His buddies, apparently unaware of the warrant for his arrest, quickly gave him something to do.

Cozie didn't know what to do with herself. She felt useless. Staying out of the way was probably the best thing she could do, but she hated being passive.

"My God, Cozie, I'm sorry." Thad Vanackern appeared beside her. In her shock she hadn't noticed him or his champagne-colored Mercedes. His face was streaked with soot and tears. "I called in the fire. I was passing by and saw the smoke, and I knew it couldn't be from the woodstove. I don't know, I think it was a chimney fire."

"It's not a chimney fire," Daniel said with grim certainty as he came up beside Cozie. She fought an urge to sink against him, to let him handle everything. What was there to handle? Her house was burning.

How would she tell her mother? Her little niece and nephews?

"I suppose you would know," Thad said coolly, clearly not appreciating being second-guessed.

Cozie touched Daniel's hand when she saw his grim, knowing expression. "What is it?"

"The fire was set." His steel eyes stayed on the older man. "There was an explosion."

"My God—how can you be sure?"

"Because I've seen too damned many of them." He turned to Cozie, his eyes softening. "I'll see if I can give a hand."

He moved off silently, the professional at work. She was ready to grab a bucket and get busy herself.

Beside her Thad said, "Will Rubeno is on his way." But his gaze was riveted on Seth as he joined in the fire-fighting fray, bullet wound and all. "I doubt there's any harm in Seth's helping to put out the fire. If

it was an explosion—well, that's not for me to say."
He breathed out, exhaustion apparent in his red-rimmed eyes and the gray pallor of his skin. It hadn't been much of a peak foliage season for him. "Cozie, if the authorities need to speak with me, I'll be at the house. Please let them know."

"I will. Thank you, Thad." Her voice was dull, as if it belonged to someone else. "If you hadn't come along when you did . . . if you'd just gone on by . . ."

He sighed. "I never would have just gone by, Cozie. I'll see you. I'm . . . I'm so sorry."

When he'd gone, she noticed Aunt Ethel standing with her knees locked, staring sober and gray-faced at the burning house that had been in her family since the American Revolution. Cozie was afraid her elderly aunt was slipping into shock and took her bony hand; it was frozen.

"I used to have nightmares as a little girl about this place going up in flames," Aunt Ethel said in a steady, clear voice. "The wood's so old and dry; it would have burned to the ground before the fire trucks could get here if Thad hadn't happened by."

"Do you think there's a chance they'll save it?"

"Don't know." She frowned. "There's your Texan up on the roof. Likes to take the hard jobs, doesn't he?"

"I wonder why he said it was an explosion."

"Because of the way the fire's spread." Aunt Ethel pulled her gaze from the burning house. Her green eyes were tired but confident. "A chimney fire or an electrical fire would spread out from one place; an explosion would start the fire in a bunch of different places at once. That's what happened here."

A chill swept through Cozie despite the hot flames. "Would a detonator cap do the trick?"

"It and some kind of starter, yes."

311

"How do you know this stuff? I know you've been reading the *Citizen* forever, but . . ."

Her aunt squeezed her hand, her fingers as stiff and brittle as sticks. "Frannie's dad taught us when we were in our teens. He worked up in the marble quarries. He taught Frannie, me, your father. Thad, too. His father wanted him to experience manual labor and had him work with Frannie's dad part of one summer. We were all eager to learn. And Mr. Tucker—that was what he knew, explosives. He was a drinker and he never held a job for long, but he could almost always find work in those days because he could blow through rock like no one else."

Cozie managed to speak. "I never knew."

"No reason for you to know. He died a long time ago. He came to work drunk and blew up himself and one of his men. It was right after Frannie and Thad were engaged. Her mother had been dead several years already; she didn't have any brothers and sisters. So then she became a Vanackern." She withdrew her hand from Cozie's and shook her head, a palpable sadness overcoming her. "I guess none of us wanted to remember Ernie Tucker."

The muscles in Cozie's jaw ached from clenching her teeth. "What are you saying?"

Her mouth compressed. "I'm not saying anything."

Meg's minivan bounced up the driveway, pulling into the expanse of lawn out back. With the fortitude that was her hallmark, Ethel Hawthorne squared her shoulders and marched out to greet the elder of her two nieces. But Cozie couldn't face Meg. She saw Daniel on the peak of her roof doing God only knew what. He looked so tall and competent and absolutely at ease with what he was doing. He was in his element.

She didn't even know what hers was anymore.

In the noise and confusion, no one noticed as she got back into her aunt's car. The keys were still in the ignition. She started it up, backed out the driveway, and in a minute was streaking up Hawthorne Orchard Road. It was as if her mind were locked in some kind of tunnel vision. She didn't think about her burning house, her wounded brother, her frightened aunt and sister. She didn't think about Daniel Foxworth or J. D. Maguire. She only heard the disembodied voice on the phone.

*You know who I am. Think about it. You really do know.*

She came up on the bumper of a slow-moving car from Massachusetts. The driver checked his rearview mirror and immediately pulled over and let her pass. She wondered just how crazy she looked.

Without bothering with the blinker, she took the turn onto the narrow dirt road up through the orchard. Aunt Ethel's old car bounced over ruts and rocks as it never had. But Cozie kept her speed under control. She couldn't risk wrapping herself around a tree.

The Vanackern house was postcard perfect in the afternoon sunshine. Cozie stopped out front. The Mercedes was in the driveway. Julia's Austin Healey. Cozie imagined Thad washing the soot and tears from his face as he wished to God his family had chosen the Berkshires or the Adirondacks instead of Vermont for their country home.

She spotted Julia on the old tire swing down along a stone wall, through the side garden where, once, she had had the Hawthorne kids over to play. Seth had been just a little tyke, afraid of going too high. The tire hung from a huge old oak whose leaves were still green. Cozie followed a flagstone path through myrtle and flowering shrubs down to the stone wall. The swing had new ropes, and Julia gave herself a little push with her heel.

"Mum hung this for me," she said without really looking at Cozie. "Daddy wouldn't. He wanted me to buy a proper swing set, but I wanted a tire swing like the Hawthornes had. I used to think I'd have children one day and they'd play here. Every time someone pulls my swing down, I put it back up."

"Julia, we need to talk."

She shut her eyes. "Leave me alone, Cozie. I just want to swing. Mum always said it's one thing I know how to do."

"My house is on fire."

Julia opened her eyes and, looking out at the picturesque landscape, kept swinging. "Dad told me."

Cozie debated grabbing the rope and dumping her off the tire, but she didn't move. "Seth's there. The police are on their way. They'll arrest him."

Julia hooked her elbows on the ropes, her gaze still fixed on the field, out away from Hawthorne land. "I wish there was something I could do."

"There is. You know there is."

"You're so tough, aren't you? You always have all the answers." Her tone was matter-of-fact, as if none of what she was saying really bothered her, really had any impact, even any value. Cozie had never heard anyone sound so defeated. "Mum wishes I were more like you: smart, successful, hard-working, willing to speak my mind. A real go-getter like Cozie Hawthorne. She wishes I had your integrity and strength of character."

Cozie bit her lip until it nearly bled. "I don't feel particularly strong right now, Julia."

But she seemed not to hear. "I think she wishes

she'd married your father when she had the chance. She could have had you as a daughter instead of me."

"I'm my mother's daughter as well."

"Not in my dear mummy's eyes. In her eyes, you're all Hawthorne. She's always wanted a close family like yours, you know."

"We have our problems."

Julia laughed bitterly, tears streaming down her pale cheeks. She pushed off once more with her heel. Nothing was going to keep her from swinging. "Don't, Cozie. Don't pretend you don't have what you so clearly do have. That would be like me saying the Vanackerns have their financial problems. No—Mum made her deal with the devil. She became a Vanackern, and she's suffered for it. She has a husband who barely acknowledges her existence and a daughter who's brought her nothing but disappointment."

"I'm sorry if she's unhappy, but I don't see you or your father—"

"What do you know of me or my father? I have to say, the one benefit of this whole miserable business has been seeing you suffer." She used her heel to stop herself, the tire swing jerking back and nearly tossing her on her rear end. But she held on. A burning intensity came into her pretty blue eyes. "It's something I never thought I'd see: Cozie Hawthorne scared and shaken and not knowing where to turn. But you never once believed your brother could hate you enough to wreck your life, did you? No one could ever shake your faith in your family. Not even me."

"It wasn't you, Julia. It's a little late for that. You tried to feed us Seth and now you're trying to feed us you."

"So." If possible, her cheeks drained of more color.

315

"So you know." And she laughed, the tears still coming, until she slid off the tire swing and crumpled up in the grass.

Kneeling beside her, Cozie placed a hand on Julia's heaving shoulders. "Julia, you can't keep protecting her. Seth was shot. My house is on fire. This has to stop."

"Oh, it will," Frances Vanackern said behind them. "It will."

The volunteers had the fire under control. The house from the kitchen on out would be a total loss, upstairs and down. The rest was a mess. There'd be water and smoke damage. Daniel couldn't say for sure if it would be worth rebuilding. He was, he realized, dealing with Hawthornes.

He glanced over at the driveway where three of them had gathered. Ethel Hawthorne was having a fit because her niece had stolen her car. Meg was screaming at Seth for having gotten himself shot. Seth didn't say anything to anybody. He looked ready to drop.

Will Rubeno was cruising up Hawthorne Orchard Road, siren on, probably of a mind to arrest the whole damned lot of them.

Seth managed to extricate himself from his sister, who announced she had kids to take care of and the whole damned town could burn down but it was potty time at the farm. The police, the fire department, and her entire family knew where to find her.

"She's pissed," her brother told Daniel unnecessarily. "She's also scared. She's waiting for Rubeno to get here so she can send him after Cozie, keep him from arresting me for a while. But I don't know, once he sees me here—"

"Yeah." Daniel caught on right away. "We're going to be a long time explaining."

316

Seth looked almost relieved, but it required too much effort, Daniel could see, for him to look anything but done in.

He said, "Cozie thinks she has to do it all, doesn't she?"

Seth gave a small, grim nod. "Especially when she thinks she's the one who caused the mess."

Daniel could well understand. Why was he in Vermont but for a heightened sense of responsibility? He listened to the wail of the police siren. "Rubeno's getting close."

Seth didn't budge. "You don't still believe I'm the one who tried to kill you and your partner."

"I never did *believe* it." Daniel tore open the door to his truck. "I was just keeping my options open."

"I wished I'd gone up with you the way Julia wanted. Then I'd never have come under suspicion."

Daniel froze. "What?"

"I was going with you. You didn't know? Hell, I assumed she told you and you just figured I'd weaseled out after I'd planted the explosives."

Another car arrived ahead of Rubeno, and a dark-haired woman in her mid-thirties climbed out, shaking her head. "Take me back to New York," she muttered before turning to Daniel. "So much for bucolic Vermont, huh? You Daniel Foxworth, aka Daniel Forrest?"

"I am."

"Sal O'Connor. I'm the one who fell for your litany of false references. Water over the dam at the moment. Some guy from Texas called and said I should get my ass up here pronto and give you a message."

"J.D. Maguire?"

"That's the name. Kind of guy I don't cross even if he is a couple thousand miles away. Said to tell you he took the liberty of bribing certain Houston hotel

317

employees, using your funds, and learned the phone records for the Vanackerns show calls made to cities Cozie visited on her September road trip. Frances Vanackern paid for them." Her brow furrowed. "Is this thing getting as ugly as I think it is?"

But Daniel was already in his truck, and Seth climbed in next to him, and they exchanged glances, their fear unarticulated but intensely real. Daniel could feel it in his gut. But he didn't give in to it. He started his truck and headed up Hawthorne Orchard Road.

"The police will arrest your brother," Frances Vanackern said, eerily calm as she picked at the rope on the tire swing. "They will believe me."

"Because you're a Vanackern," Cozie said.

She wanted to keep her talking, buy herself time— for what she wasn't quite sure. Thad to come out. Julia to do something. Aunt Ethel to notice her car was missing and send in the troops. If she made her own move too soon, there was no telling what Frances would do: she had a revolver tucked in her waistband.

"You Hawthornes have always resisted accepting the way the world works—the way things are. Of course the Vanackerns have certain privileges."

Julia crawled to her feet. "Mum—"

"Go back to the house, Julia. There's nothing you can do except make matters worse," Frances said harshly. "I've a bit more to do before we can put this entire ugly experience behind us."

"Please, Mother."

Frances didn't even look at her. "Go, Julia. Now."

Julia was sobbing, strands of pale hair sticking to her wet face. "I'll get Dad—"

"Do you suppose you could get his attention? My. That would almost be worth returning to the house to see." Frances gave Cozie a supercilious look that she didn't quite pull off; her face was too filled with pain, with a sadness so profound she probably couldn't recognize that was what she was feeling. "Thaddeus is quite adept at the passive neglect of both his wife and daughter. The public would never know, but we do. Don't we, Julia?"

"Mother, please don't. He's done his best. I don't hate him. I don't hate you. I know you're unhappy. I'll help you."

Frances whirled around. "Unhappy? Where on earth did you ever get the idea I was unhappy? Cozie Hawthorne has been rubbing your nose in her achievements, her rich family life, since you were a little girl. Don't you think I haven't noticed how you've suffered?"

"I haven't suffered." Julia's voice was barely a whisper as she choked back a sob. "Cozie and I have never wanted the same things. We're two different people. Mother, *please* don't do anything else that would hurt you, hurt all of us."

Frances screwed up her face, like a two-year-old, refusing to listen. "Go!"

Cozie reached out a hand to Julia, who seemed on the verge of total collapse. "Perhaps you should do as she says."

Julia nodded dully, her sapphire eyes glazed and puffy. "I'll get help," she mumbled, and staggered up the garden path.

Frances relaxed visibly with her daughter gone. She even smiled. "She means well, my Julia. She's never had your strength of character, of course, but I'm afraid with you around, people have neglected to see her good qualities."

Like her mother for one. Cozie took a step backward, preferring to make her exit before Frances remembered her gun. But she didn't want to do anything to help her memory. "I've always admired Julia. She's fun to be around, has a great perspective on life—"

"Don't be patronizing." Frances's smile vanished, her blue eyes darkening. "Julia's a worthless rich girl. That's what you really think. She's had it too easy. She doesn't have the perspective that comes from knowing how to do the little things that make life more meaningful. Julia's never made apple butter from her own apples. She's never pulled an egg warm from a hen's nest. She's never had to worry about balancing a checkbook."

"So?"

"So you think less of her because of that."

Cozie shook her head. "I don't."

Frances made a dismissive sound. "Of course you do."

Arguing wasn't going to help matters. "Neither of us knows how to burn down a house."

"That's right." Frances almost smiled, pleased with herself. "You don't. It's amazing, don't you think, that with all I've accomplished, only Julia has discovered me? Of course, Thad never would."

Cozie tried to maintain an outward calm, but her pulse was racing, her hands were clammy. She took another step backward, up the slope toward the Vanackern house and Aunt Ethel's car. Maybe she shouldn't have brought up her burning house. "Julia obviously cares about you. She knows how to do other things, besides making apple butter. If you'd wanted her to learn how to make apple butter, you could have taught her. She could have opened up a cookbook and found out herself. She has different interests."

Frances's eyes flashed with a keen distaste for just what interested her daughter. "Men. Your brother.

She loves having sex. *That's* her main interest. *That's* what my Julia knows how to do best." She was dry-eyed and breathing hard. "Every time I look at you, think about you, I see what Julia should have been. I see what I could have had."

Poor Julia, Cozie thought. Her mother despised her. But Frances Vanackern had projected all her anger with her daughter, with herself and her husband and their lives, all her disappointment and rage, onto Cozie. If Cozie weren't who she was, Julia would be different. So let Cozie suffer. *Make* Cozie suffer. Ruin her book tours, torment her at home, frame her brother, burn down her house.

As Cozie took another step, ready to bolt up the hill, Frances Vanackern reached under her anorak and withdrew her ivory-handled revolver. "You can stop your retreat."

"Okay." Cozie's pulse raced even faster. "Let's go up to the house together."

She seemed not to hear. "We're going over the stone wall into the woods."

"Why?"

"To end this, to end everything. It's time."

"Mrs. Vanackern—"

"Frannie. Your father always called me Frannie. I cried for days after he died. Days. How long did you cry?"

"I still do," Cozie replied softly.

"He never neglected you, did he?"

She shook her head.

"Over the stone wall, dear. Carefully. Your father and grandfather taught me how to shoot. Once I considered shooting my father when he was sleeping, but I couldn't bring myself to do it. Daddy tried his best. I—Thad and I weren't going to invite him to our wedding. It would have been so embarrassing, having him there, worrying about whether he'd drink too much. But he never knew. I'm sure he didn't. He died before we would have had to tell him."

Cozie climbed over the stone wall, which, unlike the stone walls down the road at her place, was free of sumac and gray birches and choke cherries. An image crept into her mind, unbidden, of her brother dutifully pulling out any unwanted growth. But she needed to keep Frances Vanackern talking instead of shooting.

"Thad didn't want your father at your wedding?"

"No. Thad didn't care. *I* didn't want him there."

Frances clambered over the stone wall, her gun never wavering. She was a very fit woman. She motioned for Cozie to continue through the small field, toward the woods. The wind gusted, cold. Cozie tried to control her shaking. Crows wheeled overhead, and she could smell the field grass and the goldenrod all around her. To keep herself from panicking, she tried to concentrate on the beauty of the trees and surrounding hills instead of Frances Vanackern's twisted hatred.

She thought of Daniel Foxworth and knew he'd be ticked off if she got herself killed now, when she could have grabbed him off the roof and had him join her.

But she hadn't really thought Frances Vanackern, whom she'd known all her life, hated her enough to kill her. Make her miserable, absolutely. But not to kill her.

"You shot Seth?" she asked. She could hear Frances breathing directly behind her.

"I tried to kill him, Cozie. Twice. He's quite indestructible. I can understand, now, Julia's attraction to him. I tried to kill him in Houston. Julia had discovered my little calls to you and broke off her romance with him, believing it more than your phenomenal success had triggered my . . . reaction." She paused, but Cozie couldn't guess what she was thinking. "But Seth knew she was upset about something extraordinary. He showed up in Houston insisting on an explanation. *Of course* he only wanted to help."

They were nearly to the edge of the field. Cozie slowed her pace, hoping someone would see them before they disappeared into the woods. She wouldn't mind being rescued right now. Not in the least. Daniel, Will Rubeno, Aunt Ethel and her shotgun—she'd take all the help she could get.

"But Julia didn't confide in him, did she?"

"Oh, no. She was protecting me. But she would have broken eventually. Seth can be very persuasive. I was hoping Daniel Foxworth would take an interest in her—he's much more appropriate a match for a Vanackern. Unfortunately he never even got to meet Julia until it was too late and he'd already met you."

"He could have if she'd been aboard his helicopter as planned."

"But I had to make sure she wasn't on board, didn't I?"

"I suppose so," Cozie said quietly. They were so close to the edge of the woods.

"Seth was going with her. I sabotaged the helicopter with the express purpose of trying to kill him. It really was a simple matter. Everyone was racing around getting ready for the fire, and I managed to slip into the helicopter and do my thing." She chuckled, smug. "Amazing what one remembers from one's childhood."

"Did Julia know you'd sabotaged Daniel's helicopter?"

"Not at the time, no. She's since figured it out." Her tone sharpened. "Move along, Cozie. Dawdling won't stop me from doing what I must do."

Cozie picked up her pace only slightly as they

started down a gradual slope, only a few feet before they reached the path through the woods. Julia Vanackern, Cozie realized, had known about her mother's calls when they were the work of a troubled but, at that point, still harmless woman. If she'd spoken up, the helicopter crash and everything else might have been prevented. Instead she'd stood by, willing to sacrifice Seth to shield her mother, whom she'd known—not guessed but *known*—was guilty.

"When Daniel came to Vermont," Cozie said, "you realized Seth was in a position to take the blame for everything. The thefts—"

"They were to prove he was desperate enough to steal. The money and valuables gave the police something concrete to find."

"And you could plant the detonator caps."

"Precisely. I'd hoped to kill him and claim self-defense when I saw him prancing through the woods, but I'm not as good a shot as I used to be. He was a ways off, not at point-blank range the way you are now, so don't get your hopes up."

Cozie wasn't. "Were you the one who pushed me at the monk hut?"

Frances sighed. "That was Julia. Meddling again. I think she wanted to warn Seth, try to explain, I don't know. I have a feeling Seth believed Julia responsible for everything and was trying to protect her in his usual inept way. When Julia saw you at the monk hut, she couldn't very well explain her presence, not if she were to protect her crazy mumma."

"You don't have much respect for Julia, do you?"

"I love my daughter!"

Cozie stepped into the shade of a yellow-leafed maple at the edge of the field and, knowing she was taking a chance, looked around at Frances Vanackern. The revolver was still leveled at her. "Seth is at the house with Daniel Foxworth. There's no way you can pin this on him."

Frances's smile was underlined with hate. "You of all people should know: where there's a will, there's a way. This revolver belonged to your Grandpa Willard. It's not registered, but it has his name engraved on the handle. The story will be that you armed yourself while under increasing pressure from your caller and met with an unfortunate accident."

"It won't work," Cozie said.

"It *will* work. I will make it work."

Daniel and Seth intercepted a stumbling, running, sobbing Julia Vanackern before she reached the back terrace. "Mum has Cozie," she cried. "I thought I could make her stop. . . . I thought everything would work out." She spoke between gulps for air. "They wouldn't have enough to convict Seth, and Dad and I could get Mum the help she needs."

Seth, exhausted and in pain, hung back, squinting out at the picturesque Vermont landscape.

Thad Vanackern had emerged from the house, showered and in fresh clothes. He was still buttoning a sleeve. "Julia, you're hysterical."

Julia wailed and slammed her fist into his chest. "I am not hysterical! Don't you see? Are you *blind?* Mum hates Cozie!"

Thad looked stricken. "But Seth here . . ."

She groaned and turned away from him.

"There they are," Seth said, and bullet wound or not, sprinted off the stone terrace and down the sloping lawn toward a small field.

"Frances?" Thad finished buttoning his sleeve, his brow furrowed in confusion. "Julia, perhaps you should explain."

Daniel didn't stick around to listen. He ran after

Seth, catching up with him easily as they headed across the field. Seth's breathing was labored, the creases of his eyes and corners of his mouth were caked with soot, and he reeked of smoke and sweat. Daniel knew he didn't look much better, but no one had shot him in the past twenty-four hours.

"I know the path they're on," Seth said. "There's a shortcut."

"Tell me."

"I can make it."

"Seth—"

He kept running, but he said, "Between those two hemlocks, straight down a hill, then up again. It's steep. You'll come to the path. It winds around to avoid the hill."

Daniel pushed ahead, running at full speed until he came to the hemlocks. Then caution, silence became as vital as speed, but the howling wind would cover much of the noise he made. He slipped between the two trees and skidded down a steep hill covered with pine needles, dead leaves, wilted ferns, rocks, and fallen tree limbs. There was a narrow stream at the bottom. He ran through it and used his momentum to carry him part of the way up the hill on the other side.

He could hear Seth not far behind him.

Clambering up the hill against the wind, he felt the cold and his own fear burning in his lungs. Only years of discipline kept him focused.

Seth crept up the hill beside him. "Voices," he whispered.

Daniel stopped, listening. Above him, he, too, heard voices above the wind, any words indistinguishable. He and Seth were just two yards below the crest of the hill. They crept up a yard, hidden among a stand of young pines struggling to survive.

Seth held up a hand. They went very still. Through the pine branches they could see Cozie and Frances Vanackern. They were facing each other about three yards up the road. Frances was in back, nearer Daniel and Seth, and Cozie in front.

The two men looked at each other, nodded, and crawled up the last yard out onto the path.

Cozie saw them. She gave no indication of it, but Daniel knew she did.

"I believe I'm satisfied with the way things are turning out," Frances Vanackern was saying. "You've suffered, Cozie Cornelia, and now you'll die."

That was enough for Daniel.

He lunged the last few feet and tackled Frances Vanackern from behind, catching her by surprise. He knocked her flat on her face and Cozie grabbed the hand with the gun, removed it from the older woman's grasp, and fell back, cursing a blue streak.

For a second Daniel thought she'd shoot him and her brother both. "Geez—what the hell were you two doing, diving in here like a couple of goddamned crazy men?"

Daniel stood up. Frances Vanackern, motionless and silent on the ground, wasn't going anywhere. Seth stood over her. Cozie was white-faced and shaking. The woman, Daniel thought, had to learn a little gratitude. "You were about to be killed. If we hadn't intervened—"

"I had everything under control."

"What were you going to do, duck when she shot you?"

"No, I was going to kick her down the ravine, but I saw you two idiots and figured I'd better wait before you got yourselves killed and me along with you! You two ever hear of thinking before you act?"

Her body—and her mouth—were running on pure adrenaline. Daniel could have scooped her up right then. "You're one to talk, sweetheart."

She raked a hand through her hair, and Daniel took the revolver. He couldn't wait any longer and pulled her into his arms, holding her close.

It was a tough call who was angrier: Will Rubeno or Meg Hawthorne Strout. They were waiting at the Vanackern house when Cozie, Seth, Daniel, and Frances Vanackern emerged from the woods. Rubeno threatened to lock up the whole damned lot of them. He wanted statements, he wanted them *now,* no more bullshit, no more playing cop, no more nothing. Cozie told him he should be glad *he* didn't have to go off in the woods at gunpoint with a crazy woman who hated his guts.

"That's it," he said. "I'm getting the cuffs out."

But Meg—Meg was truly fit to be tied. "Just what I need, my little brother and sister scaring the living daylights out of me. Our goddamned house about burns down, they disappear, Frances Vanackern turns into a wild-eyed lunatic, and I've got a bunch of pissed-off rich Texans in my dining room. Here I am stuck with a slew of pre-schoolers who want snack, trying to explain to some goddamned *general* that his grandson is off in the woods like goddamned Davy Crockett." She took a breath and grabbed her sister by the shoulders. "Are you sure you're all right?"

Cozie nodded. "I'm sure. It's over, Meg."

But Daniel had surged forward. "My grandfather's here?"

"Austin Foxworth, retired general of the United States Air Force and chairman of Fox Oil?"

"That would be him."

"He's here. So is Stephen Foxworth, CEO of Fox

Oil, and his wife Joan, and their daughter Susanna, vice president of Fox Oil, who says her brother Daniel will never learn, they all gave up trying years ago. I put them to work serving snack and hope to hell the kids' parents don't have a heart attack when some Texan hands them their kid."

Daniel was looking mystified.

"Obviously," Meg said, disgusted, "they're worried about you. Bet *that* never occurred to you when you went charging off into the woods. Things like that don't occur to *my* brother and sister."

Tom's truck pulled up alongside the dirt road. Cozie burst into tears when she saw her mother in the front seat. How could she explain? How could she possibly explain?

Meg calmed down. "That's the other thing. Turns out Aunt Ethel's been snitching to Mother all along. She got into Burlington airport a couple hours ago. Tom went and picked her up; he left me a note, which I didn't see until I was already up to my eyeballs in Foxworths. She says she leaves the country for the first time and her family goes to hell."

"Say hello," Will Rubeno said, still in no mood. "Then get your butts down to the police station."

The Foxworths vacated the Strout farm, despite the seemingly sincere invitations for them to stay, for rooms at the Woodstock Inn & Resort. Daniel remembered watching Cozie arrive for the Vanackern dinner in her Ingrid Bergman dress. Had he already been in love with her then?

His grandfather insisted they all go downstairs for a drink, but first Daniel had to call J.D. Maguire.

He was doing okay. But he didn't take to the idea that Frances Vanackern had sabotaged their helicopter to stop her daughter from confessing to Seth

Hawthorne about her mother's little calls to his big sister.

"Shit at and missed and by an old lady to boot. Hell. When you coming home?"

"Soon," Daniel said.

J.D. grunted. "You're in bad shape, Danny Boy."

He didn't argue.

Downstairs, his grandfather had managed to get a bourbon to his liking. "First time I've ever been in Vermont," he said. He was a tall man, as tall as Daniel, and fit for his age.

Susanna, also tall and gray-eyed, said, "I came here skiing once, to Stratton. It was nice."

But Stephen and Joan Foxworth weren't going to tolerate small talk. They wanted every detail of what Daniel had been through in the past weeks. He told them what he could, leaving out only his impressions of Cozie Hawthorne's green eyes, of the feel of her trim little body under his hands. She was with her family now, as, he thought, it should be.

And he was with his, and he could see, as he never really had before, that as much as they went their separate ways and disagreed and pressured each other to give more, be more, they'd always been there for him, even when he was feeling at his most alone. As he was now, knowing Cozie would need space, time, a chance to decide who and what she was now that she could no longer pretend that fame and fortune hadn't changed the direction of her life.

"I think I'm in love with you," she'd told him on their way to the police station. She wasn't looking at him when she said it. "But I don't trust myself right now. I don't even know who I am anymore."

Daniel had simply held onto her hand. He was sure about how he felt. Very sure.

He was in love with Cozie Hawthorne.

330

His grandfather leaned forward after Daniel's rendition of the past days. "Cozie Hawthorne the one who yelled at the chief of police for putting out a warrant for her brother's arrest?"

Daniel smiled. "She's the one."

"She's pretty for a Yankee," Austin Foxworth said, settling back in his chair. "But I'd bet the ranch that mouth gets her into a lot of trouble."

# CHAPTER

# 19

After a few weeks of pensive commentaries, Cozie Hawthorne, in her new role as a columnist for a major national syndicate, decided to take on the state of Texas.

Daniel figured it was her way of sorting out whether she really was in love with him or still just thought it. Or maybe just of getting him back to Vermont.

Texas, she started out, was too big. In the time it would take her to get to Virginia from her home in Vermont, she'd only be halfway across Texas. The people couldn't get to know their political leaders on a personal basis. The average Vermonter, she claimed, could easily meet the state's two senators and lone congressman.

That didn't get her into too much trouble. Texans didn't mind outsiders telling them their state was big, and they didn't much care if they met their politicians.

But she had to point out that Vermont had declared itself an independent republic a full fifty years before Texas did. It lasted four years longer, until 1791, when it became the fourteenth state.

A Vermonter, she reminded everyone, had died at the Alamo.

Then she got on tumbleweed, tornadoes, and—Daniel had known it was coming—Texas snakes.

Texans said it was obvious that she'd never been to their beautiful state. She countered that she had, too. She'd had a two-hour layover at the Dallas airport. What an area sold for souvenirs, she maintained, was highly instructional: a replica of an Old West pistol set complete with holster said a lot about Texas. She'd bought three sets for her niece and nephews.

She also claimed to have been served chili on Fritos and said anyone wanting quality, authentic Mexican food should come to Vermont and try a little restaurant she knew over in Quechee.

Within weeks she was the most popular columnist in Texas.

Daniel hoped her popularity stemmed not just from Texans' love of a good fight but their understanding, deep down, of her point: that the United States was a nation of outsiders, and Texans and Vermonters had more in common than they didn't. Underlying her smart-ass comments was an affection for a place she'd never really seen.

J.D. Maguire didn't see it that way. Sprung from the hospital, gaunt but on the mend, he joined Daniel at his dilapidated ranch on a warm and beautiful November evening. "You ought to go on up to Vermont," he said, "and drag her down here by her ear and show her the real Texas."

"J.D., she doesn't want the life I lead."

"Hell, neither do you. You never have. I've decided." He adjusted his outstretched leg, still bandaged but healing. "I'm buying you out."

"You can't afford to buy me out."

His black eyes leveled on Daniel. "I didn't say I'd pay a fair price and I didn't say I'd pay it right away. It'll take some time. But I'm buying you out. Doctors say I'll be fighting fires again in six months. I give me four. It'll take that long to sort things out."

"Are you sure?"

"Yes, I'm sure. You have to move on, Danny Boy. So do I."

The next day, they got a call: a well fire in Oklahoma. An ugly one. It about killed J.D. not to be able to go. But Daniel got the team together, and the equipment, and went. Their work over the next three days helped restore his reputation and satisfy lingering doubts about the trustworthiness of his and J.D.'s small fire-fighting company.

When he got back to his ranch, he poured himself a bourbon and sank into his bathtub, a sturdy old thing up on legs. His body ached. His mind was numb.

"I don't want to hear any more about me not locking my doors."

He was sure he was imagining her voice. Then he opened his eyes, and she was there, at the edge of the tub. She'd cut about four inches off her reddish blond hair and it hung in waves, framing her face.

"Whiskey and a hot bath?"

"One has to make do with what's at hand."

"They're a bad combination when you're tired." She scooped up a handful of water and let it run through her fingers. "You could go right down the drain."

"The way I look at it," he drawled, his body already

responding to the sight of her, "I'm just missing a woman."

"Any woman would do?"

"No. Not any."

She smiled.

"How'd you make it out of the airport without someone stringing you up?"

"Well, J.D. is an effective deterrent. Even on crutches he's an impressive individual, isn't he?"

Daniel arched a brow. "He picked you up?"

"He can't drive yet. He got some buddy of his to drive. They brought me here. Daniel?" She peered at him; his eyes were half-closed. "Are you going to sleep?"

"Uh-uh. No, ma'am. I'm just thinking about whether to haul you into this tub with me clothed or unclothed."

"Do I have a say?"

"You want one?"

She licked her lips. "Surprise me."

She stayed for five days, went back to Vermont, and hit back with a smart-assed column about Texas having unreliable weather. This from a New Englander.

"Didn't you take that woman to bed while she was down here?" J.D. asked, disgusted, on the Sunday before Thanksgiving.

Night and day, Daniel thought. Remembered. He showed her Texas, his life. And the wench—it was the only word for her—had gone home and written about the goddamned weather. "Cozie Hawthorne will do what she will do."

"I figure the only way to save her from a lynching is if she marries a true-blue Texan," J.D. said. "That's you, Danny Boy. Go up to Vermont," he went on, "and marry the woman."

Daniel threw down the paper. "I think I will."

A calm had settled over Vermont when Daniel arrived on Thanksgiving Day. It was between seasons: the leaf peepers had all gone home and the skiers were just starting to come out. The landscape was more subdued. It had lost its vibrant color. Now shades of evergreen and brown and yellow and gray dominated. When he drove up Hawthorne Orchard Road, his was the only vehicle out.

The white clapboard farmhouse was boarded up, awaiting restoration or bulldozing. There was no sign of Cozie's battered Jeep. He turned down to the sawmill. Still no Jeep. But the woodpile was diminishing, and there was a Thanksgiving wreath on the door. Cozie had moved back in. He could feel her presence. But he didn't get out of his rented car, and instead went back out to Hawthorne Orchard Road, up to the narrow dirt road that would lead to the orchard and Seth's sagging house.

It was there the Hawthorne family had gathered for Thanksgiving dinner. The yard was full of cars, including Cozie's Jeep. Zep was rolling around in the grass.

He almost made a U-turn out of there. Let them enjoy their holiday. Find a room at an inn and confront Ms. Cozie in the morning.

But he couldn't wait any longer. He'd thought of her every moment of his torturous journey north. Not once had he considered turning back. He wouldn't now.

Meg greeted him at the door. "I was wondering when you'd show up," she said. "Dinner's in the oven."

Daniel managed a smile. "I can smell it."

"Cozie and Seth are out in the orchard. Do you want to let them know you're here or come in first?"

"Give me a minute."

"We'll set an extra place at the table," she said, and smiled. "Good luck."

"You know why I'm here?"

"I hope I do," she said, and headed back inside.

He crossed the road and saw at once that work had been done in the orchard. A number of trees had been uprooted, the dead wood cleared out of others. He spotted two figures out across the field. A soft, cold drizzle had begun.

He resisted the temptation to run. Cozie and Seth were unaware of his presence. Even as he moved closer, the two of them kept at their work. They were planting trees. Seth would raise a huge pick above his head and slam it into the half-frozen ground, making a hole, and Cozie would drop in a seedling and push the soil up around it. Then they'd move up the row and plant the next.

Cozie had on a brown chamois shirt too big for her. Drizzle had collected on her hair, pulled back with one of her salvaged rubber bands. Daniel's pulse quickened at the sight of her. Nothing had changed. It never would. He wanted her now as much as ever. He wanted to be a part of her world, to make her a part of his.

Seth noticed him first. He laid the pick on his shoulder, sweat pouring down his face. "Hello, Daniel."

Cozie had started off to her bucket of seedlings, to replenish her stock. She gave a small gasp and flew around. Strands of damp hair hung in her face, and her eyes were as green as in all his dreams.

"I'm going to get cleaned up," Seth said. "We can finish later."

He loped across the field, looking strong, sure of himself.

"Well, hello," Cozie said.

"Hello, Cozie. Things are a little different around here."

"Yes. It took some doing, but I finally got it through my thick skull that my life has changed and that's meant changes, too, for my family."

"It's okay?"

She smiled. "So far." She nodded to her brother's retreating figure. "He's decided to finish his degree in forestry. We—Meg and he and I—have worked out an arrangement so the three of us own the land. I finally made them realize it's not charity on my part: the land is a gift from Elijah and all the other Hawthornes down through the years who've kept it in the family. We don't know how we'll work out the details, but we'll do it. Seth is restoring the orchards. We're putting in some of the rarer apple varieties. He's got some good ideas. We're just taking things step by step."

Daniel smiled. During her entire speech, she hadn't given him a direct look. "I'm glad to hear it. What about you? How are you doing?"

"Just fine. I've been getting mail from my fans in Texas by the truckload." She grinned. "Nothing that I've seen from you or J.D."

"I wouldn't call J.D. a fan," Daniel said.

"Well, I've agreed to be on a Houston talk show next month."

"Should be fun."

She grinned. "Yeah, I think so."

"I see you've moved back into the sawmill."

"It's been nice, but I think it's haunted. Seems I can't get Texas and Texans off my mind."

Daniel smiled, some of the tension going out of him.

"The Vanackerns have put the paper and their house here up for sale. Aunt Ethel tried to get veto power over the new owner. I tried—it's just not in the cards for me right now to buy it."

"You could rescue the land but not the paper."

"Next year I maybe could swing it, I don't know. Maybe there's a way. . . ." She sighed, obviously pained that there was something her energy and optimism couldn't get done. "We shut down, you know. First time since the War of 1812. I miss my office, but—well, it's been nice writing at the kitchen table."

"What about your house?"

"Meg and Seth and I are getting together with an architect next week to discuss our options. We're hoping to save it."

Now why, Daniel thought, wasn't he surprised?

The drizzle was coming down heavily now, more a soft rain. A couple degrees colder and they'd be in a mess. Daniel, however, decided to wait Cozie out. The next move was hers.

Damned if he'd propose to her in the rain.

"Would you care to join us fo      sgiving dinner?" she asked.

"Sure."

She peeled a damp strand o
tucked it back more or less
said, and darted past him

For two cents he'd hav
over his shoulder, and h
and made love to her i
instead he followed he

"I have to run back to the sawmill and change," she said, and he saw the touch of fear in her eyes.

"Is it an Ingrid Bergman day?"

"Nope." The fear receded, and she shot him an impudent grin. "Donna Reed."

Her one and only Donna Reed dress was from the last scene in *It's a Wonderful Life,* when Jimmy Stewart decides not to commit suicide after all and finally gets his due from the people he's helped. Cozie had had it done in a warm, deep red, with a hand-tatted lace collar. It was as prim and romantic as she ever got, and she loved it for the holidays.

She was breathless and somewhat lightheaded when she came down from the loft. Daniel was still there. He'd filled the wood box. His gray eyes were lost in the shadows as he watched her come down the stairs. Her response to him, so elemental and raw, threatened to overwhelm her on every level.

"Before we go," she said, "I have a confession to make."

"Oh?" He seemed ready for anything.

"I've bought a ranch," she blurted. "In Texas."

His brow furrowed. Clearly her admission wasn't within the realm of what he'd steeled himself for.

She said, "J.D. says it's not my idea of a real Texas ranch because it doesn't have tumbleweed, although he promises a few rattlesnakes."

"J.D.? Cozie, what the hell—"

"Still, it's got possibilities. It's a hundred acres. I know that's small by Texas standards, but it's on a stream—or a creek, as J.D. says. It has a sad, dilapi-
 old log cabin that could use fixing up, but I want
 the tub; it's a classic claw-foot. J.D. says he'd
 whole damned place, but I believe it has
 chitectural significance. We New En-

glanders aren't always so willing to rip things down and start over. A little continuity with the past is good—so long as it doesn't keep you from plunging ahead into the future."

Daniel stood frozen in front of the woodstove, the hard lines of his face stark. She wanted to touch him but knew she had to wait.

"J.D. says—"

"What's all this 'J.D. says'?"

"Oh. We've talked several times. He says if you don't straighten me out on Texas, he will."

Daniel took a step toward her. "This ranch—"

"We're still doing the paper work," she interrupted, breathless. "The owner was reluctant to sell. But it seems he wants to relocate to Vermont. I'm not sure he really does, not full-time."

"Then it is my ranch."

"Was, Daniel. I suppose, technically, you could stop the sale, but I'd probably sue." She made a soft sigh. "You see, that's what happens to you rich people. You turn your affairs over to underlings. . . ."

"You and J.D. cooked this up?"

"Mm. He really is an interesting fellow. He warned me not to show my face in Texas again until I was safely married to a native or had recanted my columns. I think he's exaggerating."

"J.D. never exaggerates." He took another step toward her.

"Well, I'd never marry anybody just to save myself, and I'm not one to recant."

"Even when you're wrong?"

She grinned. "Aunt Ethel would say especially when I'm wrong."

He was directly in front of her now. Another step and he'd knock her over. She could sense the warmth of his body, see the small scar at the corner of his eye,

and she yearned—ached—to feel his mouth on hers.
"Why would you marry?" he asked.

"Because I was in love."

He touched her chin; she'd washed up, done her
hair, applied makeup. "Are you?"

She didn't hesitate. Couldn't. "Yes."

He swept an arm around her and pulled her to him.
But she held back. "Wait. I need to know. What
happens when there's a big oil fire?"

"If J.D. needs my help," he said, "I'm going to help
him. I can't pretend I wouldn't."

"Good. You won't get bored leading a regular life?"

"I was bored before. I belong here—"

"In Vermont?"

"With you," he said, drawing her hard against him.
"It doesn't matter where you are, where we are. You're
enough, Cozie. You alone are enough."

Daniel was asked to carve the Thanksgiving turkey.
More guests had arrived. He didn't know how the
little house, neat and clean, held them all. The woman
who sewed Cozie's clothes and her four children were
there; the father apparently had finally checked into
an alcohol addiction treatment center. There were
four old men and women gathered in the living room,
including the infamous Thelma and Royal. Emily
Hawthorne, who twenty years ago could probably
have passed for her older daughter, was showing them
brochures of Scandinavia. She planned to venture
there next spring, provided her children learned to
behave while she was away.

Seth had cleaned up and changed clothes. He
seemed pleased to have his house bursting with people
from two to ninety. The Hawthornes were accustomed
to taking in strays. Daniel liked that.

It was a huge bird. He did a walk-around of it before

he started to carve. "Native Vermont turkey?" he asked Cozie.

"I don't know. Your parents sent it." She pointed to an enormous basket of fruit. "Your grandfather sent that. You Texans do things up big, don't you?"

He was about to give her an answer that would shut up even big-mouthed Cozie Hawthorne when her aunt burst into the kitchen. She had on a full head of steam. "Some Texan's bought the *Citizen*," she announced. She glared at Daniel. "That wouldn't be you, would it?"

He grinned. "It would."

"You don't know anything about the newspaper business!"

"Then I'll have to let you Hawthornes run things."

Cozie was staring at them both, stricken, no doubt for the first time in her life, speechless. Her aunt grunted. "Well, that's the way it's been for two hundred years."

She marched into the other room, and Cozie narrowed her eyes on Daniel. "I hope you didn't buy the paper to save me."

"Nope." He grinned at her. "I figured there'd be no peace in Woodstock, Vermont, unless Ethel Hawthorne was safe at her desk across from the common."

"Any more surprises up your sleeve?"

"Me? Lots. What about you?"

She removed the knife from his hand and hooked her arms around his neck, drawing his mouth toward hers. "More, I hope, than either of us can imagine."

POCKET STAR BOOKS
PROUDLY PRESENTS

*A RARE CHANCE*

CARLA NEGGERS

Coming from
Pocket Star Books
mid-November 1996

The following is a preview of
*A Rare Chance* . . .

He had followed her three times in the past week. Today made four.

Gabriella Starr decided four was enough.

She dumped her untouched pasta salad in a nearby trash can and started across jam-packed Faneuil Hall Marketplace, straight toward the South Market Building where he had stationed himself in front of the Crate & Barrel display window. His tall, lean good looks reminded her of Sean Connery back in his 007 days, just without the natural charm. She had spotted him in front of her apartment building almost a week ago, then on her way home from work a few days later, and just last night as she'd emerged from the dry cleaners.

It was the same man each time. Gabriella had no doubts about that.

She'd kept her chocolate chip cookies and clutched the small white bag to her as she edged her way through the crowd. The cookies were still warm. She'd meant to find a bench in the courtyard-like area of trees and stone and brick walls amid the three long, renovated nineteenth-century buildings that made up the heart of Boston's famous marketplace. The warm, sunny weather had brought out the crowds. Surely her stranger wouldn't try anything with so many potential witnesses.

She groaned to herself. She did *not* need this wrinkle in her life. For a whole year her life had been nearly wrinkle-free. Work she loved, an apartment she loved, friends, money in the bank. She was content.

More or less.

But she quickly pushed back thoughts of her father, as insidious as the cold wind off Boston Harbor. She loved him, missed him, worried about him, and might stay mad at him forever—and chasing down a man to find out who he was and why he was following her was just the sort of thing he'd do.

Well, she had no choice. She had to do it. Better to confront him here, now—at Faneuil Hall Marketplace on a beautiful spring afternoon—than at a time and place not of her own choosing. It didn't matter that her father would approve.

Barely ten yards to go, and he was clearly in sight. Had he seen her? Was he waiting for her? Was this his plan, to provoke her into a confrontation?

The man snapped his fingers, dispersing a swarm of pigeons that had gathered at his feet. He seemed in no hurry, just a man killing time. He had on neat khaki pants and a black windbreaker, unzipped. His dark hair was trimmed close.

A pigeon flew up in Gabriella's face, startling her.

When she recovered, the man had his back to her and was threading his way through the crowd toward the waterfront, away from her.

Gabriella lunged forward. "Wait!"

She resisted the temptation to push people aside, knock them over, do what she had to do to get to him before he could disappear or slip onto a quiet, isolated street where she wouldn't dare confront him. She broke into a half-run, cursing her mid-heel taupe shoes. She was dressed for work, not for chasing some strange man who seemed determined to follow her.

She reached the South Market Building, stopping hard in front of the display window. She squinted in the bright sunlight as she searched the crowd for a black windbreaker and khaki pants, for that ramrod-straight stance.

But she'd lost him.

He could have ducked into a store, down a street, behind a tree. It didn't matter. He was gone.

"Damn." Gabriella crushed her bag of cookies in one hand, her heart racing as much from nerves as from exertion. "Damn and blast."

"You always charge after guys following you?"

The voice was deep, male, languid, irreverent. Gabriella spun around, almost into the chest of a thick, compact man with shaggy, tawny hair and eyes she immediately noticed were the color of the sea.

"Who are you?" she asked.

"Name's Cam Yeager. You?"

She didn't answer. He wore jeans, a faded black Bruins sweatshirt, and running shoes that needed replacing. She had never seen him before, had never heard of a Cam Yeager. He had what she estimated was a two-day growth of beard and exuded an earthy sensuality that had her automatically taking a step back from him.

He studied her a moment. "So what would you have done if he'd stayed put?"

"Who?"

"The man following you."

She took a breath. Playing dumb wasn't going to work, not with this man. "I'd have demanded to know why he's been following me."

"Not smart."

"Why not? Do you know him?"

His sea-blue eyes narrowed on her, and she sensed she would be foolish to let his casual irreverence deceive her. "His name's Pete Darrow. If you spotted him following you, it's because he wanted you to spot him. He's got a gift for tailing people."

"Mr. Yeager—"

"Forget this Mr. Yeager business. Makes me think of my father. Here, let's sit down before your knees give out."

"I'm not the type to faint, if that's what you're worried about."

He glanced at her. "It's not. I'm just making up excuses so you'll share your cookies with me. Chocolate chip, right?"

Her grip tightened on the white baker's bag. "Who *are* you?"

He dropped onto a vacant wood-and-iron bench and patted the spot next to him. Gabriella noticed a three-inch scar running along the edge of his jaw. It didn't have the look of a childhood injury.

When she didn't take him up on his invitation, he leaned back, unconcerned. "Pete's an ex-cop. He resigned as a detective with the Boston police department a couple weeks ago. Now will you sit down and give me one of those cookies?"

"Why would an ex-cop follow me?"

"Seeing how I don't know who you are, I couldn't say."

Gabriella hesitated. This time, she couldn't blame Scag for her difficulties. Her father was in South America. She hadn't seen or heard from him in a year. He couldn't be responsible for a former police detective upsetting the peaceful, stable life she'd established for herself in Boston.

She sat down next to Cam Yeager, taking care that

her thighs didn't touch his. If Pete Darrow were an ex-cop, what did that make this guy? She pried her fingers loose from the bag and fished out a couple of tiny chocolate chip cookies, no bigger than a quarter.

"I bought a dozen," she said. "You can have as many as you want."

He popped one into his mouth. "Not very big, are they?"

"That's why I bought a dozen."

"I don't blame you for ditching lunch and keeping dessert."

Gabriella squelched a wave of uneasiness at the idea of two men having watched her. What would Cam Yeager have done if she hadn't gone after Pete Darrow? She could feel his eyes on her. She wore a simple double-breasted navy suit with a cream silk top and a silver lapel pin of a lady slipper, a wild New England orchid. Her hair was a medium brunette, cut just above her shoulders, and she wore neutral makeup that downplayed the fullness of her lips and the warmth of her brown eyes. She wasn't tall, but she stayed slim and fit with regular workouts and not too many chocolate chip cookies.

She ate half of her cookie, barely tasting the sugar and the gooey semisweet chocolate. "So what else do you know about this Pete Darrow? What's he do now that he's no longer a police detective? Why did he quit?"

"Whoa. Easy on the interrogation."

Gabriella gave him a tentative smile. "Sorry. I'm just nervous. This isn't the first time he's followed me. I first spotted him a week ago outside my apartment. It was creepy." She breathed out, trying to stay calm. "So I'd appreciate anything you can tell me about him."

"Okay." He helped himself to another cookie. "Pete quit the force to take a job with TJR Associates."

Gabriella stared at him. *"What?"*

"Thought that might strike a nerve. You work there, don't you?"

"Yes, I—I've been there a year." Her words came out in something just above a whisper, almost as if she were talking to herself. "My name's Gabriella Starr. I can't believe I wouldn't know—" She forced herself to stop. She didn't know who this man was or why he was at Faneuil Hall or what he wanted from her. She didn't need to give him information. She needed to get information from him. "Are you positive?"

He nodded, his expression alert, even wary. "It's my understanding Titus and Joshua Reading hired Pete to beef up their personal security after the attempt to kidnap Joshua a few weeks ago."

"How do you know all this?"

"Pete and I used to be partners."

Gabriella almost shot out of her seat. "Partners? You mean *you're* a cop?"

"Ex. I resigned just over a month ago. I start in the d.a.'s office the first of June as a prosecutor. I'm supposed to be taking an extended vacation, going fishing, painting the bathroom. Stuff like that."

Gabriella got out two cookies that had stuck together and ate them both. A cop turned prosecutor. Good God. She was sharing a bag of cookies with him, discussing another former cop who was following her.

The cops? her father would say. Get out now.

"I haven't seen Pete since I left," Cam Yeager went on. "When I heard he took the job with TJR Associates, it didn't make sense to me he'd quit to become a glorified bodyguard. So I decided to check it out."

"By following him," Gabriella said.

He shrugged. Behind the casual facade, she sensed that Cam Yeager was one intense, deliberate man, alert to every nuance of his surroundings. "That wasn't my plan. I saw him coming out of TJR Associates' offices, realized he was following you, and tailed you both to New England Merchants Bank."

"I had a meeting there."

"He waited for you, then followed you here. I just tagged along."

She shuddered at the thought of both Pete Darrow and Cam Yeager—two ex-cops—following her all morning, without her knowledge.

He stretched out his thick legs, crossing his ankles. "Think the Reading brothers put Darrow up to following you?"

The question caught Gabriella off guard. "Of course not. Why would they?"

"You tell me."

"Mr. Yeager—" She breathed in, trying not to be too snappy. "You might be who you say you are. But I have no proof anything you've told me is true. For all I know, you're in cahoots with Pete Darrow and this is some elaborate scam."

He stretched one arm across the back of the bench. "I'll bet you work with numbers at TJR Associates. The brass-tacks type. Have to see proof before you believe anything. However, you're right. I could be lying." His sea-blue eyes narrowed on Gabriella, all business, nothing calm or irreverent about him now. "But I'm not."

Gabriella believed him. She didn't know why, and that was enough to propel her to her feet. She was relying on her instincts, and too often her instincts had betrayed her. She left the remaining cookies behind on the bench and hoisted her leather tote onto her shoulder.

"I've got to get back to the office," she said.

"Just a couple cookies for lunch?"

"They'll do."

"Here." He had a pen out and was scratching something onto the cookie bag. "This is my address and phone number. If you need me, give a yell."

"Why would I need you?"

He leaned back, amusement creeping into his sea-blue eyes. "You never know."

She ignored him, pretended the unmistakable attraction gnawing at her insides wasn't there. It was purely physical, an involuntary response. She did not go for cops, cops-turned-prosecutors, law-enforcement types in general. And they didn't go for her. She was too smart, too driven, too naturally defiant.

She'd spent too many nights in jail.

"Just tell me one thing," she said. "Is Pete Darrow dangerous?"

His eyes reached hers, serious again. "If you cross him, yes. He can be dangerous."

*And you?* she wanted to ask. *Are you dangerous?*

Instead she snatched the bag from him and got out of there, refusing to glance back as she made her way to TJR Associates' waterfront offices. What a fine pickle you're in, she thought. Thanks to her own efforts, she no longer had just one man keeping an eye on her for reasons unknown. She had two.

Cam Yeager stared out at the crowd as he contemplated dark-haired, dark-eyed Gabriella Starr and what trouble she might be in with Pete Darrow. She worked at TJR Associates. So did Pete. And Pete was following her.

None of it was good.

Cam had done some basic research on TJR Associates, a real-estate-and-development outfit specializing in historic buildings. It was run by two brothers, Titus and Joshua Reading. On the surface, they were the embodiment of the American dream: middle-class guys who'd worked hard, done well, maintained high principles as their bank accounts grew by leaps and bounds. Titus had the drive and the vision, Joshua the charm and personality.

But there was a dark side. There was, Cam thought, always a dark side.

The information had come to him without names attached to it, without evidence, without proof. It was just talk. Maybe someone was trying to spread lies to bring down the Reading brothers; maybe someone was just telling the truth; maybe there was a glimmer of truth in what was being said and the rest was exaggeration.

The talk had started with a relatively harmless statement from a fellow detective. *Joshua Reading's a gun nut.* Cam was unruffled. These days a lot of people were gun nuts. Depended on how one wanted to define a gun nut. Someone with any gun at all? Someone with illegal guns? A bona fide psycho armed to the teeth?

Then the talk escalated. Joshua Reading was no ordinary guy who happened to like keeping a gun on hand. He was into seriously illegal stuff. Grenades, antitank weapons, miniguns. Whatever he could get his hands on. *He could arm a small militia and make a run on Boston.*

Word was, the kidnap attempt was a warning from his dealers not to get too cocky, not to think he could get away with not paying up, with playing his gun games any way but their way. They wouldn't tolerate any arrogance and recklessness from some rich boy who liked to play Rambo.

The police investigation into the incident hadn't turned up any tangible leads. Joshua hadn't pushed for answers. He didn't thwart the investigation or refuse to cooperate. He just let it be known he and his older brother didn't want to play up such a sensational story when the police were unlikely to make an arrest. The police would look incompetent, and TJR Associates didn't need that kind of publicity. They were a high-prestige, low-profile company.

Cam hadn't learned a thing he could sink his teeth into. Just rumor, innuendo, speculation, maybes, and what ifs, the kind that sometimes ran rampant in the law-enforcement community. There weren't even enough grounds for an investigation.

Pete Darrow had worked on the periphery of the investigation. He could have heard the same talk. Had he believed it? Had he hired on with the Reading brothers so he could play the hero and bring Joshua Reading down?

Or had he decided to use the information for his own purposes? Find the secret cache of weapons, steal them, sell them to the highest bidder. Or just bleed Joshua Reading. Make him pay to keep his habit a secret. Pete had walked the tightrope a long time. He'd put up with the stress, the bullshit, the ugliness of the work itself. He'd been tempted before. He could have fallen off on the wrong side. It happened. He could have seen his chance at the good life he had always talked about and seized it.

So why would he follow Gabriella Starr?

Gabriella Starr. Cam rolled the name on his tongue. She'd tossed her lunch and kept her chocolate chip cookies. She'd charged after Pete Darrow. She wore a funky little pin of some flower on her lapel. She'd shared her cookies with him.

Maybe Gabriella Starr wasn't as brass-tacks as she seemed.

A shadow fell over him, and Pete Darrow dropped onto the bench. "Follow me again, Yeager, and I'll beat you to a bloody pulp. I swear I will."

"Hello to you, too."

Darrow's dark eyes zeroed in on his ex-partner. "I'm only giving you one warning."

Cam settled back against the bench, drawing his right foot up onto his left knee. He wasn't afraid of Pete Darrow. Never had been, never would be. "What did you do, duck into the bookstore, give Gabriella Starr the slip? She's quite the pepperpot, you know. She'd have nailed your hide to one of these trees if she'd caught up with you. Tried, anyway. I don't think much deters her from trying. Even you."

"Mind your own goddamned business, Yeager."

"Not my style. First I became a cop, now I'm a lawyer. Minding other people's is just a function of my personality."

Darrow glared at him, fuming in silence. Cam had felt the sting of his ex-partner's temper before. Pete was taller, maybe as strong and as tenacious, definitely more unpredictable. He hated being crossed. He hated finding out Cam was with him, never mind a step ahead. They'd known each other for ten years. For three years, they'd had a difficult, enduring partnership based on a trust and loyalty that sometimes defied logic. The trust came from an understanding, if not an acceptance, of each other's strengths and weaknesses. The loyalty was just there, inexplicable.

But both had been frayed in the past few months. To

Pete Darrow, born and raised in a tough Dorchester neighborhood, Cam Yeager was a trust-fund cop who'd had to prove his commitment to police work. When Cam had started taking law classes at night, Darrow had maintained his partner would never be able to tear himself away from the job. When Cam had gotten his degree, when he'd passed the bar, when he'd announced he was resigning to become a prosecutor, Darrow took it all as a personal betrayal. Cam had defected. He'd thumbed his nose at Darrow's world, as much as told Pete Darrow he was inferior for being a cop, staying a cop. Nothing Cam said could convince him otherwise. Cam had used the job, had used his partner, and now he was out. Darrow refused to see it any other way.

A month later, however, he turned in his own badge. Pete Darrow, the cop's cop. He was devoted to the job, unable to imagine another life. He needed the adrenaline, the action, the authority. He needed to know he was doing a job worth doing.

It didn't make sense that he'd quit, not to Cam.

"I'm just doing my job," Pete said.

"Gabriella Starr doesn't know that."

"Not my problem."

Cam had the feeling it was now. Gabriella Starr had something of the fox hound about her. Put her on the scent, and she'd stay at it until she dropped. "You trying to rattle her?"

Darrow jumped to his feet, just a twitch at the corner of one eye giving away the depth of his anger. "Stay the fuck out of my life, Yeager."

"Pete Darrow tossing it in to look out for a couple rich real-estate-and-development guys doesn't make sense. Your work's always been sacred ground, Pete. Why quit to play bodyguard?"

"I don't have to explain anything to you."

"Yeah, you do. Because until I understand—until I believe you're not doing some dumb-assed thing designed to make you a hero or a fortune, I'm staying on your case."

"Go fishing, Cam. Go play with your pals on Beacon Hill. I can run my own life."

Cam didn't relent. "Why follow Gabriella Starr? What's she to the Reading brothers? You pick her out yourself or did your bosses put you up to tailing her?"

Pete Darrow ignored him, starting into the crowd.

"Pete, listen to me—"

Darrow turned, his eyes narrowed, his temper under tight rein. "I see you on my tail again, it won't be pretty. I promise you, Yeager."

Cam sighed. He knew his ex-partner well enough to believe he would do exactly as he promised. "If you need my help, you know where to find me."

But Pete Darrow had already melted into the crowd.

Cam got to his feet, feeling the fatigue come over him. This morning, following Pete had seemed like a good idea. Now, Cam wasn't so sure. He'd alerted Darrow that his ex-partner was on his case, and he'd alerted a dark-haired, dark-eyed Gabriella Starr that her bosses had hired the man who was following her.

He bit back a curse, pushing his way through the crowd. Hell, he thought, maybe she was the one who'd tried kidnapping Joshua Reading. Maybe she knew who had. Maybe she was his weapons supplier. For all Cam knew, she could have had a half-dozen grenades tucked inside her navy suit, and in following her, Pete Darrow was just doing his job.

But Cam didn't believe it.

He had the feeling before too long, Gabriella Starr was going to be glad she had his name and address on her cookie bag.

Look for
*A Rare Chance*
Wherever Paperback Books Are Sold
mid-November 1996